Chasing The Magic

Book 2 of the Chronicles of Crett

By

L R Attridge

Grosvenor House
Publishing Limited

This book is published by
Grosvenor House Publishing Ltd
Link House
140 The Broadway, Tolworth, Surrey, KT6 7HT.
www.grosvenorhousepublishing.co.uk

A CIP record for this book
is available from the British Library

ISBN 978-1-83615-344-3

Acknowledgements

Thanks to my brother Colin for his constructive comments, and for listening to my problems.

By the same author

Rumours of Magic (book 1 of The Chronicles of Crett)

1

Unless you have a telescope that enables you to see through things or around things, you won't have seen the planet Crett. It is permanently on the other side of our sun, circling in the same orbit, and, as luck would have it, in the same direction and at the same speed as our world. Crett has much in common with Earth. Its geology, ecology and anthropology have evolved along similar paths. And, but for the trolls, dwarfs, dragons, wizards and other things, you might think you were on Earth.

If you could zoom in on Crett, you would see rivers, lakes, forests, deserts and fertile lands. You would see signs of occupation, too, the most populated of them being the city of Kra-Pton in the land of Kermells Tong.

Kra-Pton is a sprawling metropolis that has few things in its favour, and many that aren't. The river Quaggy, easily its most unfavourable feature, oozes through the city. To say it flows, would be optimistic. The Quaggy barely manages to ooze even after a week's rain. Another feature for which the city is renowned is the University of Havrapsor. Situated on the edge of the city, Havrapsor is the fine old institute of magical learning where this story begins.

To bring you up to speed with its history, or reacquaint you with it, the university was recently the scene of a great battle. A power-hungry wizard named Dennis seized the Archchancellorship of the university by ruining the reputation of his predecessor, and intimidating his fellow senior magicians.

Dennis had hoped to use his position as Archchancellor to get his hands on two powerful, ancient artefacts – a staff and a drum. These would have given him almost unlimited power over the university, the city, the land, and possibly the world. He failed because those working against him were able to keep the staff from him. In desperation, he summoned Jamzamin, the Demon King, hoping a liaison with the creature would squash all opposition and finally put the staff and drum in his hands.

But demons are capricious beings. The final confrontation, which took place in the grounds and buildings of the university, and provoked an unprecedented amount of searing hostile magic from both sides, took a huge toll on the Demon King's hordes. Jamzamin lost patience with Dennis. He retreated to his underworld realm, dragging Dennis with him.

In the months that have passed since then, the University of Havrapsor's buildings have mostly repaired themselves. Though the buildings remain disgruntled by the onslaught, and they are prone to alter the direction of passageways and the locations of privies now and then, to let the residents know they are not yet forgiven. These occasionally-caught-short residents are the staff and pupils – the wizards and their charges – of the magical university. Life has returned to near normal for them since Dennis's removal. Though for Dennis himself, deep below the university in the caverns and labyrinths of Jamzamin's Kingdom of the Parallel Dimension, life has become mind-achingly dull.

'Is it always this boring down here?' said Dennis.

'It will be until someone up there finds the staff,' replied his companion and jailor, a demon named Hell. 'That'll probably liven things up with another battle or two.'

Dennis sighed and shifted himself on the uncomfortable boulder that served as a seat. 'Haven't you ever wanted to get out of here? You know, be your own demon?'

'Course I 'ave,' said Hell. 'But you daren't even fart round 'ere without asking Jamzamin's permission first.'

'Interested in that sort of thing, is he?' Dennis asked, though not really bothered.

'Might as well be.' The demon shrugged and his scaly shoulders made a leathery squeak.

'Haven't you ever thought about, um… how can I put this? Getting rid of him?' Dennis proposed, hoping to sow the seeds of insurrection. 'After all, who ever heard of the Kingdom of Jamzamin?' He paused to allow what he'd said to sink in before adding furtively, 'The Kingdom of Hell has a much better ring to it, don't you think?'

The small demon's eyes widened. 'I 'adn't thought of that. You're right, it does 'ave a certain ring, don't it?'

'Yes,' said Dennis, 'then *you* could be master down here, and *I* could be master up there.' He pointed a broken fingernail at the ceiling of the cavern.

'There is just one fing, though,' said Hell.

'And what's that?'

'Jamzamin don't allow elections.'

It hadn't occurred to Dennis that Hell might be a complete idiot. Nevertheless, the creature did have the kind of grey matter that the wizard could mould. It would have to be done slowly, though, and with due care and attention. 'Perhaps we could dream up a new title for him, you know, something like *retired King*, would be nice. Or, what about *the late King*?' That part was spoken in hushed tones.

'We've never tried retirement down 'ere, but *the late* – what's that? Maybe we could get 'im to take that,' said Hell, resting his scaly chin on the palm of a clawed hand.

'Well, you can give people retirement,' Dennis attempted to explain. 'But, *the late*, has to be... well... imposed on them.'

The demon screwed up his face, not that you'd notice. 'How's that work, then?'

Dennis wasn't expecting the conversion to get this detailed, and he was struggling with the finer points. 'Well,' he began. 'Let's put it this way. *Retired* means you *stop* doing what you were doing before.'

'I see,' said Hell. 'I think. But he never does much anyway.'

'All the better.' Dennis smirked. 'He's semi-retired already.'

'When shall we ask 'im, then?' said Hell.

'*Ask* him?' said Dennis, raising an eyebrow. 'We don't *ask* him. We tell him. But we can't do it on our own.'

'We're not on our own, we're together.'

Dennis blinked. *No wonder you're still number two down here*, he thought to himself. 'No, what I mean is, we'll need some *more demons* to help *make* him retire,' the wizard stressed. 'Then, if he still doesn't want to take retirement...'

'We make 'im *the late*?'

'Exactly,' said Dennis, brightening. 'You must have lots of demons down here who would follow your lead.'

'Don't fink so,' sighed Hell. 'I was left in charge 'ere once before, when Jamzamin went to Meth's funeral.'

'Meth?' said Dennis.

''E was king before Jamzamin.'

'Was he very old, then, when he died?' Dennis wondered.

'No, not really. It was sad, though,' Hell reflected.

'What did he die of?'

'Jamzamin,' said Hell, flatly.

'You can't die of Jamzamin, surely?'

'Well, perhaps not so much died as retired wiv a large axe in the back of 'is 'ead.'

Dennis was back on familiar ground. 'So he became *the late*.'

'Yup. So you fink I should whack Jamzamin on the back of 'is 'ead wiv me axe, then?'

'What a good *idea*.' Dennis smiled.

'Hmm. That's gonna be difficult,' Hell grunted.

'Do it when he's asleep,' Dennis suggested, helpfully.

'Like an assassin, you mean?'

'That's the general idea, yes,' said Dennis, scrutinising the backs of his hands and noticing how white they'd become from the lack of sunlight.

'That's 'ow Jamzamin did it to Meth,' Hell recalled.

'Well then, don't look at it so much as an assassination, more of a comeuppance, kind of thing.' Dennis half smiled.

'Yeah, I fink I can see it like that, sort of getting even for Meth,' grinned Hell. 'But I don't think Jamzamin will like it.'

'If you're quick, and stealthy, Jamzamin won't even see it coming,' said Dennis, 'Now, where's your axe?'

Hell looked around the boulders where they sat, then stood up, bent down and looked underneath them. 'Oh, no,' he wailed, slapping his forehead with a leathery thwack. 'It's in the bloody staff!'

It's a long story, but in short, Hell was the resident demon inside a wizard's staff that Dennis had stolen by mistake. He thought he'd taken the powerful staff that belonged to the former Archchancellor of Havrapsor. When he discovered his mistake, he also discovered he could use this otherwise useless staff to summon Hell. But the staff was still in the university. As was Hell's murderous axe.

Dennis sagged visibly, and Hell's dreams of becoming royalty burst with a gentle pop. The pair sat in miserable silence, each with his own thoughts of escaping the Kingdom of Jamzamin.

This was when the germ of an idea came hurtling from wherever these things hurtle and landed, also with a pop, in the cavern. It crept warily into Dennis's mind and looked around while waiting to develop. It was about to tiptoe out again, when Dennis pounced.

He cast his mind back to his old rooms. *Where did I leave that staff?* he thought. *It was against the wall. No, it fell down. It was lying on the carpet, last time I saw it.* 'I have an idea!' he said, and closed his eyes to concentrate. He always protected his room magically from other wizards whenever he was absent, and he doubted that any of the 'amateur fools', as he thought of his old colleagues, would have penetrated his superior spell. The place would still be as he left it.

'Are you gonna tell me?' asked Hell.

Dennis opened an eye. 'What?'

'Your idea. Are you gonna tell me?'

Dennis held up a hand to shut him up, and felt about his robe. Patting it for clues. Then he found it. The user guide for his flying carpet. He pulled it out and began thumbing through the pages looking for a section that might tell him if he could control the carpet remotely from his position in the bowels of the Parallel Dimension.

* * *

2

High above the bowels of the Parallel Dimension, the University of Havrapsor went about its daily business of nurturing young magical minds. But there was another side to the university. The wizards knew of it – where it was and what it did – but they went there only rarely and reluctantly. On most days this unsung section was a hive of industry, and there were few things that made wizards more uncomfortable than being in the presence of hard work.

The place they all shunned was, of course, the laundry and cleaning department.

'You're quite new here aren't you, girl?' said the major domo, a large woman who kept adjusting the supports of her ample bosom with alternate flexing of the overly large biceps on each arm. The girl didn't answer, feeling that what the woman had said was more of a statement. Then on second thoughts the girl gave a nod of her head. 'Well, there's this room up in the east wing, third floor…'

'Second, Madge, second,' interrupted a wiry woman, standing just to the left of the major domo. Madge looked up at her. The wiry woman shifted uneasily onto her other foot. The major domo turned her bloodshot gaze back to the girl.

'*Second* floor,' she repeated. 'It's been locked up for a while, and needs a good doin' out.' She glanced at the other woman and winked. The wiry woman acknowledged it with half a grin.

'Is it easy to find, mistress? Only I haven't been to the east wing before,' the girl asked. She seemed a little uneasy about the assignment.

'Oh, yes,' said Madge. 'It's the one with the big padlock on the door.' She reached into the secret crevice of her large bosom and extracted a very large, uncomfortable looking key. If it had a face, it would no doubt have had an expression of discomfort mixed with a sudden shiver from coming out into the cold.

'Here,' she said, lifting the loop of string it was attached to carefully over her rather obvious large, ginger wig. 'You'll need this.'

The girl took the key and dropped it into her apron pocket. 'Anything else, mistress?'

'Yes. Make sure you lock it securely when you've finished,' she ordered.

After a few wrong turns, the girl found herself standing nervously before a dark black oak door. Dark black was one of the stranger colours, not found on most worlds, but black *does* come in two shades: the aforementioned dark black, and the regular pale black. This is not to be confused with light black, which is generally regarded as grey.

She put down the carrying cradle that contained all the items required for the job – tins of polish, bright yellow dusters and bunches of feathers tied on sticks, that sort of thing – and suspiciously eyed the large padlock. It looked harmless enough hanging there. A bit dusty, but that was all. She reached into her apron pocket and pulled out the key, lifting the padlock towards her as she did so. At her touch, the tops of the rivets holding the lock together suddenly opened, revealing a pair of steely grey eyes.

'Who's that?' it snapped. 'What do you want?' In surprise, she dropped it and let it swing back against the door with a thud. 'Ouch!' it exclaimed.

She bent forward and peered closer. 'Did you just speak?'

The keyhole moved like a mouth. 'I did. Now, what do you want?' it repeated, tetchily.

'I want to go into this room to clean it,' she replied.

'No, you don't,' it argued.

'Well, if it's as nasty in there as you are, you're right. I don't.'

'Why did you say you did, then?'

'Because I've been told to,' she said firmly, adding, 'It's my job.'

'You really don't want to go in there,' the padlock insisted.

'I do.'

'Believe me, you don't.'

'But I need to,' she persisted.

'No. I can't let you do it.'

'I don't see how can stop me,' she argued, picking it up again to insert the key.

'Nooo... don't.' Click! The padlock fell open. She removed it from the staple, and turned the door handle. The hinges squeaked as the heavy door swung back. When it was fully open, she picked up her cradle and went in.

As she did so, she felt a peculiar sensation. It was as if she was pushing herself into a huge bubble that sealed itself behind her. For this was Dennis's room. She had passed through the magical barrier that he had created to stop wizards and students from entering. He'd clearly forgotten to mention cleaning staff when he cast the spell.

The room hadn't been used for some time by the look of it. Cobwebs brushed against her face and hair. There was a broad shaft of light cutting through the gloom, where the sun found a crack in the shutters. She slid back the iron bar that kept the shutters closed and opened them as far as they would go. Sunlight streamed in, illuminating the millions of dust motes she'd disturbed when she strode to the window.

There was a skittering sound of many tiny feet, as spiders and cockroaches scuttled for cover. She looked back at the door, and was about to close it when it slammed shut on its own. Her heart missed a beat, then began thumping faster as she went over to try the handle. It turned. She breathed more easily, and then the draught from the open window slammed it shut again.

A quick glance around the room told her that it needed nothing more than a quick flick round with a feather duster to clear the cobwebs and chase away the last of the more determined creepy-crawlies. As she dusted down the side of the fireplace near the bed, she noticed some sort of rod on the floor. Dennis's staff, in fact.

She picked it up and leant it in a corner out of the way. As she did so, a tinny voice called out, 'Don't touch that!' Which startled her and she dropped it.

'It's not a good idea to mess with that, you know.'

'Oh, it's you,' she said to the padlock. She picked up the staff again and studied it. And recognised it. 'It was stolen, you know. By a wizard, of all people.'

'Some of 'em are like that,' the padlock agreed, adding, 'Ere, how'd you know about that?'

She ignored the question, saying quietly, 'No, only *one* wizard is like that. But he will change his ways.'

'If you think you can change that one, you must be stupid,' it warned.

'Everyone has some good in them,' she replied.

'Not Dennis,' said the padlock.

'We'll see,' she said, picking up the staff again.

'No! Don't do that!'

Too late. A brisk rub with a yellow duster and the staff was gleaming again.

* * *

3

'What's that you're reading?' asked Hell, leaning over Dennis's shoulder.

'It's called a *book*,' Dennis replied.

'I can see that!' barked Hell. 'What's it about?'

'It's a *User Guide*.'

'Right,' said Hell, trying to get the general idea. 'You use it to find your way about, then.'

'Sort of,' said Dennis.

'Perhaps I'll get meself one next time I go up top,' mused Hell.

'That could be a long wait,' Dennis grunted as he turned a page.

'What could be a long wait?' said a voice that wasn't either of them.

'Oh, 'ello, your royalness,' said Hell, as Jamzamin pulled up a rock and sat down.

'Just the chap I wanted to see,' said Dennis, instinctively flexing his right-hand fingers in the hope of summoning a fireball. But his magic didn't work down here.

'What about?' asked the Demon King, almost as if he cared.

'When are you going to release me?' said Dennis.

'I'm not,' replied Jamzamin, bluntly but pleasantly.

'What? But we had an agreement,' Dennis protested.

'Yes, we did,' the king acknowledged. 'And you're keeping it.'

'Yes,' agreed Dennis. 'But you're not!'

'Remind me,' said Jamzamin, exploring with a claw, the inner cavity of his left nostril.

'I said, if you help me become master of the surface world, I'd give you anything you wanted,' said Dennis, testily.

'That's right. I remember, you did.' Jamzamin, examined something he'd found.

'But *you* failed,' Dennis griped. 'We lost the battle.'

'Lost is not a word I like to use,' said Jamzamin. He thought for a moment, and added, 'Came second, sounds much better.'

'All right. We came second.' Dennis sighed. 'But it amounts to the same thing.'

'Perhaps,' Jamzamin allowed. 'But, you see, the thing I wanted was your soul, and if I'd helped you win, that's what I would've got anyway. Haven't you heard what making a pact with a demon is all about? Didn't you read the small print?'

'There's no small print in a verbal agreement,' argued Dennis.

'It was in the stuff I whispered,' explained Jamzamin.

Dennis sulked in silence.

The Demon King folded his arms and studied him. 'He's really let himself go since he came down here,' he said to Hell. 'Not much like the dapper Archchancellor anymore, is he?'

'I'm trying to fit in,' said Dennis sarcastically, eyeing them up and down with distaste.

It was true, Dennis's robes were looking shabby. His blonde hair and beard had suffered at the hands of a demon barber, and were streaked with soot and smoke from the many fires burning around the place.

'Are you saying that win or lose, I'd have finished up down here anyway?' Dennis stammered.

'Well, yes. That's about the strength of it,' Jamzamin conceded.

'But you can't do this to *me*.'

'I've done it,' said Jamzamin. 'Feet accomplee, or something like that. So, behave yourself. Find yourself a hobby. Eternity will pass quicker if you have a hobby.'

'There's just nothing to do!'

'Course there is!' snapped the king. 'What about rock collecting?'

'Course, your royalness, 'e could try that,' Hell interjected. 'And there's pot-holing, as well.'

'What about axe grinding?' hissed Dennis.

Hell's face froze over. Was Dennis about to expose him?

'Anyway,' said Jamzamin. 'There's a couple of things you can mull over. I'll leave you to get on with it then, shall I?' He sauntered off down the nearest tunnel without waiting for a reply.

When he was out of sight, Dennis turned on Hell. 'He's got to go. I'm not spending the rest of my existence down here.'

'Don't particularly *want you* down here either!' retorted Hell.

'Well? Are you going to retire him or not?'

'Nope. I'm gonna make him the late,' replied Hell.

'Even better. When?'

'Hang on a minute, someone's rubbing that blasted staff,' said Hell. 'I'm being summoned. I've gotta go.' And he scuttled off around the flame pits shouting, 'Coming!'

Dennis saw his chance and got up to follow, but he was too late to see which way the demon went. He walked slowly back to his rock and sat down hard. The rock made a sort of 'Oomph' sound and began to move. Dennis jumped up and away, pressing himself against the wall as the rock unfolded and stood upright.

* * *

In Dennis's old rooms in the east wing of the university, a padlock was worriedly pressing itself against a door and watching as the 'cleaning girl' stood in the middle of the room leaning on the staff, waiting for a demon.

As she'd expected, a rumbling started up below and grew louder as Hell clawed his way to the surface world. Satisfied that the noise was about as loud as it was going to get, she covered her face just as the wall exploded and the demon tumbled into the room, accompanied by a cloud of dust and rubble. He banged his hands on the floor as he coughed and choked, too stupid to realise that if he stood up, he'd be above the settling dust.

'Do you have to do that?' the girl scolded him.

'Cough! Cough! Cough!' replied Hell.

She looked at the ceiling in despair, and sat down heavily in one of the armchairs, waiting for the demon to regain control of himself. This took another five minutes of coughing and sneezing, which aggravated the girl even more as the demon had arrived without a handkerchief, *yet again*. When he'd finally stopped, he sat cross-legged, waiting for her to speak.

She let him wait. After all, he'd kept her waiting. Eventually, he couldn't stand the silence.

'Yes?' he said, lamely. 'What do you want?' She tilted her head and stared at him. He flinched back. 'You!' he yelled.

'Yes. Me!' snapped the girl. 'Now – what took you so long?'

'Er, it's been a bit busy down there, but I came as soon as I could,' he spluttered.

'Well, perhaps you'll do better next time.'

'What, like before you rub?' he said, aggrieved. 'Well, now I'm 'ere, what do you want?'

'Where's Dennis?' she snapped.

'Down there,' replied Hell, without hesitation, pointing a clawed finger at the floor.

'I *know* he's down there, *stupid*. How far down there?'

'The bottom is probably the best name for it,' said Hell. 'As far down there as you can go. The pits, in fact.'

'I want to see him,' the girl demanded.

'I can't bring 'im up 'ere,' said Hell.

'Then take me down there! I want him out!'

'All right,' said Hell, slowly. 'No need for that tone, but what are you going to give me?'

'Give you? I'll think about that once you get me down there.'

'That's not very specific, is it? I mean, I might not *want* what you have to give.'

'Let me put it like this, then,' she began, in her best threatening tone, 'If you don't take me, I will summon you every hour, on the hour, until you do.'

It took the demon only a moment to work out how aggravating that would be. 'It's a deal,' he said, reluctantly. And without further ado he led the way down the hole he'd just created. As the girl passed the door, she snatched the padlock and dropped it into her apron pocket.

The descent was steep and cluttered at first, as she'd expected, but after a while the rough-hewn shaft connected with an existing tunnel that sloped more gently, and wound around like a spiral staircase. 'Are you taking the scenic route?' she snapped, 'because I would like to get there someday soon.'

'Only thinking of you,' said the demon. 'I can go on all fours.' He eyed her critically. 'But you don't seem to be put together right for that.'

'Hmph,' was the only answer she had to that.

* * *

5

The troll, for that's what was, unfolded and stretched. Trolls' temperaments were always difficult to gauge, so Dennis looked for somewhere to hide, but he was too late.

'Who are you?' The troll yawned.

'Er… er...' Dennis stammered.

'Don't be shy. You can tell me.' The troll, loomed over him at a full seven feet. Dennis looked up, still pressing against the wall, unable to speak. The troll took a crunching step closer. 'I'm Krystal,' she cooed. 'I've been expecting you.'

'Y… y… you have?'

'Oh, yes. I'm a princess – can't you tell? – from the Lava Tree Mountains.' She smiled disengagingly.

'What are you doing down here, then?' said Dennis, starting to relax a little as she hadn't punched him yet.

Krystal ground out a deep sigh as she recollected, 'Well, it was my sixteenth birthday, you see, and this mean old witch tricked me into pricking my little pinkie. It didn't hurt *that* much, but it sent me to the Parallel Dimension. And I'm stuck here till a handsome prince comes and wakes me up with a kiss.' She paused, took a breath, studied him, and continued. 'And here you are… well, a prince anyway.'

'What? No, I think there's been a mistake, madam, er… miss?'

'*Oh*, no. I know how it goes, see. My birthday… wicked witch… little prick… ouch! Then long kip and a big kiss from a handsome prince from the Ironroot Mountains.' She stopped for another breath. 'Quick romance,' she continued, 'get married, happy ever after, and that's about it.'

Dennis was having visions of what the future might hold. And from his side it looked like it was going to get worse. 'Look, er… Krystal. May I call you Krystal?'

'Course you can.'

'Er… well… Krystal, I'd better explain. First, I'm not a prince. I've never been to the Ironroot Mountains. Second… no third… I'm not even a troll. And lastly, I don't remember *kissing* you.'

'You did *too,*' she pouted her stony lips. 'I felt it. Soft and warm it was.'

'That wasn't a *kiss,*' Dennis assured her. 'That was me sitting on your head.'

'Oh, no. This is terrible,' she moaned, clutching her brow with a stony clink. 'Not a prince? I was expecting, at the very least, Prince Elvin the Blue.' Another thought came to her. 'It's a good job I woke up when I did, then. Goodness knows what you might have done to me.'

'Madam… miss… you were *never* in safer hands.'

'You haven't laid hands on me as well, have you?'

'Krystal,' he began calmly. 'I haven't touched you. Apart from using your head as a stool. In all innocence of course.'

She sat down, sounding like a bag of crisps being scrunched. 'Well… if you're sure you haven't touched me…'

'No, dear lady,' he said, holding up his hands. A problem for Dennis was that he didn't naturally look innocent. It struck her then, as it does most people, that she wouldn't buy a used cart from him.

Her huge emerald eyes stared up at him while she put her thoughts in order. 'Do you know the way out of this dump?' she asked, eventually.

'Not yet,' he replied, carefully examining an adjacent boulder before sitting. 'But I'm working on it.'

'Only I must find Prince Elvin. I expect he's looking for me by now, too.'

'Probably,' said Dennis. 'But I haven't quite worked out how to get out yet.'

'Then I think we'd better find someone and ask, don't you?'

'Er… no, not yet,' said Dennis, gently. 'I have a friend… well, an acquaintance,' he corrected himself. 'He'll be back soon. He knows the way out.'

'Well, he'd better get a move on. I can't keep my prince waiting forever.'

'How well do you know this prince?' asked Dennis, almost conversationally.

'I've not actually met him. But I dream about him a lot. Tall feller, quite handsome as trolls go. But what does it matter if he's handsome or not, it's him being a prince that counts.'

'And *rich* of course?' Dennis added for her.

'Well if he's not, my father will have something to say about it,' she muttered, haughtily.

'Oh, I'm sure he'll be rich,' Dennis assured her. His mind was going into overdrive. *If I can help her get back to where she belongs, perhaps her prince, if he's rich, that is – or her father even – might reward me for my trouble. Might even have an army I could borrow.*

'You know,' said Krystal, after a lengthy silence, 'my father might even reward you for helping me find my way home.'

'Do you really think so?' said Dennis, trying not to sound over-eager.

'Yes, I really do.'

'It really wouldn't be necessary,' Dennis lied.

'I'll tell him not to bother, then.'

'What? Let's not be too hasty. We wouldn't want to offend the good man! – I mean, troll. Such a worthy king will probably insist,' he maintained, while silently calling himself an idiot.

* * *

6

Their conversation was interrupted by a small rock fall, hotly pursued by a scream.

'Yaargh!' It was Hell, plunging through a hole in the wall of the tunnel.

'You fool!' yelled a young woman following behind him. 'You nearly had me over then!'

'Sorry, I'm sure,' Hell apologised sourly as he staggered drunkenly to his feet. He brushed himself down. 'You would insist on me diggin' a bloody short-cut. I've 'urt me leg, now,' he moaned. Then he looked up and saw the troll, 'Who the wossname are you?' he gasped, and took a step back.

Dennis stood up. 'This is Krystal.'

'It looks like bloody granite to me. And a lot of it, too,' remarked Hell.

Dennis privately agreed. Krystal was a bit of a misnomer. 'No, Krystal is her name. I'm not sure what she's made of.'

'I've got someone wiv me as well,' said Hell. 'Looking for you, she is.'

'For me?'

The girl stepped forward, and Dennis stepped back.

'YOU!' he yelled, in disbelief. 'You fought against me in the battle! What the…'

'Hell?' prompted the demon.

'… Are you doing here? You've got a nerve! Of all the…'

'Hello, Father,' she said, quietly.

The appellation didn't register with him. 'What did you just call me?!'

'I said hello, *Father*.' She stepped closer and he backed away.

'Don't talk rubbish. I can't be a *father*. I'm a wizard!'

'Stop disowning me and hear me out. You're becoming rather tiresome,' she said, levelly.

Dennis was taken aback. 'You can't speak to me like that,' he hissed. 'Do you know who I am?'

'Of course I do, Dennis. You're a scheming, conniving wizard, and you're my *father*.'

'Will you stop calling me that!'

'Perhaps, Father. Once you've admitted it. Then I might ease up a bit.'

'I'll admit nothing,' he sneered.

'I can prove it if you wish.'

'Perhaps you should try, then I shall be rid of you and all this nonsense.'

She sat down on the rock next to Krystal, who obligingly shuffled along to make room. 'That's right, dear. You tell him,' Krystal whispered in her ear.

'Sit down, Father,' said the girl, 'this might take a few minutes.'

Dennis pulled a face and grudgingly sat down.

'Good,' she said, defiantly staring him down. 'My name is Florence. My mother is called Esmerelda.' She paused, watching for a reaction.

He jumped in with both feet. 'There, you see. I don't know any Esmerelda,' he scoffed.

Krystal looked at Florence. 'Is that it?' she asked.

'Of course not!' snapped Florence. 'There's lots more, yet.'

Krystal grabbed a handful of the clothing close to Dennis's throat and hissed, 'Will you shut up and listen?' The wizard nodded. Vigorously. Krystal released him. 'Carry on, dear.' She smiled, sweetly – for a troll.

'Thank you. You knew her as Esme.' Florence went on. 'Remember her now? Esme?'

'Do you?' snapped Krystal. Dennis nodded again, but kept his lips tightly closed. 'Carry on, dear.'

'My mother, Esme is Triona's twin sister. The one you put old Archchancellor Wimlett to bed with that night the trolls wrecked the *Piggin Wissall*. Remember?' probed Florence, coldly. 'Trying to sully his good name, you were. And all the time you were up no good yourself with Esme. Remember?'

'Do you?' asked Krystal. Dennis hung his head. 'DO YOU?!' she yelled, when she didn't get a verbal response.

'Yes! For goodness' sake!' Dennis yelled back.

'Don't you shout at me,' Krystal threatened, bunching her hand into a fist.

Dennis calmed down. Quickly. Krystal looked at Florence, 'He remembers… carry on, dear.'

'Thank you,' said Florence. 'Mother told me about you becoming Archchancellor and all, and how the Drum and the staff could be mine one day. I had to pretend to help that little band of no-hopers who were against you – Wimlett's daughter, Eydith, and that junior wizard, Link. All the time I was waiting for the right moment to get the staff, but you, you fool, you lost the Drum as well!'

Dennis opened his mouth to speak, but Krystal grabbed his chin and turned to Florence. 'Have you finished yet, dear?'

'No.'

Dennis rolled his eyes in silence.

'I fought my way right up to you in the battle,' she continued. 'I could have helped kill you then and there, but I didn't. And I let the demons take you away, rather than see you dead.'

Dennis hung his head, as she continued to berate him. She brought him up to date. 'As a student at the university…' She broke off, registering his questioning look that a *girl* would be studying there… 'Yes, some girls are allowed now. As a student, I took a part-time job in the cleaning department, hoping to get into your old rooms. I knew you had my mother's staff that summoned the demon. And I knew it had to be still in your rooms, because you didn't have it with you when you were dragged down here.'

Dennis winced at the mention of the event.

'I also knew I could use it to get myself down here to rescue you. So, here I am to do just that. If you can show me you're worth it.'

There was a pregnant silence when Florence stopped speaking, while they all waited for Dennis's reaction.

'Finished?' asked Krystal.

'Yes, thank you,' Florence replied, quietly.

Krystal stood up and lifted Dennis by his collar. 'Only a daughter would've done the things she's done for you,' she scowled, dangling the wizard at eye level.

A tear rolled down Dennis's cheek and his face began to turn blue. Krystal lowered him to the ground again where he gasped for air. She hadn't realised how tight she'd been holding him, and only released him because she thought he was sorrowful.

He sat down and massaged his neck.

'Have you got anything to say for yourself?' asked the troll, about to prod him with a very hard finger.

'All right. You're probably my daughter. Only my daughter could know those things, I suppose,' he conceded, obviously under strain.

'But are you worth trying to save? That's the question, isn't it?' said the troll, prodding the air just inches from Dennis's chest.

The sustained badgering seemed over, and Dennis finally rallied himself. He stood up, defiantly. 'Of course I'm worth it. Get me out of this place and I'll show you how much I'm worth it.'

'You were supposed to be getting *me* out of here,' Krystal reminded him.

'Things have changed. Hell and Florence are here now, and the odds have improved.'

'Is this… er, funny little thing your acquaintance?' said Krystal, pointing at Hell.

'Yes, this is *it*.'

'*It?*' said Hell, turning slowly. '*Demon*, if you don't mind. I'm not an *it*.'

'Well, demon, what about getting us out of here?' said Krystal.

Dennis cut in, 'There's a price. He'll want something in return.'

'He already knows my terms,' said Florence, miming rubbing the staff. Then she turned to Hell and added, with a barely discernible grin, 'Now what would your terms be with Krystal for helping *her*?'

Krystal grabbed Hell by one of his horns and drew him towards her. 'What's your price, funny little thing?'

'Yeeow!' screeched the demon. 'I want to be king down 'ere, that's all.'

'That's all?'

'Yes,' said Hell, trying to nod.

'Nothing else? Nothing whatever at all?'

'Nope.'

'Then, what's the problem?' asked Krystal.

'The problem is…' Dennis explained, 'that there's already a king down here. Jamzamin.'

'That could be a bit tricky, then,' Krystal murmured.

'We were talking about it earlier,' Hell piped up.

'How far did you get?' asked Krystal.

'Only to the bit where I 'it 'im on the back of the 'ead wiv me axe,' said Hell.

'Did you think that was a good idea?' Florence wondered.

'Not while 'e's awake, no. But when 'e's in the land of nod, it should be safe enough to give 'im a bloody good 'ammerin',' replied Hell. 'Less of course you can fink of a better idea.'

'How big is he?' asked Krystal. Hell stood on tiptoe, with his arms raised above his head trying to give a general indication of Jamzamin's stature.

'Hmm. Not that big, then,' said Krystal, sitting down. She needed to rest now. All this thinking was giving her the start of a headache.

'Do you know where Jamzamin is now, Father?' asked Florence.

Dennis whipped his head around, then thought better of what he was going to say about being called father. 'In his office, or whatever he calls it, I suppose.'

'Where's that?' asked Florence.

'I don't know. Where is it, Hell?'

The demon thought for a moment. 'It *was* at the back of Reception, but 'e's moved it somewhere else and 'e ain't told me yet. P'raps 'e don't trust me.'

'Well, you are a demon,' Florence pointed out.

He couldn't argue with that. 'We could ask at Reception, I suppose. They might know.'

Dennis sagged visibly; he was rapidly losing what little confidence he had in Hell.

'All right,' said Florence. 'Let's go to Reception.'

'What?' said Krystal, catching the threads of something going on around her again.

'We… are… going… to… Reception,' Hell told her. 'Is she fick, or something?' he whispered to Dennis, not quietly enough. He noticed the ground was no longer touching his feet. And his spiky leather collar was a few notches tighter.

'Don't you take that attitude with me, funny little thing. Or you might not get to become king. Or anything.'

'Okay, okay,' he squirmed. 'Put me down, I'll take you to Reception.'

She did as she was asked.

'Ouch!' he moaned. 'You might've done it gently. It's a bloody long drop from up there!' He saw a hard expression on her already stony features and scurried away.

'Wait for us!' Dennis called after him.

* * *

7

Hell had only turned the next corner and was standing by a rectangular hole in the wall. Over the top of it hung a lopsided sign with the word *Reception* scratched into it. Dennis walked over and stood beside Hell. 'I thought this place would be miles away,' Dennis remarked.

'It is, if you're right up the other end,' said Hell.

'I hadn't looked at it like that,' said Dennis, patiently. 'There seems to be nobody here.'

'Should be a bell-rope somewhere,' said Hell, standing on tiptoe, trying to peer over the counter.

'There is,' Dennis noticed. 'Shall I pull it?'

'It's gonna be a bloody long wait if you don't,' replied Hell.

Dennis tugged the rope. There was silence, so after a minute he tried it again. There was that same silence again. After what he considered a reasonable time, he said, 'Did you hear anything?'

'What, like a bell ringing?'

'Yes.'

'No.'

'Okay, perhaps the duty demon's not in.'

''E's in all right,' said Hell, ''e's probably kipping. Give me a lift up, will you?'

Dennis looked at the little demon and thought he wouldn't touch him with a flag pole.

'Come on!' said Hell, getting agitated at Dennis's lack of enthusiasm.

The wizard screwed up his eyes and his courage, reached down and picked him up. He was unexpectedly and unpleasantly moist and slithery for something so scaly and dry-looking. Dennis deposited him on the counter, then wiped his hands on the hem of his robe.

'Hold my hand, will you?'

'What?' said Dennis. 'That's hardly a hand.'

'Okay, my claw. I need to lean around the back and fix it.'

Dennis took the claw reluctantly and tried not to think about it.

'Tighter than that!' Hell leaned through the hatchway hole and around to one side. 'Thought so. He always disconnects it when he has a nap.' He fiddled around for a few minutes. 'That should do it.'

Thankfully, he let go of Dennis's hand and hopped down without assistance. 'Give it a try now.'

Dennis did, and a sonorous clang echoed around the reception area. 'How do you fix it when you're on your own?'

'I don't. I come back later.'

A bleary-eyed and lugubrious demonic face appeared behind the counter. The demon glanced up to one side quizzically, thinking he was sure he'd disconnected that rope. He looked straight at Dennis, then down at Hell. 'Oh, it's you, is it.'

'I'm looking for 'is royalness, Jamzamin,' said Hell, slowly and deliberately, as if talking to a child. ''E's moved office, and I don't know where 'e's gone.'

''E could be anywhere,' replied the demon, sleepily.

'Where's that?'

The demon gave him a puzzled look. 'All right, then. Somewhere. That's where he could be.'

'That narrows it down a bit,' said Dennis, but the sarcasm was lost.

'Look mate, 'e doesn't tell *me* where 'e is, yuh know. I only work 'ere. I don't *own* the place.' Such a long speech required a deep yawn.

'All right,' said Dennis. 'I don't find that too difficult to believe. Now, let's put this another way…'

'Put it whichever way you like, mate. I still don't know where 'e is.'

'Where's his *new* office, then?'

'Not gonna complain or something are you?' asked the demon, guardedly, blinking himself into slightly more wakefulness.

'Complain?' said Dennis. 'What is there to complain about?'

'Well, if 'e finds out I've been sleeping on the job again, 'e says I'm next in line for cleaning out the slime pits.'

Yuck, thought Dennis.

The Reception demon saw the look on Dennis's face. 'Exactly, and it took a lot of persuading and palm-greasing to get this cushy little number, I can tell you.'

'You just tell me where his office is, and I won't tell him about you sleeping.'

'Supposin', just supposin' mind, that I don't tell you?'

'Well, when I *do* find him, I'll tell him about you sleeping, and then I'll tell him about the other times you've slept on duty this last week,' said Dennis, menacingly.

'But I didn't,' the demon protested.

'I know that. You know that. But Jamzamin doesn't,' said Dennis, softly. But for all the smoothness of his tone, the demon knew that it bore the edge of bloody great circular saw.

''E's more of a demon than we are,' said the creature, looking down at Hell.

'You ain't too wrong there,' said Hell. 'Now, where's Jamzamin's new office, Gluck?'

Gluck, for that was the things name, shook his horned head.

At this moment, Krystal, who'd hung back and had grown tired of waiting for them, came to see what was keeping them. They quickly updated her. 'Why won't you tell them?' she asked Gluck, almost pleasantly.

'He's gonna tell Jamzamin about me sleeping,' explained the demon, defensively.

Krystal leaned across the counter and grabbed one of the demon's horns. 'I'll tell you what,' she said, pulling him halfway through the hatch hole and holding him at her eye level. 'If you don't tell us where he is, you could be in danger of becoming permanently asleep.'

The Reception demon thought about that for about a second and a half before spitting out his reply. 'He's down at Fourmorends! Hell knows where it is.'

'There, that wasn't difficult, was it?' she cooed.

'Will you put me down now, please?'

She raised him a little higher then released her grip. He screamed as he fell backwards through the hole and met the ground.

'Come on, then. Let's go,' said Florence. 'Lead on, funny little thing.'

'Hell's the name,' he snorted.

'Whatever.'

'I'll get you for that!' Gluck yelled after Krystal. 'I'll tell Jamzamin you forced me to tell!'

Krystal stopped in her tracks, turned around and walked slowly back. 'Pardon?' she said.

Foolishly, the demon repeated his threat. The troll reached out to grab one of his horns again, but he stepped smartly back out of reach. The angry troll brought down her sledge hammer fists and smashed the counter to splinters. 'Jamzamin will hear about this!' he screamed.

She marched through the gap she'd created and grabbed the cowering demon by the scruff of his neck. 'No, he won't,' she snapped.

'Yes, 'e will!' yelled the demon, defiantly.

'NO, HE WON'T!' said the troll, emphasizing each word with a crushing blow to the top of his head. Then she took a step back and murmured, 'Now tell him.'

Gluck didn't answer. Krystal shrugged her massive shoulders and walked slowly after the others. Florence was waiting for her, but Dennis and Hell had gone further along the tunnel.

'Father!' Florence yelled after him. But Dennis ignored her. It wasn't a name he was used to hearing.

Something registered with him. *Had someone called?* He stopped. Yes, she meant him, but he still didn't answer, although he felt obliged to wait, 'What kept you?' he asked.

'I had to wait for Krystal,' she explained.

'Ah,' he breathed, and began walking on again.

* * *

After walking for what seemed an age, it occurred to Dennis to ask, 'Does anyone know where we're going?'

'Fourmorends,' obliged Hell.

'Yes, I know,' sighed Dennis.

'Why'd you ask, then?' replied Hell.

'Do you know where it is, is what I mean?' said Dennis.

'Nope.'

'Your mate at reception said you did,' Dennis reminded him.

'Look, mister bloody perfect, I've forgotten, all right?'

'No, it's not all right,' snapped Dennis. 'You should've asked.'

'You said to me...' Hell began slowly, 'find out where Jamzamin's office is, didn't you?' Dennis's chin moved but he made no sounds. 'You didn't ask me 'ow to get there, *did* you?'

Dennis's jaw continued to move soundlessly.

'Come on,' sighed Florence. 'Let's go back and ask at Reception.'

'Er...' interrupted Krystal.

'*Yes*?' said Florence.

'That won't be necessary,' said the troll, examining the backs of her hands.

'Ah, good,' said Dennis, cheerfully. 'You know where it is, then.'

'Well, in fact... no.' She shook her head slowly and grindingly.

'No?' queried Dennis.

'No. There's no point going back.'

'Why not?' asked Florence, joining the inquisition. 'The demon at Reception must know.'

'He did. Probably,' said the troll. 'But now he's, er, sort of dead, like.'

'*Dead*?' mouthed Dennis.

'You killed Gluck?' said Hell, open mouthed.

'Not *fully*, I don't think. Near enough, though,' Krystal had to admit. 'But he wasn't very nice to me,' she said in mitigation, and marched off down the tunnel.

Dennis and Florence looked at one another and shrugged. 'Now what?' said Dennis.

'I suppose we'd better stay with her,' said Florence, resigning herself to the situation. They quickened their pace to catch up with the troll, who looked like she was on a mission.

'Wait for me!' called Hell, scuttling to catch them up.

*

'Does anyone know where we are now?' asked the wizard.

'Yes,' replied Hell, who was the only one likely to know, him having lived there for a few hundred years. 'We'll be at the Slime Pits, soon.'

'Oh, good,' said Dennis, with mock cheerfulness, 'That should clear our sinuses, then.'

'Yes,' said Hell, surprised that Dennis had some local knowledge. 'We all go there to clear our 'eads, that's why we call it the…'

'Please don't go on,' Dennis interrupted, swiftly.

'Suit yourself,' muttered Hell. 'There's bound to be someone down there muckin' 'em out. They might've even seen Jamzamin.' The demon went to the front of the group and led them into the pungency of the Pits.

Dennis and Florence screwed up their noses and, in desperation, after only a few seconds, pulled handkerchiefs out to cover their mouths and noses. Hell strode on with his head held high – well, as high as it would go – and was sniffing the air appreciatively.

'Can't you smell it?' Dennis mumbled through his handkerchief.

'Yeah, great, ennit.'

'That's what comes of having your nose pickled in sulphur fumes for a few hundred years, I suppose,' he mumbled, trying not to breathe.

There was a fairly wide ledge skirting the gently rippling pools, and it looked quite solid, but this didn't stop Dennis and Florence making a conscious effort to stay ahead of the weighty troll.

Around the next bend, Hell paused, 'Coo-ee!' he called. 'Anybody there?'

'Oh, hi, Hell,' replied a round-shaped, brown thing sitting on a low, flat-topped stalagmite in the middle of a steaming pool.

'Ow's it going?' Hell called out to him.

'Not bad,' the brown thing called back. 'Bit of trouble with the Smelk, though.'

As if on cue, the sulphurous yellow liquid in front of him began to bubble. He stood up quickly and raised the paddle he'd been using to stir the pool, then watched intently as the bubbles circled around him. Something was moving below the surface. The others stood on the ledge, nervous but curious – and, above all, glad that they weren't out there with him. The pool began to boil, then slowly a large, red, horsey head with three horns rose up. It opened its jaws wide and took a deep breath, presumably preparing to fill the cavern with flames and smoke. The brown thing acted quickly, and brought his paddle down with all his might onto the beast's head, but only impaled it on one of its horns. The angry Smelk roared and plunged back into the slime, taking the paddle with it.

'Oh, bloody 'ell!' exclaimed the brown thing. 'I've got nuffin' to 'it wiv now!'

Bubbles surfaced in the slime again and began circling the rock that the brown thing was balancing on. 'It's coming back!' he yelled. 'I've 'ad it this time!' The red, horsey head rose from the slime again. It was quite colourful really. It circled the rock, then swam towards the ledge in order to build up speed to charge at the brown thing. A fatal mistake.

Krystal reached down and plucked it from the slime just as it turned to charge. She held it up and eyed it curiously. Its body was only half the size of its head, and it had no apparent weight. Mind you, compared to Krystal, nothing had any weight to speak of. The Smelk writhed in her grip, spitting and cursing in a growly voice until Krystal balled her empty hand into a stony fist and brought it down with a smack on top of its head. The Smelk went POP! It became limp and very still. Krystal raised it up to her eye level again, as she usually did with things, and stared at it.

'That's better.' She grinned into the lifeless face. The Smelk's head was smaller and flatter, but at least it was now in proportion with its body. Most of its contents were now in its distended stomach, and blue gunge was leaking from it.

Yuck. Krystal thought, and tossed its limp body back into the slime.

'Nooo!' yelled the brown thing, as the lifeless Smelk sailed through the air. 'Not in 'ere. I've just cleaned it out!' His mouth hung open as the blue gunge began to mix with the yellow liquid of the pool and turn the whole mess into a rather attractive shade of green. 'Jamzamin will go mad when 'e sees this lot,' the brown thing moaned.

'I don't see why,' remarked Florence. 'It looks rather nice.'

'I know 'is problem,' sighed Hell. 'Jamzamin likes all the colours kept separate. Yellow in one set of pits. Green in another. He doesn't 'old wiv four yellow ones wiv a green one in amongst 'em. Can't see as it matters, meself.'

'That's why you should be in charge down here,' said Dennis at his ear, seeing an opportunity to egg him on.

'Is there anything we can do?' asked Florence.

'Gettin' out before 'is royalness finds 'em would be a good idea,' advised Hell.

'Do you know where Jamzamin is?' Krystal asked the brown thing.

'Well, I might…' it hesitated.

Dennis cut in, 'Before you ask what's in it for you, you might like to bear in mind we just saved your life.'

'All right, 'e's at Fourmorends.'

'We know,' sighed Dennis.

'Well, that's all right, then, ennit?'

Here we go again, Dennis thought. 'Let's approach this differently,' he sighed. 'Where's Fourmorends?'

'Ah.' The brown thing squatted down on the rock and seemed to be thinking hard. The others watched patiently from the ledge. There was a sound reminiscent of ripping silk, followed by a gentle 'Plop'. The brown thing stood up. 'It's that way,' he announced, pointing at a low tunnel that led off from the other side of the Pits. 'Come on. I'll show you.' And he stepped right onto the ever-greening surface of the pool.

Florence gasped. Dennis watched, expectantly. The brown thing was obviously a lot lighter than it looked, or on the other hand, perhaps the pool was… no, we won't go there. The brown demon walked across it, barely sinking, as though he was treading on a wet concrete path.

'Can we do that?' Dennis wondered. 'Or do we have to walk all the way around?'

'You can try it if you like,' said Hell. 'But after what 'e's just dumped in there, I'm going the long way round.'

Dennis cleared his throat. 'Ahem… yes, you're probably right.'

The brown thing reached the other side, stepped off the sludge and stood impatiently tapping what passed for a foot. Dennis was first to catch him up and stood back as he caught the smell of him. 'Phew!' he cried, turning away, searching for a second hanky.

'Sorry about that,' the brown thing apologised. 'I'll try not to do it again in mixed company. But you know how it is. That bloody Smelk really put the wind up me.'

'Pity it didn't stay there,' Dennis complained, through his handkerchiefs.

'Look. I said 'sorry'. I can't keep apologising. If it 'appens again, try to ignore it. All right?'

Dennis tried, but couldn't. 'Look,' he said, at last. 'Perhaps if *I* went first…'

'You don't know the way,' the brown thing pointed out, as Dennis held his breath and squeezed past.

'Mind that…'

'Ouch!' Dennis moaned.

'… stalactite,' the brown thing cautioned.

'Phaw! It's everywhere!' fumed Dennis. Even as he spoke, there was a soft crunching noise underfoot. He looked down in utter dismay as he discovered he was wearing… something best not talked about, but it looked like a small, brown canoe. He put a hand on the wall to steady himself as he tried to shake it free. 'Oh, no!' he complained. 'It's all over the bloody walls as well! What have you been doing down here?'

'Lots,' said the brown thing. 'I've been very ill.'

Dennis had no further questions. Just revulsion. He stood aside and allowed the brown thing to take the lead again. The way was getting darker. 'Aren't there any torches in this place?' he complained.

'Yes, but it's probably best if you don't light one,' advised the brown thing.

'Why?' He wished he hadn't asked when the creature pointed at its rear end and smirked.

'There must be some other way we can see where we're going,' Dennis persisted.

'Just stop moaning, we'll be out of 'ere in a minute!' the brown thing snapped.

And almost as his words faded, the group emerged into a large, dome-roofed cavern, where the rocks glowed with a soft, green light. There were waterfalls tumbling into large scallop shaped troughs, which in turn created lots of smaller waterfalls to tumble from between their wide fingers into a slow-moving stream. The stream wound its way across a wide shelf below them and disappeared over the edge somewhere in the distance to the floor of the cavern.

'This is better,' remarked Dennis.

'Yes, much,' agreed Florence.

Krystal broke off a piece of the pale green rock and popped it into her mouth. She turned it around on her tongue for a moment, savouring it. 'Mm... Nice,' she commented. 'Sort of minty.'

'Don't do that,' said Hell. Krystal ignored him and broke off another chunk.

'Don't Do That. *Please*!' Hell repeated, only a little firmer this time.

'But it is rather moreish,' she protested.

'I expect it is,' countered Hell. 'But it's not yours.'

'No, and it's not yours either. Yet,' said Krystal, menacingly, but she put her fists behind her back, to resist temptation.

'What's this place called?' asked Florence. 'It's kind of... out of step with the rest of it down here.'

'Pits Mingle!' Krystal called from the back of the group.

Hell turned. He was impressed. 'How did you know that?'

'It says so, on that sign up there.'

'Oh,' said Hell. He turned and began to lead them off again. Dennis held his hand under one of the waterfalls to wash off the... whatever it was he'd leant against on the wall, and was now about to rinse from one of his pointy toed boots.

'Why is it called that?' Florence wondered.

'Well,' Hell began, 'after a while, every so often that is... the pits tend to overflow a bit, you know how it is?' Florence nodded as though she did. 'And it's channelled down 'ere where it gets diluted before it runs out over that ledge,' Hell explained.

Recalling the pits, Dennis promptly removed his hand from the waterfall and wiped it down his robe.

'Come on!' enthused the little brown thing. 'It's not far now.'

Dennis fell to the rear of the party and Krystal walked behind the little brown thing. They followed the winding stream and arrived at the high ledge where the water plummeted down and they watched in awe. The scene was bathed in a pale, yellow light here, and had there been any shrubs or trees, it might have given the impression that they were on the surface of the planet. But there wasn't, so it didn't. And nobody remarked on it anyway.

To their right, the ledge narrowed and spiralled down in an anticlockwise direction inside the great well-like hole of the cavern. That was the direction their aromatic little guide motioned them to follow and loped off.

'This is crazy,' said Dennis, impatiently, hanging back. 'Isn't there an easier way to get down to this place?'

'Yeah,' said Hell, 'but you probably won't be able to walk afterwards.'

'I didn't mean jump, idiot! Isn't there an easier path?'

'There's this path,' murmured Hell, resignedly, starting to lose his own patience, 'or there's one a couple of miles longer that we'll probably get lost on.'

Dennis huffed, and the pair moved off to catch the others.

Up ahead, something went POP! They stopped talking and listened.

***

9

'What was that?' whispered Dennis, when no further sound followed.

The others were only a short way ahead down the curving ledge. When they reached them, Florence looked a little agitated.

'It's Krystal, Father. There's been an accident,' she said, in hushed tones.

'It wasn't my fault,' Krystal moaned, looming up behind her.

'I know,' said Florence, trying to console her. 'It was an accident. I saw it.'

'I didn't see him stop, honest,' she sniffed, as she tried to shake the deflated body of the little brown thing from her foot.

'What happened?' asked Dennis.

'She trod on him, Father,' said Florence, glumly.

'Oh, great! So, now we don't have a guide,' whined the wizard.

'Is that all you've got to say?' snapped Hell, angrily. "ave a little compassion, mate. I'm supposed to be the demon around 'ere!'

'He smelt awful,' said Dennis, flatly, by way of justifying himself.

'Yeah, 'e probably *did*, to you. Don't you fink you might've smelt bad to 'im?'

'No,' said Dennis. 'Now, lead on.'

Hell shrugged and shook his horns. He walked to the edge, peered over and muttered, 'Still looks as steep as ever.'

'Just get on with it,' urged Dennis. 'Perhaps we can ask someone for directions when we get down there,' he added sarcastically, then realised it wasn't such a bad idea.

Hell moved off, taking the lead. 'Well,' he said over his shoulder to Krystal, by way of consolation, 'if you 'adn't saved 'is life, 'e wouldn't even 'ave been 'ere to kill.'

She responded with a sob.

As soon as she was out of Hell's line of sight, she broke off another chunk of green rock.

* * *

10

The unlikely quartet – a troll, a demon, an arch-magician and his young daughter – walked steadily down the spiral path hewn into the wall of the great circular cavern. The path was not so narrow and treacherous that they had to edge their way down in single file, but they had to keep their wits about them. There was occasional rock debris to negotiate, and there were fissures to step across. But they settled into a rhythm and made good progress – until about half way down when the path abruptly ran out.

Hell brought the party to a halt in good time. He strolled right up to the sheared off edge and peered over, and was immediately joined by Dennis.

'Oh, bloody brilliant!' railed Dennis. 'All this way for nothing!'

Hell sighed deeply. 'Gimme a moment, will you?'

'What are you going to do – distribute wings, or something?!'

'No, I'm gonna do this.' He raised a claw and pushed hard on a round protrusion on the rock wall beside him. From deep within the wall came the sound of an ancient engine stirring sluggishly into life. A harsher noise followed – rock scraping over rock – as flat rectangular slabs began sliding out of the wall at intervals, in front them, each a little lower, forming a stairway that, when complete, led all the way to the bottom.

Hell turned and grinned. He looked as if he might take a bow.

'That's amazing!' said Florence.

'Yeah,' grunted Krystal.

'Are we going to stand here admiring the view all day?' griped Dennis.

'It was supposed to come right from the top,' said Hell, ignoring him, 'But no-one's bovvered to finish it.'

'Another job for you as king,' said Dennis, without missing a beat. 'Now, can we get moving?' He started forward.

'Hold on,' said Hell, holding up a claw.

The demon carefully put a clawed foot on the top step. He stamped on it a couple of times to be certain it wasn't going to break off. The slabs were substantial, but they were also very old, as was the mechanism that held them in place. He put both feet down and jumped twice with his full weight. This caused a few minor dust falls, but the step stayed firm.

'Alright,' said Dennis. 'That's enough. No need to push your luck.'

'Look, mate,' said Hell, looking up at the wizard. 'I'm the one what's in front, and I rather like the idea of getting to the bottom at my own speed and not havin' to lead the charge of a few fousand tons of rock that might be trying to overtake me.'

He carefully extended his foot down to the next step. The stone stayed firm. Satisfied that they would all support his weight, he carried on down. 'Come on!' he called. 'It's all right!'

Dennis followed, with Florence next and Krystal bringing up the rear. No-one wanted to be behind Krystal in this situation. Florence, who was nearest, was sure she could hear the steps creaking ominously under the weight of the lumbering great troll.

The four descended in silence, apart, that was, from the tip-tap of leather on stone, the scratching of Hell's clawed feet, and the methodical clonk of stone on stone as Krystal thudded down. No-one uttered a word. But their footfalls were eventually drowned out by the sound of Krystal idly crunching another chunk of rock. Much to Hell's annoyance.

* * *

11

High above the Parallel Dimension, through many strata of rock and the fossils of long-forgotten creatures, Eydith stood on her balcony in the west wing of Havrapsor University. She was watching the sun go down over the city skyline from the rooms into which she had recently moved. *I never had this sort of view from father's old room,* she thought. *I don't know how he stuck it in there for all those years.* Though, she reminded herself, when he became Archchancellor, he had a small stipendiary house on the campus, and spent a lot of his time in his office in the main building.

'I wonder where he is now?' she said to herself, thinking she was alone. But Sprag, her magical staff was listening from the corner where she'd left him propped against the wall. Sprag had belonged to her father, and by right of succession he now belonged to the new Archchancellor, but recent events in which Eydith had played a significant role, and in which she had shown herself to be a wizard of extraordinary talent and power, had resulted in her forming a bond with the staff and being allowed to keep it. Not that anyone had the temerity to disallow it. She referred to Sprag as male at the staff's own request, and it made sense because the voice was male, and its now-fading misogynous streak could only have been male. Although any allocation of a gender seemed somehow fatuous for what was in fact, a large, gnarly stick.

'I don't know, mistress,' Sprag's voice scratched her mind. 'Would you like me to find him?'

'No, it's getting late now, but I'd like to know in the morning.'

'Yes, mistress.'

'I thought I heard a rumbling noise, earlier. It sounded like it was coming from underneath the university,' she said, with a note of concern in her voice.

'Yes, mistress, I felt the disturbance myself.'

'Any thoughts?'

'It was not unlike the sound of demons breaking through from the Parallel Dimension, mistress.'

'I don't think it could be that. Since losing the battle and taking Dennis, they seem to have lost interest in up here.'

'Perhaps, mistress.'

'You think we've not seen the last of them, then?'

'No, mistress. I believe Dennis will find a way out, and that could re-ignite their interest. Let us hope it takes him a long time.'

Eydith wandered slowly back into her rooms, took one last look at the setting sun, at least for today, and closed the door. 'I wonder if Link heard it.'

* * *

12

'I'm glad that's over,' said Dennis, hopping off the last step. Florence was so close she almost collided with him. She was anxious to get clear of the mechanical stairway. The reason was Krystal, who was rhythmically and loudly clonking down not far behind her.

On arriving at the bottom, the troll jumped off with both feet. Her weight as she launched herself, snapped off the last step, and the deafening crack echoed around the cavern. As a result, sympathetic creaking and cracking sounds began occurring high above, as slabs weakened by Krystal's footfalls, began breaking off.

'I think we'd better run!' shouted Hell, above the rising din.

'Where?' yelled Dennis, seeing no obvious shelter.

'Away from 'ere!' shouted Hell, unhelpfully, looking over his shoulder as he scooted off to the other side of the cavern. He had the presence of mind – or the lucidity of self-preservation – or the luck – to head for an alcove that the falling rocks wouldn't reach until last as they spiralled down around the perimeter of the cavern.

Dennis looked up just in time to see the horrific process begin, the steps falling like a row of vertical dominoes. He hitched up his robe and ran like Hell – well, perhaps in more of an upright manner than the demon. The entire perimeter of the cavern seemed to be falling in around them. Even Krystal quickened her pace, which wasn't that noticeable on the flat, but Florence waited for her, staff in one hand, hem of her skirt in the other, prepared to make a dash for it as soon as the troll was close.

'Come on, Krystal!' she urged, trying to make herself heard over the rumble and crash of the falling stones.

'You go! I'll catch up!' the troll shouted.

'Come *on*!' yelled Florence.

'I'll be all right! Save yourself!' Krystal yelled, breaking into a lumbering sort of waddle. At least it was a shade faster than a walk. And as Florence watched in horror, a torrent of great slabs dropped to the ground behind the troll as she tried her best to hurry. A great cloud of dust enveloped her and billowed towards Florence, who ran after Dennis who was now disappearing into the alcove just ahead of her, sprinting as though her life depended on it. Well, it did, and she skidded in beside him as the dust cloud swept past.

'You made it, then,' said Dennis, coldly stating the obvious. She didn't answer. With all the noise going on outside, she may not have heard, but she probably chose to treat the remark with appropriate contempt. She peered intently into the heap of fallen rocks, looking anxiously for signs of the fallen rock that was Krystal. She stood by the alcove entrance, listening. The slabs and other dislodged debris had stopped falling, and all was quiet now.

* * *

13

The thunderous rockfall in the cavern in the Parallel Dimension shook the surface world, too, chiefly in Havrapsor University, which was directly overhead. And happening in the early morning, it roused some of the wizards.

Linkwood awoke with a start and groped around in the gloom for his bedside candle. He knocked it over, and a glass, still half full, or half empty, depending on your point of view, crashed to the floor with it. *Sod it*, he thought, *I wonder where that went.* He sat up and gathered his thoughts while his eyes grew accustomed to the gloom. He could make out the shape of the lamp fixed to the wall opposite and muttered a spell as he pointed his fingers at it.

Since the recent battle with the demons from the Parallel Dimension, his magic had improved to the level where he was ready to take the examination that would elevate him to the next level of wizardry. The only positions above that were of the various faculties of tutorship, or the Archchancellorship itself.

He had already been passed over for the latter, on account of him being too young. But he wasn't too put out about it. And if the Archchancellorship belonged to anyone, it belonged to Eydith. But she was too young as well. And the conservative senior wizards were finding it hard enough getting used to the idea of female *students* around the buildings! Years of tradition could not be forgotten in a few months.

A narrow fork of soft, green light zigzagged from Link's fingertips and struck the lamp. It flickered momentarily, appearing to enjoy the experience, then spluttered to life. He leant back against his comfortable pillows, and did a quick double-take. He'd noticed lately that, for some reason, sometimes the shadows in the room had shadows of their own. He guessed it was probably the building doing it. It had been playing up since the battle, peeved that it had been seared and blasted so badly in the fight. It probably knew that he'd had a hand in it, too.

Thin lines of light streaked the sky. Dawn was about to break. He didn't mind as long as it did so quietly. Somewhere in the distance, a cock crowed. In that same somewhere, someone yelled, 'Shut up, you noisy bastard!' Which saved him the bother.

Just then there was another rumbling under the building. It was felt more than heard. Link figured out it was just such a rumble that had woken him up. It had intruded into his dream, as external things sometimes do. *Bloody inconsiderate. Probably the building messing with us again.* 'Get over it,' he said, aloud.

Dust particles drifted down from the ceiling. He dressed quickly and hurried outside into the hallway. Eydith's rooms were next to his and he rapped on her door.

'Did you feel it?' he asked.

'What?'

'The earth, moved?'

'Oh, that. What do you think it was?'

'That's what I've come to ask *you*,' he said.

'I don't know. It felt like the foundations moving.'

'Yeah,' said Link. 'Is the building getting more annoyed with us? What does Sprag think?'

'No, it's not that. He's not sure, but he thinks there might be something going on in the PD.'

'Did he actually call it the PD?'

'Don't be silly. This is Sprag we're talking about.'

'I *can* hear you!' said a wooden voice in both their heads.

'Sorry,' said Link, and Eydith just smiled.

Link considered for a moment. 'Do you think Dennis has something to do with it?'

'Don't know,' she replied. 'But it's likely. I think we should find out.'

'Okay,' he said, cautiously. 'But where do we start?'

Straightaway she said, 'The Archchancellor, of course. Let's see what he knows.'

'Hmm,' breathed Link. 'Do you think he'll be awake yet?'

'That earlier big rumble woke most of us.' She walked out onto her balcony and looked across the courtyard. 'Yes, it looks like he is. There's a light in his window. And in a few others.'

That settled it. 'Okay, then. Let's go.'

Eydith picked up Sprag, and followed him along the hallway. 'Wait for me!'

He paused and looked back. 'Shh… you'll wake everybody up.'

'They're awake already.' She chased along the hallway and down the stairs after him.

He was waiting at the bottom. The ground grumbled again. 'There it goes again,' he said. 'We'd better hurry.'

*

In minutes they were at Archchancellor Trinkel's door. Eydith raised the brass knocker, which was cast in the shape of a cat, and let it drop. Trinkel was fond of cats. He might even have been named after one. The cat fell slowly back against the door and struck with a resounding boing, out of all proportion to the meagre tap, which seemed to echo right across the campus. Everyone in that wing would surely be awake now. A muffled voice called out from somewhere nearby. 'Keep the bloody noise down, will you! Some of us have got to get up in a minute!'

'I didn't think it would be as loud as that,' she said, pulling a pained face. There was a shuffling noise on the other side of the door.

'Just a minute,' said a reedy voice inside. A small round hole appeared in the knocker. 'I wasn't expecting anyone. Certainly not this early,' said the Archchancellor, dropping the cover of the hole and lifting the latch. 'Come in, come in… er, *both* of you.' Eydith and Link entered the room and looked around. Though they knew the Archchancellor fairly well, this was the first time they'd visited him at home.

The place was cluttered. Pictures of strange things hung from the walls, and odd-looking stuffed animals hung from the ceiling. Shelves were filled with leather bound books, and there were jars containing, what can only be described as *bits* of things. 'I expect you've come about the rumblings. Hmm?'

'What? Oh, yes,' said Eydith, dragging her attention back from something suspended from a hook on the back of the door. 'Do you know what it is?'

'Nope,' said Trinkel. 'But I'm checking my reference books. It might be some kind of cat or a bloody great mouse. I found it by the side of the road, you know. Must have been hit by a lot of carts.'

'Sorry?' said Eydith, and then realised he was talking about whatever it was that was hanging on the back of the door. 'No, not that – the rumblings.'

'Ah, those... yes. Well, first I thought it was that curry I had last night. Then I thought, no. I didn't have curry last night. It was the night before that. And then, I thought... fried garlic and trotters. Then the ground shook again. Funny, I thought, it's not me, then. Anyway... what was the question again? Oh, yes. Do I know what the rumbling is? No. Leastwise, not quite sure yet. Could be a bit of subsidence I suppose... yes, that's it. Subsidence. Nothing to worry about. Probably. The buildings generally take care of themselves.'

Trinkel was cluttered like his room. The pockets of his robe bulged and draped with things, some even seemed to be alive. He was tall, though slightly stooped with age, and with his unexpectedly well-trimmed white beard and hair – and especially in his robes of office – he bore a passing resemblance to his old friend, Wimlett.

But Trinkel wasn't a born leader. He didn't have to be. Although increasingly eccentric these days, he was both a good wizard and a good man, who'd earned the respect of his peers through a distinguished career. However, the main reason he'd been elected to the Archchancellorship was because *he was safe*. For seventeen years, the senior magicians had suffered from the serious mistake of allowing themselves to be manipulated and cajoled into electing Dennis. So when he was finally out of the way, they unanimously got behind Trinkel. He was not so respected and beloved as Eydith's father had been – who was? – but *he was safe*. Though one sometimes had to wonder, how safe?

Trinkel seemingly floated across the floor to his little table and poured himself a cup of tea. 'Cheers.' He smiled, raising the cup. 'First one today... I think. Help yourselves.'

This is going to be difficult, Eydith thought, *there's only one cup, and he's using it.*

Sprag's voice entered her mind and he ran a spell for extra cups across the backs of her eyelids. There was a pair of popping sounds as two cups materialised on the table. These were accompanied by the pops of a small milk jug and a salt shaker disappearing. 'Oh, dear,' she apologised.

'Not to worry, my dear. It's happening all the time just lately. Every time I want something, it seems I have to forfeit something else. Odd that. Some strange magic floating about, I think. Started the other…what was it now? Day? Yes. That's right… the other day. I was stuffing this… er… long thing… four legs…'

'Sofa?' prompted Eydith.

'Sofa? No, it wasn't as big as that… Ah, yes. I remember. A goat! That was it, I was stuffing this goat. You know how it is?' He glanced at Link, who rapidly shook his head. 'Someone knocked on the door,' Trinkel continued, 'I was only gone a minute, came back in, the cat's knocked my alcohol over, *and* half a jug of wotsitsname – I'll never see that again – some sulphur crystals and… and… oh, something or other. Anyway, there was a loud bang, lots of smoke and my spells haven't recovered enough to work properly since. By the way, you haven't seen a half-stuffed goat anywhere, have you?'

Eydith and Link hadn't.

'Oh, well. If you do, be sure to let me know.' He carried on fussing with some cotton wool and wood shavings, pushing them into some sort of empty, scaly thing. He stood back and admired his handiwork, 'Hmm,' he sighed. 'Not bad.' He followed this by muttering what must have been one of his very own secret spells and waving his hands about mysteriously. This caused a minor explosion which was more wind than substance, and the scaly thing jumped down off the table and scurried into a hole in the skirting board.

Trinkel opened the book that was lying on the chair and eyed it with suspicion. He ran a finger down the page. 'Hmm, it doesn't say anything about that in here.' He scratched his head, turned slowly and almost jumped out of his skin. 'My goodness! You gave me a turn.

I thought you'd gone.' He was clutching his chest with one hand and the chair for support with the other.

'We came about the rumblings,' Link reminded him.

'So you did, so you did. Minor subsidence, that's all. Nothing to be alarmed about.' He showed Eydith and Link to the door and the pair walked out, unconvinced. 'Don't forget!' called Trinkel. 'If you find any half-stuffed goats out there, they're mine!'

* * *

14

'Any sign of her, yet?' asked Dennis, deeply concerned about the reward he hoped to collect from Krystal's father if he got her home safely.

Florence peered into the dust cloud that was slowly settling over the heap of rubble outside the alcove.

'There's no sign of her yet, Father.' She knew Krystal was tough, but she was getting seriously worried about her.

Dennis cringed at that word *father* again. 'She'll be alright, she's…'

'Shh…' hissed Florence, as she strained her ears, listening intently to something in the dust cloud. She heard it again. 'Crunch, crunch, crunch.' They all heard it. It sounded like heavy footsteps approaching. Was she coming through the cloud? Then they recognised the sound.

'She's eating bloody rocks, again!' exclaimed Hell.

'Oh, there you are!' Krystal called, as she lumbered through the dust, kicking rocks aside. 'Haven't seen a storm like that in years.'

Course you haven't, Dennis thought, *you've been asleep for years*. 'Storm?' he said. 'Storm? That was a bloody avalanche! You could've got us all killed!'

'Well,' said Krystal, looking down her nose at him. 'We'll never know, will we?'

'You're safe. That's what matters,' said Florence, hugging her awkwardly. It felt like hugging a statue. 'What now?' she said, looking at the others.

Hell's opinion was that they couldn't do anything till the dust settled properly. 'And there might still be more to come down,' he said, looking up at the wall. 'So we'd better hang on for a while.' The others agreed and they all sat down and waited.

After a while, Dennis looked around him and said to Hell, 'Do you happen to know where the exits are from this place?'

'Yeah. They're behind all these rocks and stuff.'

'I thought so,' he said, and lapsed into a brooding silence.

After another while, Dennis piped up again, 'Have you ever noticed…?' he began, 'that for a place that's called the Parallel

Dimension, there's quite a lot of *up* and *down*, but not too much that's *parallel*.'

'Everything's parallel to somefing, somewhere,' remarked Hell.

'Yes, and this place seems to be parallel to a mine shaft, rather than the surface world, which is what one might expect.'

'I s'pose it depends on 'ow you look at it,' the demon argued.

'You can look at it however you like,' said the wizard. 'But all we ever seem to do is go down. And the surface world is surely up! Not down! Not sideways!'

'We have plenty of sideways,' said Hell, aggrieved, and missing the point. 'All right, we can go sideways if you like.'

'That would be an improvement on down. Up and out of here would be even better.'

'And the tunnels that go out of 'ere do go sideways for a bit.'

'Wonderful,' said Dennis, with unconcealed sarcasm. 'So, let's make a move. I think it's safe enough now.'

*

Eydith and Link made their way back to the west wing. 'I don't think he can hack it anymore,' said Link, when he judged them to be out of Trinkel's hearing range.

'I don't know; he seems to have hacked enough stuff in those rooms of his,' said Eydith. 'It was horrible. All those dead things and that other thing bursting into life like that. I wonder what it was.'

'More worrying,' said Link, 'is where it went?' He gave his robe a good shake and Eydith laughed.

'Yes, but what on Crett was it?' she said.

'Probably harmless,' said Link. 'It didn't look as though it had teeth. Anyway, I wasn't referring to that. I meant he seems to be losing his grip. Is he still up to the job?'

'Hmm, yes, I suppose he is a bit vague,' she agreed.

'A *bit* vague? He's in danger of becoming invisible.'

'I think we'd better try and find my father,' suggested Eydith. 'He'll know what to do.'

'Let's see what we can find out for ourselves, first, before we bother Wimlett,' said Link. 'Use him as a last resort. You know him and Sprag annoy each other.'

She thought about it and agreed.

'Good,' said Link. 'Now, let's go and get some breakfast.'

'It's all about food with you, isn't it?'

'One has to observe priorities,' he said, and ducked as she took a playful swipe.

'Hey, that's a point,' she said, having thought of something as they headed for the food hall, 'It's still quite early. Maybe Trinkel just isn't a morning person.'

'Huh.'

* * *

15

Dennis glanced around the cavern. 'Hell, can you tell exactly where the exit tunnels should be?'

'They should be behind all these rocks,' said Hell. He stood and turned slowly on a clawed heel. 'If I ain't mistaken, there should be one over there, and one over there.' He indicated to his left and right. 'And that one would be best. We just need to shift a few tons of staircase and stuff. Any ideas?'

'Indeed I have,' said Dennis. 'The one who got us into this mess is going to get us out of it.'

'The troll?'

'Me?' said Krystal.

'Yes, you,' said Dennis. 'We need you to clear a path to that wall. Eat anything you like along the way, if you must.'

''Ere,' objected the demon, but he didn't get in her way.

She trundled forwards and sized up the heap in front of her.

'And don't throw any of it this way!' yelled Dennis, suddenly fearing what might be about to happen.

She grunted something that probably only another troll would have understood and barged her way into the heap with her arms and legs flailing. She seemed to be enjoying herself. A cloud of dust was the immediate result. But when it cleared, they saw a rough path had been bulldozed through the rockfall. Even better, it led to a tunnel entrance.

Dennis actually smiled. But he didn't go all the way to thanking her. Florence did that. 'Right,' he said. 'Let's get moving.' He stood aside for Hell, and they all fell in behind him.

As the demon had said, the passageway went sideways for quite a way. Then it joined another, smaller cavern, where they were surprised to meet another small group coming the other way. It shouldn't have surprised them, because the subterranean network that was the Parallel Dimension was home to an entire race of demons, together with a few minor species. So, it was unlikely they would travel for long without meeting some of them. But this particular group did surprise them. And it turned out to be not the friendliest of meetings.

'What the blazes is going on down here?' yelled a familiar voice.

It was Jamzamin with a couple of his henchmen – a pair of demons known as Brown and Green, for obvious reasons. The king looked and sounded furious. He scowled at the motley quartet in front him. 'Are you idiots trying to destroy my kingdom? What was all that noise and commotion?'

'Oh, it's you. 'Ello, your royalness,' said Hell, bowing awkwardly.

'I'm told there's been a major collapse in the stairway cavern. That's where I'm headed. And that's where I find you lot coming from,' he said, accusingly. 'Anyone going to tell me what's going on? Who's responsible? Because they are in serious trouble!'

Hell seemed to have lost his voice. Dennis and Florence stood quietly for a moment. The wizard was sizing up the situation, wondering what lie would work best to get them out of this crap, or how best to drop Krystal in it. Florence was waiting for him to choose one of those. It was Krystal who broke the silence. She stepped forward and looked down at the king. 'I fink it's me you want,' she said. 'I broke your stupid stairs. And you are?' she asked.

The others waited, holding their breath.

Jamzamin's neck cracked as he looked up at her. It would be wrong to say he turned ugly, because ugly was his resting face, but he did turn snarlier. 'Then you're the one I'm gonna deal with. First, that is. Because you're *all* in trouble. Guards, take her!'

Brown and Green looked at the towering troll, then at one another, then gulped, and took a tentative step forward. Their king was still pontificating, and seriously annoying Krystal, which wasn't a sensible thing to do. The troll princess was no respecter of persons, even kings, as her father would confirm.

'I am Jamzamin, king of the Parallel Dimen…' He was stopped in mid-sentence by an unexpected stone fist crushing his head into his shoulders.

'Not anymore, you're not,' she growled, watching him sink slowly to the floor.

Hell stood with his mouth agape, unable to speak. Before he knew it, Krystal had closed a mighty hand around one of his horns and lifted him off the ground. It was becoming too regular an occurrence. 'Well, *your majesty,* that's my part of the trade, where's yours?'

The guards faltered and backed away, giving Hell a parting cursory bow of acknowledgement as their new ruler. Then they fled for their lives, and to spread the news of their ex-king's lateness.

'Put me down!' Hell whined. 'This is no way to treat a new king.'

'Get us out of here,' she demanded. Then, with a sweet smile, said, 'Please.'

'Well, as you put it like that…' said Hell.

'Don't push your luck,' advised Dennis. 'And don't expect me to start calling you 'your royalness', either.'

The demon composed himself, muttering, 'Ahh. Out of here. Yes. Out of here.'

They waited, until at length he said, with impressive insight, 'We need to go upwards.'

Dennis rolled his eyes.

Krystal said, 'Yes. You're right,' without a hint of sarcasm. She was genuinely impressed.

'We do, indeed,' said Florence, trying to keep the peace.

'Right, then,' said Hell. 'Follow me.'

'Really?' said Dennis.

'Yup. Really. I fink I've worked out where we are.'

'What about the way to where we need to be?'

'Probably that, as well.'

Unenthusiastically, except for the excited Krystal, they went after him.

*

The tunnel sloped upwards, and joined another that was steeper. They trudged on for what was, had they known it, the best part of the afternoon on the surface world, until weary and frustrated they arrived in a high and wide hallway carved into the solid rock. They dropped to the ground and rested. Not only had they walked for miles, they'd had only some scraps begged from a passer-by – a demon who hadn't heard that Hell was king now, and parted with very little before scampering off.

Hell could just about summon the energy to speak. 'We're here.'

'Oh, yes,' said Dennis, who'd almost lost interest in being anywhere, and wanted to go to sleep.

'Gonna need your help,' said Hell, addressing Krystal. 'I need you to bash your way through that wall over there. It's a bit fick, so be careful.'

Krystal was as tired and sluggish as the rest of them, but she brightened at the thought of some bashing through. She ambled off in the direction the demon's claw was pointing. Arriving at the wall, she patted it experimentally, as if she knew what she was doing, and perhaps she did, then she took a mighty swing at it. Then a few more, until things got rather loud.

The others covered their ears. They cowered away, too, to avoid flying shards. They knew she'd succeeded when a shaft of sunlight streamed across the cavern, giving them a shadow-show of Krystal on the cave wall opposite.

She strode back smiling and wiping her stone hands, or rather, grinding them together.

The other three dragged themselves to their feet, crossed the cavern, and picked their way through the rock-strewn floor of the exit she'd created. 'You were right, it seems,' conceded Dennis, though not apologising for doubting the demon.

Hell said he remembered that years ago, there'd been a door in this chamber that opened out into the bottom of a deep valley. 'It was blocked off for security reasons,' he explained.

Dennis could hardly believe that anyone would want to break into this place, then realised it was probably blocked to keep people like him inside. 'Wouldn't it have been easier to break through where the old door was?'

'Maybe.'

'Where would be the fun in that?' interrupted the troll.

Out in the sunshine, Dennis knelt down to touch the grass. A shadow appeared on the ground in front of him and he looked up. It was Florence. He said, 'It's odd, isn't it, you don't really notice it until you can't have it, do you?'

'No, Father,' she replied, hunkering down beside him. 'And, just in case you've forgotten, those are trees and that's a bird,' she pointed.

'All right, all right,' said Dennis. 'I know.' He stood up and scoured the horizon, shielding his eyes from the sun. It had been a long time since he'd experienced it.

'What are you looking for?' asked Florence.

'Kra-Pton,' he announced.

'We can't go back there, Father.'

'We must. If I want to get Krystal back to the Ironroots.'

That's a nice thought. Perhaps he's going to change after all, she thought.

'And I need the carpet and the Drum,' he added.

* * *

16

'I think we should go down to the cellars and have a look,' said Eydith, peering over her glass of orange juice.

'Not a good idea,' said Link, shaking his head.

'It's the only way we'll find out what's going on.'

'Trinkel should get someone from the Works Department to check for structural damage. It's not really our problem.'

'Have you asked the Works Department to do anything lately?' she said, furrowing her brow.

'Point taken,' he granted. 'It'll be two weeks before they even think about it. I don't think even Trinkel could get *them* to hurry themselves.'

'And it *will* be our problem if a collapse down there opens up a way out for Dennis.'

'Yeah, but…'

'I think you're scared,' she grinned. 'Cluck, cluck, cluck.'

'What?'

'Scared, afraid, *chicken*,' she repeated.

'Of what?'

'Demons and ghosts,' she wriggled her fingers at him.

'No. Not demons,' he said.

'What, then?'

'The whole building collapsing on us while we're down there, that's what.'

'I don't think that's likely. It's a magical building.'

'Then why does it keep moving?'

'Because it's old.'

He wasn't to be put off. 'And when old buildings move, it's usually sideways and then downwards.'

'Well, I'll go on my own, then,' she said, getting up.

'All right, I'll join you. But just a quick look, and then out. All right?'

'All right,' she agreed, grinning. 'And I'm sure Sprag can protect us if it falls in.'

The staff gave a non-committal mumble.

* * *

17

'Well, I'll be off now, then,' said Hell. 'I've got a coronation to organise and a kingdom to rule. I can't stand around here all day chatting with you peasants.'

Florence looked over her shoulder at him as she walked away. 'Get on with it, then!'

I was going to say that, Dennis thought.

'Well, if you're sure you don't need me,' said Hell.

'No. Can't say as we do,' said Dennis.

'I'll be going, then.'

'Yes, so will we!' called Dennis, looking back.

'P'raps I'll see you again!' Hell called after them.

'I hope not, Father,' Florence whispered.

'We'll do our best, but you never know,' Dennis said, ambiguously.

They didn't get far before the exertions of the afternoon caught up with them and they had to sit down. The trek out of the valley was all uphill, and they needed to recover first.

They sat for a while looking across the valley. There was a road winding through it, and it was likely that it followed a stream where they could get a drink. After about ten minutes something occurred to Florence. 'Father,' she said, rousing him from the torpid state he'd lapsed into. 'Father, now we're out here, do you have any magic back?'

'Huh? Oh… yes, I suppose I should.' He'd been too tired to give it a thought. He flexed his fingers and a dull glow appeared.

'Can you produce food and drink?' she asked. 'I've seen even Linkwood do it, so I'm sure you can.'

'Of course I can, girl,' he spurted indignantly. 'But my powers are only as strong as I am physically. It will drain me even further if I attempt too much.'

'Just a snack will do for now,' she tried. 'And a drink.'

He flexed his fingers again, and a weak light appeared in his hands. A few moments later a couple of bacon rolls appeared, along with tumblers of water. Krystal was okay because she'd harvested a collection of green rocks from the caverns and had them secreted about her person. No-one took her up on it when she offered them round.

They were fortified enough to make a start twenty minutes later. There was indeed a road nearby, though not a stream. 'Perhaps someone will come along and give us a lift,' said Dennis, hopefully.

'I don't think so,' said Florence. 'I can't imagine anyone stopping to give a troll a lift, somehow.'

She was right. No-one stopped. But then, nobody even came by. Though, once they were out of the valley and on a main road, a poor-sighted farmer took pity on them and let them on his wagon. Fortunately, it was a sturdy, two-horse wagon returning empty from a delivery to a distant town, and its destination was not far outside Kra-Pton.

It was late afternoon when they trudged up to the outskirts of Kra-Pton, and not wishing to enter Havrapsor in daylight, they waited outside the city walls until dusk. Dennis and Florence desperately needed to eat something substantial.

Just inside the city gates was one of those stationary, mobile fast-food stalls, which change shifts through the night and never seem to close. Except when you're actually looking for one.

'Do you have any money?' asked Dennis.

'Five silvers,' Florence replied, digging them out.

'We only need a couple of large meat buns apiece, and some drinks,' he said. 'We don't want to buy the place.' He took one of the coins and tapped it on the counter. The owner wiped his greasy hands down his even greasier apron and looked at the coin. It was more money than he'd seen in a very long time.

'I can't give you change from that, mister,' he lied.

'That's all right,' said Dennis. 'Give me what you can now and I'll come back for the rest later.'

The man smirked.

'Oh,' said Dennis. 'And don't think we won't be back, because we will. We have to come back for our friend, here.' He beckoned Krystal forward. '*She* will keep an eye on you while we're gone.'

The man's smirk faded. Dennis and Florence sat by the kiosk, eating while they waited for the cover of darkness. Due to the urgency of what Dennis had planned, the coming of night seemed to take longer than usual. They went outside the city gates again, and waited for the officer of the Watch to announce: 'Twelve o'clock an' all swell!' Dennis couldn't help but wonder if the man had got the script quite right, or someone had left the typo in, to make the officer sound stupid.

He asked Krystal to wait in the shadows and keep an eye on the fast-food vendor, while he and Florence headed to the university to get the carpet back, and hopefully, recapture the Drum.

'Don't you think we might need help, Father?' said Florence, as they strolled, avoiding the campus lights where possible, and watching for anyone else who might be about.

'A good idea,' he said, slamming a fist into his hand and flinching from the stinging pain. 'Jook and Psoddoph!'

'As you wish, Father,' she said, a little hurt. 'But I'd rather stay.'

'No, that's their names.'

'Oh, of course it is. Yes.' She grinned. 'I remember.'

Dennis halted and spun around. 'Right, first stop, the barracks.'

* * *

18

Eydith led Link down the dimly lit steps behind the library. A blast of cold air was causing their breath to vaporize. Something was wrong. In the past, the ancient tomes and magical grimoires housed within the library's walls had issued forth their own magical draughts to combat the chill from the Parallel Dimension, but they were not in evidence now. Slowly, the pair continued down.

Eydith was using Sprag to brush away the cobwebs that touched her face and clung to her hair. 'It doesn't get any better does it,' remarked Link, putting out a hand to steady himself as the building trembled and the steps lurched sideways. 'I still think this is a bad idea,' he whispered nervously, in case anyone apart from Eydith was listening.

'Perhaps,' she agreed, quickening her step. 'So we'd better hurry.' The building groaned again.

When they reached the lower levels where the cellars were located, they looked around and at each other, wordlessly recalling that, not many months ago, this was where the demon king had massed his forces to join Dennis against them. The cellars had been used to imprison the captured staff of the university. Beyond it were the tombs of the Ancient Ones where not even demons would dare to venture.

Everything looked intact down there. There were no obvious cracks or collapses. Nothing to report back to Trinkel. 'It must be coming from down there.' Eydith indicated the floor of the cellar area, meaning the Parallel Dimension.

'And we can't get down there to check,' he said, thankfully, with a little nervous laugh.

Eydith said nothing. They made their way back the way they'd come, up the staircase where the last moments of the battle had taken place. It still bore some scars that the building hadn't repaired yet. Perhaps they ran too deep – this was where the most intense lethal magic had been unleashed. They climbed the stairs in silence.

Eydith stopped when they reached the part of the wall she recognised as being where Dennis and the demons had exited. They'd escaped through a hole which the demon king magically closed behind them.

Link examined it. 'Still looks solid,' he confirmed, looking over his shoulder. 'Let's go.'

'Not yet,' she said. 'Look, there's a gap.' Link had seen it, too, but hoped she hadn't.

'Did you bring a knife?' she asked.

'I'm a wizard,' he frowned. 'What would I need a knife for? And you surely can't be intending to…'

'Have you got anything *like* a knife that I can use to, maybe, prise a stone out?'

'Nope,' he replied, feeling relieved that she might give up and head back up.

'All right,' she sighed. 'I'll use mine.' She hitched up her skirt and pulled a dagger from a sheath strapped to the outside of her thigh. 'Well, these aren't permitted on campus,' she said, by way of explanation. Of course, she could have secreted it in her belt, or up her sleeve, but there you have it. Sometimes, you *just* can't *tell.*

'It's a wonder you can walk with that thing strapped on there,' Link remarked, eyeing the dagger's location for perhaps a little longer than necessary.

'You shouldn't be looking!'

He quickly averted his eyes, but it didn't stop that picture from hanging around in his mind.

Eydith eased her dagger into the crack in the wall and jiggled it about. Something clicked. 'What was that?' she whispered, nervously.

'My elbow,' said Link. 'It does that sometimes. Seems to get locked.'

'Well, stop it. I'm trying to concentrate.' She inserted the dagger into the crack again and began working it around. Then she stopped.

'What's the matter now?' asked Link, hoping she'd given up.

'It's stuck,' she complained, trying to move it again.

'Here, let me try.' He thought he'd better offer. He took the hilt in both hands and tugged. 'It's definitely stuck.'

'*I know*,' she sighed.

Link tried again, this time raising his knee to give himself more leverage. After a sustained effort, something started to give. Dust floated down from the ceiling.

'Look out!' Eydith alerted him. 'Something's happening.'

'Yes, I'm getting hit by bits of rock!' he yelled, stepping back quickly.

A section of the wall fell forward in a cloud of dust.

'Now look what you've done,' she accused.

Link smiled, even though appalled at the damage. 'Don't know my own strength sometimes.' He stepped into the rubble and began kicking around in the stones. 'Ah, here it is,' he said, picking up the dagger. She took it from him and wiped the blade on her skirt. Link turned away like a true gentleman while she replaced it back in its secret place.

'Right, shall we go in?' she asked.

'You really are serious, aren't you? This hole leads to the Parallel Dimension, and Dennis could use it to get out.'

'The problem's obviously down there. We won't find out what's going on unless we go down there. And I can probably use Sprag to close it afterwards.'

The staff made another of its non-committal noises.

There was no dissuading Eydith, so Link stepped aside and bowed mockingly. 'After you, my lady.'

* * *

19

Dennis and Florence stood at the barrack gates waiting for someone to answer the bell. 'Try the handle,' Florence suggested. Dennis only touched it and the gate swung back, creaking softly.

'I hate it when that happens,' he whispered. He peered around the door, half expecting... what? He didn't know, but he was relieved when they weren't challenged. 'There's nobody about.'

'Well, let's go and find somebody,' she suggested.

'Yes, I suppose we'd better.'

They crept past the empty sentry box, through the low wooden arch and on to the dimly-lit parade ground. In the furthest corner from where they were standing, was a building like a garden shed. There was a sign illuminated by a row of oil lamps on a shelf over the door. Someone had gone to a lot of trouble. The building was shining in the dark like a beacon for lost souls. As it happens, most of the men in these barracks met that criterion with distinction.

'Father,' Florence panted. 'Just because this is a parade ground, you don't have to *march* across it.' Dennis hadn't realised and slowed down, he was almost at the shed now and could read the sign.

OFFICER IN CHARGE

'Ah, this looks like the place we need.'

'It would've been a bit annoying if it wasn't,' said Florence, petulantly. Dennis stamped noisily onto the bottom step and rapped on the door.

'Ooo goes there?' asked a voice from within.

That's Psoddoph, Dennis thought. 'I said, Ooo goes there?' the guard repeated, when there was no reply.

'It's me... Dennis.' Then to Florence, he said, 'We're in luck, It's Psoddoph.'

'Maybe,' she said. 'It depends on how he remembers you.'

'I paid him. That's all he'll need to remember.'

'Oh,' said the voice. There was the sound of a chair being dragged from behind the door and various other items of furniture being re-arranged. 'Why didn't you say, boss. All this buggerin' about with this 'Ooo goes there' rubbish, and that. Just a minute, I'll open the door.'

Dennis stood back and waited. A key was inserted into the lock and turned. Heavy bolts were pulled back – three altogether – and finally a chain was disconnected. The door inched slowly back and a face peered sheepishly out from behind it. 'Really you, is it?'

'No,' said Dennis, looking up at him.

'It is you!' Psoddoph grinned. 'I thought you were *dead*.'

'Not yet,' said Dennis.

Psoddoph's addition to his reply was not what Dennis was expecting: 'Well, maybe next time, then.'

'We'll see,' said Dennis, interpreting the remark as nothing more than banter. 'Are you in charge?'

'What, of everything like… no, only this shed. Most of the lads are on holiday this week, so I'm, what you might call, acting in charge. But I get the rate for the job,' he added, proudly.

'Who's in charge of the barracks, then?' asked Dennis.

'That'll be Woolf, he's the Sergeant,' Psoddoph told him.

'Is he in?' Dennis wondered.

'Course 'e is. Otherwise, I'd be in charge of all of it, wouldn't I?'

'Yes, I suppose you would,' said Dennis, wondering how anyone could even leave this man to look after a whole shed on his own. 'Can I see him?'

Psoddoph took a pace forward onto the top step and looked around the parade ground. 'Nope. Leastways, not from 'ere. I suppose the next question is gonna be, can I go and get 'im, then. Right?'

'Right,' agreed Dennis.

'Wait 'ere, then. I won't be long.' The guard squeezed by and stepped down to the ground, then marched off into the gloom.

'It's getting chilly,' Dennis remarked. 'Let's go inside.'

'He said to wait here, Father,' Florence reminded him.

'Well, yes. But here generally, not here specifically,' he replied, taking both steps to the top in a single stride and walking into the office. Florence sighed and followed him in. Dennis glanced around the place to satisfy his curiosity, and was about to sit down when the guard returned with his senior officer.

'I thought I told you to wait outside… No, I distinctly remember saying it,' said Psoddoph, to make it quite clear that the Sergeant knew that he hadn't invited Dennis in.

'I must have misunderstood,' said Dennis, smarmily.

'Well, that's all right then. This is the Sergeant,' said Psoddoph, pointing at the man next to him. He looked, apart from the three stripes sewn on his sleeve, like an older clone of Psoddoph. Woolf took a step forward and offered his hand, then saluted leaving Dennis shaking thin air.

'What can we do for you, sir?' he said, in the kind of staccato voice that only a man with twenty years' service can perfect.

'It's like this, Sergeant,' Dennis began. 'I'm taking a small expedition into the Ironroot Mountains to deliver er… a package. Yes. That's it, a package,' he decided.

'Yes, sir?' the Sergeant prompted.

'And,' Dennis continued, 'I need a couple of your best men: you know, for bodyguards, that sort of thing.'

'My best men, eh?' echoed Woolf, stroking his chin. 'I don't know about that.'

'I'll pay,' said Dennis, his voice momentarily going falsetto.

The Sergeant's eyes widened. 'And how long would this expedition be, do you think?' he asked.

'I don't know, a month perhaps, maybe two.'

'How much are you willing to pay, then?'

'Shall we say, one silver? Each?' the wizard offered, hopefully.

'No,' said Woolf. 'I think we'll say four.'

'Oh, no we won't,' said Dennis, getting into his stride. 'We'll say one each for the men, and a half for you… all right?' Then, seeing the man's expression, he reconsidered. 'No, okay, I'll make it one for you as well, Sergeant.'

Woolf gave it some thought. *He's not getting my best men for three silvers.* 'I'll tell you what… I'll release Jook and Psoddoph here. They're my two best men in the barracks at the moment.' To himself, he added, *Apart from me, they're the only two men in the barracks at the moment. So he's getting what he bargained for – sort of.*

'Thanks,' muttered Psoddoph.

'Don't forget your manners, soldier.'

'Sorry. *Thanks, sir,*' Psoddoph corrected himself.

Dennis felt relieved. They might not be the best, but he'd worked with them before. He knew their capabilities *and* their shortcomings. The only drawback was, they knew his, too. But he'd live with that. 'Excellent men!' he said. 'Certainly no complaints, there.'

'Good, when do you want them to start?' said Woolf.

'No hurry,' said Dennis. 'Say, ten minutes?'

'Shall we say twelve?' Woolf responded.

'Call it eleven,' said Dennis.

'Done!' snapped Woolf, feeling he'd won a minor skirmish and spat on his palm and held it out for Dennis to seal the agreement.

He squinted at the Sergeant's palm with some trepidation.

'Shake on it… Seal the deal, man,' Woolf demanded.

'Oh, that's all right, Sergeant,' said Dennis, grinning over-enthusiastically. 'No need for that. I trust you.'

'But I don't trust *you*,' snarled Woolf. 'Shake, or there's no deal!'

Dennis spat half-heartedly at his own palm. And missed. He tried again. *Why did people insist on these yucky formalities,* he wondered. And why was his mouth suddenly so dry? He stared at a spot between the Sergeant's eyes and muttered something. A spell? The man took a step back, but he didn't lower his hand. Dennis snapped his fingers and said, 'Okay, Sergeant. Thank you. All sealed.'

The Sergeant blinked rapidly and shook his head as if he'd tasted something sharp. 'What? Just like that?' he said. 'Haven't you heard a word I've said? No shake, no deal. And if you just tried to hypnotise me – which I think you did – then I'm what's known as not susceptible. So don't try a stunt like that again with me.'

'Shit,' muttered Dennis. That was unexpected. Fighting back his annoyance and distaste, he managed to force some dampness from his mouth, spat on his palm and slapped it against Woolf's outstretched hand. 'It's a deal!' he snapped.

'Good. That's settled then,' said Woolf, smugly. 'Psoddoph! Sod off and get your gear, and get Jook.'

'But Sarge…' Psoddoph protested, 'it's the middle of the night!'

'That's an order, soldier!'

Psoddoph snapped rigidly to attention and saluted. 'Yes, sir.' He marched to the door.

'Thank you, Sergeant,' said Dennis. 'We'll wait for them by the main gate.'

'There is just one more thing…' said Woolf, holding out his hand.

Dennis looked at it suspiciously. It was dry. 'What's that, Sergeant?'

'My hand, sir.'

'Yes,' said Dennis. 'I can see that.'

'It's empty, sir.'

Good, thought Dennis. *I won't get wet again, will I?* But then he twigged. 'Oh, *yes*, Sergeant. I see, of *course*.' He rummaged in his cloak for Florence's silver coins which he'd hung onto after buying the food. 'There you are.'

* * *

20

'I'm not going in there first,' said Eydith. 'You're the man around here.'

'All right, stand aside,' said Link, boldly. 'I'm going in.'

She stood back and waited for him to rush past. It didn't happen. He crept forward and peered around the gap in the wall. She heard him sigh as he ducked inside and flattened himself against the inside wall.

Eydith walked in behind him. 'What are you doing?'

'Being careful. I'm not rushing in there where I don't know what could be waiting.'

'Stop playing games,' she scolded.

'Shh…' he hissed.

They stood in silence for a minute. Eventually, Eydith asked, 'Did you hear something?'

'No. And I'm not likely to if you don't keep your voice down. Ouch!'

Eydith caught him with her elbow. 'Let's just see where it leads,' she whispered.

'We already know where it leads, and it's not where we ought to go.'

'Not afraid of a few demons, are you?'

'No. I am afraid of hordes of them.'

She squeezed past him in the narrow tunnel – which wasn't at all unpleasant, he thought – and took the lead. Without being prompted, Sprag glowed with a subdued light to guide them. The tunnel soon joined a larger one, which was lit, and they proceeded cautiously for another ten minutes, thankfully not meeting anyone – or anything. At the next junction they came to an even larger tunnel.

'Look, there's a sign,' Eydith pointed. The pair hurried across the dusty ground.

'What does it say?' asked Link, narrowing his eyes and trying to focus.

'Wait a minute.' She reached up and unhooked it.

'RECEPTION?' he frowned. 'Well, at least we know where we are.'

'Counter looks a bit knocked about,' she noticed.

'Someone got fed up with waiting, I expect,' said Link, by way of a possible explanation.

'There's a bell,' said Eydith.

'Don't ring…'

BOING!!!

'…it!' cried Link.

They scrambled to a nearby rock and crouched behind it, waiting to see what happened. There was a scurrying sound and then silence. They looked at one another. 'Did you hear something?' she whispered.

'Yes. I think there's something at the counter,' he whispered.

'Is there anybody there?' a timid, little voice called out.

'What shall we do?' whispered Link. He removed his hat and peered over the top of the rock, then ducked down again.

'Just stay quiet,' she whispered, putting a finger to her lips.

'Is there *really* anybody there?' repeated the little voice. It seemed to be pleading hopefully that there wasn't.

Link glanced at Eydith. 'Perhaps it will go away.'

She considered a magical solution, but Sprag's voice in her head told her it wouldn't work. 'The place has a dampening effect on surface-world magic, mistress. I could barely light the way here myself.'

The little voice piped up weakly again. 'Anybody?'

'We'll have to do something,' she hissed.

Link cleared his throat as quietly as possible. Which was not easy, squatting behind a rock in a tunnel like an echo chamber. 'No,' he squeaked. Then added in a much deeper voice, 'NO… there's nobody here.'

'Oh, good,' came the little voice.

Eydith and Link sat in total silence, hardly daring to breathe as the scratching of clawed feet on the rock floor faded away.

When the coast seemed clear, Link was in the act of standing up when…

'Are you *sure* there's nobody there?'

He could hardly deny it now. 'Okay, yes. There is someone here,' he admitted.

'I knew I'd catch you in the end,' said the little demon, with an air of triumph.

Link looked around. 'Where are you?' he asked, in his manliest tone.

'Down here, on the other side of the rock you're standing behind.'

The young wizard looked down and saw a rather flat demon that resembled a large, scaly Frisbee with arms and legs. Link looked at the sorry-looking creature and saw, what looked like the imprint of a fist on what could've been its head. 'Have an accident?' he asked.

'No, thanks,' the demon squeaked. 'I had one earlier.'

'It looks nasty,' said Link, sympathetically.

'Nasty? It was 'orrible. I got 'it by a troll!'

'What, down here?' queried Link, surprised.

'Yup. Smashed me 'ead in wiv 'er fist,' it squeaked. 'Anyway, enough of my problems, what're you doin' down 'ere? You don't look dead enough, yet.'

'Dead?' queried Link. 'Oh... *dead.* No, I'm not dead. I've just come down for a quick look round, then I'm going back up.'

'Once you get to Reception, mate, that's it. Full stop,' the demon squeaked. 'There's no goin' back.'

'Well, I think there's every chance I'll be going back,' Link assured it.

'You 'aven't got a troll wiv you by any chance, 'ave you?' asked the demon, swivelling its eyes.

'No, I don't need one. I'm a wizard,' Link replied, hopefully impressively.

'Well, try usin' yer magic, an' see what good it does yer. We 'ad a wizard down 'ere recent-like. Real sneaky 'e was. An' it was 'im who set 'is troll on me. I used to be tall like you, before 'e got brought down 'ere.'

Eydith was listening.

'You had a wizard down here?' said Link, keeping the conversation going and prompting the demon to continue.

'Yeah, and 'e 'ad a girl wiv 'im. She was all right. But that troll…'

'Where did they go?' asked Link, urgently.

'They got out, and they wrecked this place doin' it.' The demon went quiet as if waiting for Link to speak again, but Link was processing what the demon had said.

'Even killed King Jamzamin, they did. *And* the poor bugger that stirred the slime pits,' the demon added.

Yuck, thought Eydith, *I wonder how that happened.* But a little voice in her head told her, *you don't really want to know.*

'Jamzamin's *dead*?' said Link. 'Who's king now?'

'That little creep, Hell. The demon of the staff. Always at 'er beckon call. Always running when she rubbed the staff. 'E's even changed the name of this place. Now 'e calls it, the Kingdom of Hell.' The demon thought about that, then added, 'Catchy, though, ennit? Trouble is, you're in it, now.'

'Yes, but I'm not stopping,' Link assured it again, and turned to walk back the way he'd come. The cavern shook and rumbled again.

'There goes another bit,' the demon squealed.

'Bit?' said Link, raising an eyebrow. 'It sounded like quite a lot. What was it?'

'Since that troll was down 'ere, bringin' down the stairs in the staircase cavern and knockin' great 'oles in fings, the place 'as started fallin' apart. Some of the caverns and tunnels 'ave fallen in. Don't suppose it'll be long before this one goes as well,' the demon moaned.

As if on cue, dust fell from the ceiling, indicating that the demon might be right. 'Don't matter though. His new royalness 'as got us digging new ones. Only a bit nearer the surface world this time. So, when the time's right to take over, we won't 'ave so far to go.' He bared his teeth and a couple fell out.

Link was beginning to put the pieces together. 'With all the destruction the troll caused, and now with all this new tunnelling under way,' said Link, squatting down in front of the demon, 'you're moving the foundations of the university, and probably the city. There's been reports of houses subsiding.'

'Do you fink the university will fall down?'

'That is a possibility, yes,' said Link.

'Good!'

'*Good?*'

'Yeah, no more wizard magic. They'll all be down 'ere wiv us. Dead.'

'You're mad!' snapped Link. 'Don't you think the wizards will stop you?'

'When Hell gets it together, they won't know what's 'it 'em,' the demon squeaked, happily.

'They'll know all right,' Link assured it, as he stood up. 'Because I'll tell them.'

'What? You can't!' the demon screamed. 'If you get out of 'ere alive, my life won't be worth living.' And it made a rush for Link's legs.

The wizard stepped aside and kicked it as it went careering by, sending it crashing into the rock that Eydith was hiding behind. She stood up to join the fray. The only weapon readily available, was in her hands.

The demon cannoned off the rock. 'Oh, bugger, not again!'

'Oh, no,' moaned Sprag, as he was brought down forcefully across the demon's flat head. There was a loud bang and a bright green flash as the two connected, killing the demon instantly and plastering the walls with most of it. It seems the staff still had some residual magic.

'I think now would be a good time to leave, don't you?' said Link. But it didn't need saying, Eydith was already trotting back.

* * *

Dennis and Florence waited impatiently at the barrack's gate. Soon, the still night air was disturbed by the sound of two pairs of heavy feet stomping across the parade ground. 'At last,' Dennis murmured. 'Go and tell Krystal we're ready.' Florence nodded and disappeared into the semi-darkness, and headed for the city gates.

'Evening, Dennis,' said Jook, with a wide grin.

Dennis cringed. It wasn't that he minded the name Dennis, he just didn't appreciate people he considered of a lower status – *most* people – using it in an over-familiar way. Even *Father* was more acceptable – though perhaps not from Jook. 'You know I don't like you calling me that!' he snapped.

Jook held up his hands. 'Whoops. Sorry, boss. It just slipped out.' He grinned again.

'Right. Forget it. Come on, there are some things I want to get.'

The two guards looked at each other with a here-we-go-again expression. The wizard strode off with the two guards a couple of paces behind him.

'Just like old times,' said Psoddoph, cheerily.

Dennis cringed. He was regretting this already.

'An' we thought you were… you know…' he began.

'Well, I'm not, am I?' Dennis cut him short.

'Sure is like old times,' whispered Jook. Then to Dennis, 'Where we going, boss?'

'Havrapsor,' replied Dennis, glancing over his shoulder.

'Right, boss. What's this *stuff* you want to get, then?'

'A couple of odds and ends that's all,' said Dennis, keeping his eyes on the road ahead. 'But first, you have to meet a couple of people.'

The trio walked briskly on, and soon the city gates were in sight. 'Who're these people?' Psoddoph enquired, as Dennis wasn't volunteering any information.

'Florence and Krystal,' replied Dennis. 'You don't know them.'

The same thought hit both men at the same time. *Women*? The next thought also scored two direct hits. *I wonder what mine will be like.*

The male of the species has what might be likened to an automatic gearbox. When he's suddenly made aware that he is going to meet a female, his legs gather speed. On the other hand, if a female walks past him, the mechanism slows his forward momentum. This depends of course on whether he's attracted to her, otherwise the reverse can happen. Females have a similar mechanism, but sadly for males, it either has a good filter, or they have more control over it.

'Florence is my daughter,' said Dennis, forestalling any imminent blunders.

The two guards slowed noticeably and looked at each other mouthing *daughter*? They walked on in silence, turning this bombshell over in their minds. Over and over again. Jook was first to crack.

'Didn't know you got married, boss.'

'I don't want to talk about it!' snapped Dennis.

'No, boss,' Jook mumbled. Psoddoph had a thought, *I wonder what the other one's like.* Jook soon had the same thought, but neither of them spoke. As they drew nearer the city gates, it was apparent that chests had been expanded and stomachs flattened, each man meaning to impress this woman Dennis called Krystal.

'Ah, good,' said Florence, stepping out of the shadows. 'You've brought them.'

'Men,' said Dennis, 'this is my daughter, Florence. You may remember her… from our little trip to Prossill.' Dennis sounded almost proud. Only almost. Both men acknowledged her, and Psoddoph did recognise her from that last mission. His mind soon went off that, though, when a large grey shape lumbered lethargically from the gloom and stood next to her. 'And this,' Dennis announced, 'is Krystal.'

Two torsos deflated, and two stomachs visibly sagged, along with two pairs of shoulders as they looked at Krystal and then at each other, both thinking, *It's a bloody great troll!*

Before either man could say the wrong thing, Dennis informed them, 'Krystal is a princess…'

What's 'e up to now? thought Jook. *There's got to be a catch, an angle, or a reward, even. He wouldn't be tagging her along for nothing.* And while Dennis was giving his carefully tailored explanation of how she came to be with him, Jook's mind wandered back to the last time he'd worked for Dennis. It had some good moments, but some pretty awful hours. He felt like returning the silver coin and heading back to his quarters… *Hang on, what silver coin?* he asked himself. *Never mind what Dennis is getting out of this – and the Sergeant – what are we getting?* But his superior hadn't given him the choice of opting out.

'…and get her home to the Cludells in the Ironroot Mountains,' Dennis finished.

'Shouldn't be a problem, boss,' said Psoddoph. 'Shall we be off then?'

'He said we needed to get some things first,' Jook reminded him.

'I need the magic carpet,' said Dennis. They remembered the carpet. Two hearts slipped their moorings and sank.

'Is it still in your old rooms, boss?' asked Psoddoph.

'Yes, but the door will be locked, so take something with you to open it with,' advised Dennis.

Psoddoph held out his hand.

'What?' said Dennis, looking into it.

'Your key?'

'I have no key,' said Dennis. 'It's padlocked; you'll need a crowbar.'

Florence spoke up, 'It's open, Father. Look.' She lifted the padlock from her apron pocket. She'd forgotten she still had it.

'There you are,' said Dennis, taking the padlock and passing it to Psoddoph, 'it's open.'

Psoddoph shrugged and looked at it. It blinked at him, and he thought it was a trick of the light. All he could think to say was, 'You want me to lock it again, then?'

'Yes, of course.' After which, he moved on quickly, saying, 'If everyone's ready, we'll get going, shall we?' He turned and began the walk to the university.

The others fell in behind him, the two guards smelling the aromas and looking wistfully at the mobile fast-food stall as they left.

As they approached the university gates, Jook asked, 'Will you be coming in with us, boss?'

'Er… yes, I will. But I won't be going to my rooms. There's something I need to get from somewhere else,' he said, evasively. 'Nothing for you to worry about.'

Then why am I worrying? thought Jook.

'Okay,' said Psoddoph. 'Do you want one of us to go with you?'

'No!' snapped Dennis. 'I'll manage, thank you.'

I get it, thought Psoddoph, *He's going to steal something.*

They arrived and halted at the university.

'No,' said Dennis, quickly. 'Not the main gates. No point disturbing anybody at this time of night. We'll use the side entrance.' He led them down the alley at the side of the building to the small door the cleaners and cooks used. Sizing up Krystal, he said, 'You'd better wait here. We'll be back in a few minutes.' As he ducked under the low portal, a nagging thought crossed his mind and he stepped back into the alley. 'Krystal, don't eat any of the stonework, we won't be long.'

She grunted and Dennis went back inside where Florence and the guards were waiting. He directed the guards up to his old rooms and told them to wait outside with Krystal as soon as they had the carpet.

'One more thing,' he said, before they left. 'While you're in my rooms, go to my wardrobe and get me a clean robe. This one… smells a bit from where I've been.'

'I didn't like to say anything,' said Jook, without thinking.

Dennis didn't pick up on it. Instead, he turned to Florence and, looking pointedly at her cleaners' outfit, asked if she'd like the guards to pick up a change of clothing for her, too, from her room.

The look he got was withering, bordering on horrified.

'Do you really think I'd want two men poking about in my room, among my clothes?!'

'Er, no. I suppose not,' said Dennis, noticing how eager his guards were to help out.

'Once we're done,' said Florence, emphatically, 'I'll slip across to my room and get cleaned up and changed. No-one will bother seeing me around.'

'Don't worry, boss, we'll get you a robe,' said Psoddoph, quickly, tugging Jook's sleeve, and heading off at the double.

As soon as they'd gone, Dennis turned to Florence. 'Right. Where's Eydith's room?'

Her eyes widened. 'You want to pay her a visit?'

'Not if I can help it. But I need the Drum, which you tell me is kept in *her* room, of all places!' She looked doubtful.

'Come on,' he said, urgently. 'You want the Drum, don't you?'

She thought about it. 'What time is it?' she said, looking about her in a mildly abstracted way for a moment before answering her own question, 'Almost five to ten.'

Dennis followed her eyes expecting to see a clock on one of the walls, but didn't. 'Really? You can sense what time it is? Accurately?'

'For as long as I can remember,' she said, matter-of-factly. 'As powers go, it isn't that wonderful, but it comes in handy. This time of an evening, Eydith usually takes a walk around campus with Link. Or they'll be in the Senior Common Room.'

'Senior?' He raised an eyebrow.

'They were both raised a couple of levels after they defeated…' She stopped herself. '…After the battle.'

He grunted something inaudible, and not nice. 'Are we going?'

'Yes. Yes.' She scurried towards the steps that led to the quadrangle, with Dennis doing his best to keep up.

The quadrangle was bathed in a soft yellow light from the crescent moon, and a few oil lamps that would soon need refilling. They crept silently around, keeping to the shadows till Florence found the door to the west wing. 'In here,' she whispered, slipping quietly through. Once inside, they took the stairs two at a time up to the second floor. Florence stopped. 'It's down here, at the end,' she whispered. Dennis nodded, and motioned for her to continue.

At Eydith's door, Florence put her ear to the keyhole and listened. The room was silent.

She whispered, 'If she's in, I'll just say I was passing and thought I'd stick my head in to say goodnight. She won't suspect anything. She doesn't know I'm helping you, yet.' She gently turned the handle and let the door swing slowly back. Satisfied that all was well, she stepped inside. Thankfully, a lamp was burning in its sconce on the passage wall. She hated groping around in the dark. She reached Eydith's bedroom door and pushed it open. The bed looked as though it hadn't been slept in. 'It's all right, you can come in,' she whispered. 'She's not here.'

Dennis strode in. 'Find the Drum and let's go,' he muttered, glancing around.

'Open that door wider,' Florence whispered. 'There's no light in here.' Dennis obliged. In the borrowed light, they searched the wardrobes and cupboards, even the drawers (but that was just being nosy). The Drum wasn't anywhere. 'What about under the bed?' she asked. He didn't answer, but she knew he was checking, as she'd heard his knees crack when he knelt down.

He lifted the valance and stuck his head into the darkness. There was a gentle hollow ringing sound, like a town clock chiming one. Then, came the low muttering of a voice, cursing, 'Ouch! Sod it!'

Florence grinned, guessing what he'd found under the bed. 'Can you see it, Father?'

'No,' he snapped. 'I don't think it would fit under here anyway. Try the other room again.' He eased himself out, and stood rubbing the top of his head. He joined her, looking about. 'There's the door to the balcony,' he whispered. He opened it quietly and looked around. In the corner, was a canvas sheet covering what looked like a large box. He lifted a corner and peered cautiously inside. 'I've found it,' he said, almost too loudly.

'Shh...' she whispered, and rushed to his side. She looked into the box, then into Dennis's face. Between them, they lifted the ancient Drum out and onto the floor.

'Let's get out of here. Now.' Dennis flexed his fingers, as if threatening the Drum, magically, and picked it up, steadying it with his knee. 'I've got it,' he puffed. 'Lead the way.'

She moved quickly, opened the front door for him, and looked outside. 'Come on, it's all clear.'

The Drum was uncannily quiet for such a powerful artefact. It unnerved Dennis a little, that it made no attempt to thwart him, no light show, no magical hindrance. He knew it hated him.

What he didn't know was that the Drum was conflicted. It belonged to whoever was Archchancellor. Dennis had never formerly resigned or been voted out. It had been assumed that he would never return, and so Trinkel had been voted in to replace him. But here was Dennis. The situation was unprecedented. The Drum would have to work things out before doing anything. It was even unsure of its own powers in such a situation. Equally concerning – it was very aware of Dennis's powers. It dared not even alert Sprag.

* * *

22

'I hope we don't have to shift a load of furniture off his carpet,' whispered Jook, as they crept along the hallway to Dennis's old rooms.

'This is the one,' said Psoddoph, stopping by a dark black oak door. And just as Florence had told him, the door wasn't locked. He pushed it open with one finger. They entered with only the slightest magical resistance, because Dennis's protective spell hadn't included soldiers.

'Dark in 'ere, ennit?' remarked Jook.

'Just a bit, get that lamp from outside.' Jook went back and lifted one of the lamps from the wall and put it on a shelf over the fireplace. 'Now give me a hand with this table, that desk and those four chairs.'

'What about the bookcases?' asked Jook, miserably.

'One thing at a time,' sighed Psoddoph. 'Now… lift.'

They lifted the table and stood, holding it.

'Yes?' said Jook. 'Now what?'

'Shit,' muttered Psoddoph. 'Put it down.'

'What about rolling it up to the table legs, and lifting the table over it,' suggested Jook.

'Okay. We could try that,' agreed Psoddoph, 'when we get this end out from under this bookcase, or that end out from under that one.'

*

Once the guards had worked it out, it wasn't long before they'd freed the carpet and rolled it up.

'Let's get it out of here before someone comes,' said Psoddoph. 'Oh, and put that lamp back. And take Dennis's robe off and stop messing about. We don't have time for this.'

Remembering to lock the door – the padlock blinked again – they went back down through the building as quietly and as quickly as they could with the carpet on their shoulders, and arrived without incident at the little door that led into the alley. Krystal loomed out of the shadows. 'Oh, I thought you were Dennis.'

The guards stopped in their tracks. 'Don't do that,' puffed Jook. 'I nearly 'ad one of me turns, then.'

'What you got there, then? said the troll.

Psoddoph put his end of the carpet on the ground. 'This is a carpet,' he explained. 'A magic carpet.'

'I've heard of them, but I thought only princes and thieves had them,' she said, knowledgeably.

'Well,' said Jook, dropping his end. 'This one belongs to Dennis, and you may rest assured miss, that 'e ain't no prince.'

'That only leaves the alternative then, don't it?' she concluded.

Florence came hurtling through the little door with Dennis puffing along behind her. 'Oh, good. You've got it,' she said, stepping over the carpet. Dennis was carrying the Drum in front of him, so didn't see the carpet and stumbled over it.

'Damn fools! Did you have put it right across the door?!'

Jook assisted him back to his feet. 'You all right, boss?'

'Just a graze, that's all,' Dennis whimpered, rubbing his stinging hands. 'You'd better unroll it, unless you propose that we ride astride it.'

Jook kicked the carpet. It unrolled a couple of feet and stopped, obstructed by the walls of the narrow alley. 'That's no good,' Dennis moaned, irritably. 'Take it into the street… Krystal, will you check that the street is clear?'

'Did you bring the robe?' said Dennis. Psoddoph held it out. He snatched it, ducked into the shadows and emerged a couple of minutes later looking, and smelling, better. Florence had managed to change and freshen up quickly *en route*, and to the accompaniment of her father's impatient huffs and puffs outside her washroom.

The troll lumbered to the end of the alley and looked up and down the street. Satisfied, she beckoned the others forward. 'Right. Come on, move it,' Dennis ordered, as he picked up the Drum. The guards, grinning behind his back, hoisted the carpet onto their shoulders and followed him and Florence out onto the street.

Annoyingly, as soon as the carpet was unrolled, an officer of the Watch strolled around the corner at the top end of the street.

'Two o'clock an' all's… Oi! What's going on!' he yelled, as he spotted Dennis putting the Drum down on the carpet.

'Shit!' muttered Dennis. 'Quick! Everyone get on!' There was plenty of room for all now. Unlike the last time Dennis used the carpet, when, as well as the two guards, it was also carrying a cart. Jook and Psoddoph stepped smartly forward and sat down. They'd done this before. Florence followed their example. The officer was getting closer. 'Come on, Krystal, hurry up!' rasped Dennis.

She ambled onto the carpet. 'Why should I hurry? He can't hurt me.'

'No, but he can damn well hurt me!' Dennis snapped, noticing that the officer now had a large sword in his hand.

'There's no need for that tone,' sniffed the troll.

'Come on, Krystal, *please*,' pleaded Florence. At the sound of a friendlier voice, the troll seemed to go up a couple of gears and move quicker. She creaked into a sitting position at the back of the carpet.

The officer was only yards away now and was fumbling in his pocket for something.

When he'd found it, he put it to his lips and blew a long, shrill blast, then removed it and shouted, 'STOP! Thief!'

Dennis froze, then he looked at Florence. 'How dare he; I'm only taking back what's mine.'

'Come on, Father. Don't argue. Let's go!' Florence urged.

Dennis sat down. 'Come on, boss, what are you waiting for?' said Jook. Then he had a thought: *Don't tell me he's forgotten how to fly this thing.* 'You've got the book, haven't you?'

'Yes, of course!' Dennis snapped, glancing back at him. 'Carpet! Up, please!' Then suddenly remembering, he quickly added, 'Slowly.' The carpet didn't have that many options. Under Krystal's weight, it seemed pinned to the ground. The edges rose and then flattened again. 'Come on!' Dennis yelled, 'I said, UP! Please.' The carpet struggled again, sending ripples along its length, as though flexing unseen muscles. After the third attempt, it began to rise and Dennis urged it forward. Then he changed his mind and urged it to go sideways. He'd forgotten that the carpet had been cut wrongly and that the wider edges were in fact the front and back, meaning that the shorter edges were the sides.

The officer of the Watch slowed when he neared the carpet. Other officers had joined the chase and unless they slowed down, they were in danger of actually catching up – and a magic carpet with a wizard, his daughter, two guards and a bloody great troll on board, could easily ruin a man's chances of collecting his pension, and greatly improve his prospects of downsizing to a small plot in a cemetery.

The leading officer slowed down, hoping to become the second officer, or third would do, but as the carpet lurched precariously into the air, he stopped and waited for the others.

'That was *too* close, men!' he stormed, as they caught up with him. 'We nearly 'ad 'em.' The other officers looked at each other, silently congratulating themselves on their lack of success. The leading officer spoke again. 'If we get that close again to a suicidal apprehension, there will be trouble! Understand?'

'But Sarge, I thought that was the idea… to catch the bad guys,' said a very young-looking Watchman.

'Are you new here?' asked the Sergeant. 'I don't recall seeing you before.'

'Yes, Sarge, this is my first day,' said the young man, standing rigidly to attention.

'You've got a lot to learn… er… what's your name, son?'

'Antknee, sir,' said Antknee, relaxing slightly.

'Well, *Antknee*, the first thing is… you count 'ow many miscreants you're chasing… you can count, can't you?' Antknee nodded. 'And then you look around you to make sure there are twice as many of you as there is of them. If there are *not* twice as many of you, you just chase 'em… you do not try and catch 'em… an' especially if one's a troll… understand?'

'But Sarge, the book…'

'Sod the book, we do it *my* way!' the Sergeant interrupted. 'We make a *mental note* of who they are and we get them one by one, when they're on their own.'

'Yes, Sergeant,' said Antknee, quietly.

'Because we don't want to take *actual* notes and get all tied up with writing incident reports, and things, do we?'

'The book says…'

'Did *you* make notes?'

'Yes, Sergeant.'

How did I guess? he thought. 'Well done,' said the Sergeant, in a kindly, though faintly peed off tone. 'And what did you see?'

Antknee stepped forward, and studied his pad. 'Well, Sarge. I saw a wizard…'

'Yes.'

'A girl?'

'Good.'

'Two soldiers… and a bloody great troll!'

'Excellent!' said the Sergeant. 'That's dead right. You can write up the report later. Now, let's get down to the *Piggin Wissall* before closing time!'

* * *

23

Eydith and Link reached the steps that led up to the library level without incident. Their magic abilities restored, Sprag and Eydith were able to seal the entrance on the stairs. The blasts of cold air emanating from the Parallel Dimension were now a sustained draught, and a light frost clung to some of the lower cracks in the walls of the passage. Sprag glowed with a dim red light, but not for human benefit: he was keeping the frost from collecting on himself.

'How come the Parallel Dimension's mostly pretty hot,' said Link, 'but it creates such a cold draught?'

Eydith had no idea.

The ground shuddered again as another part of the Parallel Dimension subsided. Or it could have been the new excavations. They quickened their pace, which was not easy on the uphill climb to the library and beyond. When they felt no further rumbles they slowed down to catch their breath.

Once they reached the library they felt safe enough to stop. They sank to the floor and a few moments passed before either of them spoke. It was Eydith who broke the silence. She peered into the library and noticed the time by the clock over Paske, the librarian's, desk.

'Have we really been gone that long?' she said, in disbelief.

'Probably not,' said Link, 'I've heard the Parallel Dimension can sometimes mess with time.'

'We've lost a few hours,' she said, a little indignantly, though not sure who to blame. 'I think we'd better leave reporting to Trinkel till the morning. I reckon the buildings will be safe enough for a while yet.'

'I shall sleep soundly tonight with that reassurance,' he said, a little derisively.

She let it pass. 'Sleep's just what I need right now,' she said. 'Come on, let's get going.'

'Through the library?' suggested Link.

'Is it any quicker?'

'About the same, really.'

'Okay. We can warn Paske on the way.'

'No, don't say anything to him. He panics. Besides, the books will look after him. After all, he's looked after them for long enough.'

Most of the books in the library were about magic, but some of them were magical themselves. These were kept away from the others because, in the past, they'd been known to breed magic of their own, and some of their spells could only be read safely through inch-thick, dark-tinted glass. A rare enough commodity in itself, but without this protection, some wizards' minds had been turned, and vows of celibacy forgotten. That's not to say that some of them hadn't forgotten them anyway.

Just as Eydith and Link were passing through the library, Paske looked up. 'Oi!' he called, rising from his chair, 'is that you, Linkwood?' knowing full well that it was. Link ignored him and hurried on. 'Have you still got that book?!' he shouted. They kept walking fast till they exited the door on the far side, slammed it behind them and leant on it.

'What book?' she asked.

Link thought about it, then it dawned on him. He grinned. 'He means the one about sewers.'

'You haven't still got that, have you? The fine must be enormous by now.'

'I'll get it back sometime. I doubt there's a queue for it.'

She agreed wholeheartedly.

The pair made their way back, each to their own rooms. Eydith crashed out quickly. Link didn't have any trouble getting off to sleep either, though he spent five minutes looking for that book first, to no avail. The Parallel Dimension had shortened their day, but somehow it hadn't delayed their need for rest. Link slept soundly. But he awoke with a start in the morning.

Someone was knocking repeatedly and insistently on his door.

'Who is it?' he called, testily, struggling to come round.

'Me, Eydith.'

'Come in, it's open!' he called, dragging himself up so he was seated on the bed.

She stepped into the room. 'It's gone!' she announced.

Link's unthinking reaction was to look around the room to see if he had it. 'What's gone?'

'The Drum!'

His mouth gaped. He was suddenly wide awake. He got up off the bed, rushed past her and into her rooms all in one fluid movement, it seemed. She followed him out to the balcony. 'Anything else missing?' he asked, going back inside, relieved to see she still had the staff.

'The bedroom's been disturbed, but they've only taken the Drum,' she replied, pale faced.

'Any magical hints from Sprag as to where it might be?'

'Sprag says he's lost connection with it.'

'Come on!' he ordered, marching into the passage again.

'Where are we going?'

'To the Watch to report it. For all the good it'll do us. They usually try and wash their hands of anything that goes on in Havrapsor. But you never know. It's a burglary, after all. And the sooner we tell them the better. It shouldn't take too long. We can see Trinkel afterwards. This can't wait. He'll want to know about it, too.'

About halfway along the passageway to the stairs, Link realised he was still wearing a nightshirt and popped back to get dressed.

The university was stirring to life as they walked hurriedly across the dawn campus, as was Kra-Pton itself as they headed for the city gates. It was fully daylight by the time they reached the Watch House.

* * *

24

'Yes, officer. A *Drum*. Very old and tatty, but still a *Drum*,' stressed Link.

'Anything else missing, sir?' asked the officer at the desk.

'No, that's all,' said Eydith.

The officer turned to face the men in the office behind him and called out, 'Lionel! Anyone found a drum? – or seen one being lugged about suspiciously?' There was a moment's silence as the occupants of the back office searched their minds. Then came a chorus of negative replies. The desk officer shook his head.

Just then, the Sergeant of the Watch came in off the street, followed by his five trusty Watchmen. A couple of them rocking unsteadily and smelling of a large intake of ale. The Sergeant noticed Eydith first and drew himself up to his full height, expanded his chest and removed his helmet.

'Good… er,' he paused, and turned to the man nearest him. '… what time of day is it, son?' he whispered.

'It's mornin', Sarge,' Antknee whispered.

'Are you *sure?* We've been out *all night*?' He turned back to Eydith, 'Er … mornin' miss.' And greeted her with a smile. 'What appears to be the trouble?'

'She's lost a Drum, Sergeant,' explained Link, stepping forward. 'A very precious Drum,' he went on, fearing they might not take it too seriously.

'You just wait your turn, young man,' said the Sergeant. 'I'm speaking to the young lady. I'll get to you in a minute.'

'We're together,' said Link.

'Ah.' The Sergeant slowly reverted back to his original shape, that of a pear: his chest deflated and his stomach expanded, just in time to take up the slack in his belt before it fell to the floor taking his trousers with it. 'About this Drum, then,' he began again. 'Where was it?'

'It was in a box on the balcony of my rooms at the university, Sergeant,' she replied.

What a charming girl, he thought. *Respectful, too*. 'And now it's gone?' he said.

'Yes. It must have been taken late last evening while we were out,' said Eydith, still agitated. 'What can you do to help us?'

The Sergeant walked slowly to the front of the counter and leaned back against it. 'Any of you men see a stolen Drum last night?!' he barked.

The other officers looked at one another, all shaking their heads, except one.

'I did, Sarge,' said Antknee.

'Where?' asked the Sergeant, smiling at Eydith.

Antknee stepped forward. 'It was on that carpet we chased, Sarge, you remember? The one with the wizard and the troll, and that.'

Eydith's chin dropped. 'Oh, no. Dennis!'

Link put his arm around her shoulder. He felt crestfallen, too. 'Did you notice which way they went?' he asked.

Antknee went to the window and looked out, but he couldn't see what he was looking for. 'Which way does the sun rise in this place?' he asked nobody in particular. The others shrugged. This time of day they were usually still sleeping or too hung over to care.

Link looked out. The sun hadn't cleared the buildings opposite yet, but he could see where the shadows were falling. 'That way: east.' He pointed, for the benefit of the young officer.

'Right,' said Antknee. 'Then they flew that way.' He pointed at the blank north wall.

'Could be anywhere by now,' said the Sergeant, shaking his head, and wishing he hadn't after all that ale. 'We'll get word to the men on the street today and tell them to keep an eye out for it.' The duty officer nodded, and wrote something. 'But my guess is they've left the city with it.'

'Thank you,' said Eydith, sounding a little deflated. But her native determination was beginning to kick in again. 'That'll do to be getting on with. Come on, Link.'

Link followed her, giving their thanks to Antknee as he went. Outside, as they walked, he asked her where they were going. 'Back to the university to get some things, and then to get the Drum back.'

'We'd better tell Trinkel about the Parallel Dimension before we go,' said Link, softly.

'If it hadn't been for the stupid time loss there, we'd probably have been back in our rooms, and this would never have happened.'

*

Shortly after, they arrived outside Trinkel's rooms. Eydith lifted the brass, cat-shaped knocker and tapped it against the door as lightly as she could. It struck again like the boom of a canon being fired. *Why does it do that?* she wondered, ready to be annoyed at almost anything at the moment. The flap at the back of the spy hole slid back, then closed again.

Trinkel opened the door and greeted them with a broad smile. 'You've found it?'

Eydith and Link looked blankly at each other, then back to the Archchancellor, 'Sorry?' she said, with a frown.

'My goat.'

'Goat? What goat?' she said, trying to stay calm. Then, the all-too-graphic image of a half-stuffed goat slowly materialised in her mind. *Yuck.*

'Oh, *that* goat. No, Archchancellor, we haven't seen it.'

'Oh,' said Trinkel, his face stiffening. 'Well, come in anyway, I expect it'll turn up.'

The pair followed him in. Eydith tried not to look around. She kept her eyes firmly fixed on the ageing mage. 'What can I do for you?' he asked, pouring some orange liquid into a test tube.

'It's the Parallel Dimension…' Eydith began.

'No, I don't think so,' said Trinkel, holding the test tube to the light. 'Should be orange juice.' He tasted it and grimaced. 'Not enough sugar.' And laid it down, carelessly spilling some onto the floor, where the carpet began to smoke and retreat from the liquid like lead flowing away from a welder's torch.

'No, Archchancellor,' Eydith sighed. 'We went down to the cellars yesterday to see what's happening under the building, and we've come to *warn* you about the Parallel Dimension.'

'Oh, I know all about that… nasty place, full of demons and dead people.'

'Yes, Archchancellor, but the problem is, it's caving in,' she continued.

'Best thing for it, if you ask me.'

'Archchancellor,' she tried again. 'The university is built directly over it, and it's also falling down. Do you understand?'

The old mage took a moment to digest this. When he did, his face clouded over and he slumped down into a chair, wearily, as though all the breath had left his aged body.

'And there's something else you should know,' said Eydith, feeling bad about adding to his woes, because he looked so down. 'The Drum has been stolen… from my rooms… last night.'

He seemed not to hear her at first, lost in thought, but then he nodded quite slowly.

Eydith added one more blow. 'Dennis is back. He was seen leaving the city on his carpet. The Watch saw him go. And he had the Drum.' She bit her lip and waited to see how he would take all this. She exchanged concerned glances with Link.

Trinkel nodded slowly again. He stared at the floor, unseeing, and became quite solemn.

Right before their eyes, he was shedding his persona as the absent-minded professor. There was a different look to his face and light in his eyes. A more authoritative and business-like Trinkel was coming through. The Archchancellor liked to play, but he never truly lost sight of his work. Eydith and Link watched the transformation and were both amazed and reassured.

'Yes, I do understand,' said the old mage, in an unfamiliar no-nonsense voice. 'Leave it to me. I'll get everybody moving. Firstly, we need to set a full evacuation in progress. It might even be possible to relocate… temporarily relocate… the entire university buildings, should it come to it.' He got up from his chair nimbly, like a man twenty years younger. 'You'll no doubt be wanting to get after Dennis. If I can help with that I will,' he added, obscurely and without elaboration, then looked around his rooms. 'I'd better get some boxes to pack this lot in, I suppose,' he muttered to himself. Eydith and Link got up to leave. 'Just a minute,' said Trinkel. 'Would you mind telling my secretary what's happened, and that he needs to get things moving? He's far better at dealing with this sort of thing than I am.'

Eydith nodded and gave him a weak smile, a little intimidated by the new Trinkel.

* * *

25

'Where did you say we're going, boss?' asked Jook, as Dennis snapped out an instruction to the carpet to avoid some trees that had inconsiderately grown in his path.

'We're taking Krystal back to her *royal* family in the Ironroot Mountains,' he replied, staring directly ahead.

'That's nice,' said Jook. 'Ain't been there for a while.'

'Place is full of trolls,' remarked Psoddoph, glumly.

'Exactly,' said Dennis. 'That's why we're taking her there. Near the Lava Tree range, I expect.' Krystal neither confirmed nor denied it. She hadn't flown before, except downwards a couple of times when she was very young. But falling off cliffs didn't count, and the only time she'd changed direction was when she'd bounced off something on the way down.

At that moment her eyes were pressed tightly shut and her banana-like fingers were gripping the sides of the carpet in near panic. She just couldn't get used to it.

'I don't want to be an old worrier, boss,' said Jook, quietly. 'But 'ave you noticed that we're losing height?'

'Yeah,' agreed Psoddoph. 'Can you take us up a bit, boss?'

Dennis glanced down and had to agree that the ground looked a lot closer than he remembered it, and, as he watched, it got closer. He muttered a few polite commands to the carpet and it began to rise again, very slowly. He'd learned from some previous alarming experiences that the carpet didn't react well to being ordered about, especially being shouted at. He had to be polite to it at all times. Fate clearly had a sense of humour providing Dennis with such a transport.

'Something's wrong, boss,' said Jook. 'It feels like we're dragging something.'

'Take a look underneath,' Dennis called.

'Why me?' muttered Jook. 'It's *always* me.'

Psoddoph answered with a look that said *keep your mouth shut, then.* Jook took his helmet off and handed it to Psoddoph. Then he stretched out on his stomach and peered over the edge. There was a great, protruding bulge underneath. He quickly calculated its position and knew what was causing it. The weight of the troll! Jook had visions of Krystal stretching the carpet to its limits and falling through. *Better tell Dennis, I suppose, but he ain't gonna like it*, he thought. He brought himself back on top.

Jook sidled up to Dennis and whispered in his ear, so Krystal didn't overhear. Dennis's face froze momentarily and he silently repeated to himself what Jook had said. His mind raced. He couldn't dump Krystal off. He wanted that reward. And what if she survived and made it home, and told her father what he'd done? The last thing he needed was a tribe of angry trolls looking for him. What should he do? He remembered Psoddoph was sometimes a good man in a bad situation. Loathe as he was to ask for help, he might just be worth asking. He whispered the guard's name and motioned for him to come closer, giving Jook a stare that meant move away now.

Psoddoph eased his way across the carpet, wondering what he was he going to get saddled with this time. 'What's up, boss?'

Dennis gestured for him to keep his voice down. 'We've got a bit of trouble.'

Psoddoph's heart began to sink. 'What's that, boss?'

'It's Krystal. She's too heavy. She's going to rip the carpet and fall through if we can't spread her load.' Saying that, Dennis immediately realised he'd found his own solution. Before the guard could open his mouth, Dennis said, 'Yes! That's it! I knew I could rely on you.'

Psoddoph shrugged.

'Spread the load,' Dennis repeated. 'Would you mind asking her if she'd mind… you know, spreading herself out a bit… like, you know… lay down, put an arm here, a leg there… that sort of thing,' he whispered. 'Be tactful about it.'

The guard edged over to Krystal. Even with her stony features – which were usually quite blank, apart from the pits where her emerald eyes were – Psoddoph could sense that she was terrified. If he got too near, she might make a sudden move and upset them all. And him getting too near, he thought ruefully, would increase the weight where she was. He called across to her as calmly and gently as he could, 'Krystal, can you hear me?'

An eyelid moved. 'Yes, I can hear you. I'm frightened, not deaf.'

Psoddoph pressed on. 'Would you mind, please...?'

'What?' she snapped.

'Laying down?'

'What have you got in mind, soldier?' Her lower lip was quivering slightly.

This is going to be tricky, he thought. 'Um... I... just thought you might be more comfortable if you laid down, that's all.' Then added hopefully, 'and spread yourself out a bit.'

She opened both eyes, glaring at him. 'I see, soldier. It's my *weight* you're referring to here, isn't it?' She noticed she was sitting in quite a dip, and the carpet looked strained. He nodded, sheepishly. Slowly she began to redistribute herself. 'If this doesn't work,' she began, 'I'll remember that remark. Probably.'

The guard's face reddened; he knew he'd remember it too. 'Thank you,' he said, kindly. 'You know, if you opened your eyes and watched, you might get used to it. It can be quite exhilarating,' he tried. 'And you can help direct us when we get nearer to where you live.'

She didn't reply straight away, but Psoddoph could almost hear the cogs grinding in her mind as she thought about it. 'Do you really think that would work?' she wondered.

'Why not give it a try?' said Florence, offering some encouragement. Krystal moved to another position, lying flat on her stomach with her chin propped on her hands and her legs spread. She was still in a dip, but it was shallower. Dennis sighed with relief when the carpet became less sluggish and gained a bit more height. There was no weight difference, but there was certainly an improvement in the carpet's ability to function.

'Don't you go too high, now,' Krystal warned him.

'The sensation of speed gets less the higher you go,' Psoddoph explained.

'Let's take it one step at a time, soldier,' she growled. 'I haven't forgotten the weight remark, yet.'

By mid-afternoon, Dennis was thinking about landing. He needed to get his bearings, stretch his legs, and find the right-sized bush for a comfort leak. Worrying about Krystal's weight, and trying to keep the carpet in the air, was having a bad effect on his nerves. He was edgy. And with a creature as punch-happy as Krystal, he'd have to keep a tight rein on his temper. Since meeting the troll, he was sure he'd seen the Grim Reaper standing in the shadows smirking once or twice.

* * *

26

Scanning the near horizon for a suitable landing site, Dennis saw a farm. The others saw it too. 'Looks like a good place to land,' said Psoddoph, just thinking aloud.

'I'll say what's a good place to land!' snapped Dennis.

'Well? What do you think, boss?'

'It looks a *reasonable* place,' said Dennis, grumpily, and gave the carpet the necessary request, but in a more polite tone. They drifted down by a small pond. Ducks and chickens scattered as their shadow passed over them. Dennis settled the carpet on the grass with a gentle bump.

'That wasn't so bad, was it?' said Florence, as Krystal stood up.

'Bad enough,' she complained. 'But I'll get used to it, I suppose.'

'Oi!' called a voice from the farmhouse door. 'You there!' A man emerged, armed with a crossbow.

The wizard put his hands in the air. 'Don't shoot!' he called. 'We mean no harm. We're just passing through… just travellers.'

The farmer turned his gaze to Krystal as she began lumbering towards him. *Oh, no. A bloody great troll,* he thought. He opened his mouth and hoped for the right words. 'Welcome…er… travellers,' he muttered, partially lowering his crossbow. He was not a foolish man. 'How can I help you?'

That's better, Dennis thought. 'We are in need of some refreshment and directions to the Ironroot Mountains,' he called back.

To be fair to the farmer, the travellers who stopped at his farm usually tried to rob him. Hence the crossbow welcome. The sizeable graveyard on the nearby hillside bore testimony to his skill. The crossbow was no empty threat. He was fully prepared to use it. Though he tended to hold back because he hated digging holes.

The farmer cleared his throat. 'Directions are free. Food will cost you,' he said, a little nervously. 'You'll have to pay me… with a few hours' labour.'

'That's all right,' said Dennis, chirpily, as he didn't have to part with any actual cash. 'We don't mind a bit of labour. Do you, men?'

The two guards' chests heaved, but their lips remained sealed. 'What is it that you want done, farmer?' Dennis offered. 'Stacking straw, clearing ditches... that kind of thing?'

The farmer thought, *If they're prepared to do that, they could probably do better*. 'See that old stone barn?' he said, pointing at a crumbling building a few yards from the side of the house. 'I need that taken down, and I could do with a nice gravel path around the house, down to the front gate over there. That'd be nice.' He stood back and waited for an argument to start.

'Will you excuse me for a moment, while I consult with my men?' said Dennis, pulling the two guards aside to where the farmer couldn't overhear. 'Do you think you can do it? You know... in a couple of hours?'

'No, boss,' replied Psoddoph. 'Without putting too fine a point on it, nobody could do all that in two hours.'

'What about Krystal?' suggested Jook. 'She might help, at least with taking that barn down.'

'Good thinking.' Dennis grinned. 'I've seen her demolition skills. She quite enjoys it, too. I'll talk to her. I've got an idea.' He strolled over to her and told her what he had in mind.

The guards could see her nodding and smiling. Florence, standing by Krystal's side, was smiling, too, at whatever it was Dennis was plotting.

Finally, he returned to the farmer. 'We will do what you want,' he said, narrowing his eyes. 'But for a job like that, we will require accommodation for a night as well.'

The farmer stroked his chin, then agreed, adding, 'The troll stays out here, though.'

'Agreed,' said Dennis, as that was part of what he'd planned, anyway.

Florence, and the two guards carrying the Drum between them, followed Dennis towards the front door. 'Stop!' called the farmer. 'Work first, food and rest later.'

'Sir,' said Dennis, snaking an arm around the farmer's shoulders. 'We will do your labours, but we will do them when *I* say. And *I* say, after we are refreshed.'

Krystal shuffled menacingly, eloquently conveying that she backed every word Dennis had said. The farmer reluctantly stepped down. He couldn't harm the troll with a two-handed battle-axe, never mind an old crossbow. 'And no music!' he grunted, noticing the Drum as he led them into the house. 'Kitchen's through here,' he mumbled, pushing the door open. 'Mother!' he hollered. 'We have guests.'

A kindly looking old lady was sitting in a rocking chair by the range. She peered over the top of a pair of half-spectacles as Dennis and Florence filed into the room. 'Hello, my dear,' she smiled broadly at Florence, ignoring Dennis. 'Come in. Would you like something to eat?'

Florence gave her a shy smile. 'Oh, yes, please… anything really. We don't want to put you to any trouble.'

'Oh, it's no trouble.' The old lady smiled in the sweet way that only old ladies can. 'Come and have a look in the pantry. See if there's anything in there you fancy.'

As she followed the farmer's mother, Florence glanced through the window and couldn't help noticing the graves on the hillside. She caught her father's attention and signalled him to look through the window. 'What are all those graves out there?' Florence asked, trying to sound innocently curious. 'Have you lost a lot of family?'

The mother looked about and Florence pointed to the hillside. 'Oh… those. My eyes are not so good these days, my dear. Can't read them from here,' she replied.

'No, I didn't mean tell me the names. I just wondered why they are there.'

'It's my son,' the old woman began. 'With that crossbow thingy of his…' She took a deep breath. 'He tells me they were all thieves come to rob us, so he dealt with them. We don't get so many these days, though.'

'I suppose not,' she said, looking over at the crowded hillside.

'Still… he's a good boy, really.'

Florence couldn't comment on that. But she felt happier about eating the old woman's food now. It had crossed her mind that the graves might contain victims of her cooking.

That night, Krystal put the rest of Dennis's plan into action. She was hungry. She'd tried to eat a chunk from the wall of the university while she was waiting outside for the others, but the building had reclaimed it rather painfully. She wouldn't be doing that again, ever. Under her stony gaze, the old barn looked delicious. She set about dismantling the stones. They were old and well-weathered and she crunched them up quite happily. When it came to the roof, she found a bucket, fetched some water, then sat down with the great pile of tiles she'd stacked, and dunked them like biscuits in a mug of tea.

Over the next couple of hours, the barn disappeared completely. Where it once stood, there was now a rectangle of compacted dirt. All she had to do now, was let nature take its course, and then she could lay the gravel path.

* * *

27

Trinkel's Secretary was a big man with great big, bushy eyebrows that crowned his round, yellowing eyes, giving him the permanent expression of an irate eagle. He could be quite intimidating. But he knew Eydith by reputation, and he listened intently to what she told him regarding what was going on in the Parallel Dimension. And as if to underline the gravity and urgency of Eydith's words, the building rumbled again and lurched slightly.

It didn't right itself for some moments, and the Secretary had to reach out to grab his inkwell before it slid off his desk and into his lap. 'I see what you mean,' he said. 'It is getting worse. And you say you've *been* down to the Parallel Dimension and actually know what's going on down there?' He might not have believed that of anyone but Eydith.

'Yes, sir,' she affirmed, with quiet confidence.

The Secretary thought about it, absently turning the inkwell over in his hands. Moments later, he jumped up with such force that his chair slammed into the cupboard behind him, shattering one of the door panels. Eydith and Link flinched. The Secretary grinned sheepishly, but with a pool of spilt ink on a desk that was sloping towards him, the first thing to do was to panic. It was cheaper than buying new clothes.

He looked down, briefly annoyed at the mess on his carpet, then stoically said, 'Hardly worth worrying about if the whole place is falling down, is it?'

Eydith shook her head in agreement.

'Well,' he said, quite calmly in the circumstances, 'I'd better rouse everyone and get them working some magic. See if we can't do something about it. It's a pity it's come at a time when the buildings aren't being too co-operative! You say the Archchancellor spoke of evacuation?' He stepped back to his desk and opened a drawer. 'Funny…' he muttered, slamming it shut again. 'I could've sworn it was in that one.' He tried the next one. 'Hmm,' he breathed, extracting what looked like a large toffee hammer. He hefted it in his hand for a moment, as if judging its suitability for what he had in mind. Then he strode to his office door. 'This should do it,' he said, glancing back at Eydith before stepping outside.

She looked at Link questioningly. He shrugged. Moments later, a bell was being struck vigorously and someone was yelling, 'FIRE! FIRE!'

Link grinned. 'That's one way of getting everyone's attention, I suppose.'

Moments later, other bells were being rung around the buildings in reply to the first. 'I've always wondered if there would ever be a fire-drill in this place,' Eydith said, watching to see what would happen next.

The nearest bell stopped and the Secretary marched back into the office. 'That's the first step,' he announced, obviously pleased with himself. 'Scare the shit out of 'em.' He crossed to the window, grinning with an evil smugness. Down in the courtyard, wizards and students were appearing by the score. Some from doorways, some from windows and some were shinning down rainwater pipes.

The very elderly and infirm were being wheeled out in their wheelchairs towards the main gates. It was the Archchancellor's ruling for any such emergency that they must go first. Not because he cared so much about them, or that he might even be among them himself, but rather to obstruct the young and agile, and stop them from taking the opportunity to nip off down to the *Piggin Wissall* before anyone had noticed they'd gone.

Seeing their way blocked, the younger element milled around waiting for something to happen. They didn't have to wait long. The Secretary threw open his window and leaned out. 'Will you give me your attention, please!' he yelled, at the top of his voice. All the assembled wizards continued chatting feverishly amongst themselves, totally ignoring him. He tried again, 'Oi!' he yelled.

Eydith whispered to Sprag and then moved to the Secretary's side.

'Damned rabble!' he snapped. 'Don't they know I'm trying to talk to them?'

'Try again, touching this,' said Eydith, placing her staff between them.

The Secretary complied. He was used to the ways of magic. This time his voice was so loud that he rattled the windows on the other side of the courtyard. The wizards fell silent and looked up. 'Thank you,' he said, glaring down at their upturned faces.

He began to address them, 'Some of you may have heard some rumblings around the university of late. Just because you are wizards, doesn't mean you can be complacent about this sort of thing. It's not just the buildings playing up… It's more than that.'

'What's going on, then?' interrupted one of the older mages from his wheelchair, and a few others murmured similar things. 'And where's the fire?' someone wanted to know.

'If you'll all just shut up, I'll tell you!' the Secretary yelled, touching Sprag again and almost deafening everyone.

The courtyard went very silent. The Secretary stared down at them and they reminded him of expectant children in a playground. 'Well,' he began again. 'We have something of an emergency on our hands. The Archchancellor has told me to tell you that he feels it might be a good idea for us all to leave the university for a while and study our magic somewhere else.'

'Why? Those bloody Alchemists are not complaining again, are they?' yelled one.

'Yeah, they make more noise than we do, all those soddin' explosions all over the place. It's about time they learned how to do it properly!'

'Yeah,' agreed another. 'They wouldn't keep blowing themselves up then, and we'd all get some sleep.'

'That's *not* the reason!' the Secretary yelled down at them.

'What is it, then?'

'Why don't you just hear me out?' he snapped. 'About the rumblings! The buildings are falling down!'

'Nah,' said the one who'd started the heckling. 'It's only a bit of subsidence. It's happened loads of times. The place sorts itself out.'

'This is much more serious.' The Secretary frowned. 'I have it on good authority that there have been some major collapses in the Parallel Dimension – which is bad enough – but in order to create new living space, the demons are digging great caverns beneath us and the whole university is threatened…' He hesitated for a moment. 'All of it… could soon fall into the ground. Into the Parallel Dimension, in fact.'

That caused a stir. The assembled wizards began murmuring in dismay. One of the older ones, in a wheelchair, rummaged in his pannier box, pulled out an oilcan and squeezed it onto his axles. He might need to move fast.

'What's the Archchancellor going to do about it?' shouted one.

'He'll be doing his bit, believe me. He'll be communing with the buildings themselves, as only he can. But this may have gone too far for that.' The Secretary finally had them concerned. 'Now, you senior wizards need to do *your* bit. It's up to you to come up with something to stop the demons! Some appropriate defensive magic is called for.'

The shouty wizard went quiet, but his chin carried on moving.

'Well, don't just stand there!' the Secretary yelled. 'Get on your way and do something!'

In a matter of moments, the crowds cleared back into the buildings. Not long after that, the wizards began emerging again. They were carrying bags and cases, and filing out through the main gates and onto the streets.

'That appears to be that,' said the Secretary. 'They've got the message. Now, if there's nothing else?' Eydith and Link looked at each other. 'No? Good.' The Secretary nodded. 'I'll be off then.' He went back to his desk, rummaged through the drawers, and realised that after all his years of loyal service, dedication and self-sacrifice, there wasn't really anything worth keeping in any of them. He sighed a long sad sigh, then marched briskly out of the room and out of the building.

Eydith sat on one of the Secretary's over-stuffed armchairs and looked sadly at Link. 'Do you know?' she said, trying to keep her mouth from turning down at the corners. 'I really thought they'd do something right away. With all the magic that must be in this place!'

Link knelt down in front of her and put his hand over hers. 'They did…' he said, softly.

'Yes, they left!' she interrupted. She almost added something unladylike, and knew that Link was thinking it, too. 'Well, it looks like *we'll* have to do something then, doesn't it?' They both stood up. 'I tried too hard to get accepted into this place to let it fall into the hands of demons!'

Link smiled, but only in admiration of her determination. He wasn't sure what they could do, but he was sure it would be fraught with problems. He didn't mind problems so much as the danger that usually accompanied this sort. *That*, he did mind.

He followed her down the steps and across the courtyard, back to their respective rooms. They each packed a small bag and went to the kitchens to collect some food. Even the cooks had left.

Out on the streets, carts loaded with furniture were already being towed out of the city. People were leaving *en masse*. Once news that the wizards were leaving Havrapsor had leaked out, the citizens of Kra-Pton felt there was no point staying. The wizards were their chief source of income. The news that hordes of demons might soon be on the loose also influenced their decision somewhat.

The only people not leaving were the Officers of the Watch. Antknee had shamed them into staying to try and protect the city, if not from the demons, at least from the hordes of barbarians that would sooner or later descend upon Kra-Pton to loot, pillage and rape. Though the lack of opportunity for the last of those things might deter them. All the women would be gone.

When they reached the university's main gates, Eydith turned right and hurried down the street, forcing her way through the oncoming tide of people. 'That's not the way!' Link called after her, in an effort to make himself heard above the hubbub of the crowd and the rumbling of wheels on the street.

'I'm going to the stables to see if there are any horses left! We can't walk all the way to the Ironroots!' she told him, glancing over her shoulder. Link stopped. Eydith didn't. He had to run to catch up again. This might not be a good time to tell her that he'd never ridden a horse in his life. He hoped they would get to the stables in time to see the last horse disappearing into the proverbial sunset. Alas, his wish was not granted. When they reached the stables, there were two horses left. And one donkey.

The blacksmith was taking the last of his unsold harnesses and bridles from their pegs, and loading them onto a cart. When he heard Eydith and Link, he turned. 'Can I help you?' he asked, in a deep, rich voice.

Eydith peeled her eyes back from the man's bare chest, which even in the gloom was still glistening with golden sweat. 'Er… yes, I… that is, we, are looking for a couple of horses.'

'Sorry, only got one left for sale,' he said, his white teeth gleaming. He walked over to the stalls to show her what was on offer. There were two horses. One a beautiful chestnut with large muscles, a flowing golden mane, and a kind face. All horses have kind faces, of course, but some have wild eyes. Then, there was the other one…

'A magnificent beast,' said the blacksmith. 'Runs like a racehorse…'

Link couldn't help feeling that the man hadn't finished that sentence. The word *but* was hanging in the air at the end of it. 'Yes...?' said Link, by way of a prompt. Then it came.

'But she won't go anywhere without Mabel,' the blacksmith added.

'Mabel?' queried Eydith.

'Yes, that's Mabel.' The blacksmith introduced them to the donkey.

Link's expression was one of mild satisfaction. 'She's just right,' he said, quickly, before Eydith could stop him. 'How much?'

The blacksmith went through the ritual of stroking his chin, as many men do when faced with that question. They settled on eight copper coins and one silver.

As they rode away, Link, struggling to stay on the donkey, couldn't help wondering why the horse was so reasonable, and Mabel so expensive.

* * *

28

In a farmhouse due north-east of Kra-Pton, and about seventy-five miles from the city, the morning went differently. It was a misty start, brightened by a watery yellow sun, which appeared to be racing through the haze as the mist was swept along by the breeze. In the house, the farmer was first to rise. In the farmyard a cock crowed, then another one, louder. The first cock tried again and there was a momentary silence before a fight broke out. The noise woke Dennis, and first thing in the morning was not his best time of the day. Angrily, he threw back the blankets and stepped across to the window of the cramped spare bedroom he'd been allocated.

The yard was in uproar. The two fighting cocks had upset the hens who'd started squabbling among themselves. The farmer threw open his front door and the dog escaped between his legs, eager to join the fight. He picked up his mother's walking stick and gave chase, knowing that if the beast got in among the hens they'd scatter and it would take him the rest of the day to catch them.

He hadn't run far before the soles of his bare feet shot an urgent message to his brain, telling him to go back indoors and put some boots on. He hopped and skidded to a halt, but not before his surprise new gravel path had shredded some skin.

In exasperation, he threw his mother's stick at the dog and missed. It hit the gate and cartwheeled back at him, missing his shoulder by inches and catching him a glancing blow to the side of his head.

Dennis threw his bedroom window open and leaned out. 'What the hell's going on?' he yelled. 'It's… it's…' frantically wondering what time of day it was. 'It's bloody dawn! That's what it is!'

The farmer looked up, rubbing his ear. 'The cocks are fighting again, that's all. I'll sort it out in a minute!' He went back indoors, trying to ignore the pains in his feet, and yanked his boots on.

Now that Dennis was awake, he thought he might as well get up. He threw some clothes on and thumped moodily down the stairs. He found the farmer in the front yard armed with his crossbow.

The hens had fled – those that were still alive, that was – and it would be many a day before *they* laid another egg. One cockerel was dead and the other was squaring up to the dog.

'What are you going to do now?' asked Dennis.

'I've got three choices, mister,' the farmer said, grimly. 'I can shoot the cock, or I can shoot the dog. That way I'll still have one of them.'

'And the other choice?' asked Dennis.

'Oh, yes… er, one of us goes in there and separates 'em.'

Dennis considered a magical solution. But, after a prolonged silence, he asked, 'Which one will you shoot, then?'

The cock lunged at the dog again, making it yelp and shy away. Then the dog spun round and snapped at the bird, which used its wings to lift itself out of harm's way. It landed on the dog's hind quarters, drawing blood, and flapped to a halt a few feet away. The dog charged again, and they grappled furiously, creating a cloud of dust.

'I don't want to shoot either of them!' the farmer snapped. 'I can't see either of them now, anyway. Look, you go round that side, and I'll go in from here. We should be able the get between 'em.'

Dennis shook his head. The farmer raised his crossbow, menacingly. Dennis changed his mind. The short distance the bolt would have to travel to reach him, would no doubt make it a lot quicker than any spell he could muster. Except, perhaps, the one that produced a bouquet of paper flowers.

The morning mist was clearing. It was going to be a nice day. Dennis might even enjoy it if he survived the next few minutes. He reluctantly sidled round to the other side of the cock-and-dog fight, and quickened his step when the farmer motioned with the crossbow for him to get on with it. Dennis was thinking of spells that might be of use in the very near future. He'd gotten a little out of practice from his months in the Parallel Dimension. A spell that changed his robe into chainmail would be useful.

But then he thought of the Drum, which was nearby in the front room of the house. Without Sprag – Eydith's staff, which had a restraining effect on it – the Drum had a nasty habit of interfering with his magic. It took delight in making his spells only *sort of* work. And in a situation like this, where he was at risk, it was more prudent to use a lump of wood than magic.

Half hidden by the screen of dust, Dennis tugged one of the palings from the fence and gingerly poked it into the squawking, yelping cloud. He felt one of the animals moving, so raised the plank and brought it down as swiftly as he could. The dog yelped and ran. He'd had enough anyway. The cockerel didn't see which way it went. Neither did Dennis, but he saw the cockerel. It was charging straight at him.

Dennis swung the plank in desperation, connecting with a mild thump on the side of the bird's neck. It squawked once and stopped. Its head lolled to one side and then it ran around in circles. Dennis stood back and used the plank as a staff to lean on. He was pleased with himself. He'd broken up the fight and both creatures were still alive. Then the cockerel keeled over. Looking down he saw that, on the two nails in the plank that he hadn't noticed before, there was blood and feathers. Gingerly, he looked up as the farmer ambled through the settling dust. Dennis turned the tell-tale side of the paling away from him and secretly scraped the feathers off the nails with the side of his boot.

The farmer knelt by the dead bird. 'That damn dog's gonna have to go,' he muttered. 'I hate cold chicken.' He picked the cock up by one of its legs and walked slowly back to the house. With the farmer's back turned, Dennis discreetly tossed the plank over the fence from which it came, and followed the farmer.

'Nice job,' the farmer commented, stopping to take in the new gravel path.

'The barn's gone as well,' said Dennis, pointing at the patch where it once stood.

'Yeah, nice job,' the farmer repeated, still silently assessing his losses and mentally preparing himself for the forthcoming chicken hunt. He looked at the cockerel. 'Put up a good fight by the look of him… here you take him,' he said, holding it at arm's length.

'Er… Thank you,' said Dennis. 'Just put it down there, one of my men will pick it up before we leave.'

In the kitchen, Florence and the two guards were being served breakfast by the farmer's mother. 'You're just in time, young man,' she smiled. 'I was just going to give yours to the chickens.'

The farmer sat himself next to Florence. 'You'll have a job, mother,' he said, sullenly. 'They've all bloody-well gone.'

The bucolic smile disappeared from the old lady's face. 'That's no way to speak in front of a young lady,' she said, haughtily. 'Even if they have all bloody-well gone.'

Florence grinned. 'It's all right, I've heard it all before. And worse.' She glanced at Dennis.

Dennis glanced at the guards and they stared back at him with hurt looks.

'I worked at a tavern in Prossill for a few days,' Florence went on. 'The language of some of the barbarians could be quite colourful.' Dennis's glare abated, and the guards sat at ease.

'We have a new path, mother,' said the farmer, happy to change the subject, while diligently chasing something around his plate with a fork. Eventually he speared it by holding it down with his fingers. 'And the old barn's been taken down as well.'

The old woman sighed. 'I liked that old barn. Your grandfather built it.'

Dennis didn't like the sound of that. Supposing the dear, sweet old lady convinced her son to rebuild it? He might want them to do it. 'Right,' he said quickly. 'As soon as we're done here, I'll go and see if Krystal's ready, then we'll be off.'

'So soon?' said the farmer's mother. 'We get so few visitors; can't you stay a little longer?'

'Thank you,' said Florence. 'But we really must be going. I'll come and see you again one day,' she promised. The farmer grunted, as if to say, *I've heard that before.*

When breakfast was over, Dennis pushed his chair back and stood up to signal it was time to go. Florence took a few minutes saying her goodbyes. The guards followed Dennis outside. 'Looks like it's gonna be a nice day,' remarked Jook.

'Tell me again tonight,' muttered Psoddoph.

Jook ignored him. 'Where's the troll, boss?'

Dennis pointed to what looked like a large rock in the middle of the carpet. One of Krystal's duties had been to guard the carpet overnight, and certainly no-one was going to steal it with her sleeping on it. Jook went to wake her.

'NO!' yelled Dennis, in a sudden panic. 'Don't touch her.' Jook stopped dead in his tracks. Dennis recovered and spoke in quieter tones. 'Better let Florence do it.'

'Okay, boss. I'll get her,' he said, and turned to go back to the house.

'Why don't you bring the Drum out with you while you're at it!' Dennis called after him, muttering, 'Unbelievable!' to himself. And while Jook was gone, he asked Psoddoph if he could think of any way to strengthen the carpet.

Psoddoph looked around for material they might use, but apart from the roof of the deserted chicken house, the only real contender was the plank fence. 'A few of those planks would help spread the load, boss.' He glanced at Krystal, hoping she was still asleep.

'You could be right,' Dennis mused. 'Grab as many as you think we'll need' He looked around to see where the farmer was. Psoddoph guessed this meant a hasty escape, as opposed to a goodbye routine.

'I wonder how much he'd want for these,' said Psoddoph, quietly, as he worked one of the palings loose.

Dennis stopped. 'Sorry?'

Psoddoph repeated himself.

'You mean, *pay*?'

'Yes, boss.'

'That trigger happy little bugger will have us mending his roof, wallpapering his rooms, rounding up his chickens…'

'Alright, boss. I get the picture… you pull that end, and I'll get this.'

They prised five planks from their posts and hurried over to the carpet. 'Where's that girl?' hissed Dennis. 'We've got to wake Krystal.'

'I'll do it, boss.'

'No, I told you, don't touch her.'

'I wasn't going to, boss. I was going to poke her with a plank.'

'She's killed for less than that.'

Undeterred, Psoddoph stepped back to what he hoped would be a safe distance and was about to nudge what he hoped was her arm – it was difficult to tell because a sleeping troll resembles a misshapen boulder – and Dennis was about to knock the plank away from him, when....

'I'll see to her!' Florence called.

Dennis spun round. 'Hurry up, girl, we haven't got all day,' he muttered, testily.

Jook came waddling out with the Drum held high on his chest. 'Come on,' urged Dennis. 'I want to get going.'

Florence knelt beside the sleeping troll and touched her gently, while calling her name. Krystal stirred. The rocklike appearance she adopted while asleep began to move like flowing lava. A stony eyelid peeled back revealing an emerald green eye. It blinked, and then the other one opened. 'Oh, it's you,' she moaned. 'I was expecting a prince.'

'No, it's me, Florence.'

'Not that bloody prince fixation again,' thought Dennis, then realized he'd said it aloud. Thankfully, she didn't catch what he said.

Upon hearing Dennis's voice, Krystal flowed upwards. Having reached her full height, she looked down at him with an expression of disappointment on her face. 'You're not a prince either, are you?'

'No,' snapped the wizard. 'It's me, Dennis. Remember?'

She stared at him and rubbed the grit out of her eyes. 'Oh... yes, the thief.' She yawned. Dennis held his tongue, knowing that a verbal retaliation might well result in a swift blow to his head.

'We want to strengthen the carpet, Krystal,' Florence began. 'With these planks. For your safety.'

A glimmer of appreciation shone in Krystal's eyes. 'I was hoping you'd do something. You know, there were times when I thought I might fall through.'

The others thought so as well, but said nothing. When the troll was clear of the carpet, Psoddoph hurriedly placed the planks on it.

Florence took Krystal's hand and got her settled. Dennis motioned to his guards. 'Don't just stand there, *get on!*' They moved forward and sat down. Dennis crouched beside Psoddoph and Jook nursed the Drum.

'Ready, boss?' asked Jook, tensing himself for the take-off. Dennis remained resolutely quiet. 'Boss?' Jook repeated.

'Which one of you got the directions from the farmer, then?' Dennis wanted to know.

The guards remained silent.

'No. I didn't think so.'

Psoddoph stood up. 'I'll go, boss.'

As the guard left, the farmer appeared at the front door. 'Directions?' said Psoddoph.

'Well,' said the farmer. 'Easy, really. Go that way for about ten miles and you come to a stream. Follow it north and it'll take you straight, sort of, to the Ironroots.'

'Thanks,' said Psoddoph, touching his forehead in salute before walking back to the others.

When the farmer turned to go, he caught sight of his fence. Or, rather, a section of his *not* fence. A gap, in fact.

'Oi!' he yelled after Psoddoph. 'Where's my bloody fence?!'

Psoddoph and the farmer began to run. Both in opposite directions – the farmer into his house and the guard to the carpet. In only moments, though, the farmer was running in the same direction as the guard, and he was carrying his crossbow.

'Stop! Or I'll shoot!' he yelled.

'Hurry up!' yelled Dennis, unnecessarily.

Something zinged past Psoddoph's ear. He glanced over his shoulder and saw the farmer reloading. He also caught sight of the graveyard on the hill at the side of the house. He ran the remaining few yards to the carpet at a speed he hadn't been capable of since he was a much younger man.

Dennis started rattling out polite commands to the carpet, while the others screamed encouragement at the sprinting guard. Without Psoddoph's weight on it, the carpet rose a little easier. His legs were moving like the pistons on an express train now, and his last few strides took him *under* the carpet. The farmer yelled again. 'Stop! Thief!'

Another bolt buzzed close to Psoddoph's head. Jook leaned over and extended his hand.

'Go a bit lower, Father,' Florence pleaded, anxiously. Dennis sighed and politely asked the carpet to comply.

'Got 'im!'

Upon hearing Jook, Dennis asked the carpet to rise. It did. Slowly at first, but it soon reached a height of about fifty feet, tilting dangerously with Psoddoph hanging from the edge. Unsure what to do for the best, Dennis was giving the carpet conflicting instructions. It went forward very quickly, and on a line of descent that meant it would probably hit the ground about a mile further on – if it missed the rapidly approaching group of trees directly in its path. Dennis hurriedly asked the carpet to rise again. It appeared to be ignoring him, thrusting itself harder towards the ground, its angle of descent getting steeper by the second.

Psoddoph was not a happy man. His life was hanging by two wrists. He'd have felt a lot safer if the other one wasn't Jook's. The carpet belatedly tilted upwards again and sideways, avoiding the trees and using its momentum to glide steeply into the sky.

They were barely visible to the farmer, but in his frustration he fired his crossbow up at them anyway.

'I can't 'old onto 'im much longer, boss!' Jook yelled.

Dennis shot a quick glance over his shoulder. 'Let him go, then,' he said, calmly.

'What?' replied Jook, unthinkingly releasing his grip. Psoddoph began his swift descent to the ground. Thankfully he passed out. Jook peered over the edge and watched his friend gradually shrinking into oblivion. 'Ooh shit,' he murmured. Dennis rapidly issued a few polite commands to the carpet. It veered around steeply as it turned. Everyone hung on more tightly.

Florence clung to Krystal, who was living her worst nightmare. Florence's reassurances helped to keep her calm, even though the girl was having trouble enough keeping calm herself. In fact, for the worst of it, they all clung to Krystal, who was spread-eagled face down in an indent in the centre (despite the planks under her), and was the most stable thing on the carpet. Thankfully, she mistook their gripping onto her for a sign of their concern.

'Do something, Father!' pleaded Florence. Dennis ignored her and continued the extremely trying task of issuing polite commands to the carpet while he was so close to screaming at it for instant action. It continued to swoop and swerve rapidly for a few very long seconds, then mercifully it stopped and hovered. There was a gentle thump and a small cloud of dust as Psoddoph landed safely on the carpet. He was fortunate not to slam into the troll – and also fortunate not to be aware of it all.

The carpet continued to hover, as if orienting itself. 'Come on... please go up,' Dennis pleaded. 'Come on...'

The carpet strained. When it had gained a little height, something struck the underside, with a muffled thud.

'What was that?' said Florence. Dennis shrugged. A moment later, it happened again. Jook peered over the edge and ducked back as another crossbow bolt zipped past his ear. They were in range again.

'It's that farmer, boss!' Jook called. 'Why's he shooting at us?'

'Er... we borrowed some of his fence,' said Dennis. 'It's under Krystal.'

'Oh, yeah.' Jook looked back and saw the farmer reloading. Out of self-preservation he pulled the Drum in front of him. A triangular-headed tip stabbed through the carpet beside him and hung there.

'Come on, boss. He'll hit one of us in a minute,' pleaded Jook.

'Don't you think I'm trying!' snapped Dennis.

'Yes, boss,' replied Jook, and silently added... *bloody very*.

The farmer loaded again and, as the carpet began to move away, aimed quickly and released another bolt.

'Look out!' yelled Jook. 'Here comes another one!'

They held their breath. Except Psoddoph, of course, who was comatose. Jook ducked behind the Drum and felt two dull thuds in quick succession. One was the bolt passing through the first skin, which fortunately slowed it sufficiently, and the second was the bolt lodging in the other skin.

Jook opened his eyes and swallowed hard. The point of the bolt was protruding from the Drum at a spot just in front of his forehead. He slumped back and lie there gratefully thinking how wonderful the sky was today.

The carpet levelled at a good height and hurried from the scene, leaving the farmer waving his fists and shouting unheard threats as it sped silently away to the distant mountains.

* * *

29

Link rubbed his elbow and stood up.

'Haven't you got the hang of it yet?' Eydith grinned down at him from her mount.

'It's all right for you. I wasn't brought up on some farm in the back of beyond.' He brushed himself down and went to climb up onto Mabel's back again.

'Not that side!' Eydith called, as the donkey moved around, making it difficult for him to get on board. He put both feet back on the ground and, still gripping the reins, moved around to the other side. Mabel eyed him viciously as he passed in front of her. Then, with one foot in a stirrup, he pulled himself into the saddle again.

'Are you doing this on purpose?' Eydith snapped.

'What?' said Link, innocently.

'You know what! Now get off and face the front!'

Unwilling to dismount, he lifted his legs and swivelled himself around. Somehow, he got it right and managed to be astride the donkey when he'd finished.

Eydith was almost impressed. 'Now, let go of her neck and sit up straight,' she said.

Link slowly pushed himself up.

'Now – feet in the stirrups… yes, that's right… one each side.'

He smiled in a determined kind of way, and managed to arrange his feet accordingly.

'Now, if you push down, you'll be able to balance.'

He tried it and found she was right.

'Now, just nudge her with your heels and she'll go forward.'

Sure enough, Mabel began to walk. Though after a few yards she stopped and looked around. With minimal encouragement, Eydith's horse also began to walk. The donkey then moved on again, happy in the knowledge that her stablemate was following. Link glanced back and gave Eydith an uncertain grin. He was gaining confidence. But he'd had this feeling before and had learned to be sceptical of it.

After a few hours riding and finding himself still in the saddle, he began to believe he'd grasped the idea and even nudged Mabel into a gentle trot. The horse broke into a slow canter and came up alongside, but in Mabel's donkey-mind she was always supposed to be in front and the only time the horse was beside her was in a stable.

So Mabel began trotting a little faster and Link began getting bounced up and down. He was thinking about calling for help, but had second thoughts about that, fearing he might accidentally bite his tongue off.

Eydith could see he was in trouble, and called out. 'Pull back on the reins!' But before she could say, *'gently'*, he'd yanked on them. Mabel responded instantly. Link somersaulted over her head and ended up sitting in the dusty road, still clutching the reins.

Eydith quickly dismounted and ran to his side.

'You alright?' she asked.

'Nothing's broken if that's what you mean, except my spirit, that is,' he moaned, rubbing his backside. Eydith took his elbow and helped him to his feet. He stood there for a moment, trying to massage the pain away.

'Is *that* broken?' she asked, smiling.

Link forced a grin while still rubbing his backside. 'No, just cracked, that's all.'

'Come on,' she said, taking his hand. 'Let's try again.'

He approached the donkey and affectionately pulled her ears. 'Now, Mabel,' he said, quietly, 'we were doing just fine, but this time we're going to try a little harder.' The donkey flicked her ears. Link patted her neck and adjusted the stirrups.

As he was about to raise his foot, Eydith reminded him, 'Not that foot. You'll finish up backwards again.' She looked to the sky as if for some kind of help. It was at times like this that she realised just how far away the sky was.

Link changed feet and climbed back into the saddle. He found the other stirrup and spent a moment getting himself straight. Then, comfortable at last, he gently squeezed the donkey's flanks. Mabel moved grudgingly forwards again. She hadn't forgotten how Link had pulled back on the reins just now, and almost broke her jaw.

Without any prompting from Eydith, her horse followed on behind. Without her. No matter how she tried to stop it, the animal just kept walking. It wasn't worth calling for Link to stop, which would halt her horse, because that could go badly. Finally, she managed to get a foot in a stirrup and clamber aboard while the horse was still moving.

***

30

'Is he alright?' said Florence, referring to Psoddoph, who was still lying unconscious.

Jook had seen all shades of 'out-of-it' in his time as a soldier, from the mildly concussed to the outright dead. 'Looks okay to me,' he said. 'But he can't stay like that.' He gave his unconscious colleague a prod with his toe. 'Oi! Come on... wake up.'

Psoddoph stirred and his eyes flickered open. It was dark. He lay there for a moment, pleased not to be feeling any. pain. The last thing he remembered was falling from the carpet. Beyond that was a blank. *Perhaps I'm dead,* he thought. *It's very dark.* His senses gradually returned as he tested for movement in remote parts of himself, like fingers and toes. They seemed okay, but why was it so dark? He could hear voices. *Gods, I hope, if I'm dead.*

'Come on,' said Jook, prodding him again.

Psoddoph heard the voice next to him and felt the nudge on his foot. He strained his eyes to see something, *anything*, even a shadow in his private darkness would do. He noticed he was still breathing. *I'm alive*, he thought. The voice he'd heard was familiar. 'Is that you, Jook?'

'Yeah, now come on and sit up.'

Psoddoph smiled. Although to Jook, who could only see the lower half of his colleague's face, and not his eyes, the smile might have been a grimace of pain. Psoddoph falteringly pushed himself into a sitting position and groped for something to hold on to. He found Jook's arm – at least, he hoped it was his arm – and gripped it tightly.

'I think I'm blind,' he whispered, with a bit of a quiver.

'Yeah, you probably are,' said Jook. 'But if you push your helmet back, you might find it'll clear up real quick.'

Psoddoph felt for his helmet. He pushed it back with a huge grin of relief and some embarrassment. 'What happened?' he asked.

'Your helmet slipped over your eyes,' said Jook.

'No, before that.'

'You fell off the carpet and we dived down and caught you,' Jook explained. 'You were probably lucky you passed out. You might have panicked a bit.'

'I think I would have panicked *a lot*.' He looked around to see Florence smiling nicely and Krystal smiling stonily. 'I remember running for the carpet…'

Jook gave him the potted version. 'We were already in the air.' He cast an accusatory glance at Dennis. 'I grabbed you as we rose but you couldn't hold on. Then, better late than never, the boss got the carpet to swoop down like crazy and catch you. It's a wonder we didn't all finish up splatted down there.'

'Stop whining,' Dennis interrupted. 'I caught him, didn't I?'

'Yes, boss,' the guards chorused.

'Only just in time though, boss,' added Jook.

'Perhaps next time I'll be a little less polite to the carpet and we'll see what happens, shall we?' the wizard offered.

'Shall we all settle down now and enjoy the ride?' suggested Florence, casting a meaningful glance in Krystal's direction. The troll was getting agitated. The three men looked at one another and grudgingly nodded, knowing she was probably right.

They flew on in sulky silence, until Dennis remembered something. He turned to Psoddoph. 'Did that farmer give you any directions, after all that?'

'Yes, boss.'

Dennis craned his head round and looked over his shoulder. 'Well?'

'Oh, yeah. I suppose *you* need them, don't you.'

'It would be a good idea, yes,' said Dennis, his patience thinning a little.

Psoddoph thought back to when he saw the farmer, 'He said it's easy. All we do is go about ten miles north and we'll come to a stream. We follow it and it'll take us there.'

Dennis had been keeping an eye on the sun's trajectory, so was able to adjust the direction of flight slightly to head north. With nothing else to do, Jook set about extracting the bolt from the Drum.

It glowed softly, as if it appreciated what he was doing. *Don't be daft*, he thought, *it's a Drum*. As he worked the bolt loose and gently pulled it through, he heard a sound like a sighing on the wind, and the Drum glowed brightly and then dimmed. Jook glanced at Psoddoph, who had been watching, and shrugged.

'It must like you,' Psoddoph grinned.

'Don't be daft,' said Jook. 'It can't feel anything.'

'*Can't it*?' said Psoddoph. 'It's a lot more than just a drum, you know.'

'True,' agreed Jook. 'Or we wouldn't be lugging it around.'

No-one said much for a while. After their nerve-jangling experience, they were all pleased that the ten miles to the stream passed uneventfully.

'There it is, Krystal,' Dennis said. 'You'll be home soon, and then you can find your prince.'

'What prince?' she asked, distractedly.

'Elvin the Blue, I thought you said his name was.'

'Oh, him,' she said, coldly. 'I don't know that I want him anymore.'

'Why? What's happened to change your mind?' asked Florence, with concern.

'He didn't come looking for me, did he?' she moaned.

'He probably did, but I don't suppose he thought to look in the Parallel Dimension,' said Florence.

'Is that a good enough excuse?' she grunted. For someone soon to be back home after a long absence, she didn't seem too happy.

'I'm beginning to think you don't want to go home,' said Dennis.

'I do really… it's just… well, you know… I don't know how long I've been gone. I'm told the Parallel Dimension can mess up time. Will I recognise everybody? Will they recognise me? They're a quarrelsome lot and they don't take kindly to strangers at all,' she said.

'What about us?' Dennis was anxious to know.

'Oh, you'll be all right… providing my father recognises me.'

'Just supposin',' said Jook, listening in. 'Only just supposin', mind, he doesn't recognise you. Then what?'

'It would be best if you didn't hang around too long.'

If I'd known this might happen, thought Dennis, *I wouldn't have bothered.* However, he said, 'I'm sure everything will be alright.' No one was convinced, least of all him.

'Do you think you'll recognise your village?' asked Psoddoph.

'What village?' Krystal frowned.

'The one where your people live.'

'We don't live in a *village*,' said Krystal. 'We live in a *cave*, with a big hole in the front of it.'

That narrows it down a bit, Dennis thought. *A cave with a hole at the front.* 'This cave,' he said. 'Is it easy to find?'

'You can't miss it,' she claimed, confidently. 'That is, providing Grandpa's out hunting. Otherwise, he sleeps in front of it. But in that case, of course, you can't miss Grandpa.'

'You use Grandpa as a door?' Florence smiled.

'Oh, yes,' said Krystal. 'He's the biggest mountain troll you ever saw.'

'What does Grandpa hunt, then, when he's out hunting?' said Jook. 'It can't be that difficult to catch rocks.'

'He doesn't eat rocks anymore,' said Krystal, glumly, 'on account of his teeth.'

'Does he not have them anymore?' asked Florence.

'Yes, he's still got them. Trouble is, they're not in his mouth. They're in the cave. All the trolls' teeth are kept there when they fall out,' said Krystal. 'So, now he eats people on horses.'

Psoddoph felt he'd regret it, but asked anyway. 'Why people on horses, particularly?'

'Well, he started out eating people *and* horses, but he found they weren't filling enough on their own, so now he goes for people *on* horses.'

'Ah,' said Psoddoph, getting the logic, and making a mental note to stay on foot while they were there.

Dennis was beginning to scheme again, and to worry again. Krystal's teeth were diamonds, which enabled her to eat rocks. So, if Grandpa's teeth were the same as hers, then somewhere in that cave, there were more than a few buckets of diamonds. His worry was that once he'd got his hands on them, would he be able to escape with them?

They were getting close to the Ironroot Mountains now, and another scrape with the Grim Reaper was beginning to look more and more likely. Grey rocks beneath them had brought tons of scree and boulders down with them on their slide to the bottom of the mountain, and others were balanced precariously on the edges of great canyons, just waiting for a nudge from the strong winds that regularly tore through these parts to send them crashing down.

'I think it's through that gap,' said Krystal, pointing at a very narrow ravine.

Dennis swallowed hard and issued a nervy command to the carpet. It turned slightly, lining itself up to squeeze through the gap. The wizard looked over his shoulder. 'Keep your eyes open for a huge cave mouth or a huge troll, men.' But Jook and Psoddoph didn't need telling. They were looking everywhere already, keeping an eye out for Grandpa. Dying in battle was bad enough, but the thought of being sucked to death by a large toothless troll didn't bear thinking about.

They cruised slowly and watchfully.

'Did you see something move down there?' said Jook.

'Yeah, you bet I did,' said Psoddoph. 'I think we've found the place.'

A large troll craned its neck to look at the strange shape in the sky. Possibly the first thought to enter his mind was: *I wonder what that funny looking bird is up there?* This was probably followed by: *I wonder what it tastes like?*

* * *

31

Many miles back down the road, a pair of riders of differing skills and mounts were also making their way to the Ironroot Mountains. They travelled more slowly overland, and even more slowly because of the frequent unplanned stops they were obliged to make.

There had been no serious attempt to build a roadway to the Ironroot Mountains. The roads were generally no more than rutted dirt tracks that were occasionally used by the horses and carts of the villagers in the region. Link was lucky that the tracks were not so well-trodden as to make them hard landing places. They were mostly loose dirt and dust with some hardy tufts of grass along the edges and centre strip. The roads were consistent with the flat, scrubland all around them that was dotted with only an occasional tree or clump of bushes.

Eydith pulled on her reins once more, stopping her horse, while Link got up and thought about getting back on the donkey. He stood for a moment then sighed, rubbed his arm, dusted himself off and climbed back into the saddle.

'Do you want to change?' asked Eydith.

'No thanks. It's not so far to the ground on Mabel,' he replied, forcing a smile.

'Shall we stop and rest, then?'

Link thought that was a good idea. 'I think the next time I see Hector, I'll suggest he puts a railway line across here.'

'I can't see him agreeing to that,' said Eydith. 'Most folks using this route would probably be trolls.'

Hector was a big, friendly man they'd met many months before, on their previous cross-country journey together. He was an ideas man, an engineer and entrepreneur who'd built Kermells Tong's first railway. He and Link hit it off well, and liked to bounce ideas off one another. He was part of Eydith's family now, too, having married her aunt. But that's another story.

'Yeah, that would challenge his engineering skills – designing and building carriages for trolls.'

'Not to mention an engine to pull them!'

He laughed at the thought, then sat down on the ground and winced. 'Do you think we could trade Mabel for a cart?' he suggested, quite seriously. 'We'll never catch up with Dennis at this rate.'

Eydith had to agree. 'I think you're right; a horse and a donkey are no match for a flying carpet.'

'Perhaps we'll pass a village on the way,' said Link, hopefully.

'There's another track about half a mile over that way.' Eydith waved to their right. 'It looks like it'll cross or join this one. Probably at those woods up ahead.'

'I didn't see it,' said Link, squinting across the scrubland that had been their scenery for many hours.

'I'm higher up than you,' she remarked.

'Well, let's hope there are some people on that road, or a village or two. This track's been deserted. Hold still, Mabel!' He thrust a foot into a stirrup and hauled himself back into the saddle. Mabel was off at a brisk trot before he could dig his heels into her flanks. The horse took off after her, leaving Eydith sitting on the ground.

'Not again!' she moaned, jumping up and running after them.

'Why don't you ride, mistress?' asked Sprag, in his soft, woody voice.

'I will, just as soon as I catch up with my horse,' she puffed.

'I mean *on me*, mistress.'

'Why didn't you suggest that before?' she snapped.

'You were so intent on obtaining animals, that you never asked,' he replied, sliding from her saddle strapping and hovering, waiting for her to sit on him.

'Huh,' she puffed in reply.

Unsure of herself, she sat side-saddle – witchlike, in fact.

'Ready?' asked the staff.

'Let's go,' said Eydith. 'But not too fast.'

The staff bobbed slightly under her weight, then lurched forward. A moment later, it stopped next to the donkey that Link had managed to rein-in further up the road. She slid off. 'That was a tad too quick!' she said, her annoyance bordering on anger. 'I wasn't ready for that.'

Sprag didn't answer. Which was unusual: he usually had an answer for most things. 'And there's no way I could have ridden you like that all the way to the Ironroots.' She snatched the reins of the horse and steadied her before remounting.

Link looked back at her, amused. 'Did I just see you flying like a witch?'

'Well, I wasn't going to chase after you all afternoon.'

At the place where they expected the tracks to converge, they found that they intersected. The new track crossed to their left, skirting the woods. The track they were on went straight ahead through the woods.

'So which way?' Link wondered. 'Around or through?'

She shrugged. 'Which way, Sprag?'

The staff made a soft humming noise. 'The Drum is that way, mistress. It's sending out a cautious, barely-detectable signal,' he said, twisting in the saddle strapping to point through the woods.

* * *

32

'That's Grandpa down there!' cried Krystal, waving frantically. The carpet rolled dangerously, almost spilling its passengers.

'Keep still!' Dennis yelled, in panic.

Krystal stopped waving and fixed him with a cold, emerald stare. 'Watch it thief, you're in my backyard now.'

Dennis held up a grudgingly apologetic hand in acknowledgement. 'I don't want anyone falling off and onto those rocks down there, that's all.' She peered down and grunted something that might have been acceptance. He asked the carpet to circle and land a short distance from the large troll.

*

'Grandpa!' Krystal called, stepping off the carpet. 'Is that you?'

The old troll eyed her curiously, as if trying to remember his own name. Florence walked nervously beside Krystal as they approached. Dennis and the two guards hung back on the carpet, ready to leave if the old troll decided to try and taste anyone.

'It's me – Krystal, Grandpa,' she said, hopefully.

Dennis detected some apprehension in her voice. The old troll's lips moved soundlessly as he struggled to get them around the word 'Krystal'. Then the corners of his mouth turned up as he gave her a gummy smile of recognition.

'Kryshtal? Kryshtal? It ish you.'

'Bless you,' muttered Dennis, reflexively.

The old troll held out his arms as Krystal lumbered towards him and they met in a crunching embrace. Then he pushed her away. 'Let me look at you!' he said, grinning, after several attempts at forming the sentence in his mind. Krystal stood back and beckoned Florence to come closer. She stepped forward hesitantly. Grandpa smiled at her, his lips moving soundlessly as he slowly turned back to Krystal. 'What a thoughtful child you are, Kryshtal. You've brought lunch.'

Krystal grabbed Florence's hand and stepped in front of her. 'No, Grandpa. This is my friend.'

The smile left Grandpa's face. 'Are thoshe your friendsh ash well?' he asked disappointedly, gesturing towards Dennis and the guards.

'Well, that one is Florence's father, and those two are his guards,' said Krystal, by way of an introduction.

'Yesh, but are they your *friendsh*?' Grandpa repeated, feeling his stomach rumble.

Dennis looked pleadingly at Krystal, willing her to say 'yes', but she seemed to be giving old Grandpa's question a lot of thought. 'Yes, Grandpa, this one,' she pointed at Dennis, 'helped me escape from the Parallel Dimension.'

Grandpa's lips began to move again, as he struggled to engage his brain. 'What about theshe two, then? Can I have them?'

'No, Grandpa, they're my friends, too.'

Grandpa's massive shoulders sagged. 'Oh, all right.' He sighed and looked up, scanning the darkening sky to see if anything else soft and suck-able might be coming by in the not-too-distant future. All he saw was an approaching raincloud.

'Can I see my father?' asked Krystal.

Grandpa shrugged. 'Yesh, all right, I'll take you to him.' He turned slowly, and silently led them to the cave-mouth.

'Not before time,' said Jook to Psoddoph. They'd been eyeing the heavy black cloud drifting over them. The downpour started only moments later.

*

Inside the cave, a few trolls were sitting in a loose circle on the floor, idly chatting and occasionally selecting stones from the piles beside them and popping them into their mouths. At the back of the cave was a single torch, the flame from which was sufficient to illuminate the whole area as it reflected off the myriad sparkling gemstones lodged in the walls.

Directly beneath the flame sat another troll, larger than the rest, though not quite as big as Grandpa. What also distinguished him from his fellows was the ornate chair he sat on, the dais on which it was perched, and the golden crown of roughly hewn gold nuggets rammed on his head. He was the king.

Not that everyone had worked that out. 'Who's that big bugger up there?' Jook whispered to Dennis, but before he could reply, Krystal spoke.

'*That big bugger up there* is my father.'

'Oh,' said Jook, biting his tongue. 'Sorry about that…'

'You'd all better wait here while I speak to him,' said Krystal.

Out of deference, and because he rudely lumbered forward in front of her, Krystal let Grandpa go first. He trudged slowly up to the king, his lips moving all the time, while he sorted out what he was going to say and juggled the words into the right order. The king looked up and, seeing his father-in-law hesitate, he smiled and beckoned him forward.

'I have a vishitor to shee you,' the big troll announced. He reached out and pulled Krystal forward. The king frowned in concentration as he fought to recognise the newcomer.

'Hello, Father. It's me, Krystal,' she said, pinning her hopes on her smile and her voice.

A grin cracked the king's face as the light of recognition came on. 'Princess!' he cried, extending his arms. 'It *is* you. You're home! Come here. Let me look at you.'

She sighed with relief and stepped forward.

'Tell me what happened. Where have you been all this time? We were so… um…' he was looking for the word *worried* but it didn't seem to be in his vocabulary '…about you,' he finished, looking puzzled.

She sat down by his great feet and began telling him the story.

As the story wound on, Dennis became increasingly bored and, for want of anything better to do, let his gaze wander around the cave. His boredom vanished abruptly. There were veins of gold in the walls, and many precious stones cemented into place. But what really took his eye was a pile of small to fist-sized diamonds on the ground by the king's feet. What was so appealing about them was that they were loose, and *above all,* pocket-sized.

A quick mental calculation told him there was probably enough there to buy a reasonably-sized castle and employ enough guards to defend it for about thirty years, if he was careful.

His eyes fell upon Krystal and the king, he couldn't hear what they were saying, but Krystal's gestures and the king's occasional glances in his direction, indicated that they were talking about him and his guards. He shuffled uneasily, hoping Krystal was pleading their case well enough to make the king feel obliged enough to dig deep and reward them – reward *him*, he corrected himself. Also, well enough to avoid them finishing up in Grandpa's pantry.

'Can you hear what they're saying, boss?' whispered Psoddoph.

'No, but I expect we'll find out in a minute,' replied Dennis, from the corner of his mouth.

Florence was about to speak, but the king beckoned the others forward, interrupting her train of thought. Dennis moved quickly to the front of the throne, hurriedly followed by the two guards. Krystal stood at her father's side on the low dais, a narrow smile on her lips.

The king gazed down at Dennis. 'My daughter tells me you led her from the Parallel Dimension and brought her home.'

'I did, indeed, Sire. But it was nothing, really,' said Dennis, modestly. 'I would do the same for anybody,' he added, crossing his fingers superstitiously behind his back. Florence dug him in the back. He turned sharply and scowled at her.

'I do not understand you humans,' the king continued, 'But I have heard of this Parallel Dimension. Not a pleasant place.'

'No,' said Dennis. 'I was glad to get out of there myself.'

The king looked at Krystal, who was smiling. She nodded to her father, encouraging him to continue. The king reached out and took her hand, then looked down at the wizard. 'My daughter feels you should be rewarded for your trouble,' he said.

At last, thought Dennis, eyeing the pile of diamonds beside the throne, *my reward.* He looked eagerly up at the king. 'It was nothing really, as I said. I'd do it for anyone,' he muttered, trying to appear humble, but verging on the obsequious. He wasn't good at this sort of thing.

The king had reached down and picked up a diamond the size of a cricket ball, but he paused after Dennis's last remark. Dennis's eyes widened in anticipation, then narrowed in horror as the king put it back and selected another, nearer the size of a pea. Dennis's heart almost stopped beating for a moment when the king offered it to him.

Florence smiled proudly and nudged her father forward to accept it. Grudgingly, Dennis took a step forward and held out a shaking hand. It was shaking not from fear but restrained anger. He felt severely cheated. Seriously robbed.

The small diamond suddenly slipped through his shaking fingers and rolled back onto the pile. Dennis bent forward quickly, seizing the opportunity to scrabble among the larger stones to search for it. He glanced sidelong at the king, who was momentarily distracted, and slipped one of the larger stones inside his robe.

'Can you see it?' asked the king, peering over the arm of his throne.

Dennis thought derisively, *I could hardly see it when you offered it to me*. 'No, but I'll find it in a second,' he replied, as he continued to dismantle the pile of gems.

The king looked to Krystal. 'Give him some help, Daughter, he's beginning to make the place untidy.'

She stepped off the dais and joined Dennis sifting through the gems. 'You're making a lot of fuss,' she whispered. 'Look, here it is.' She picked up a diamond that was about the same pea-size as the one Dennis was originally given.

He looked at it critically for a moment, tossed it in the air and caught it again. 'No, that's not it, it was bigger than that.'

She thrust her hand back into the pile and pulled out another, the size of a blackbird's egg. 'Here,' she said, sharply. 'Take this one instead, then. After all, it's only one of Grandpa's teeth.' She looked back at her father. The king sighed and waved a hand in agreement. Dennis smiled and shoved it into his robe with the other one.

'Do you think your father would mind if we stayed for a while? Just till it stops raining,' said Dennis. Krystal turned to the king for approval. He nodded and suggested that she show Dennis around the cave while they waited for the weather to brighten.

Rather than risk upsetting the trolls, and possibly getting hurt, Dennis chose to stick with Krystal. The king returned to presiding regally over whatever was going on in the chamber.

She took him first to the wall behind the throne and indicated a square recess about her shoulder height. Dennis stood on tiptoe to peer inside. It was deep and almost overflowing with diamonds of all sizes, some even *bigger* than his fist. 'Those are my aunty Beryl's,' Krystal told him.

'Aunty Beryl's what?' Dennis wondered.

'Teeth, of course,' said Krystal. 'Apart from the one that was knocked out by some hussy from the Lava Trees, there's a complete set in there. Right from the day she was born. Oh, yes, and she still has the ones in her mouth.'

Krystal moved on. 'Come on, there's much more to see.'

This was a sightseeing tour with a difference, thought Dennis. He followed her to the next recess. There were even larger 'teeth' in this one and a lot more of them. Dennis licked his lips and thought, *what a morbidly expensive custom.*

Krystal dragged him around the rest of the recesses and continued to bore him with the histories of her various ancestors' molars. But Dennis's interest was far from orthodontic. He was imagining them being traded for piles of gold coins, while also wondering how long he could stay in the cave and plot their extraction, as it were, before the trolls asked him and his party to leave.

Through the cave entrance, he saw the figure of a man moving about in the misty rain. It was Psoddoph, who'd had the presence of mind to go out and bring the carpet inside. The wizard re-ran his thoughts, this time with a slight modification. With the carpet inside the cave, perhaps a quick getaway wasn't out of the question.

Psoddoph half dragged, half carried the sodden carpet with the Drum on it, into the cave and dropped it with a slap. Dennis beckoned him to bring it further inside. The guard grudgingly picked up a corner and began dragging it towards the throne. Jook went to help.

Florence had been watching her father and guessed he was up to no good. She frowned her disapproval at him. He looked away and towards the pile of diamonds at the king's feet. She was all too aware of what he had in mind, but she couldn't see how he proposed to steal the pile. Her frown quickly gave way to interest, though. She, too, began to picture the 'teeth' as large piles of gold coins. She *was* Dennis's daughter after all.

Krystal had taken Dennis full circle around the cave, and they were standing back at the foot of the dais.

'Do you know how many teeth there are in all those holes in the wall, your Majesty?' asked Dennis, affecting to be fascinated, which didn't take a lot of acting in this case. The king's lips moved soundlessly and he rested his chin on the palm of his hand. Dennis thought he could see the lights of calculus flashing on and off in the king's eyes, and after a long pause, his lips slowed down and formed a word.

'Yes.' Then after a pause he added, 'All of them. Except this pile of Grandpa's. We've just got the last one out.' He cast his eyes around the walls. 'As for the exact number, we may get around to counting them one day. Yes, someday,' the king said, without much conviction.

'We'd be pleased to count them for you,' Dennis volunteered. 'We're in no hurry.'

The king mulled this over. He'd heard that some of the more superior humans could count quickly. You only had to say one word to the brainiest of trolls while he was counting and he'd forget where he was, and possibly even who he was, and have to start over again. If you asked him how many teeth were in a pile, he would always come up with the same answer – three. Nobody knew why this was.

The king came to a decision. He waved his hand in approval. The wizard stooped, picked up a handful of diamond teeth and began counting them out onto the carpet, making small piles of tens. It was going to be a longish job on his own, so he beckoned Florence and the guards to join him, signalling them to sit on the carpet.

The Drum glowed, softly.

'Check those piles of ten for me,' said Dennis.

Psoddoph scooped up a pile and counted them out in front of him. 'All there, boss.'

'Well, count the next lot, then, and give them to her to put in hundreds,' he ordered.

Her? Florence thought, *her? That's nice.* But she said nothing and started heaping the diamonds into bigger piles as Dennis had instructed.

After about fifteen minutes, Florence had accumulated five conical piles of 'teeth', Psoddoph had seven and Dennis had eight. He glanced up at the king, who was in deep, slow conversation with Krystal. The moment was right. He glanced around to make sure Florence and the two guards were on the carpet. He licked his lips, and whispered with his mouth almost on the carpet, hoping it would hear him, 'Carpet… up, please.'

The carpet rose, and moments before it collided with the cave roof, Dennis asked it to stop. It was soggy from the rain, heavier and harder to handle. Adding to these difficulties, suddenly there were bats everywhere. Florence screamed and clutched her hair to her head. She'd read somewhere that bats can easily get caught up in women's hair.

Dennis asked the carpet to descend a few feet, but the air was filled with the tiny creatures. And two really big buggers.

'What the…!' Alerted by the noise above, it took the king no time at all to realise what was happening. He grabbed the arms of his throne and yanked himself upright, yelling at the other trolls to muster at the cave entrance to block the carpet's escape.

Dennis quickly gathered his thoughts and asked the carpet to get moving. The requirement to be polite in a situation like this was again a severe strain on him. He made a mental note to scream long and loud when the opportunity arose.

'Hold tight!' he shouted. 'Carpet, forward, please!' And just as it was about to hit a wall, he requested, 'Carpet, stop and turn around, please.' He growled a low note of exasperation deep in his throat and waved some bats away from his head. 'Carpet, forward, please, and hurry.' It flew forward, very fast and a little too high for the cave entrance. Dennis saw it in time and civilly asked the carpet to descend accordingly.

Trolls armed with rocks, some the size of footballs were standing at the entrance, and as the carpet neared, they started to hurl them. Their aim was poor, but it was good enough to make the wizard ask the carpet to bank around and try again. A long blast on a horn somewhere brought more trolls to the cave, some armed with spears.

The wizard lined up the carpet and headed for the cave mouth again, asking for as much speed as the carpet could make without leaving its passengers behind.

Psoddoph put one arm around Florence and held on to the carpet as best he could with the other.

Jook gripped the Drum tightly. 'Why doesn't he use his bloody magic?!' he mouthed. 'What's the point in being a bloody master magician if you never use it?!'

Psoddoph mouthed back, as best he could, 'He needs all his concentration to do what he's doing. He can't think of spells right now!'

Florence at his side, nodded in agreement.

As the carpet dipped under the top of the cave mouth, a hail of spears came up to meet it. The carpet paused momentarily, as if someone had touched the brake, then it moved forward again with a loud ripping sound. Jook ventured a look over his shoulder and saw there a was tear in the carpet just behind him.

The rocks being hurled at them were becoming more accurate and one was thrown with such force it tore a hole beside Jook, who was now praying to his favourite god. Or any who might be listening. The heavy carpet lurched wildly out into the valley as Dennis struggled to control it. Mercifully the rain had stopped, but the small split behind Jook was affecting the aerodynamics and the wizard could feel the carpet trying to twist.

'Will it go any higher, boss?' Psoddoph called, trying to make himself heard above the noise of the wind. Dennis met the question with a glare and continued to wrestle the carpet to safety, which was made all the more difficult by the carpet's own, often contradictory evasive movements.

Another rock tore a small hole through the carpet. Jook whimpered. He could see the jagged cliffs below them through this one. Rather than keep staring down, he tried to bury his head in the Drum. The carpet flew on erratically.

A long and anxious minute later, the rocks and spears being thrown by the trolls, began falling short and Dennis asked the carpet to slow down. He regained partial control and had it cruising unsteadily while he calmed himself. The carpet was finding it difficult to stay on course. At the first opportunity, Dennis clumsily, and almost fatally for all of them, settled it down on a ledge where they all sat in total silence. The look on his face dared anyone to speak.

With all the panic now over, though, they were all quietly thinking the same thing – how wet their butts were from sitting on the rain-drenched carpet for so long.

***

Eydith and Link crossed the dusty road and entered the woods. Apart from the dull thump of the animal's hooves, the only sound was birdsong. 'This is nice,' Eydith commented.

'Thank you,' said a little voice. 'We do our best.'

Link looked around. He hadn't said anything, and wondered why Eydith was talking to herself.

She stared back at him. 'What did you say?'

'I didn't say anything,' he replied, as bemused as she was.

Eydith looked around. There were only bushes and trees. 'Somebody spoke,' she whispered. 'Was that you, Sprag?'

The staff sounded a little peeved. 'Have you ever heard me speak in a voice like that... mistress?'

'Well, no, but...' She couldn't stifle a little smirk at the thought of it.

'It was him,' said another small voice.

'Are you sure it wasn't you?' she said.

'Yes, it was definitely the oak,' said another voice.

Eydith reined in her horse and looked about. Mabel stopped without any prompting from Link. He looked around and after a few seconds said, 'Do you think it's the trees?'

Eydith studied them closely. *Is it a trick of the light*, she wondered, *or does that tree have a face?* Something moved at the base of the tree nearest Link, attracting his attention. He dismounted slowly and went to look. Eydith watched quietly as he edged forward. Just as he was about to look behind it, a figure no more than six inches high, dressed in a brown jerkin and green trousers, stepped out to meet him.

'Hello,' said Link, smiling. The little figure returned his greeting in a piping voice. Link called out to Eydith, 'Come see, it's an elf.'

The tiny man thrust his hands on his hips and frowned. '*Elf?* I'm not an elf. I'm a brownie.'

Link knelt down. 'Sorry, no offence meant, it's just that I thought... well, I didn't know there was a difference.'

'Course there is,' the brownie asserted. 'You don't get elves in woods.'

'Is that right? I didn't know that,' said Link.

'Elves usually live under floorboards in shoemaker's shops. Every kid knows that.'

'I thought that was goblins,' said Link, as he moved to sit on a log. The brownie came and stood beside him in a patch of shorter grass.

'Goblins!' cried the brownie. 'Don't talk to me about goblins… Nasty bits o' work, goblins. Always messin' fings up.'

'Are you sure?' said Link. 'I thought that was gremlins.'

'Just as bad,' the brownie told him, then paused to give it further consideration, 'No,' he went on, 'probably worse than goblins.' And as an afterthought, added, 'Uglier too… Hello, who's this then?' he said, standing on tiptoe and adding a full eighth of an inch to his stature, when he saw Eydith coming towards them.

'This is my companion. She's called Eydith.'

The brownie looked her up and down, then grinned at Link.

'She's *pretty*. Is she your girlfriend?'

Link could feel himself blushing a little. 'Yes, I suppose she is.'

'Like her a lot, then, do you?' the brownie persisted.

'Shh… she'll hear you. And it's personal,' whispered Link, putting a finger to his lips, and putting his ear closer to keep the conversation more private.

'Well? Do you?'

'Of course, I do,'

'Does she know?'

'No!'

'Well, she won't if you don't tell 'er, will she?'

'Tell me what?' asked Eydith, squatting down beside him. Link's face reddened. 'Tell me *what?*' she repeated.

'Ahem…' Link coughed, 'er… nothing really. Just chatting, you know... as you do… to brownies you meet in the woods.'

He watched a little nervously as the brownie beckoned her closer and she leant forward so he could talk into her ear. She smiled and turned to look at Link. His face couldn't get any redder and his ears felt like they were on fire, so he turned away and looked up to study the canopy of the woods. Disconcertingly, there seemed to be smiling faces up there.

Suddenly, Eydith put her arms around his shoulders and planted a quick kiss on his cheek. The brownie jumped up and down laughing. 'I think I've known for some time,' said Eydith.

'Well,' Link began. 'It's bad form for a wizard to be involved with women. They don't like it back at the Uni.'

'Well, do *you* like it?'

'Oh, yes!'

She put her hand on his and whispered, 'It'll be our secret.'

Link looked into her eyes and followed his heart instead of his head and kissed her. Very clumsily.

'All right, all right, that's enough,' said the brownie, as the kiss lingered on. 'Save some for later.'

Link pulled his head back. 'Hmm… I like it very much,' he confirmed, all traces of embarrassment gone.

Eydith smiled down at the brownie and bid him hop on her hand.

'Thank you,' she whispered.

'No need for thanks,' he squeaked. 'I just did what needed doing. This *is* an enchanted wood, you know, so it probably would've happened anyway.'

Eydith looked at the trees again. She felt sure they were looking back, smiling encouragingly, if a bit woodenly.

Eydith set the little figure back on the ground. 'You're not quite what I expected a brownie to look like,' she said, smiling.

He looked puzzled. 'How do you mean?'

'I thought you'd be more colourful.'

The brownie looked down at his drab green and mostly brown clothes, 'What's wrong with this? And what colour's a brownie going to wear, if not brown, I ask you?'

'Hmm, yes, I suppose so,' said Eydith. 'And, yes, it *is* a lovely shade of brown,' she decided, trying to cheer him up, again. 'Very muddy, and woody.'

The brownie ran his hands down his tunic, smoothing it down. 'Thank you,' he said.

'Don't mention it,' said Eydith. A thought crossed her mind. 'Where are the others? I heard lots of voices before.'

'That was the trees,' he told her. 'The other brownies are in the middle of the woods. I'm just one of the guards around the edge,' he explained.

'But you let us in,' said Link.

'You looked like nice people,' said the brownie. 'Nice, but tired. On a quest, are you?'

'Yes, that's right,' said Eydith. 'A Drum from the university has been stolen and we're going to get it back, but we're a little lost.'

'Course you're not. You're here,' stated the brownie.

'But where is *here*, exactly?'

'The Enchanted Woods. My woods.'

'Yes, we know that,' said Link. 'But we could be going round in circles for days in here. And I'm guessing that all the magic in this place is playing havoc with our… er… navigation stick,' he decided to call Sprag, to avoid going into detail.

'Your wizard's staff,' said the brownie, matter-of-factly. 'Yes, it would do that.'

Sprag glowed slightly in thanks for the little fellow's correction of his description.

'That must be why I'm here, then,' squeaked the brownie. 'To help you on your way. Oh, and don't take any notice of the trees if they tell you anything,' he warned.

'Why not?' asked Link.

'They tend to send people in the wrong direction,' the little man explained.

'You mean… they *lie*?' said Eydith.

'Not intentionally, no. Obviously, they don't get around much, being trees, and the only directions they know are 'over here' and 'over there'. Not much help really, especially when all their branches point in different directions.'

Eydith looked at the trees again. They gave her more of their wooden smiles.

'Come on,' the brownie squeaked, 'lift me up and I'll show you the way.'

She carefully sat him on her shoulder and climbed back onto her horse. Link looked sadly at Mabel, sighed and climbed into her saddle. Surprisingly, he found the going easier now. Perhaps getting his feelings for Eydith out into the open had given him a new confidence. He smiled to himself, thinking how much better his life was becoming.

Twenty minutes of trotting later, Eydith asked the brownie, 'How far into the woods are we going?'

'Only half way,' he replied. 'Then we start coming out again.'

Eydith closed her mouth.

After a lengthy silence, the brownie asked, 'Do you know where this Drum is now?'

'We think it's been taken to the Ironroots,' replied Link.

'Ah. I went there, once,' said the brownie.

'Only once?' said Eydith.

'Yeah. Just the once,' the brownie confirmed, and the way he said it killed the conversation.

A few minutes later, Eydith caught sight of him waving his hands in the air. 'Stop!' he cried.

'What's the matter?' asked Eydith.

'Nothing. This is where I get off. You can put me down now.'

She dismounted and set the tiny figure on the ground. He looked deep in thought. 'That's troll country – the Ironroots,' he squeaked. 'I'll draw you a map.'

'Are you afraid of trolls?' asked Link, dismounting.

'No,' said the brownie. 'They wouldn't get a lot of nourishment out of the likes of me. And the woods wouldn't let them in anyway. They thump and crash around too much.'

'Then why won't you come any further with us?'

'This is where I live.' He bent down and picked up a tiny twig. 'Look, you are here.' He drew an X in the moist earth. 'The Ironroots are here.' He drew another X. 'You go this way.' And he drew a line connecting the two X's and pointed north. He tossed the twig away and trotted off towards the bushes. 'Bye!' he called over his shoulder and started to run. Eydith and Link heard him shout, 'Mum! I'm home!'

'Well,' said Link. 'I suppose we'd better be going, then.' He steadied Mabel as he prepared to climb back on board.

'Just a minute,' Eydith whispered. Link turned and she took his hand, bringing on a minor panic attack. Slowly, she put her arms around his neck and kissed him full on the lips. He dropped Mabel's reins and held Eydith close, any moment expecting a little voice to interrupt them. It did. But it was his own, and it told him that he needed to stop and take a breath. He drew his head back and dwelt on those blue eyes for a moment. He'd seen those eyes alight with strange and powerful magic before, but he was seeing a different magic now. He wasn't sure which disturbed him the most. She rested her head on his shoulder and hugged him. Without looking up, she said, 'I think you're right. We'd better be going.'

Hand in hand, they walked to their mounts. 'Haven't you forgotten something?' said Link.

She glanced back and without thinking, called out, 'Come on, Sprag!' The staff didn't move. Although it glowed slightly green. Was that the colour of envy? She trotted back and picked him up. 'Are you not speaking to me?' she asked. He still didn't answer. She tried again. 'Are you in thought?' she said, giving him the benefit of the doubt.

'No,' he replied, sulkily.

'Are you *jealous*?' she wondered.

'Jealous? Me? Jealous? Of course not. He's not my type at all.'

'Well, why did you ignore me when I called?'

'I was talking to that pretty little oak over there,' he glowed, slightly red.

'What did it say?'

'Not very much. It was a waste of time, really. She kept complaining about the squirrels pinching her nuts.'

Unsure of his sense of humour, Eydith carried him back to the horse, slid him safely through the saddle strapping, and climbed into the saddle. 'I'm ready, Link.' At the sound of her voice, Mabel began to move on before Link had a chance to dig his heels into her ribs.

* * *

34

Dennis stood up. 'Look at the state of this thing,' he whined, pointing at the carpet. 'Ripped to bloody shreds.'

'Can you mend it, boss?' asked Psoddoph.

'Yeah,' Jook chimed in recklessly. 'Use some of your jiggery-pokery on it.'

Dennis's nerves were already frayed and this nearly pushed him over the top.

He looked appalled. 'I haven't spent the last forty-odd years learning *jiggery-pokery*,' he spat out. 'I'm a master magician, for goodness' sake! And one of the things I *have* learned, I'll have you know, is that it isn't good practice to use magic on something that *is* magic – because it can drive the magic right out of it!' He glowered at the guard before finishing. 'So, if I try to fix it with *my magic*' – he let the words hang in the air – 'we could end up with *not* a magic carpet, but just a carpet! And good luck flying off this mountainside on that!'

'Sorry boss,' the deflated guard mumbled. 'I didn't mean to...' He wasn't sure how to finish so he didn't. And he saw Psoddoph signalling him to shut up before the irate wizard hurled a fireball at him. Fortunately for Jook they were all too close for him to do that without some collateral damage.

Psoddoph stepped in to try to smooth things over. 'It's only a single tear at this end, boss. And a couple of holes that aren't too big. I'm sure we could get it to fly again safely enough,' he said, as brightly as he dared. And knowing Dennis's susceptibility to a bit of flattery, he lied, 'Especially with you in charge of it.'

Dennis said nothing, which in itself was a good result as far as Psoddoph was concerned.

Florence examined the carpet, taking in the extent of the damage. Dennis had rather over-dramatized the situation. Psoddoph was right, it was only a small tear about a foot long in the middle at one end, which created a couple of flaps that were destabilising it in flight. The rest of it looked perfectly serviceable.

'Lend me your knife, please.'

Jook drew his knife and offered it to her, the way Psoddoph had shown him. Handle first.

'What are you *doing?*' said Dennis, watching in horror as she began to saw through the carpet.

'Mending it,' she replied, icily. 'It's alright, it's not a *magic* knife,' she said, a little caustically. 'I also know enough not to drive the magic out. But we do need to fix it. I'm not *walking* down this mountain.'

'But... but…' Dennis stammered.

'If you want to sit up here until you freeze to death, Father, that's your problem,' Florence told him.

Dennis exhaled heavily and let her get on with it. *The problem with having kids is that they have too much of yourself in them*, he thought in frustration.

Inside twenty minutes, it was done. She'd cut off the two flappy bits and used them to patch the holes caused by the flying rocks. She handed Jook his knife. 'There, good as new,' she said, stepping back to admire her handiwork.

Dennis cast a critical eye over it. 'It's smaller,' he muttered. Which scored him ten out of ten for observation.

'Of course it is. I've taken the flaps off. There's enough room,' said Florence. 'We'll just have to sit closer together, that's all.' Immediately it occurred to her that it would be nice to sit a little closer to Psoddoph if she could. Was she developing feelings for him?

Dennis stepped onto the carpet and sat down. It was dryer now, at least, and so was he. Jook took a step forward, but Psoddoph thrust out an arm and stopped him, allowing Florence to get on next. It wasn't about 'ladies first' in this case, but more a matter of it being a bad idea for Jook to sit too close to Dennis right now. When she was ready, Psoddoph passed her the bag of diamond teeth and sat behind her, leaving Jook to pick up the Drum and occupy what space was left.

Jook scratched his head while he thought about it. The way he saw it, there were two options…

a) Sit on the carpet and dangle the Drum over the side.

b) Put the Drum on the carpet and…no, that's not going to happen. 'Can you move up a bit, please?'

The carpet rose a few inches and stopped.

'Just what do you think you're doing?' snapped Dennis. 'This is *my* carpet, and I'll fly it, if you don't mind – carpet down, please.' He cursed himself for not having activated the voice-recognition security feature yet, and promised himself to find it in the manual and do it soon.

Three voices yelled, 'Ouch!' Dennis hadn't said anything about not dropping down too fast. He stood up and rubbed his backside. Jook put the Drum down and began to examine his boots. 'Sorry, boss. There's not enough room at the back.'

It instantly crossed Dennis's mind how to make more room, but he felt Psoddoph might desert if he left Jook there. Florence might have something to say about it, too, because annoyingly for him she had some of her mother's qualities, too.

Florence re-organised the seating arrangements. Dennis sat at the front on his own, while Florence and Psoddoph sat close together in the middle. Jook sat sideways at the back and nursed the Drum, which spread the load fairly evenly.

'Happy now?' asked Dennis, as if he cared.

Nobody answered.

The carpet rose gently, and responded well to Dennis's carpet-voice, as he now thought of it. The group flew on in silence, leaving the mountains to fade into the distance behind them. 'Where are we going now, boss?' asked Psoddoph.

'Corin,' said Dennis.

'Any reason, Father?' asked Florence.

'To try and find a bigger carpet,' snapped Dennis.

'Oh,' said Florence.

He came straight back. 'I thought you'd be happy with that. You know, something more than just, *oh* would've sounded more appreciative.'

'Well, it's just that you're not very good at flying one, are you?' she said casually, as if it were common knowledge. The guards looked the other way to hide their smirking faces. They'd always thought so themselves, but had never found the courage to say so in such a direct way.

'What do you mean?' Dennis was hurt. 'I haven't lost anyone, or hit anything, yet.'

Jook was about to help with some history here, but found Psoddoph's hand over his mouth.

'No, Father, but I get the feeling that our luck might be running out, and it's only a matter of time before you do.'

Dennis was really hurt. He sulked. After a few minutes, he looked back over his shoulder at the guards. 'Have you got any complaints?'

Jook and Psoddoph looked at one another.

'Okay, okay. I don't want to know.' Then, after a further sulk, he said, 'When we reach the town, I'll buy a horse and cart.'

Thumbs went up all round behind him. And in unison, the three of them silently mouthed, *buy*? Dennis was better known for his cashless negotiations, as he liked to think of them. Most people thought of them as stealing.

'Yes, *buy*!' said Dennis, as if he knew what was going on behind his back. He could afford to now, with all those teeth in the bag.

* * *

35

'I was beginning to think we'd be stuck in there for days,' said Link, as the pair emerged from the woods.

'We seemed to be going uphill for a long time, too,' said Eydith, as they came to a band of scree that had slipped from higher up. If there had been a track of any sort, it was somewhere beneath it. 'Do you think we're still heading in the right direction?'

'I don't know, but it looks like it could be hard going for a while,' Link replied.

'Oh, well. Straight ahead it is, then.' Eydith gently tapped her horse's flanks.

Mabel started to trot. She seemed quite at home in the rocky terrain. Link tightened his grip and hung on. He was getting better at it. Eydith followed, a few steps behind.

Soon, they were walking through a craggy valley, strewn with rocks and boulders, some the size of a small house. The place looked as though it hadn't changed since the Creator turned His back on it. The place seemed abandoned by every lifeform. It seemed even more desolate because of the stark contrast with the Enchanted Woods they had recently left. They were both wondering how such places could exist right next to one another. Eydith was right when she suggested that enchantments had a lot to do with it. There was no birdsong, no insect noise, not even the scurrying sounds of small furry things. Nothing competed with the gentle tapping of Mabel's hooves and the steady clip clop of Eydith's horse.

Link's voice seemed over-loud when he spoke. 'I think we came so far in those woods, that we're almost at the Ironroots. And I don't like it very much,' he added.

'I don't like it at all,' said Eydith. 'It's creepy.'

Link hadn't felt that, but now she'd mentioned it... he discretely ran a hand over the short hairs on the back of his neck. 'Did you see something move just then?' he asked, quietly.

'Where?'

He pointed to a large rock a few yards away. She looked. The rock moved again. Then another, a short distance away from it. Then two more. As if obeying some secret signal, the four trolls unwound and stood up in an unexpectedly fluid motion for creatures so ungainly. Link dug his heels into Mabel's ribs, but the little donkey wouldn't change her steady gait. He tried again, but to no avail. The trolls fell in behind them.

As they followed the contours of the mountainside around a bend, a very large troll stepped into their path and just stood there. Link pulled on the donkey's reins and this time she stopped. He twisted round to Eydith and gasped, 'That's a very big troll. Now what?'

She looked behind her. The other four trolls were ambling down the slope to cut off their retreat. She walked the horse forward a few steps and stopped next to Link. 'Will you let us pass, please?' she said, hardly controlling the quaver in her voice.

'Dinner!' growled the big troll, the word sounding more of a belch.

'Do you speak troll?' asked Link.

'Yes,' she answered, quietly.

'Well? what did it say? Yes, or no?

'It said, dinner.'

'Oh.'

'They speak our language,' she explained, 'but not too clearly – well, not this one anyway. And I don't think he meant it as an invitation.'

Link took her meaning, though not entirely. He patted the donkey's neck. 'But I've grown fond of Mabel. They can't eat her.' The donkey's ears flicked.

'It wasn't referring to Mabel,' Eydith warned him.

'Shit,' breathed Link.

'Quite,' said Eydith, sliding Sprag from the saddle strapping, and raising him.

'Wait, mistress. Do not be too hasty.' The staff spoke directly into her head. She could sense him using her eyes. 'This one is very old.'

'Perhaps, but it still referred to us as *dinner*,' she reminded him.

Sprag's advice was to avoid a run-in with the troll community, if at all possible. 'We're after Dennis,' he reminded her, 'who might be among them with the troll who was in his party. We might need their help to get to him.'

'So, we should get eaten to keep the peace?' she thought back at him.

'That's not what I had in mind, mistress.'

'Could we reason with it?' said Link, though not thinking it looked like the reasoning kind.

Sprag communicated his assent and his readiness to step in.

'We can try,' said Eydith. She dug her heels in and the horse walked forward a few steps. 'Hello,' she said, friendly but clutching the staff tightly.

The big old troll slowly moved his head and looked down at her. 'Dinner?' he repeated. Another troll – a young female, by the look of it – stepped forward and stood beside him.

'Wait a moment, Grandpa,' said the other troll. 'This human looks very like the one that was here before. This afternoon, remember?' She stared at Eydith for what seemed an age, her lips moving all the while she thought. 'She looks a lot like the one that helped me get home. She was kind to me.'

Grandpa painfully turned his head slightly. 'She shtole my teef,' he reminded her.

'She was there, yes. But it was the shifty-looking one dressed in black that stole your teeth.'

'Dennis?' said Eydith, 'you've seen Dennis?'

'You know him?' asked the smaller troll.

Link touched Eydith's arm and slowly shook his head, warning Eydith to think carefully before answering. Knowing Dennis could be confused with being a friend of his.

Eydith replied, careful to make it plain where they stood, 'Yes, I know him. He's no friend of mine, though. He's not a good man.'

'He's a strange one, I'll give you that,' the female troll asserted. 'He helped me escape from the Parallel Dimension, and then he helped himself to things that didn't belong to him.'

'That's Dennis alright! He's stolen from me, too. A Drum. A very special Drum. It's important that I get it back. That's what we're doing out here. We're trying to find him and get it back.'

'He did have a drum thing,' said the young troll. 'He took it from that place… where the wizards live.'

'University?' said Eydith, helpfully.

'That's the place.'

'What did he steal from you?' asked Eydith, seeing an opportunity to bond a little.

'He stole Grandpa's teeth,' she said, and looked perfectly serious about it.

'His *teeth*?' said Eydith, in astonishment. Link grinned without thinking.

'Shnot funny,' said Grandpa, testily.

'No,' agreed Eydith. 'It isn't.'

Link forced the smirk off his face. He could only stare up at the huge creature in disbelief, wondering, 'How on Crett did Dennis manage that?'

The younger troll stepped in to explain how it happened. The older one punctuated the story with nods and grunts while she spoke.

Eydith and Link followed it as best they could. One of the more unexpected things to emerge from the story was that the young troll's father was the king of the Ironroot Mountain trolls.

'I'm sorry, princess, I didn't know,' Eydith said, promptly dismounting.

Link took his cue from her and slid off Mabel's back and bowed. 'Can we be of any assistance?' he asked as he straightened up.

'Dinner?' asked Grandpa.

Link stepped back out of reach. 'No!' yelled the princess. 'My father will decide what happens to the trespassers… I mean our visitors.' She smiled reassuringly.

Grandpa shrugged his shoulders clunkily and slouched away.

'Come,' said the princess. 'My father will want to see you.' And without waiting for a reply, she turned and ambled after Grandpa. The four trolls behind Eydith and Link closed ranks, and strode forwards like a rock wall, giving them no option but to follow.

Eydith led her horse and caught up with the princess. She walked by her side. Sprag was right: there was no point in upsetting them. *After all, he will help channel some magic to keep us safe if necessary*. She heard a noise in her head that she interpreted as agreement.

Link fell in beside them, leading Mabel.

'My name is Eydith,' she said, looking straight ahead. 'And this is Link.'

'I'm called Krystal,' replied the troll.

'Pretty name,' said Eydith.

'Thank you,' said Krystal. 'You're very like the girl with Dennis. She was pleasant to me, too. Do you two know one another?'

'Oh, yes,' said Eydith.

'That's nice.'

Eydith left it at that.

A mile further up the canyon, they paused. 'There's our cave,' announced Krystal, pointing at a great hole in the cliff face.

They led their mounts to the entrance. Krystal strolled in, unchallenged.

Link looked up in wonder. The cave was enormous up close. One of the trolls behind prodded him gently, reminding him that he was to go inside. As they passed under the high portal, two trolls beckoned by Krystal came forward and took the animals' reins. Eydith and Link didn't protest, but she did tighten her grip on Sprag.

'My father is down there.' She waved into the gloom at the back of the cave. There was a solitary torch burning, but it gave enough light to cause a myriad sparkling pinpoints to glisten in the walls.

The king looked down from his dais and regarded them suspiciously. 'I suppose you've come to steal from us as well?' he said eventually, with enough menace to make Link swallow hard. He felt guilty just standing there. Eydith lowered her head respectfully then looked up into his sapphire blue eyes.

'Your Majesty,' she began, 'we have no intention of stealing from you.'

'Then why are you here?' he demanded, in a slow monotone.

'We were brought here by your daughter, sire,' she replied.

Krystal stood at her father's side. 'She looks like the other one, Father, the one they called Florence. She helped me to get out of the Parallel Dimension.'

'She's my cousin,' Eydith told her. 'We're looking for her. Well, her father. Her father has stolen a valuable Drum from Havrapsor University and it must be returned.'

'He stole my Father-in-law's *teeth*,' the king complained. 'He tricked us.'

'Perhaps I can help you,' said Eydith, stepping forward. 'Is your father-in-law here?'

The king beckoned the big old troll forward. He lumbered across the cave, rubbing his empty belly. He glanced at the king and whispered, 'Dinner now?'

'No,' said the king. 'This human says she can help us.'

Can we give him some teeth, Sprag?' she thought.

The staff glowed momentarily. 'Yes, mistress, but only one set.'

She didn't pursue that. Instead, to the old troll she said, 'I can give you some *new teeth*.'

He grinned a gummy smile and nodded in a yes-please kind of way. Eydith raised Sprag, hoping it wouldn't alarm anyone, and closed her eyes. The words of the spell paraded across the backs of her eyelids. She intoned them quietly. When she raised her other hand, a searing white light enveloped the old troll. The king was about to intervene when, just as suddenly, the light ceased. Grandpa experimentally worked his mouth and gingerly touched his once hollow cheeks. They weren't hollow anymore. He smiled a glittering diamond smile. Then he laughed and grabbed Eydith's hand, shaking it vigorously.

'Careful, Grandpa!' admonished Krystal, and he slackened his grip, apologetically.

She prised her hand free and suggested the old troll tried them. He looked at Link, and licked his lips. Link took a *big* hurried step back.

'NO!' yelled Eydith. 'Not him! A rock. You don't have to eat soft things now!'

'Rock?' He scratched his head and blinked a few times, creating rasping and clicking noises. 'I haven't a good rock in years.' He stooped, picked up a pebble and popped it into his mouth. He moved it around with his tongue a couple of times, then crunched it up. Eydith tensed then smiled with relief when the new teeth didn't break. The old troll smiled again. He selected a larger stone, tasted it, then crunched it up. He swallowed and smiled up at the king. 'They're very good.'

'I know,' said the king. 'I eat them all the time.'

'No, I mean the teeth.' The old troll looked towards Link, 'You!' he said, pointing with a fierce-looking finger. 'Not dinner anymore.' Link laughed nervously, somewhat relieved. Though the old troll hadn't said anything about dessert.

Eydith and Link's audience with the king was over. Krystal and her father walked them to the cave-mouth. 'Can you tell us which way Dennis went?' asked Link.

Krystal pointed across the bare valley. 'He started flying that way, and then he turned that way. The carpet might be slower now. Our guards hit it with some rocks and spears. It was wobbling about.'

'That's good to know.' Link looked at the sun. 'So they went south,' he muttered.

'South?' said Eydith. 'What's down there?'

Link scratched his head. 'Nothing really, till you get to the sea town, but that's miles away.'

'He's got the carpet,' she reminded him.

'If it's still capable,' he said.

In her mind she thanked Sprag for his help. *Are you going to make us rich now by producing some diamonds for us*? The staff was quick to remind her of the magical protocols that forbade that. He was also careful to point out that he hadn't materialized the troll's teeth from nowhere: he had removed them from a niche in the cave. *Worth a try*, she thought. Though Sprag couldn't work out why.

The trolls looking after Mabel and the horse, passed the reins back to Eydith and Link, and took a deferential step back as the king ambled by. 'Thank you for giving Grandpa his teeth back,' said Krystal. 'That's just the sort of thing Florence would have done.'

Eydith made no comment.

'You humans are not all bad,' agreed the king. 'Perhaps we will meet again.'

Link silently hoped not, but chose to say, 'Probably,' as he climbed into Mabel's saddle. Eydith smiled, nodded respectfully to the king, then at Krystal, and hauled herself onto the horse. She waved as she followed Link back down into the valley.

* * *

The carpet flew low over the hill and a sprawling town loomed up before them. 'This looks interesting,' remarked Psoddoph.

'Yeah, I like towns,' said Jook. 'You know where you are with a good town.'

'What are you going on about?' said Dennis.

'Well, boss,' said Jook, who was pleased to be conducting what passed for a civil conversation with him after some hours of alternating snappiness and broodiness, 'with a town, people go to the trouble of putting names at the ends of streets, and that. And you can always tell a nice friendly building.'

'Friendly building? There's no such thing. They're all full of barbarians, bandits and drunks – usually at the same time.'

Jook let it go.

'But there will be stables,' said Dennis, in a more positive voice.

'And carts, as well. Let's hope,' said Florence.

'Indeed,' agreed Dennis. 'But I'm not getting rid of the carpet.' The two guards exchanged looks, but kept their thoughts to themselves.

Dennis landed the carpet at the edge of a small wooded area overlooking the town. It would attract less attention than flying in, he told them. What he didn't tell them was that the town looked short on landing places that he was happy to negotiate even on the smaller carpet. Before walking in, he distributed Grandpa's teeth among the available pockets. And before they got too excited, he made it absolutely clear to the guards that he wasn't giving them *their share,* because there was no such thing. They'd get their agreed one silver when the job was over – nothing more, and not before. They were only minding the teeth. Jook rolled up the carpet, and Psoddoph picked up the Drum, in preparation for the half mile walk into town. Dennis strutted off ahead of them.

'Father!' Florence called out – but he was still unused to the word, and ignored her. She called again, this time with more success.

'What is it *now?*' he moaned.

'Why don't you go and buy the horse and cart while we wait here for you?' she suggested. Psoddoph allowed the Drum to slide through his fingers and onto the ground.

Dennis glared at him. 'I haven't said yes, have I?' Psoddoph bent to pick it up again. 'All right, leave it,' he snapped. 'Just remember who's giving the orders around here, that's all.'

Florence gave Psoddoph a secret wink.

I'm beginning to like you, he thought.

'I just thought, Father, you know, walking through a town carrying a large Drum and a carpet, we're not going to pass through unnoticed, are we?'

Dennis couldn't argue with that, much as he wanted to. 'Are you staying here, too?' he asked.

'I'll come with you, if you like,' she said.

'Yes,' said Dennis, abruptly wheeling round to go and leaving her to catch up.

Jook let the carpet drop off his shoulder and sat down on it with a thump, a bit annoyed at missing out on the trip to town. 'Suppose we'll just have to sit here and mind the stuff,' he griped.

Psoddoph joined him. 'Well, it is why we're here.'

'S'pose so.'

*

Dennis and Florence found the market square. It was busy even this late in the afternoon. 'This looks like a good place to buy a horse,' said Florence.

'Hmm,' Dennis snorted. 'They look like a load of cut-throats to me.'

'Why is it that every time someone expresses an opinion,' said Florence. 'You want to start an argument?'

'No, I don't.'

'You *do*.'

'I don't.'

'There you go, doing it again,' Florence enlightened him.

'All right, I do,' said Dennis. He thought for a moment. 'I don't know why I do it. I just do. Things… get to me. People get to me. And, anyway, you started this one.'

'What?' Florence let it drop. 'Look, there are some horses over there,' she motioned to a line of docile-looking animals tied to a long hitching rail. A string of bunting draped overhead indicated they were for sale. The wizard pushed his way through the crowd and took a look at them. He made for a large brown one that caught his eye.

'That one looks alright,' remarked Florence. Dennis wanted to agree, but wouldn't commit himself until he'd looked the beast in the eyes. He'd bought docile-looking horses before only to find he'd been tricked by the vendor. Florence patted its neck and pulled its ears. The horse responded with a friendly snort, which would probably come off with some warm water and a bit of a scrub. 'Well, what do you think?' she asked, trying to prompt a decision. He looked it in the eyes again. The horse gazed steadily ahead, as though in a trance.

Dennis decided, 'Okay, let's find out who the vendor is.'

A tall man dressed in black materialised seemingly out of nowhere and stood by his shoulder. Dennis had a disquieting feeling about him, but dismissed it after a better look. Too much flesh on the skull. Death didn't appear to be abroad today. At least, not yet.

'Two silvers,' was all the man said, in a tone that wasn't far off Death's.

Dennis turned his back and checked his money, then turned back. 'I need a cart as well,' he said.

'Down here,' the man grunted, in a manner that was never going to earn him employee of the month. He led Dennis, with Florence leading the horse, down an alley and into a large ill-lit building. In one corner there was indeed a cart. Very basic, but still a cart. It looked designed for speed more than luggage.

'How much?' he asked.

'Another silver,' the man told him.

Dennis looked again, closely inspecting the wheels and the overly-greased axles. 'Okay,' he muttered, 'I'll take it.' He fished in his pockets for another coin. All he found was a few coppers. He whispered to Florence, 'I don't have enough.'

Florence dug into the purse attached to her belt and lifted out a gold coin. This was worth *five* silvers. She offered it to her father.

'Is that all you have?' he whispered.

'No, Father, I've got another seven.'

'Shh. I meant haven't you got anything smaller?'

'No.'

'Then it'll have to do,' Dennis sighed. He turned to the man with the Death-like presence. 'Do you have change for a gold?'

As expected, the man shook his head. 'No, but I can get it. Wait here,' he muttered, snatching the coin from Dennis and setting off briskly for the door. Once out of the wizard's sight, though, he broke into a fast trot. It wasn't his cart to sell.

'I've got a bad feeling about this,' said Florence, quietly. A shadow moved in a corner.

'Me too. Do you know how to hitch a horse to a cart?' She nodded. 'Then do it quickly,' he murmured. 'I don't think we're alone in here.' Another shadow passed quickly across the wall. Florence backed the horse between the shafts and started to attach the various bits of harness as quickly as she could, but it was gloomy and some bits looked alike.

'Is there anybody there?' asked Dennis, in a loud whisper and hoping for a no, though not really thinking that through. But it was worse than that. There was no answer at all. *I know you're there*, he thought, raising a hand that was already glimmering with magical intent. 'I will ask you once again,' he called, louder this time. 'Is there anybody there?' He recognised the ominous swishing sound of steel against leather as a long dagger was drawn. 'How are you getting on?' Dennis whispered to Florence.

'Nearly there.'

'When you've finished, get on board and be ready to drive.' He turned his attention back to the living shadows. A grey shape emerged from the gloom, and two more drifted in beside it.

'I'll take your gold, old man,' said the shape nearest him.

'Gold?' said Dennis. 'What gold? And what old man?' he added indignantly.

'The gold that needs changing,' said the shadowy figure.

'Ah…' said Dennis. 'That gold.' He paused a moment and flexed his fingers behind his back. 'Well, you see, that gold isn't mine to give,' he began to explain.

'We don't care who gives it, just as long as we get it,' interrupted the figure.

'It's my daughter's, you see,' Dennis continued, 'and I'm very fussy who she gives it to.'

'Well, we're not. So hand it over,' snapped one of the other shadows. 'We'll take anybody's gold.' The others laughed.

'I'll tell you what,' said Dennis. 'How about one of these?' He pointed his fingers at one of them and a bright arc of golden fire flashed past the villain's head.

'Sod this, Trevor! It's a bloody wizard!'

'Well, rush 'im, the pair of you!' Trevor yelled. 'You know what to do, I've told you enough times.'

'What, you mean grab 'is 'ands, like?'

'Yes, Weasel. That's exactly what I mean. Now do it!'

Weasel and his colleague, Reg, sidled warily towards Dennis, with daggers drawn, 'We don't want to 'urt you, wizard,' Weasel grinned.

'The feeling is *almost* mutual,' said Dennis. He raised his hands again and pointed his fingers at Weasel's chest.

'You won't get all of us,' said Weasel, bravely.

'Well,' said Dennis, almost casually, 'Perhaps you're thinking: he's just an old wizard, so that was probably all the magic he had left in him for now. Is there any more, you wonder? Ask yourself – am I feeling lucky?'

Weasel and Reg glanced at one another. 'Don't take all day!' snapped Trevor, from a few paces behind them – a few *safe* paces behind them.

Weasel took a deep breath and started towards Dennis again. The wizard pointed two forked fingers at them, and a twin burst of golden fire leapt at Weasel and Reg, hitting both men full in the chest and knocking them to the ground.

'Shit, Trev…' moaned Weasel, ''e's done it again.' He rolled over, coughing. Then he spotted he was on fire and sprang to his feet, prancing about. 'Ow! I'm on fire!' he yelled, beating his chest with his hands. Reg quickly realised he was, too. 'Ow! Ow! Ow!' He tried in vain to beat it out, then ran out shouting, 'Horse trough! Horse trough!' Weasel raced after him. There were two distant splashes followed by a lot of thrashing around.

Dennis turned to the remaining robber. 'Do you feel lucky?' he said, with a thin smile.

Trevor reddened with anger. 'I'll get you for this, wizard,' he threatened. 'One day when you're alone in an alley, or a bar.'

Dennis affected a puzzled look. 'But I'm alone now, *idiot.* And I never go into bars on my own. I'm a wizard – no, I'm a *master* wizard – you'll never catch me off-guard.'

Florence coughed.

'Just watch your back, wizard,' snapped Trevor, lamely trying to salvage some dignity from his defeat.

'Open the doors, Father!' Florence called out. He strode across the floor and threw them back forcefully, still drunk with the power he'd exercised over the hapless robbers. There was an unexpected yelp from behind one of the doors. Dennis's curiosity got the better of him. He peered behind it and saw a large barbarian slumped on the ground clutching a bloody nose. 'Whoops, sorry,' said Dennis. 'I didn't see you there.'

The barbarian shook his head and staggered to his feet, at the same time drawing a rusty old sword. 'Oh!' exclaimed Dennis. 'It's like that, is it?' He raised a hand and was about to unleash a fireball, but the barbarian staggered off swinging his sword randomly and swearing loudly, clearly not only stunned from the blow, but drunk from the local inn.

Florence called out, and Dennis assured her that all was well. He was about to join her at the cart when a couple showed up looking to buy a second-hand cart. They saw Dennis and mistook him for the salesman, and made a hasty exit. 'Of all the…' he said, but he was cut off by the horse and cart thundering past.

Florence's light slap of the reins across the horse's back had caused the animal to rear violently and burst headlong into a gallop. She managed to hold onto the reins, and after a dozen yards, managed to pull hard enough to slow the horse down almost to a trot. She emerged from the alleyway into the busy market square, and from her position above the crowds, she could see Dennis running behind her.

She'd managed to slow right down for him when a member of the local Watch showed up. He told her officiously that she wasn't allowed to drive a horse and cart in the square on market day because it wasn't safe for pedestrians. He then unwisely slapped her horse hard to get her moving, sending her charging through the square knocking stalls and shoppers over. Seeing the mayhem, he blew his whistle and summoned two other officers to join him in pursuit. Dennis ran past and was only slightly in front of them.

They weren't actually chasing him, he realised in a moment of lucidity. Spotting the hitching rail where they'd bought the horse, he seized this moment of turmoil in the crowd to grab one of the other horses. 'Oi!' shouted the tall man in black, appearing again from seemingly nowhere, and giving chase. Though Dennis reckoned he'd more than paid for it.

Florence's final mishap with the milling and panicking crowds in the market square was to plough through a group of barbarians sitting outside an inn. She scattered them and drenched them all in their own ale. They stumbled to their feet yelling obscenities and looking for their mounts.

With Florence in the lead, the Watch some way behind on foot, Dennis gaining on them on horseback, a pack of barbarians screaming bloody murder, and the Deathly horse-trader bringing up the rear, the chase left the market square, carried on through the streets, and careered out of town for about a half a mile.

*

'Hey,' said Jook, 'will you take a look at this?'

Psoddoph stood up to see what had caught his colleague's attention. It looked bad. But he couldn't help laughing at the scene below. 'He just can't keep out of trouble for five minutes, can he?' he said, as they watched the cart bouncing along towards them with Dennis riding for all he was worth alongside it, and a posse of barbarians following them. They looked on riveted as the Watch gave up, and the horse trader went back for a horse.

'I wonder what 'e's done now,' grinned Jook.

'Probably taken that horse and cart without paying.' Psoddoph shook his head.

'And that other horse,' guessed Jook.

As the cart started up the hill towards them it slowed down, allowing Dennis to overtake. 'Quick! Get in the cart!' he yelled to the guards. They hauled themselves aboard, slamming the carpet and the Drum carelessly onto the boards and held on as best they could.

Florence slapped the reins across the horse's back. She was ready this time as it reared and lurched headlong into a gallop, leaving Dennis standing for a moment. She drove furiously down the other side of the hill. Jook grappled the Drum on to its side to stop it rolling and covered it with the carpet. Psoddoph crawled to the front and clambered over the seat to sit next to Florence.

'What happened?' he asked her.

'Don't ask,' she told him, cracking the reins again.

Psoddoph thought carefully about what he was going to say next, but he said it anyway, 'Did he steal the cart, then?'

'No,' said Florence, trying not to sound too surprised. 'Not this time.'

'Then why are you being chased?'

'They tried to rob us, but father stopped them,' she replied.

'How?'

She thought she might as well tell them. A brief version of it anyway.

Psoddoph glanced behind him again. Dennis drew closer, either to help protect the cart, or for the guards to protect him. 'I hope you've got some of those fireballs left, boss!' Psoddoph called. 'I think we're gonna need 'em in a minute.'

The barbarians were catching up. *Shit*, Dennis thought, and his mind began to race. Not that thinking the word *shit*, caused this, but it was fast becoming his number one 'go to' word. It summed up most of the things that happened in his life recently.

Just ahead was a valley thick with trees. Exactly what Dennis needed.

Psoddoph was likeminded. 'Let's head for those trees, boss!'

'I am!' snapped Dennis. Florence slapped the horse, urging it to go faster. Behind them, the barbarians had slowed down, one of their horses had stumbled and unseated its rider. It gave Dennis and the others the extra time they needed to reach the woods ahead of them.

Under cover of the trees, Dennis dismounted and hastily tethered his horse to a bush. Jook and Psoddoph scrambled down off the cart and crept back to the edge of the woods to wait.

The pursuers came into view, saw the trees and stopped.

'If they've gone in there, we might never find 'em,' moaned Badger Hercop, one of the barbarians.

'No need,' said Krumlin Droggett, the leader, knowledgeably. 'Those woods are haunted by Eric the Strangler.'

'Not *the* Eric the Strangler?' gasped the other man, a man known as Chickweed Scrawnier. There were only three of them now. The others had been too drunk to ride that fast and were sitting on the ground at intervals along the way. The three sat in silence, deciding what to do next. The chase had sobered them quite a lot, but they weren't the best of thinkers even when stone cold sober.

'But, yuh know? I ain't never 'eard of anyone actually getting killed by a ghost,' remarked Badger, after a lot of stressful thought.

'No,' agreed Krumlin, having spent a similar amount of time thinking. 'Neither 'ave I.'

'Shall we have a look?' said Chickweed. 'You know, just a quick look and then come out if we can't see 'em?' Krumlin spurred his horse forward without answering. The others followed at an easy canter a few yards behind.

'Ready?' whispered Psoddoph, unsheathing his sword. Jook nodded from his perch on a branch overhanging the track. As the last of the three barbarians passed beneath him, Jook silently swung his legs around the man's neck and squeezed him into unconsciousness while Psoddoph grabbed the man's horse. Jook hung there for a moment, just to make sure he'd restricted the man's breathing long enough to make him sleep for some time, then dropped him and half swung and half clambered back onto his perch. Psoddoph dragged the barbarian into the bushes and out of sight.

Moments later, Krumlin and Badger came back looking for their comrade. Jook was about to drop onto Badger when Dennis stepped onto the track behind them and released a fireball. It sailed harmlessly over Badger Hercop's shoulder and exploded in front of him. This wasn't quite what Dennis had in mind, but it worked out for the best, as the man was temporarily blinded. Psoddoph grabbed the reins from Badger's hands and Jook caught him a glancing blow to the forehead and knocked him to the ground.

Krumlin Droggett, finding himself alone, slapped his horse's butt with the flat of his sword and rode back to town as fast as he could. The Barbarian code of conduct was every man for himself.

Jook dropped from his perch, grinning widely. 'That was fun, boss.'

Dennis actually returned Jook's grin and flexed his fingers.

'Well, boss,' said Psoddoph. 'We have more horses than we know what to do with now.'

'You can ride, can't you?' said Dennis.

'Yeah, course, boss,' the two guards chorused.

'Good. You can ride one on each side of the cart,' said Dennis, hitching his own horse to the back of it.

Florence brought the cart out from the cover of the trees and onto the grassland at the edge of the woods. Dennis was about to climb on when he spotted a box bolted to the underside of the seat. 'We can put the teeth in there,' he said, 'for safe keeping. We don't want them bouncing out of our pockets, do we?'

The guards emptied their pockets into the box. 'Is that all of them?' asked Dennis. They nodded. 'Are you sure?' They nodded again, giving him the opportunity to put his hand in their pockets, which he was very sure he did not want to do.

'Right. Get to your horses and follow me.'

'Where are we goin', boss?' asked Psoddoph, as the two mounted.

'Still Corin,' Dennis reminded him, gruffly. 'Now I've got the teeth, I don't need the Drum. Besides, it's not much use to me without the staff.'

'Why not give it back, then?' suggested Jook.

'Don't be ridiculous, man. I don't want to give more power to those with the staff. No, I'll sell it.'

The Drum glowed, a pleasant pastel hue. The possibility of finishing up with someone worse than Dennis was fairly remote.

* * *

37

Daylight was fading when Eydith and Link reached the base of the mountain. They turned their mounts east to follow Dennis. As they struck out along the dusty track, Sprag shivered slightly in Eydith's grasp.

'Mistress,' he said, 'the Drum is moving more slowly. In another direction.' He twisted in the saddle strapping to show the way.

'What? Over there?' said Eydith.

Link thought for moment, recalling his geography of Kermells Tong. 'The Land of *Corin*? That confirms they're heading for the coast.'

'We'll stop at the next town and check our bearings,' said Eydith.

Link agreed. 'Perhaps we'll get some food as well.'

'You used to conjure it up,' she reminded him.

'Yes, but what a waste of magic that was. And it's never *totally* like proper food, if I'm honest. Anyway, I don't know what I fancy yet.'

The pair travelled on steadily for the next hour, wanting to get as far as possible before nightfall, but not wanting to push their mounts too hard.

Sprag trembled again. 'Mistress, the Drum is definitely moving slower and I would suggest it isn't flying.'

'Maybe the weather's not so good where they are. Or the carpet's out of magic – or damaged,' offered Link. 'The trolls said they'd damaged it.'

'Which direction?' asked Eydith.

'Same as before.'

'Still south,' said Link.

Eydith reined in her horse. Link instinctively leant back. He'd got used to the fact that Mabel would stop every time the horse did. Eydith slid to the ground. 'Where do you think we are now, Link?'

He swung off the donkey and looked around to get his bearings. A glance towards the setting sun gave him his orientation. 'This is the mountains,' he said, drawing some triangles in the dust with his finger. 'The Land of Corin is here.' He drew an outline with a coastline below it, and pinpointed the city of Corin itself. He looked around again, then added, 'We've travelled across from here.' He drew a line. 'And I would say we're about here.' He added an X, and finished by scratching an area of forest.

Eydith looked it over. 'You're pretty good at this. It even looks to scale. So we just need to keep heading this way,' she said, using Sprag to draw in the dust. 'And we'll probably meet with Dennis about here.' She banged the staff on the ground to show just where she meant.

'I do wish you wouldn't do that, mistress. I'm not a pencil,' Sprag complained.

'Er… sorry, Sprag, I wasn't thinking,' she replied.

'Does this mean we won't be going through a town, then?' Link wondered. 'Only I can't seem to recall the last time we ate.'

Eydith laughed. 'Alright, we'll detour to the next town. In fact, we're heading directly for Corin, so if you can manage with a bit of roadside foraging and a magic meal or two till then…?'

'I reckon so,' said Link. 'But Mabel could use some… er…'

'Grass?' said Eydith, helpfully.

Link looked around him at the expanse of heathland. 'Not exactly short of it, are we?' he said. He got off the donkey and sat on a boulder at the side of the track, allowing Mabel to graze as far as her reins would allow. Eydith sat down beside him.

They watched a beautiful sunset. 'Looks like we'll be spending a night under the stars,' said Eydith, a little wistfully.

Link wasn't enthusiastic. He shuddered. 'It's starting to turn chilly, too.'

'Then we'll have to snuggle up together,' she said, smiling and keeping her eyes straight ahead.

'Ah,' he said, warming to the idea.

* * *

The following day, back in the city of Kra-Pton, the rumblings of subsidence had quietened. Nothing serious had happened for almost a week and people were beginning to return to their homes and businesses. Those with friends or family in neighbouring towns and villages were beginning to outstay their welcome. For those who'd camped out in the open, the novelty was wearing off. Not only that, most of their belongings were still in their houses, and while most of the citizens held the Watch in high regard, there was always a nagging suspicion that one or more of the Watchmen might be going through their things, and seeing things they might take a fancy to. Or things they wouldn't keep secret for very long. It was the perennial problem of who watches the Watch?

In the Great Hall of the university, some of the wizards who had returned were sitting by the great open fire, warming their toes. Some were chatting and others were surveying the damage.

'Which bit do you think will come down next?' the Archchancellor asked of no one in particular.

'I reckon the south wing, Archchancellor,' said Cho, a small, wiry man, on the lecturing staff, who happened to be closest. Cho had come to the university seventeen years ago as an exchange student from the Eastern kingdoms. Like many a student, he'd decided to stay on and work in the region where he studied. He'd been back home a few times and found himself less and less attached to the manners and customs of his old homeland. He was hoping to make senior lecturer should there continue to be a university to work in.

'No, the south wing's not worth it,' Rumpitt argued, unsurprisingly, for he was contrary by nature. He was a tall, elderly, senior lecturer and faculty head, with a naturally negative turn of mind, and face to match. His age was uncertain, but he had to be somewhere in his mid-eighties. He came from a family of centenarians, so thought of himself as still in his prime. If asked what he put his fitness and longevity down to, he'd say it had nothing to do with genes, diet or exercise, it was his grumpiness that kept him going. It gave him something to live for. 'It'll be the library they'll go for, or the outside privy.'

'What makes you think that?' asked Pelgrum, another elderly senior lecturer, a short, rotund and generally pleasant man.

'Well, it stands to reason, doesn't it?' said Rumpitt. 'Most of the stuff elsewhere is no good to demons.'

'I agree with Rumpitt,' said Cho, changing his mind. 'Stands to reason, first they'll undermine the privy block, then the library.'

'In that order?' asked Pelgrum.

'Yep, first the privies, then the library,' Cho repeated – his pronunciation perfect, Rumpitt couldn't help noticing.

In the past, Cho hadn't been able to get his tongue round 'L's and 'R's, but now he was coping admirably. What most people didn't realise, though, was that he used to mispronounce words intentionally and mostly around Rumpitt, because he knew it annoyed the old wizard. Cho was naturally upbeat, so the pair were opposites and hadn't always got on. Nowadays they hit it off reasonably well, and Cho had no need to pretend. Though he wasn't above trying it mischievously now and then.

'How can you be so sure?' Pelgrum persisted.

'Got to have the privies first,' Cho began. 'Then they'll need books. Some of the books in there… well, they're thick enough to last at least a whole year!'

'That's terrible,' moaned Pelgrum. 'Some of those books are hundreds of years old.'

'Yes, so not much use now,' said Rumpitt, philosophically. 'Pages will be too brittle for…'

'I'm not having those demons using my books for wiping their… well, you know,' said Paske, the librarian, angrily.

'No, I don't know,' muttered the Archchancellor. 'What are we talking about?'

'Books in the privies, Archchancellor,' said Rumpitt.

'Excellent idea! I love a good read… Secretary! See to it. Every privy, at least four books!'

The Secretary sighed, and humoured him. 'Yes, Archchancellor.'

Trinkel's chin dropped back onto his chest. He'd dozed off again.

'We've got to stop them, you know. Remember what happened last time?' Rumpitt recalled.

'Yes,' said Cho. 'All hell broke loose.'

'Yes, and his bloody mates,' Rumpitt added.

'We need reader,' said Cho, having trouble with his 'L's again – or feigning to.

'Reader?' snapped Rumpitt. 'I thought we'd finished discussing books.'

'No, I mean *leader!* Someone to lead us.' Cho stopped messing with Rumpitt, and, indicating the slumbering Archchancellor, he shook his head in frustration. 'This is getting serious.'

The ground moved and the rumblings started again.

Those wizards that were standing, threw themselves to the floor. The statue of some long dead Archchancellor rocked on its pedestal then toppled over and smashed into many pieces. Just beyond it, a hole appeared in the marble floor and another statue tilted and slipped into an abyss.

When the dust had settled, the sounds of voices arguing could be heard drifting up from the depths.

'Can't you be more careful wiv that spade? Those bloody statues 'ave sharp edges, you know.'

'Sorry, Hell,' said a little voice.

'One of you lot is gonna 'ave to come up 'ere and make sure nuffin' too 'eavy surprises me like that when I break the surface again! Do you understand?'

'Yes, your kingship.'

'Now get back down there and delegate.'

The sound of clawed feet on rocks became fainter as they receded slowly back into the bowels of the Parallel Dimension. Hell descended with his minions.

'Well,' remarked Rumpitt, 'we've got to do something now, or we'll soon be overrun by the little buggers again.'

* * *

39

On the road to Corin in their newly-acquired horse and cart, Dennis and Florence jogged along in a comfortable enough silence. Dennis wasn't one for small talk, not even with his daughter. The road was long and straight, and Florence, who held the reins, had been doing a lot of thinking.

'They're bound to be looking for us by now,' she said.

'Who?' Dennis queried.

'Cousin Eydith, and that young wizard.'

'Linkwood?'

'Yes, that's the one.'

'I suppose they are,' Dennis sighed. 'But that staff of hers is not so clever without the Drum.'

'It's clever enough,' she countered, and started telling him what was on her mind. 'Haven't you ever wondered how they managed to defea… well…'

'Defeat me? It's alright, you can say it,' he said, though he had trouble getting the word out himself.

'Yes, they defeated you. How could that possibly have happened? A mere Seventh Grade wizard, an Entry Grade girl, and Wimlett, a ghost – however did they defeat an Archwizard like you?'

'That girl might be Entry Grade on paper, but she's the daughter of an Archchancellor,' he reminded her. 'They had you as well – another daughter of an Archchancellor, as it turned out.'

'But Eydith hasn't anywhere near mastered her powers yet,' she pointed out. 'And I certainly haven't.'

'But she had the staff *and* the Drum.'

'Yes, and that's what I've been thinking about. We were all in Prossill at the same time as you and your guards, so why didn't they attack you there and then?' He shrugged and kept his eyes on the road. 'I may be wrong but I think I know why. I think the staff and the Drum draw their power from the university. It's a powerfully magical building, as you know. What I think is that the further away from

Havrapsor they got, the weaker the power of the staff and Drum became. So they followed you back and faced you there.'

'I don't know,' said Dennis, doubtful. 'In that case, why follow me to Prossill at all if they knew the power in the staff would fade?'

'That's just it. I don't think they knew until they followed you.'

'Hmm.' Dennis sounded unconvinced.

But she hadn't finished. 'I think we should ride as far as we can from Havrapsor and let them follow us. As they will, I'm sure. And when they catch up, we can face them with the biggest power on our side – you!'

That appealed to Dennis. His ego was certainly stroked by her last comment. Enough to consider it seriously. 'Though, what if you're wrong?'

'If I'm wrong, we've still got to face them sooner or later. So we might as well try to improve our chances.'

He couldn't argue with that, though he still had his doubts.

'Then you can take the staff for yourself at last!' she said, fired up with the plan.

'And then I'll order the guards to kill her… oh, and Linkwood of course.'

'That's a bit drastic, Father.'

'All's fair in war and… that,' said Dennis, awkwardly.

'Why don't we go to one of those islands in the Sea of Lan-vor?' Florence suggested. 'That would easily be far enough from Havrapsor.'

'Because, as I recall, nobody ever comes back! Is that reason enough?'

'They weren't us, Father,' said Florence. 'You're an Archwizard and I'm the daughter of an Archwizard.'

'Yes, you are, aren't you. I hadn't given that side of things much thought,' he said, quietly, then added, 'And a witch, of course.'

'Pardon?'

'Your mother… a witch.'

'Oh, yes.'

'Have you learned much magic at the university?' he asked.

'A bit,' she paused, thinking back. 'No, not much really. Just how to do fireballs and a few basic spells.'

'They teach fireballs at entry level now?!'

'Well, not the lecturers, so much,' she said, sheepishly. 'It's more something we pick up in the Junior Common Room.'

'Ah,' he said, comprehending all too well.

'But mother taught me a lot, you know, herbs, potions – that sort of thing.'

'Oh, witches stuff,' said Dennis, with distaste.

'Yes, witches stuff,' she repeated. 'Would you like a demonstration?'

'Er… no. Not just now,' he declined. The conversation petered out at the right moment.

Jook and Psoddoph caught up with the cart. 'Riders coming, boss,' called Psoddoph.

Dennis swivelled and looked over his shoulder.

'Other side, boss,' said Jook.

Dennis gave him one of his injurious glances and looked the other way.

'They don't look like barbarians, Father,' said Florence.

'They're riding like barbarians.'

'No, I think they're just in a hurry, boss,' said Psoddoph.

The riders reined in their horses in front of the cart. 'You'd better come with us!' the nearest rider called.

'Are you barbarians?' Dennis called, defiantly.

'No,' replied the rider. 'Those are barbarians!' he nodded towards another large group of riders following on, just managing to stay ahead of a great cloud of dust.

'Bugger,' muttered Dennis.

'Looks like trouble, boss,' said Jook, perceptively.

'It *is* trouble, stupid!' snapped Dennis. He turned to the leading rider. 'Where are you heading?'

'South, to the port.'

'Good,' said Dennis. 'That's where we're going! Drive, Daughter!'

Florence slapped the reins against the horse's back, and hung on tightly.

'Can't you do something, boss?' said Psoddoph, his horse cantering alongside the cart.

'What do you suggest?' said Dennis, sarcastically. 'Tell them we don't want to be robbed and killed today, thank you. That sort of thing?'

'No,' said Psoddoph. 'I don't think that would work, boss. I was thinking fireballs.'

'You *know* that's dangerous when the Drum's near me!'

'Why not use the carpet to get up and away from it,' Psoddoph suggested.

Dennis glared at him. He hated it when other people had the good ideas. Angrily, he dragged the carpet off the Drum and spread it out as best he could and sat down on it. 'Carpet! Up, please,' he mumbled, politely. The carpet didn't move.

'I said, UP! Please… oh, damn it!' He staggered to his feet again. Turned the carpet over and tried again. 'Up, please!' The carpet flew up with the wizard lying spread-eagled on his back, watching the clouds rapidly descending to meet him. 'Yaargh! Stop! Please!' he yelled. The sudden halt shot him a couple of inches into the air, but he managed to land safely back on the carpet. He sat up and asked the carpet to descend, gently this time, and came to a hovering standstill in the midst of the pursuing barbarians, who had now reached the spot that Dennis had left a few moments ago.

'Argh!' he screamed. 'Up, please. But not too fast!' The carpet obliged and when it was about thirty feet up, Dennis asked it to stop and start flying forward. All the time he was flexing his fingers for the onslaught. When he was a few yards in front of the barbarians, he raised his hands and launched twin flashes of orange flame from his fingertips.

The leading riders seeing the carpet sensed what was about to happen and pulled up. Those behind crowded into their backs, knocking them to the ground and into the path of the following horses. Dennis was enjoying himself. He shouted maniacally and released two more forks of flame. 'Thought you could mess with me, eh?!' he yelled, and for good measure he released two more, which exploded in a shower of silver sparks just above the barbarians' heads.

Some of their horses were spooked and reared up, unseating their riders. Others bolted, trampling anyone that got in their way. Dennis asked the carpet to circle the carnage in case he'd overlooked anybody, and then flew back to the cart.

He was flying along just behind it, his mind working overtime trying to judge the right moment to land. The cart raced along beneath him. *Now*! He thought, *now's the time*. He snapped out the request to the carpet.

*

As he sat in the dust, watching the cart racing up the track, Dennis reflected that it might have been wiser to tell the carpet what he wanted and let it get on with it.

He stood up and found the carpet. Hearing the sound of many horses thundering towards him, he instinctively raised his hands.

He calmly whispered the spell. Two streaks of hot fire arced from his fingertips. One was a searing yellow that hurt his eyes. *Gods, where did that come from*, he wondered. The other was equally effective in its way, but what it lacked in colour was more than compensated for in smell. It was disgusting. The remaining barbarians reined in their horses and galloped away, each of them cursing and blaming the others.

Dennis wondered which of his hands had caused that, but it didn't really matter. The barbarians had gone; that's what mattered.

'Slow down!' Psoddoph called to Florence. 'The boss is coming back.'

This time Dennis landed on the grass beside them. It was much less tricky and painful. He rolled the carpet up, heaved it into the cart, and climbed aboard. 'That showed 'em,' he smirked, as he made himself comfortable. Florence gave him an appreciative, daughterly smile, tapped the horse, and they moved on. The guards rode alongside, rendered speechless by the fact that Dennis had actually loaded the carpet himself for once.

* * *

40

A couple of days later, Eydith and Link arrived in the Land of Corin. They knew they were getting near when the track became more like a proper road. A signpost confirmed it. And inside half an hour they were seeing the welcome signs of civilisation.

'Whose castle is that?' asked Link, looking at the top of a long, draggy hill overlooking the town.

'It's Treadwell's,' replied Eydith, sounding a little wistful. 'My mother used to work for him a long time ago. I was very young then.'

'What does he do around here, then?' Link wondered.

'He's the king.'

'Useful man to know,' said Link. 'Maybe he could be helpful to us.'

'I hadn't thought about that,' said Eydith.

'He'd probably know if someone like Dennis has shown up, or passed through. Or, he could find out. And if he's still here, he'll be keen to help us get rid of him, I'm sure.'

'Mother said he was a good king. Never killed anyone. Except by accident, of course.'

'Oh, of course,' echoed Link. What he knew of kings was only hearsay, and mostly not good.

Eydith thought about what else her mother used to tell her about this king. 'He had a strange way of dealing with criminals.'

'How do you mean?' he asked, intrigued, and with a view to making mental notes, so's not fall foul of the man.

'Well, say you stole something. He'd cut off one of your fingers, and if he caught you stealing again, he'd cut off another one.'

'Curing by degrees?' suggested Link.

She ignored him. 'If he caught you listening at keyholes, he'd cut your ear off.'

Link involuntarily rubbed his ear. 'And no doubt your other ear if he caught you again. Ah, but what if he caught you a third time?'

She gave him her patience-being-tried look. 'If he caught you listening at a keyhole with your no ears, you mean?'

'Ah, yes,' he said, catching up. 'Cutting offending items off seems a bit drastic, though. I suppose he must have stamped out adultery completely by now?'

'Mother never said…' said Eydith, not really wanting to pursue that.

'Do you think the king will see us?'

Eydith looked up at the castle. 'No, I don't think so. Not from there.'

He was about to say what he meant, but caught the flicker of a smile. 'That's the sort of thing I'd have said to you.'

'Annoying, isn't it? You're obviously a bad influence.'

'Yeah,' he said, feigning concern, 'to both of those.' Then, noticing, much to Eydith's amusement, that Sprag glowed, seemingly in agreement, he added, 'And you can keep out of this, too.'

'King Treadwell did tell mother to look him up if ever we were in the area.'

'Excellent! Is the cook any good?' he wondered.

'The best for miles around, probably.' She smiled, as he urged the donkey on a little faster.

* * *

41

Beneath King Treadwell's castle lay the town of Corin. It was a welcome sight for two slightly saddle-sore travellers. And much as they liked each other's company, it was good to have other people around them again.

Eydith dismounted and led her horse through the busy streets. Mabel trotted along contentedly behind for a change, doubtless due to the attention she was getting from children patting and stroking her as she went by. Link hoped nobody would offer her carrots, because then she'd never move until she'd eaten them all.

Eydith slowed, allowing Link to bring Mabel alongside, and they walked hand in hand up the slope to the castle.

'Funny,' said Link, when they arrived in front of the building.

'What is?'

'I thought there'd be a drawbridge or a guardhouse, not just a great big door.'

'As I remember it, there is a drawbridge on the other side of this door.'

'How do we get in?' he wondered, looking for a bell-rope, or a knocker, or even a horn to blow.

Eydith raised Sprag, and before he could complain she struck the door with him. Three times, in quick succession.

A small hatch opened and a pair of beady eyes peered out. 'Who's there?' came an irate sounding voice from within.

Eydith was about to announce herself when the voice repeated its challenge, 'C'mon, I 'aven't got all day!'

'My name is Eydith…' she began.

'S'not my problem,' snapped the voice. 'Now, what do you want?'

'I want to see King Treadwell,' she replied, straining to stay polite.

'Well, you can't.' There was a pause, and the addition of, 'not from there, anyway. Come to think of it, I can't see 'im from 'ere, either.'

She sighed and shook her head in disbelief. 'I'm someone the king used to know. I was expecting you to let us in,' said Eydith, barely keeping her calm. 'Because I'm sure *King Treadwell* will want to see us.'

'Us?' queried the voice. 'How many of you are there?'

'Only two,' said Eydith.

'Stand back so I can see you.'

Eydith and Link stood back. The hatch closed and many bolts slid back before the door finally creaked open.

'Do you have an appointment?'

Eydith looked around for the speaker.

'Down here,' stated an agitated voice.

Oh, she thought. *Of course – A dwarf*. 'My mother worked here a long time ago,' she said. 'The king said we should come and see him if we were ever in Corin again.'

'What was her name?' asked the dwarf, trying to be intimidating. He was wielding a double-headed battle-axe.

'No – what *is* her name. She's still alive,' she corrected him.

'Okay, what *is* her name then?' the dwarf asked again, huffily. She was starting to play by his rules and he wasn't liking it very much.

'Triona,' said Eydith, and spelt it out for him in case it helped.

'All right. I can spell, thank you,' said the dwarf. He stroked his beard and stared up into her face. Then a spark of recognition lit up his eyes. 'Triona? Triona, the... er... witch?'

'Well... yes,' said Eydith cautiously, because it didn't always please people to know that about her mother. They often took a step back.

The dwarf looked her up and down. Mainly up. 'Then, you must be little Eydith, with a y.'

'Yes, that's right. I am.'

'I'm *Ben*,' he beamed.

'Ben?' she repeated, and looked blankly at Link.

'You must remember me. Ben de Little,' he said, smiling broadly again as he slammed his battle-axe back into his belt. The end of the shaft glanced off his big toe and he hopped about for a moment. 'Ow, ow, ow.' It brought both a smile and a flash of recognition from Eydith.

'Ben? Yes, I do remember you now. Of course. But you were much taller back then.'

'No, you were much shorter, my dear. Come on in.' Then he saw the horse and the donkey and opened the door wider.

Once inside, Link couldn't help looking behind the door to see how Ben could see through a hatch so high. Then he saw a set of crude wooden steps on wonky wheels. 'Why didn't you cut the hatch lower down?'

The dwarf, hands on hips, scowled. 'Because I don't want to be talking to kneecaps half the time, that's why.'

When they were all inside, Ben set about the task of slamming all the bolts back. 'Don't just stand there,' he chastened Link, 'do the top ones or I'll have to wheel me steps over again and we'll be here all day.'

Link did as he was told. 'You could do with some oil on those.'

'Just what I need – another boss. Right then, follow me.'

The little man spun on his heels and marched across the small cobbled yard to a portcullis opposite. Arriving there he muttered to himself, 'Halt,' and looked up at the battlements on the other side of the moat. They were deserted. He cupped his hands to his mouth and shouted, 'Oi! Enry! You up there?' Aside, to Eydith he confided, 'That's Enry wiv an E. You wouldn't remember 'im, though.'

A small helmeted head peered over the edge. 'Oo is it?'

'Oo do you fink it is, idiot. It's me – Ben!'

'Oh. What do you want?'

'I've got visitors down 'ere!' Ben shouted.

'That's nice, 'aven't 'ad any of them for ages.' Enry yawned. The chief qualification for gate-keeper in this place seemed to be obstructiveness.

'Will you stop buggerin' about and lower the bridge!'

Ben tapped his foot and waited a minute. Exchanging glances with Eydith, he said, 'I'll get 'im moving.' He looked up at the battlements again. 'Enry!'

'What now?'

'My visitors…'

'Yeah?'

'Well, they're not exactly *my* visitors.'

'Well, *I'm* not expecting anyone,' said Enry, unhelpful as ever.

'They've come to see the king, *actually*,' Ben told him. 'They're *His* visitors.'

At the mention of the king, many feet started to run. The great chains that held the drawbridge up were suddenly freed to clank over their pulleys, and the great bridge was majestically lowered across the moat. Once across, Eydith and Link had to wait while bolts were slid back. The inner door of the castle opened a crack. Enry peeped through the gap, saw Ben and his guests, sighed and opened the door just wide enough for them to squeeze through, one at a time, along with Mabel and the horse.

Enry, who was another dwarf, told them to wait while he closed and secured the door.

Without being asked this time, Link slid the bolts at the top.

Enry looked up and frowned. 'Did I ask you to do that? No.' And before Link could open his mouth. 'So don't expect me to thank you.'

Link shrugged and grinned slyly at Eydith.

'Right. Follow me!' Enry shouted.

'Are we going to the king?' Eydith asked Ben.

'No, the stables first,' replied Ben. 'I don't fink the king wants to meet your animals, too.'

'And then someone will take us to see him?' she queried.

'Not my job,' snapped Enry.

'I'll do that, young Eydith.' said Ben. 'My you've grown… up,' he said, taking another good look at her.

When Mabel and the horse were stabled, Ben ushered Eydith and Link through the castle to another of the many small courtyards in the grounds and buildings. In one corner was a low door. Well, it was low for Eydith and Link. Ben fitted through perfectly. Eydith and Link ducked through behind him.

It was fast dawning on Link that this castle was built for dwarves, and that King Treadwell was going to be the dwarf king here. Eydith, of course, already knew this. *So why didn't she mention it?* He made a mental note to ask, knowing she'd probably just dismiss it, and tell him she thought she'd let him find out for himself. The truth of the matter was that she'd known these characters for a significant phase of her early life and had always thought of them simply as just other people. It didn't occur to her that others might see them differently.

'This way,' said Ben, and started to climb a narrow staircase. It spiralled around inside what must have been one of the towers they'd seen when approaching the castle. Part way up, the little man opened another door and signalled them to follow as he went inside. More steps. At the top was yet another door. Ben stopped and rapped on it with his chain mailed fist.

Footsteps were heard echoing closer and closer from the other side. A small hatch slid back and a pair of dark eyes peered through. 'Yes?'

'It's me, Ben.'

'Ben who?'

'Ben de Little.'

'Don't need to. I can see you from here.'

'Is that you, Thadax?' snapped Ben.

'Er… yes.'

'Well, stop playin' silly buggers and open up!' His face flushed with annoyance, he turned and apologised to Eydith. Back at the hatch he barked, 'I've got visitors – for *the king*!'

Thadax slammed the hatch and opened the door.

'About time!' snapped Ben, barging his way inside. 'Now tell the king I'm here and I've got some people to see him.'

Thadax trotted along to an arched door that had a badly carved crown over it. He pushed the door gently and raised the heraldic bugle he carried, to his lips. But before he could blow a single note, an imperious voice boomed out from the other end of the room. 'Blow that thing once more and you'll be wearing it!'

Thadax stiffened. The bugle slipped from his fingers and clanked tunelessly onto the stone floor.

'Pick it up and bring it here!' ordered the king.

'Yes, your majesty,' said Thadax, stooping hurriedly to collect his bugle. He rushed it to the king's feet.

The king sighed. 'Give it to me,' he said, holding out his hands. Thadax reluctantly placed the instrument across the king's palms, and whimpered.

The king gripped it tightly and proceeded to bend it over his knee. He then tried to tie it in a knot but couldn't. But he eyed what he'd done with satisfaction, knowing it would never be in any shape to have breath pushed through it again. He smiled kindly and handed it back to Thadax.

The ex-musician took it out of the king's hands and examined it for a moment. He glared at the king, then quickly changing it to a weak smile, murmured, 'Thank you.'

King Treadwell leant back on his throne, crossed his legs and folded his arms. 'Right – now that's out of the way, what do you want?'

'Er… Ben's got some people to see you, sire.'

'Well, don't just stand there, show them in.'

Ben ushered Eydith and Link forward and knelt at the foot of the throne.

'Get up, Ben, and stop messing about. We've known each other too long for that.'

'Just trying to impress the visitors, sire,' he whispered.

Treadwell smiled approvingly and looked up at Eydith and Link, who were having to stoop slightly because of the low ceiling, and were unwittingly observing the protocol for approaching a king.

'Er… this is Eydith, sire, with a y. Remember her?' Ben stood aside and held out his hands as if introducing her on stage. 'Her mother used to work here. She said you told her she could drop in any time, as it were. And this is… er, what did you say your name was again?' he asked, craning his neck up at Link.

Link gave his name and politely bowed a little lower. Treadwell acknowledged him with an almost dismissive wave and turned his attention back to Eydith. She was *so much* prettier, after all.

'An open invitation, eh?' the king mused. 'Should I know you?'

Eydith bobbed an awkward curtsy before she spoke. 'As Ben said, my mother used to work here, sire. When I was very small…' She quickly rephrased that. 'Er… very young, I mean.'

'What was your mother's name, girl?'

'Triona, sire.'

Treadwell stroked his beard and drummed his fingers on the arm of his throne, casting his mind back through the cobwebs of time. He screwed his eyes tightly shut and frowned, giving the impression that the process of recollection was hard and painful. At length, his eyes flicked open and stared at her. 'Was that Triona the witch?'

'Yes, sire,' she confirmed, nodding vigorously.

'Ah, yes.' He grinned, rubbing his hands together, happy that he'd actually remembered. 'Then you must be *little* Eydie.'

She cringed. She hated it when people called her that. And no doubt Link wouldn't let her forget it now. But she needed the king's help, so she accepted his familiarity with good grace and avoided Link's faintly flickering smile. 'Yes, sire.' She smiled, and through gritted teeth, acknowledged, '*Little Eydie*. That's me.'

'Well, it's good to see you again. My how you've grown,' he marvelled. She guessed she'd be hearing that a lot today. They talked for a few minutes about her mother's work, and the people she would know from those days. It was pleasant for both of them to recall, but then he paused and became a little kinglier. 'Now… is this just a courtesy call, because you're passing through Corin, or is there something particular I might be able to do for you?'

Eydith retold the story of the stolen Drum and how important it was that it should be recovered. The king listened without interruption, making mental notes regarding what he would do to this Dennis if ever he caught up with him. When Eydith had finished, he signalled her and Link to sit down and waved them into silence while he considered their situation. He closed his eyes and drummed the arm of the throne again.

While they waited, Eydith and Link took the opportunity to look around the throne room and admire the tapestries of battles fought at the castle. The king, or his forebears, were victorious in all of them. Which was unlikely, but tapestries showing defeats were probably at the bottom of the moat, along with their needle workers. After a while, the king's tapping slowed and stopped. Alarmingly, his head slumped forward, and before Ben could catch it, the heavy crown slipped from the king's head and landed with a painful-sounding thump in his lap.

Link winced.

King Treadwell awoke with a start, and a pain that seriously threatened his royal composure, and possibly his chances of having an heir if he didn't already have one. He muttered something obscene at some minor deity, and with both hands, rammed the crown back on his head. 'Hmm, I didn't expect *that.* Now, where was I? Ah, yes. Here's what we'll do,' he said, pausing first for a wince of pain. 'If this Dennis is anywhere in my realm I will find him. I'll send my best spy to search him out. He will report back to me and I'll keep you informed.' The king considered this for a moment, then bent closer to Ben, 'You don't happen to know where he is, do you?'

'Who?' asked Ben.

'This wizard. Dennis.' The king sighed. 'I *know* where my spies are.' Then on second thoughts added, 'Well, I know where *most* of them are. Some of them are so good they don't even know where they are themselves sometimes. And I can't even be sure *who* they are sometimes.' He scrutinized Link for a long moment and decided he was way too tall.

Ben shrugged. 'Not a clue, sire.'

'We know he's heading south, sire. Towards the town by the sea,' Eydith came to the rescue before the king could start on him again.

'In that case, I'll send the *Sea Dragon* as well. To cover the port. And more spies to hang around in the bars and places like that,' he said, cheerfully. 'You know? – I'm beginning to wish I was coming with you, Ben! Bit of excitement. Go and get Loosley.'

Ben snapped to attention and saluted smartly. With a brisk, 'Yes, sire!' he turned on his heels and marched rigidly from the room.

'Well?' said the king, turning back to Thadax, 'what are you still hanging about for?'

'Sire?' queried Thadax.

'Why are you still here?'

'I didn't hear anybody at the door, sire.'

'Well. You must have *something* to do?'

Thadax thought for a moment, 'Er… no, sire. I can't think of anything.'

'Well, go and get some refreshments, then,' the king suggested.

'I've not long had lunch, sire…'

'Not for you, idiot! Our visitors. And… oh, yes… let me think… *me*.'

'Oh, er… yes, I see. Right. I'll get some refreshments then. Shall I?'

'Just go.' The king sighed.

Thadax slouched along to the kitchens. He hated it when the king sent him away. He worried in case they were talking about him. Or worse than that, they might be talking about someone else. And he so wanted to be a spy.

* * *

42

Rumpitt looked out of a window in his rooms. 'There goes another bit,' he moaned, as the ground shook and a few more tiles slid off the university roof.

'Got any ideas?' asked Pelgrum. The short, plump man moved promptly away from the fire as a cloud of soot came down the chimney.

'South wing, I think,' muttered Rumpitt.

'No, about what we should do,' Pelgrum clarified.

'I know what we *should* do, but doing it's the problem. I've been giving it a lot of thought, but it's bloody difficult to know where the blighters are going to dig next.' Rumpitt walked away from the window still in thought. 'Perhaps we could rig up an alarm system – something that tells us exactly where they're surfacing. We can be on alert and rush them in force.'

'What… hit them with a volley of fireballs?' queried Pelgrum, enthusiastically.

'It might work. We could station ourselves in groups around the place and wait for them to stick their heads up?' suggested Rumpitt.

'And *then* hit 'em with fireballs!' said Pelgrum, ensuring that was still in the plan. 'Yes… But *no*. There might be more of them than we can manage,' he said, deflating.

The building shifted slightly again.

'Let's get a meeting organised… as quickly as we can,' suggested Rumpitt. 'Somewhere safe, where we can think without worrying the floor might fall through.'

Dust drifted down from the ceiling.

'I'll go and see the Secretary. He's good at getting meetings organised,' said Pelgrum. 'Though I'm not sure about quickly. He does seem to have lost his sense of urgency about the situation since we all returned.'

'As have far too many people, Pelgrum. Okay, I'll see if I can wake the Archchancellor long enough to agree,' said Rumpitt, not sounding too hopeful. He'd always thought that having an awful lot to complain about would make him really happy, but it didn't seem to be to working out that way.

Pelgrum went as fast as his aging legs would carry him to the Secretary's office. He'd never had a problem complying with the *no running in the buildings* rule, and today was no exception.

*

'Well, what do you expect me to do about it?' the Secretary asked, steepling his fingers under his nose.

'Get all the wizards assembled somewhere,' said Pelgrum, agitatedly. 'I don't know, you're the one that's good at this sort of thing.'

The Secretary leaned forward on his elbows, staring searchingly at the wizard. 'Yes, and then what? What's going to happen at this meeting?'

'We agree some sort of plan, of course. Organise defensive lines or circles, or something,' floundered Pelgrum, hardly believing the Secretary wasn't grasping the importance, the urgency.

'And do you think this would work? This er… defensive circle, or something?'

'Well, something has to. And they'd listen to you, Secretary, if *you* chaired the meeting.'

That seemed to push the right button. 'Yes – they would, wouldn't they,' he smirked. He knew that whatever he wanted, he'd only have to say that the Archchancellor had said it, and nobody would doubt him. It would be obeyed without question. Within reason. 'Hmm, let me think about it,' he said, quietly, as he gestured Pelgrum away.

Pelgrum left the office somewhat frustrated, but happy in the knowledge that when the Secretary said he'd think about something, he usually followed through. He walked back to Rumpitt's rooms with a bit of a spring in his step, but crashed against the hallway wall as the building lurched again. Dust settled on his shoulders like severe dandruff. He stretched out his arms for balance and staggered down the hallway, bouncing from wall to wall. He was unfortunately the right build to accommodate this kind of involuntary manoeuvre.

Behind him, he heard the Secretary curse, as something slid from his desk and landed with a dull thump on the floor. It was an uncapped inkwell, but Pelgrum didn't know that. He was just happy that the Secretary would definitely be angry enough now to get things moving.

Pelgrum turned the handle on Rumpitt's door. It opened a fraction and stopped.

'Just a minute!' Rumpitt called from the other side. 'My armchair's rolled in front of it.'

Pelgrum could hear the older wizard puffing and grunting on the other side of the door. 'It's no good,' he panted. 'You'll have to give it a push from your side.'

Pelgrum took a couple of steps back, took a deep breath and charged, unmindful of his volume. After a resounding crash, he was in Rumpitt's rooms. The door, or what was left of it, was still wedged by the chair, and the overweight wizard was rubbing his shoulder.

Rumpitt inspected the damage. 'Ah, well,' he shrugged, 'that'll give those lazy buggers in the Works Department something to do.'

'They're going to have more than enough to do around here before this is over,' reckoned Pelgrum, voicing the ugly truth of the situation. Between them, the two wizards heaved the armchair away from the door and went down to the dining hall.

'How'd you get on with the Secretary?' asked Rumpitt on the way.

'He said he'd think about it,' Pelgrum replied.

'Good. That means he'll do something, then.'

The building rocked again.

* * *

43

Jook sniffed the salty air. 'Haven't smelt that since I was kid,' he reminisced.

'Yeah, we can't be far from the sea now,' Psoddoph agreed, inhaling deeply.

'My mum used to take me to the seaside sometimes, when my dad was away,' Jook continued. 'Used to spend hours on that beach, diggin' 'oles and makin' great piles of sand.'

'What for?'

'I dunno,' said Jook. 'Probably seemed like a good idea at the time, I s'pose. Anyway, it always ended in tears.'

'Why, what happened?'

'The tide came in and washed 'em all away, and I 'ad to start all over again,' Jook said, sad-faced. 'Mind you, after the last time, my mum never took me again.'

'That upset, were you?'

'No, not really. I just got fed up with having to go back the next day to rebuild. So, I took some cement with me. Well, quite lot of cement actually. Then we had to get away quick.'

'What's wrong with a kid enjoying himself on the beach with a bit of diggin' and buildin'?' said Psoddoph, sympathetically.

'Well, these people came, with some officers of the Watch. Well… I'd never 'eard of planning permission, had I?' said Jook.

'Did they make you take it down, then?' asked Psoddoph.

'They tried,' said Jook. 'But it was too late by then… Last I 'eard, they had a couple of hundred soldiers garrisoned in it.'

Florence smiled, but Dennis was not amused. 'Do we have to listen to this nonsense?'

Before anyone could take it any further, the group of riders that had been accompanying Dennis's party, and who'd been keeping their distance, and themselves to themselves until now, changed formation. They rode their horses into a loose circle around the cart and the two guards.

'I think this is far enough,' said the leader, as one of his colleagues grabbed the horse's reins and stopped the cart.

'What do you mean, far enough?' said Dennis.

'We need your horses and the cart,' the man told him, grinning unpleasantly.

'Don't you think we need them?' Dennis challenged him.

'You're in sight of town, now. You can walk,' the man spoke sharply, his patience thin already. 'Now, if you'll just get down…'

Dennis flexed his fingers, but thought better of it when he heard the tell-tale click of a safety catch being released on a crossbow behind him. Jook's hand moved slowly to the hilt of his sword. He never reached it. He was struck on the head from behind. He slumped forward and rolled to the ground.

'Now,' said the leader to Dennis, 'put your hands together behind your back, wizard. We've seen what you can do with them.' Dennis grudgingly complied and felt a loop of twine tighten around his wrists.

The leader peered around him into the cart. 'Hmm. You can leave the flying carpet behind, too. That might fetch a gold.'

'I doubt it,' said Dennis,' It's damaged.'

'And it only responds to 'is voice,' added Psoddoph, hoping they didn't test it. 'So it wouldn't be any good to anyone. But you're welcome to it.' Dennis shot him a look that said: *who's carpet is it?*

'What else are you carrying?'

'Just an old Drum,' said Dennis. 'Also damaged, as you can see.'

'We're taking it to some musicians in the town,' Florence, quickly interrupted, before Dennis had the chance to say something stupid, like the truth.

'Looks like junk we don't need,' said another of the riders, getting a look from his leader very like the one Psoddoph just had from Dennis.

'And that?' said the leader, pointing his sword at the box.

'Teeth!' said Florence, thinking quickly.

'Teeth?' the man repeated. 'Ugh!'

'Old, used teeth,' said Psoddoph. 'There's a mouth doc down town who thinks he can screw 'em into peoples' mouths to replace ones that go bad or drop out.'

Somewhere behind him, someone was being ill.

'I won't ask where you got 'em. I don't think I wanna know. We'll just take the cart and the horses,' said the leader. 'You two! Get that stuff off there.'

Two men dismounted and clambered onto the cart. One of the them carefully helped Florence down and then went back to give Dennis a shove. With his hands tied he fell more than jumped, and was clumsily caught by Florence. They both tumbled onto the roadside.

In a matter seconds the carpet and Drum had been dumped on the ground.

The box of teeth was bolted to the underside of the seat, and was not so promptly unloaded. They had to yell for one of their number, a man who boasted the special skills for dealing this sort of thing. His expertise lay in the size of his biceps, and the crowbar and hammer he wielded. They were lucky the box wasn't shattered – or the seat, for that matter.

Psoddoph, being a soldier, knew he was in a no-win situation, so he calmly stepped down from his horse before he was ordered to, and went to help Jook.

The slap of leather across a horse's back made him look up just in time to see the riders making off with the cart and the horses. Jook had rallied, so Psoddoph hastened to console Florence.

And once Dennis had complained bitterly, Jook picked himself up and went to cut his wrists free.

The travellers sat in silence collecting their thoughts. The luxury of ample transport had been short-lived. But frustrating as that was, they'd managed to hang onto the teeth, which would buy them whatever they needed. And although bruised they were all still alive.

'Didn't you say you'd learned fireballs?' said Dennis, looking accusingly at Florence. 'You could have surprised them, you know.'

'My aim isn't always the best,' she explained, a little hurt. 'And I can't make them quickly enough yet to deal with a lot of attackers at once.'

'In that case, thank you for not trying to help. I really must give you some coaching.'

Silence descended over the group again.

'What time do you think it is, boss?' asked Psoddoph.

Dennis looked up the sun, shielded his eyes from the glare, and raised his other hand and pointed north. He glanced back at Psoddoph. 'You know?' he sighed. 'I haven't the faintest idea.'

'It's mid-afternoon,' Florence obliged. 'Ten past three.'

The guards humoured her until Dennis put them wise.

'How far would you say it is to that town?' Dennis asked.

'About four miles,' said Jook.

'Hmm, about an hour's walk, then,' Dennis mumbled to himself.

The two guards agreed. They would know. Psoddoph rolled the carpet up and slung it over his shoulder. Jook, realising he'd drawn the short straw, sighed and grappled with the Drum.

Dennis began to march off but Florence called him back. 'Do you realise how heavy this thing is?' She stood there with her hands on her hips, waiting for him.

'Ah,' said Dennis, and walked back to help her with the box of teeth.

* * *

44

'I didn't hear you announced,' said King Treadwell, glancing up.

'No, sire, sorry about that, but Thadax seems to be taking so long…' said Ben, who for some reason was having difficulty trying to stand to attention.

'Alright,' sighed Treadwell. 'But don't make a habit of it.'

'No sire,' said Ben, looking down at his boots.

'Alright, stop sulking. I'm king around here and it's my job to tell people off sometimes.'

'Yes, sire,' Ben brightened slightly, knowing his king was always right.

'Now, where's Loosley?'

Another dwarf, identical to Ben stepped out from behind him, grinning all over his face. It was Loosley Speekin, the spy. He thought if he could fool the king, he could fool anybody.

'It worked!' he proclaimed, with a self-congratulatory grin.

'This is Loosley, sire,' said Ben looking away, he was too embarrassed to be associated with him.

Loosley ripped off his false beard. It sounded like a sticking plaster being removed at speed, and from the look on Loosley's face, it was momentarily just as painful. After a few seconds of cursing and rubbing his reddened chin, he bowed before the king. 'Your majesty,' he began, 'I was trying a new disguise; I hope you didn't mind.'

Treadwell smiled. 'Mind? Me? Mind? Of course not.' Then the smile tightened, and he added, 'But if you ever do it again without warning me…' he paused, trying to think of a suitable threat, '… I might just recommend you for a job as a wizard's guinea pig.'

'Sire, don't you mean assistant?' Loosley frowned.

'I said, guinea pig. I *meant* guinea pig.'

Ben and Loosley stood to attention and both spoke at once. 'Right, sire. It won't happen again.'

'Good,' said Treadwell, in a calmer voice. 'Now, let me introduce you to my guests.' He motioned Eydith and Link to come forward.

The sight of them made him take a step back. He was not expecting *big* people to be having an audience with the king.

'Loosley,' said the king. 'I want you to get your spies into the sea towns, the ones with docks…'

'Ports,' Loosley corrected him.

'Ports? Is that what we call them? *Ports*?' The king sat corrected.

'Yes, sire,' replied Loosley.

'Why?'

'Haven't got a bloody clue, sire.'

'No matter. Like I said, I want you to put spies in all the ports,' said the king. There was silence while Loosley waited to hear what else the king might say. Like please, or something. The king remained silent, waiting for Loosley to agree.

Eventually King Treadwell gave in. 'Well, what are you waiting for?'

'I'm waiting for you to tell me why… sire.'

The king was about to launch into a tirade about him not needing to explain himself, but realised the man probably did need to know. 'Er… I've…' he tapped the side of his head a few times. 'I remember, yes. It's a wizard. Name of Dennis. He's stolen young Eydith's Drum – a special sort of Drum, I gather – and I've told her we will help her get it back.'

'I see,' said Loosley, rubbing at the dried beard glue on his face, which was beginning to itch. 'But why go to all that trouble? I could nip out tonight and get her a drum, when the shops are shut, sire.'

'You mean *steal* one?' said Treadwell, with raised eyebrows.

'Yes, sire. Unless the young lady would like something less cumbersome. Like a flute perhaps.'

'Do pay attention, Loosley. It's not any old drum she wants.'

'It's not a *musical* Drum,' Eydith pointed out.

'They seldom are, young lady,' agreed Loosley.

'It's the magical Drum from Havrapsor University,' Eydith told him.

'What? *The* Drum?'

'Yes,' said Eydith, '*the* Drum.

'I see.' The gravity of the situation finally hit home. 'Then I shall despatch my spies to every port this very night,' vowed Loosley.

'Good,' said the king. 'Get on with it then.'

Loosley bowed, straightened, saluted and marched out of the room.

'And keep me informed!' Treadwell called after him.

* * *

45

That same evening, heading for one of those very ports to which Loosley despatched his spies, was a quartet of somewhat fed-up travellers. Dennis, Florence, and the guards trudged along, each immersed in his or her own thoughts. After about a mile, Jook suddenly stopped dead in his tracks and smacked his forehead with the palm of this hand.

'Look, sorry to be a bit of a smart whatsit. But why is Psoddoph *carrying* a carpet that will *carry* us?'

'What?' said Dennis snapping out of his reverie.

Florence and Psoddoph were walking side by side – ostensibly so that with his free hand Psoddoph could take turns with Florence carrying the box with Dennis. They seemed to be lost in one another's thoughts, but they snapped out of it, too.

Psoddoph thumped the carpet down. 'I'm carrying our means of transport!' he said, kicking it to roll it out.

'That does seem to be the case,' Dennis noted, hardly believing it. 'It's been a long day,' he said, by way of exoneration.

Jook paused before getting on. 'You okay to fly it, boss?'

Psoddoph gulped and pulled Florence further away from Jook in case Dennis let fly at him, but she had a better idea and stepped over and stood next to him.

'I'm okay,' said Dennis, this time taking the remark in the context of his tiredness, as it was meant.

They flew slowly, only a few feet from the ground, to the edge of the town, and with only the slightest of near misses, when their approach startled a large white bird idling in the long grass. Its squawking would have woken half the town had they not quite turned in yet.

The party entered the town on foot. It was on the cusp of the day's activities when shops were emptying and closing while bars were opening and filling. They were looking for somewhere to stay the night. Dennis had a number of criteria in mind when selecting a place to stay, but the chief concern of the others while lugging their stuff was that it be somewhere close.

Lights flickered into life on the front of a building on the other side of the street.

'Look, Father,' said Florence, 'a hotel.'

Dennis gave the place a critical once over. It would do, he supposed. He shrugged, huffed and crossed the road. The guards followed a short distance behind. Once inside, Dennis and Florence gently placed the box on the floor. Apart from his party and another man standing in the bar just off reception, the place was empty.

The small counter area had a long sign over it, which read RECEPTOIN. Dennis read it slowly, then read it again, thinking to himself, *have they spelt that right?*

A man appeared behind the counter. He ignored Dennis and started to dust the rows of pigeon holes that lined the back wall.

'Are you ignoring me?' said Dennis.

'I didn't hear you ring the bell, sir,' the clerk replied, abruptly.

'I didn't,' said Dennis.

'Well, there you are then. I'm not a mind reader, am I, sir?'

'I'd guess not,' Dennis agreed, with certainty. 'Are you going to serve me or not?'

'When you ring the bell, sir. We do like to have things done properly.' The man continued dusting.

Dennis slammed his fist down on the bell, and the clerk spun around like a ballerina.

'Good evening, sir. How may I help you?' he said, with a friendly smile.

Dennis looked at Florence. 'Can you believe this?' he hissed.

Florence stepped forward. 'Yes, we're looking for a place to stay for a couple nights.'

'Couple?' said Dennis. 'Let's not be too hasty.'

'Ah, good,' said the clerk. 'You've come to the right place. How many rooms would you like?'

'Three!' blurted Dennis, before Florence got too carried away.

'Three?' The clerk repeated.

'Yes, these two soldiers will be staying as well,' Dennis informed him.

'I see,' said the clerk. He neatly wrote some entries in the great ledger and turned it around. 'Will you sign the register, please, sir?'

Dennis took the quill and scratched his name in the book, then he beckoned Jook.

'Yes, boss?'

'Sign your name,' said Dennis.

Jook picked up the quill, licked the nib, swirled it round in the inkwell and licked it again. Then, with his inky tongue sticking out of the corner of his mouth, he proceeded to draw a very elaborate X.

'Is that it?' said Dennis.

Jook stood back to admire his handiwork, then carefully added a full stop. He nodded his satisfaction and handed the quill to Psoddoph, who drew something long and squiggly, very quickly. Florence added hers, and while doing so she quickly scanned the page to see if she knew any of the other guests. On a previous trip like this, in the town of Prossill, Dennis and his guards had stayed in the same inn as Eydith and Link without being aware of it. But this time all was well.

'Thank you,' said the clerk, turning the ledger around again. He glanced at the signatures, shrugged and without turning his head, reached behind him and took three keys from their pigeon holes. 'Here you are, sir. Top of the stairs turn right, they're all next to each other.'

'How convenient,' said Dennis. He waited for Florence. They picked up the box and walked to the stairs. Psoddoph walked behind them carrying the carpet. Jook picked up the Drum and as he passed the clerk, he grinned broadly.

The clerk looked up and saw him, 'I hope you're not going to play with that thing all night.'

'I haven't made me mind up, yet,' said Jook. 'It depends what time the rest of the band get here.'

Dennis was waiting at the top of the stairs. 'Did you have to say that?'

'It was only a joke, boss,' Jook moaned.

Dennis wasn't in the mood. 'Dump your stuff, first,' he said to everyone, 'and then meet in my room, number eleven. And make absolutely sure you lock your door behind you whenever you go out.'

Jook gave him a worried look.

'The room with two ones on the door,' said the wizard, guessing the problem.

'Ah, right, boss.'

After a brief chat in Dennis's room, Florence headed back to hers – she'd had enough for one day. Dennis told the guards, 'Right, I don't intend to make you stay in here all night. Leave the stuff locked up and go out and enjoy yourselves.' Just as they reached the door, he added, 'Don't get into trouble, and meet me back here at midnight.'

The two guards smiled broadly, 'Yes, boss. Thanks, boss,' said Jook, enthusiastically as they raced to the door.

'And don't be late!' he called after them.

* * *

46

The fire bell clanged, then died away. The Secretary was calling the wizards to assembly and this was the best way to get their attention, short of actually setting fire to one of them. He smiled to himself. He really loved ringing that bell. It was one of the few things the wizards were afraid of – not the bell itself, of course, but what it signified.

This was the second time he'd rung it recently. They used to have occasional fire drills, but they were so badly organised and undisciplined that two of the older wizards were killed in one of the stampedes. Now, should there be a real fire with actual smoke, the nearest staff member to the main gates was charged with opening them and shouting FIRE! in the hope that the citizens will forego any grudges they might have against the wizards and come to help put it out. They'd probably come anyway in winter: there was no point in wasting all that heat.

The Secretary waited patiently for a few minutes, guessing the privies might be working overtime, and then made his way casually to his window overlooking the courtyard. Many had already arrived. 'It's alright!' he called down, 'There's no fire. I just need to speak to you all!'

'You telling us it was a false alarm… *again!?*' one of the wizards yelled up at him.

The Secretary nodded.

'I was in the privy, you bas…'

Rumpitt appeared at the Secretary's shoulder. 'Be quiet! All of you!' he shouted down at them.

The ground rumbled and shook slightly. A tile slid down the roof, causing the watching crowd to shuffle back, but it wedged in the gutter.

Rumpitt cleared his throat. 'Ahem. I asked the Secretary to get you all here to talk to you about the Parallel Dimension!'

'We know all about the Parallel Dimension!' one of the older wizards shouted at him.

'Well, if you're so bloody well-informed, what are you doing about it!' Rumpitt snarled back.

The shouter was about to come back with a clever answer, but found he didn't even have a stupid one, so he looked down at the ground.

'I'll tell you what you're doing!' Rumpitt yelled. 'Nothing! Don't you want to save your university? Your careers? The future of wizardry?'

The crowd fell silent.

'Good! Then listen to the Secretary!'

'I'm impressed,' the Secretary muttered, as Rumpitt stood back to allow him to speak.

The Secretary outlined how he proposed to stop the demons, and called for volunteer group leaders to meet him in his office in ten minutes. Then, before any of them could argue, he slammed the window shut and went to sit behind his desk and wait.

'I doubt if we'll be seeing anybody?' said Rumpitt, back in his comfort zone.

'You never can tell,' the Secretary replied. 'Especially after your rousing little speech.'

'Huh,' he grunted, dismissively.

Then, as if in answer to the Secretary's thoughts, there was a gentle tap on the door. 'Come!' he called. The door opened and a head peered gingerly into the room.

'Come in, come in.' The Secretary stood up. A junior staff member entered the room.

It was Cho, 'I volunteer for group leader,' he said, bowing slightly.

'Good man,' Rumpitt smiled.

'What else I do?' said Cho. 'Someone got to stop those demons.'

There was another tap on the door. 'It's open!' Rumpitt called out.

Three wizards sidled into the room. 'It gets better,' the Secretary remarked, leaning back in his chair.

* * *

47

'We're decided, then,' said Dennis.

'Yes, Father,' said Florence.

'You want us to keep the Drum and await our chance to steal the staff?'

'Yes, Father.'

'And we are to sail to the Boring Islands and wait for our pursuers there?'

'Yes, Father.'

'Right. I'll go and see the clerk and find out where we can hire a boat. Want to come with me?'

'I didn't sleep too well last night. I think I'll stay in my room and have a lie down.' She yawned, enforcing her claim to weariness.

'As you wish. And to be on the safe side, we'll move the box into your room while I'm gone. And I'll make sure the idiots have locked their room before I go.'

She pulled a face telling him he was being a bit hard on them.

*

Downstairs, Dennis hit the bell on the reception desk. The clerk pirouetted round to greet him. 'Oh, it's you again… sir.'

Dennis was beginning to hate the superior way the clerk always paused before saying sir.

'I trust you're finding the rooms to your liking?' This time, there was no sir at all.

'Yes, yes, never mind that now,' said Dennis. 'This town…'

'This is a port, sir. A port.'

'Right, port it is then,' Dennis granted.

'Port Akerbyn, to give it its full title… sir.'

'Alright, alright, perhaps there's somewhere in this… *port*… where I can hire a boat?'

'No… sir. In Port Akerbyn, one does not hire a boat,' the clerk informed him.

'Then how does *one* get to sail on the sea?' Dennis mimicked him, sarcastically.

The clerk would not be drawn and let Dennis's attitude wash over him. 'One *charters* a *ship*… sir.'

'What's the damned difference?' snapped Dennis, getting irritated.

'One *sails* on a ship… sir,' said the clerk, then, adding in a much quieter tone, 'one goes *fishing* on a boat.'

'How do you know I don't want to go fishing?' said Dennis.

'I can tell by your dress… sir.'

'It's a robe!' Dennis corrected him.

'I beg your pardon… *sir*… I can tell by your *robe*, that you are a wizard. Therefore, you would sail,' the clerk insisted, patronisingly.

'Even a wizard might want to go fishing,' Dennis persisted.

'No… *sir*… I think not. And you especially haven't the patience to sit with a rod and line. A wizard such as yourself would use his magic.'

He was irritatingly right. But to get uptight about it would prove the man right about him yet again. Dennis felt the clerk had got the better of him. His mouth opened and closed soundlessly a couple of times. The verbal combat had paused, and it was getting him nowhere. He decided the only way he was going to get anywhere with this man was to be nice to him. Make a friend of him, distasteful as the idea was. Pleasantness was sometimes a useful tactic. He tried again.

'Where would I be able to charter a ship, then, my good man?' he asked, trying to limit the smarminess in his voice. 'You seem to be the best source of information around here.'

'Sir… I know just the chap. Why don't you wait in the bar? He's only next door. I'll send a boy to fetch him.'

His friendliness had worked. *Almost like magic*, he thought. It was a bit like dealing with the carpet, he realised. Maybe the carpet was a metaphor for life? he mused. But he cut himself short. That kind of airy-fairy nonsense was going to get him nowhere. He walked into the bar. The door banged behind him. The room was empty, apart from a bored-looking barman lounging against the counter. He was polishing a glass. The wizard chose a corner table and sat down. The barman stared across, still polishing. Dennis looked away, his attention taken by the décor of the room. Almost everything was red. It looked expensive, but on closer inspection, the redness was only a coat of paint deep.

''Orrible, ennit,' said the barman.

'Sorry?' said Dennis, looking up from his crimson reflection in the table.

'Don't be. It's not your fault,' said the barman. 'I said, it's 'orrible, ennit?'

'What is?' asked Dennis, in all innocence. 'The weather?'

'No. All this red paint.' The barman waved an encompassing arm.

'I've seen worse,' said Dennis, honestly.

'So have I, mate. So have I. Two months ago, it was yellow.'

Dennis didn't answer. He didn't have one.

'He gets it cheap,' the barman told him.

'That accounts for it then, I expect,' said Dennis, looking away again.

'At least, that's what 'e tells me. I reckon it falls off the back of a cart, meself,' said the barman, with an exaggerated wink.

'He must be pretty quick, then,' said Dennis, even more determined not to look the man in the eye.

'What?' queried the barman.

'To get to it before anyone else does,' said Dennis, looking up at the ceiling.

'Oh, yes…' the barman winked again. 'I see what you mean.'

The door swung open and a small boy entered. A large man with a black, bushy beard, followed him in.

'Someone looking to charter a ship?!' the large barrel-of-a-man bellowed.

Dennis looked around the room to see who would reply. 'Oh… yes, me,' called Dennis, pointing a finger in the air.

The bearded man looked up at the ceiling, and apart from a thick coating of soot and nicotine, he couldn't see what Dennis was pointing at. He swayed over to where Dennis was sitting and had another look. Dennis looked as well. He couldn't see anything either, but he was curious. 'Er… excuse me…'

'Yeah?' said the big man.

'What are you looking at?' asked Dennis.

'I don't rightly know, sir. I saw you point up there. I thought you might know.'

Dennis sighed, wondering, *Why are all the stupid people attracted to me*? 'No, I was just trying to attract your attention. I wish to charter a ship.'

'Then you must be the chap I'm looking for,' he beamed, sticking a rough hand out. 'I'm Cap'n Skillet.'

'I'm sure you are,' said Dennis, ignoring the captain's hand, and trying to ignore his irritating zeal. 'How much, and when can we sail?'

The captain pulled up a chair. 'Well now…' he paused, seemingly resisting the urge to say 'me hearty.' 'That depends where you might be wanting to go.'

'Do you know the Boring Islands?' asked Dennis, leaning closer to the captain.

'Course I do, sir. You sails south for about a month, then you slows down and stops.'

Dennis's face held a question.

'Cos I don't want to get too close and hit something, do I?' said Skillet.

'No. Of course not.' Dennis didn't really know what Skillet was talking about.

'How many of you would be wanting to go the Boring Islands, then?'

'Just me and my daughter,' said Dennis. 'And some luggage, of course.'

'Daughter, eh? Well, in that case, we won't sail till the day after tomorrow,' said Skillet.

'Why? Is there some quaint old custom about not sailing – *tomorrow*?'

'Oh, no, sir. Nothing as daft as that. But if the lads know there's going to be a woman on board, I likes 'em to get it out of their systems before we sail. If you know what I mean?'

Dennis shook his head. He didn't have the faintest idea what he meant.

The captain winked. 'A month at sea is a long time, sir.'

In Dennis's mind the proverbial penny dropped, hit the bottom and clanged loudly. 'Let's sail in three days, then,' Dennis suggested. 'Let them really get it out of their systems.'

Captain Skillet laughed in what must have been a raucous, seafaring way and nudged the wizard's arm. 'Aye, aye, sir. Three days it is. We'll sail at midday.' He got up to leave, then thought of something. 'My ship is the *Racing Slug*. It's the smartest ship in the dock, so you can't miss it.' Skillet gave him a loose salute and swaggered out onto the street.

* * *

48

The quartet of volunteer group leaders who'd turned up in the Secretary's office eagerly awaited to hear their assignments.

'Right,' said Cho, jumping in ahead without waiting, 'I go west wing. I try to get others to help.'

'Good man,' said Rumpitt.

Cho's face glowed. That was one of the nicest things that Rumpitt had said to him in a long while.

'I think it will be best if two of you guard the east wing,' said the Secretary. 'That's where the demons seem to be hitting hardest lately.'

Three chins dropped as the remaining wizards wondered which of them would draw these short straws.

'What about the main privy, Secretary?' Rumpitt suggested. 'At the moment, that's looking more important – and *vulnerable* – than anywhere else.' He winked, slyly.

The Secretary leaned back in his chair. 'My word, yes!' he exclaimed, playing along with Rumpitt's game. 'If they blow that up, we're really in the…' His voice trailed off.

At the thought of this even more dire prospect, three chins dropped even further. But then the faces of the two smartest brightened. The short straws weren't so short after all! 'We'll do the *east wing*,' they chorused quickly.

'Really? Well, that's good. I knew I could rely on you. Off you go, then.' The Secretary smiled, thinly. The two wizards hurried out of the room before he could change his mind. Which left just one. Rumpitt smiled kindly at him.

'I'll be off then, too, shall I?' said the young wizard, hopefully, attempting to leave before the job at the privy was assigned to him.

'No, don't go,' said the Secretary, calling him back. 'We don't really need you to guard the privy, do we Rumpitt?'

The old wizard smiled and shook his head. Just then, the air reverberated to the splodgy thump of a rather mucky explosion. Rumpitt, the Secretary and the younger wizard, found themselves standing looking out of a brown-blotched window, surveying the damage.

'Well,' said Rumpitt, waving a much-needed cleansing spell over the glass. 'Not much point guarding it now.'

'No,' the Secretary agreed. 'I doubt there's much to do there. I'll notify the Works Department.'

* * *

49

Loosley Speekin knocked on the door.

A small panel slid back. 'Oh, it's you,' said Thadax, sounding disappointed. He closed the panel and opened the door. 'I'll tell the king you're here.'

'I'll come with you,' said Loosley.

'There's no point in me goin' to tell his majesty you're 'ere if you come wiv me, is there?' Thadax complained.

'Look, Thadax,' Loosley began. 'I know you've got a job to do, but just this once, it's urgent. Alright?'

Thadax sighed. 'Oh, alright. Come on then.'

As soon as the throne-room door was opened, the king looked up. 'It's Loos…' Thadax started to say.

'Ah, Loosley!' the king exclaimed. 'Come on in. How are things progressing?'

Loosley bowed deeply, watching Eydith out of the corner of his eye. 'I think we've found him, sire. In Port Akerbyn. My contact says he's chartered a ship and plans to sail to the Boring Islands.'

'Oh, very good.' The king rubbed his hands together. 'Thadax!'

'Yes, sire?'

'Get Ben in here.'

Thadax slouched out of the room and a few minutes later ushered Ben in.

'Ben, Loosley's found that wizard!' said Treadwell, excitedly. 'I want you to tell Captain Dognettle to round up his crew, or whatever it is he does with them, and sail the *Sea Dragon* to Port Akerbyn and recapture the Drum. Then, I want you to introduce Eydith and whatshisname here to my own wizard chappie with the bright ideas.'

'Yes, sire,' said Ben. He saluted smartly and turned to the door, frantically trying to remember what the king had just said.

'I love a bit of action,' beamed Treadwell, as Ben marched out of sight.

'Thank you for what you're doing, sire,' said Eydith.

'It's the least I can do. I probably owe it to your mother anyway.' Treadwell had a faraway look in his eyes, remembering her mother, and thought he might shed a tear if he wasn't careful.

Ben returned from his errand and waited for Treadwell to call him forward.

The king jolted himself back to the present. 'Ben!'

'Yes, sire?'

'I've decided I want you to go with Eydith… you know, to keep an eye on her, that sort of thing.'

'You're not coming with us, sire?'

The king thought: *not bloody likely, I've seen these wizard fights before.* His battles were best fought on tapestries. 'No, not this time, Ben. I'll stay here and organise reinforcements.' Then quickly added, 'Should you need any, of course.'

'Very good, sire,' said Ben, quietly.

'Now, take Eydith and er… thingy here, to that wizard chappie and let it begin.'

* * *

50

Eydith and Link followed Ben through a maze of passageways. Sometimes they crossed courtyards and sometimes they went underground. Finally, they came out into… well, it could only be described as a room. A very large room, but without a ceiling. It didn't just extend into the loft space; it was open to the sky. In the centre of the room's stone-flagged floor there were two large baskets. One contained a tandem bicycle affair that appeared to be attached by a series of chains and gears to a large propeller, and the other basket was filled with logs. The basket with the logs had another basket made of iron strapped to the top of it. The rest of the room seemed full of wizard. Not that he was overly large, he just appeared to be everywhere at once.

Ben finally managed to attract his attention long enough to slow him down. Then he grabbed him by the arm and stood on his foot to hold him still.

'Alright, you've stopped me. Now, what do you want? Can't you see I'm busy?' he growled.

'I have orders from the king,' said Ben, calmly.

'Oh, what does he want, now?'

'He wants you to transport me and these two people to one of the sea ports,' Ben told him.

'He *does?*' The wizard brightened considerably. 'That's splendid! My flying machine will be ready quite soon, now. We can use that.'

Ben took Eydith by the arm. 'This is Eydith – *with a y*,' he stated, firmly. 'You probably won't remember her. And this is er… what did you say your name was again?'

'You probably won't remember me again, either,' said Link shaking his head while offering to shake the wizard's hand. 'I'm Linkwood. Link.'

'And this is Teeter Gravy,' said Ben, introducing the wizard.

'Hello Eydith, hello Linkwood-Link,' said Teeter, immediately turning away to get on with something more important to him.

Link followed at a respectful distance. He knew from experience that hazards always lurked in another wizard's workshop. He stopped by one of the baskets, peering in and screwing up his nose at the cycle arrangement.

'Something wrong?' asked Teeter, pausing at Link's shoulder.

'I'm not sure,' said Link, scratching his head. 'But I don't see how this thing can possibly fly.'

'Well, today it can't,' Teeter acknowledged. 'When did you want to go?'

'Any time in the next couple of days will do,' said Link.

'I doubt it will fly then, either,' said Teeter. 'A couple of months, perhaps.'

Link whistled through his teeth. 'I don't think we can wait that long. Is there anything I can do to help it along?'

'It goes *along* well enough. It's *up* it doesn't go.' Teeter shrugged.

'Mind if I take a look?' said Link.

Teeter waved his hand in a 'be my guest' gesture.

Link walked around it a couple of times, scratching and shaking his head occasionally. He turned to Teeter, who had found Link's interest in the machine more interesting than what he was working on, and was following him. 'Is there something missing?' Link wondered. 'It looks incomplete.'

'Missing? No. It's over there.' Teeter pointed.

Link saw a great sheet of coloured fabric stretched over the floor. 'Hmm,' he breathed, still not satisfied.

'You seem mechanically-minded, Linkwood-Link. I think you should see my drawings,' urged Teeter, dragging Link over to his desk. 'I call it the 'Ball of Hot Air Thing',' he announced, proudly.

'It won't work,' said Link, flatly.

'Look,' said Teeter, patiently, leading Link back to the baskets, 'this one drives it forward…'

'Yes, I can see that.'

'This one holds the wood, and that one up there is where you light the fire.'

'Fire?' said Link, raising an eyebrow.

'Why, yes. To heat the air,' Teeter explained. 'The heated air rises and fills the balloon.'

'Then what?' Link grinned.

'The whole thing goes up.'

Yes, Link thought, *in flames, I expect.* 'You don't seriously expect this lot to fly?'

'I've been expecting it to fly for months,' Teeter said, plaintively. 'I don't know what's wrong with it.'

'Has it *ever* flown? Even slightly?' Link asked him.

'About two inches for about two seconds.'

'Then what?'

'I would've thought that was obvious,' Teeter replied, raising an eyebrow. 'It landed.'

Link examined the machine again and shook his head.

'What do you think is wrong?' asked Teeter, when Link didn't say anything.

'I think it's way too heavy,' said Link. 'What's that fire basket made of?'

'Iron.'

'Oh, dear.'

'Is that a problem?' asked Teeter.

'Have you tried anything lighter?'

'Yes, but it melted.'

'Well,' said Link, 'I think Eydith and I will go by horse, this time. If you get it working, do let me know. I'd love to see it fly.'

Link started to walk across to Eydith, who'd chosen to hang back with Ben and not crowd the busy man. 'There's no need to go,' Teeter called out, 'I do have another flying machine.'

Link stopped. 'Does it work?'

'Oh, most definitely,' Teeter replied, proudly. 'It's what the king had in mind when he sent you to me, not this one I'm still working on. This way.'

Link followed him to another area of his open-air workshop. Here, a section of the wall was cut away and a long slide was positioned in front of it. The slide was very steep, and the last few yards turned up to point at the sky. Link followed the curve with his eyes, then walked to the gap in the wall. The upward end of the slide extended into thin air over the edge of the cliff behind the castle. The drop was about three hundred feet.

Link turned his gaze inside and looked up at the top of the slide. There was a large white cross perched at the apex, firmly anchored with… well, an anchor.

'Don't look so worried,' said Teeter. 'It will fly,'

'You just said it *did* fly,' Link reminded him.

'Yes, that means it'll fly again,' said Teeter, confidently.

'Have you flown in it?' Link wanted to know.

'Er… no. Not exactly. But my apprentice has.'

'Where is he now?' asked Link.

'In recovery.'

'How many legs did he break?'

'He's only got two.' Teeter smiled, then he added, 'No, he didn't break his legs. In fact, he broke a finger.'

'How?'

'He tripped over the control lever as he was getting out.'

Link felt a surge of relief that blind courage wasn't going to have to play a significant part in this trip. He looked back up at the flying machine. 'How does it go forward, then?' he queried, noticing a distinct lack of anything resembling a propeller.

'Er, it flies on the wind,' explained Teeter.

'What? Like a child's toy?' said Link.

'Exactly,' said Teeter.

'And about as far, I shouldn't wonder,' Link muttered.

'No, if weather conditions are good, it'll go for miles,' Teeter assured him. 'And it's better for longer journeys than a flying carpet. Not that there are many of those around these days. It's more comfortable. More manoeuvrable. More… well, more fun, really. And my apprentice reported that dragons don't chase it like they used to chase carpets.'

'Did he run into dragons out here?' Link was anxious to know.

'No. That's just what I mean. Not a single one.'

Link pulled a face. 'That's probably because there aren't as many dragons around these days, either.'

Teeter conceded it might be the case.

'And how do you make it stop?'

'See that anchor up there?' Teeter pointed. Link nodded. 'Just throw it over the side when you get close to the ground.' As an afterthought, he said, 'Not too close, or it'll be a waste of time.'

Link looked up at it again. 'No, I really think we'll take our horses this time,' he said, quietly but firmly. He walked back to Eydith and Ben who were studying some of Teeter's elaborate drawings that were pinned to the wall.

'Find anything useful?' Eydith asked.

'No.' Link shook his head. 'He's got a couple of flying machines, but one doesn't and the other one's uncontrollable.'

'Show me,' said Eydith.

'Okay,' said Link, shrugging his shoulders. 'But I think you'll agree.'

She gave the 'Ball of Hot Air Thing' a cursory glance and carried on past. Teeter scuttled along behind her. Then she saw the big white cross perched at the top of its slide and silently admitted to herself that Link might be right. It didn't look safe. But it looked nowhere near as dangerous as the Ball of Hot Air Thing.

'How does that one work?' she asked Link, and he explained. 'How does it stop?' He told her his misgivings about the anchor. She sighed deeply, and thought, *Will we be able to fly it, Sprag?*

Sprag looked at it through her eyes. He glowed momentarily. 'It's not impossible, mistress,' he replied into her mind.

But what about the wind? she wondered.

'You'll just have to try and control yourself, mistress.'

Eydith ignored him. Was it an attempt at humour? She doubted it. But Sprag wasn't that obtuse, either.

'I apologise, mistress,' he wheezed, as she tightened her grip.

'Sprag says we can use it, Link.'

'But…' He had a list of objections that he guessed were going to be swept aside. 'Oh, all right,' he agreed, but only with his head: his heart wasn't in it one bit. 'When can we try it out?'

'There's no *trying*, about it,' Teeter interrupted. 'It's a case of up anchor and away!'

'We don't get a chance to practice, then?' said Link, glumly.

'We'll be alright,' Eydith reassured him. 'And we'll have Sprag.' She saw Teeter nodding vigorously.

Link shrugged. 'Okay, if you've made your mind up. I'll just have to come with you, then. Won't I?' It helped to know that in an emergency they could both hang onto Sprag and drift down. He noticed a pale blue light flickering along the staff in Eydith's hand, as if it had heard him. Hardly the soft orange glow it gave off when it was pleased with something, though.

'Don't worry,' she said, squeezing his hand.

Link had one of those unwizardly feelings again.

'Come on,' said Eydith. 'Let's go and tell the king we're leaving.'

Ben went to Teeter, 'You'd better put an extra seat in that thing,' he rasped, 'and if anyone gets killed in it, you're in deep sh… trouble.'

Teeter raised his hands as if to say, 'Don't worry.'

* * *

51

Much later that day – late evening, in fact – Dennis returned to the hotel.

'Everything all right, sir?' the clerk asked.

'It'll do,' Dennis muttered as he walked past. He reached the bottom of the stairs and paused, 'Er… where would be the best place to get some entertainment in this… er…'

'Port, sir?'

'Right – port,' Dennis remembered. 'If I were, say, a sailor?'

'Ah, but sir is *not* a sailor, is he?' the clerk pointed out.

'No,' said Dennis, 'but let's suppose I were. Where would I go?'

The clerk hesitated. He knew only too well where *he'd* go if *he* were a sailor. In fact, he went there anyway, all the time. 'Er… there's a place down Onion Street…' He hesitated again. 'You can't miss it… there's a big red light outside, over the front door.'

'And where will I find Onion Street?' he persisted.

'Well, if you're really sure, sir.'

'Yes, yes, I'm sure,' said Dennis.

The clerk took a deep breath. 'Out the front door, turn left, end of the street, and left again. Very easy to find.'

'Thank you,' Dennis murmured. He threw his cloak around his shoulders and made for the door. 'Left, then left again, right?'

The clerk had trouble with that, and chose to nod politely.

Dennis went out into the night. It had turned slightly chillier, and he walked briskly to the end of the street. He reached the corner and glanced up at the street sign. 'Onion Street,' he read aloud. 'Good!'

About halfway along he saw the red light the clerk had mentioned. The place wasn't as big as Dennis imagined or hoped, but nevertheless it would do. He stood at the bottom of the steps leading to the front door, taking in the place. Not that the portico gave much away. He straightened his collar, went up and pushed the door. It opened as silently as a well-oiled curtain. He checked to make sure the street was empty, as he didn't want to be recognised, and went inside.

There was a bar in one corner of the room and tables with highly-polished, copper tops spread around. The straight-backed chairs looked comfortably padded, and at various intervals around the wall there were overstuffed armchairs and a sofa. A few sailors stood at the bar and some occupied the large armchairs, and apart from one or two of them, they all seemed to be in the company of scantily-clad young women. He noticed a desk tucked away around a corner by a door. A plumpish woman sat behind it. She wore a shiny, green, low-cut dress, and what Dennis couldn't help thinking looked like the remains of a colourful dead bird on her head.

She gave Dennis a quick smile. He hoped that was free, at least.

'Hello, dearie,' she cooed. 'Have you come to party?'

Dennis didn't think so, so he took a couple steps closer. 'Party? Sorry, miss, I wouldn't want to gate-crash someone's party,' he apologised.

'Madam,' she corrected him.

'Again, I'm sorry. I didn't realise you had a title.'

'Title? What are you talking about, dearie, that's my job description? Anyway, it's always party time here.'

'Er… do I need an invite?' he wondered.

'Was the front door open?'

'Yes.'

'Then you've already received it,' she smiled.

Dennis relaxed.

'Now, what's your pleasure, sir?'

'Er… wine, I think. Yes, wine will be fine.'

'Well, that's at the drinks bar,' she smiled, 'over there.' She indicated the bar in the opposite corner.

'What are *you* selling, then?' he asked, in all innocence.

'Pleasure, sir. For half a silver, you can take your pick.'

Dennis's mind and face held a thousand questions. The madam leant forward, filling his sinuses with her perfume and his eyes with acres of pink, bare flesh. 'Is this your first time, dearie?' she whispered, saving his embarrassment.

Dennis hadn't lived a sheltered life; he'd lived more of a distracted one. Having belatedly woken up to his situation, he couldn't think of an answer that wouldn't embarrass him. 'Er…' he stammered. 'Look, I only just got here. I'll have a drink at the bar first, then I'll come back.' He grinned nervously and tried not to break into a trot.

'Hello, boss,' said Jook, cheerfully. 'I didn't think we'd see you in 'ere.'

'Likewise,' said Dennis. 'And now we're leaving.'

'But, boss, we can't go yet,' Psoddoph complained.

'Give me one good reason,' said Dennis.

'Well… um… we've already paid.'

'What?'

'Yes, boss, sorry.'

'Sorry?'

'Yes, boss. We're not leaving till we've partied,' said Psoddoph, flatly.

'Are you refusing to obey a direct order?' said Dennis, incredulously.

'Yes, boss. You said we could 'ave the night off, remember? So, we're 'avin it off.'

'In that case, I might not need your services at all,' Dennis threatened.

'Can't we talk about it in the morning, boss?' said Psoddoph, calmly.

Just then, two of the establishment's girls came over and stood by the guards, each sliding an arm around them.

'It's party time,' grinned Jook. 'Why don't you stay and enjoy yourself, boss?'

Dennis cast a critical eye over the girls. 'Are they all like these?'

'No, boss,' said Jook. 'These are the ugly ones. They're all we can afford.'

The girls nodded, happily confirming Jook's statement.

Ugly? thought Dennis, *These girls are* ugly? *They're two of the most attractive women I've seen in a very long time.* 'I'll think about it,' he muttered, quietly.

Jook and Psoddoph made their way to the stairs at the side of the bar, each with a giggling girl on his arm.

Dennis stared at the empty staircase for a few moments more then turned to the barman. 'Give me a wine,' he requested, despondently.

'Okay, sir. Anything to oblige.' He assumed a miserable expression, and said, in a weary voice, 'Weather's bloody miserable again for the time of year, ennit?'

Dennis sighed, decided he'd had enough, and left.

* * *

52

'You're back early, sir,' the clerk remarked, when Dennis walked back into the hotel. 'Was it not to your liking?'

Dennis scowled, 'You didn't tell me it was *that* sort of place.'

'I thought it might be just the place you were looking for, sir, what with you going away for so long.'

'Now, where can I find Captain Skillet at this time of day?'

'Night, sir,' the clerk corrected him. 'When it's dark outside, we say, *this time of night*, sir.'

'I know how light it is out there,' Dennis argued.

'No, sir. Wrong again. It's *dark*.'

Dennis was getting more annoyed. 'Look, I don't want to argue with you, man. I haven't the time or patience. Now, are you going to tell me where he is or not?'

'Pity, sir, I do so look forward to our little tête a têtes. You're the only resident who hasn't resorted to… ouch! I was going to say physical violence. Now, if you'll just release my neck, sir, I'll tell you.'

Dennis eased his grip, but he didn't let go. 'Good,' he hissed.

The clerk's heels came back into contact with the floor again.

'Well? Come on then,' Dennis snapped, finally releasing his grip.

'He'll be at the tavern across the road,' the clerk replied, massaging his throat.

'Thank you.' Dennis turned to leave, then stopped. 'Do you have a strong room?'

'Best you ever saw, sir.'

'I would like to make use of it,' said Dennis.

'Yes, sir. It's through here.'

'Good,' said Dennis. 'In my daughter's room, you will find a drum. I want you to get it and lock it away until I ask you to deliver it. Understand?'

'Perfectly, sir. I'll do it now.'

'And if my daughter's asleep, wake her up and tell her to help you. Then give her the key.'

'Don't worry. As I said, I'll deal with it now,' said the clerk, lifting the counter flap.

Dennis threw his cloak around his shoulders and went back out onto the street. Then he headed for Onion Street.

*

Jook and Psoddoph were in the bar. Dennis spotted them and headed over.

'Hello, boss,' grinned Jook. 'Changed your mind?'

'No,' said Dennis. 'I've come to see if you're ready to leave yet.'

'When are we sailing, then, boss?' asked Psoddoph, leaning back against the bar.

The barman leaned closer, trying to hear what was going on.

'Three days,' whispered Dennis.

'*Three* days?' replied Jook, noisily. 'And you're asking us to leave now?'

'Keep your voice down,' hissed Dennis. 'I don't want everyone knowing my business.'

'Well, I'm sorry, boss, but if we're leaving in three days, there's no way you're gonna see us till the day after tomorrow at the earliest,' said Psoddoph.

The barman nodded in agreement.

'In that case,' said Dennis. 'I'm dispensing with your services.'

'Yeah? Is that right?' said Jook. 'You've got to get us 'ome you know.'

'No, I haven't,' Dennis countered. 'You're disobeying my instructions. I don't have to do anything.' He threw his cloak around his shoulders and strode out onto the street. Then, he went to find the tavern that Captain Skillet would be using.

'Now what are we gonna do?' sighed Jook.

'Don't worry,' said the barman, who was an habitual eavesdropper. 'I have contacts… What's your immediate problem my friends?'

'After tonight?' said Psoddoph, 'We're pretty much out of money.'

'In the morning, I will introduce you to a man who needs some help,' the barman whispered, conspiratorially, lest anyone was eavesdropping.

* * *

53

'This is terrible,' moaned Pelgrum, standing outside the partly-demolished privy.

'What? The smell?' replied Rumpitt.

'In part, yes,' said Pelgrum. 'But I was actually referring to the state of the privies.'

Rumpitt looked around. The books were getting a bit thin, he noticed, but not desperate yet. He tentatively pulled a rusting chain. It clanged, gurgled, then flushed. No telling where to. 'Nothing wrong with that,' he reckoned, with a certain amount of satisfaction.

'It's the doors,' said Pelgrum, quietly.

'What doors?'

'Exactly.'

'Ah… yes, I see what you mean. Or rather I don't, if you get what I mean.' Rumpitt grinned. 'I expect they'll turn up.' He was being uncharacteristically upbeat today. Probably because his self-generated pessimism couldn't compete with the reality of the moment, so he wasn't bothering with it at all. 'We'll just have to use the privies in pairs, that's all. At least we'll find out who our *real* friends are.'

Pelgrum was not amused. 'I'm going to find one of the carpenter chappies,' he decided, as he cautiously picked his way over the rubble.

*

The university rocked again. The point of origin was beneath the west wing.

'Blow that bloody whistle!' yelled Cho. 'They're coming up in here!'

The wizard with the whistle didn't need telling twice. In fact, he had it to his lips before Cho had finished shouting.

A small green head with two horns, one a bit loose, peered out of the hole. The wizard in charge of the whistle blew harder and louder this time. The demon clapped his clawed hands over his ears and screamed. A moment later he disappeared back down the hole.

'What's the matter now?' groaned Hell.

The demon lowered his claws. 'That bloody well 'urt me ears, your kingship,' he growled.

'It's only a whistle,' snapped Hell.

'It wasn't only that, your royalness, I smacked me 'ead, too. But never mind, it's goin' off now.'

'Get back up there and sort that wizard out, now!' stormed Hell. And to show he meant business he punctuated each word with a poke in the demon's chest with his shiny new trident.

The demon snarled for effect and stuck his head out of the hole again. A moment later he ducked back down, his face blackened with soot and his loose horn leaning the other way. 'Sod it!' he cursed. 'He caught me wiv a fireball, your kingship.' Upon which, the charred demon fell back and collapsed like an ironing board.

'That's it!' raged Hell. 'I've 'ad it up to *'ere* wiv these wizards!' He started forwards, but tottered back, slightly stunned from a self-inflicted smack to the bridge of his nose, delivered while indicating just how far he'd had it up to.

'You alright, your kingness?' said the small green, slightly charred demon, staggering to his feet.

'I'm bloody livid! That's what I am!' Hell snarled, cuffing the tears from his streaming eyes. 'C'mon,' he said, lowering himself down the shaft they'd created, 'Let's get some more demons up 'ere, and do this again. We'll 'it 'em with four or five at a time.'

The two demons slunk back down to the Parallel Dimension, muttering threats and curses.

Cho peered gingerly into the hole and saw the demon who'd just started to follow his king down. He hurled a fireball down at him and counted quietly to himself… *two, three*! There was a small explosion followed by a pain-filled scream. Cho smirked. 'Got you, you little green bugger.'

He stood up and scraped the heap of loose stones back into the hole with the side of his pointy-toed shoe. Seconds later, he heard, 'Ooh… ouch! I'll get you for that!' as Hell was peppered with rubble from above.

Cho rubbed his hands together and sat down to wait.

'It might not be so easy next time, Cho,' one of the other wizards warned him. 'Now they know what they're up against.'

'Perhaps not. We see,' said Cho.

Just then, Pelgrum arrived, puffing and panting. 'I heard the whistle,' he wheezed, 'is everything alright?'

'No problem,' said Cho.

'Oh, good.' Pelgrum continued to breathe heavily and sat down.

The rumbling started again, more violently this time.

The demons in the Parallel Dimension were really getting it together now, and a long split opened up in one of the outer walls of the east wing.

'Oh, dear,' Pelgrum sighed. 'They've started on my section now… hold on men, I'm on my way!' the plump wizard struggled to his feet and scuttled away.

Cho was left wondering why the buildings themselves didn't retaliate, as they had after the last battle some months ago. That would help. But then it occurred to him that the university was more passive-aggressive than outright offensive, which wouldn't help much in this case. But at least the place could repair itself when all this was over.

* * *

54

In Teeter's workshop, it was almost time for the flight of his glider. Link followed Eydith up the ladder to the top of the slide. Ben was already waiting on the platform. 'Where do you want to sit my lady?' he asked, referring to Eydith in a more respectful manner, now, but before she could open her mouth...

Link said, 'In the front. She'll be steering.'

Eydith looked down at Ben and shrugged. Ben sighed audibly and stomped to the front seat and began removing his stuff. Battle-axes, clubs, swords and metal polish (for his armour) were thrown out onto the platform.

'Do you really think you'll need all that stuff?' asked Link, scratching his head.

'I've only brought my best stuff,' countered Ben.

'Haven't you got anything lighter? If you must take weapons,' said Link, bending down to sort through what he'd got, 'what about this?'

'A sling shot?' Ben sneered.

'Why not?' said Link. 'It's light and it's quick.'

'I'm not very good with it,' Ben admitted.

Link flexed his fingers and muttered something under his breath. Sparks crackled from his fingers and coruscated along the strips of leather. 'It shouldn't let you down, now,' Link promised.

'Really?' Ben smiled at it. 'Can I just take this as well?' he pleaded.

'All right, but that's all,' said Eydith. 'If it makes you feel better.'

'A lot better, my lady. I feel naked without it.' Ben tossed his battle-axe onto the back seat and jumped in after it. Eydith stepped onto the front seat and sat down, wedging Sprag down beside her.

'You are coming with us, I trust?' she challenged Link playfully, because he was hanging back.

'Well... if you're ready.' He sighed, as he climbed in behind her.

Teeter's head appeared at the top of the ladder, 'I see you're all ready and eager, then.'

'No, not really,' said Link. 'But you might as well let this thing go, anyway.'

'I'm not letting it go until you all put those safety belts on,' said Teeter. 'You don't want to fall out, do you?'

'No. But I can assure you it won't make me feel any safer,' he moaned.

Teeter ignored him and turned his attention to Eydith. 'So, you're to be the pilot. Wise choice.' Eydith nodded and smiled nervously. 'Well,' he continued, 'this stick thing here is all the controls you need. Push it forward… to go down. Pull it back… to go up…'

'With a bit of luck,' muttered Link.

'Push it to the left…'

'I think I've got it,' said Eydith. 'How do I stop it?'

'You'll work it out,' said Teeter, vaguely. 'It's all about working with the air currents. Once you get the feel of it… there's nothing to it… or so I'm told,' he said, doing what he could to reassure her, though not pulling it off. 'Now, are we all ready? Good.' With that, he unhooked the anchor and dropped it into Ben's lap. If it hadn't been for his chain mail tunic and a hidden item of armour beneath it, Ben might well have been in considerable pain. Then, Teeter gave the whole thing a push with his foot.

The flying machine tipped forward. Eydith instinctively pulled the stick back. Ben lurched forward and knocked himself out cold on the metal rim on the back of Link's seat. Link muttered something unseemly and cast a spell that filled the air with something that smelt as though it had been dead for a very long time. Most unplanned of all, though, was the buckle on one of Teeter's sandals catching on something sticking out at the back of the flying machine. He only managed to save himself from falling off the platform by grabbing hold of the tail plane.

The machine gathered speed a lot faster than Teeter expected, due to the extra weight it was carrying. It rapidly reached the bottom of the slide and started the upward phase of the take-off. The rattling sound of the loose undercarriage on the rails stopped suddenly. The only sound now was the whoosh of the wind as the glider leapt into the air like a salmon.

Using Eydith's eyes, Sprag saw that they had immediately gone into a steep descent and the ground was getting closer by the second.

'Pull up mistress!' He screamed into her mind. She responded immediately, although she didn't really need telling. Only seconds from the impact, she pulled the stick back and the glider soared skyward again.

'That was *too* close,' breathed Link, holding onto his hat with his free hand.

'Is everyone okay?' Eydith called, over her shoulder.

'Yes,' replied Link, but the silence behind him, made him turn around. 'Ben's okay, as well. He's asleep.'

Then, unexpectedly, came another voice from the rear. 'Can you hold on a minute?' called Teeter. 'I've got a bit of a problem.'

'What?' gasped Link, his head almost spinning off. 'Eydith!' he yelled. 'Teeter's caught on the tail! He's hanging on!'

A painful moan emanated from the back seat. Ben was coming round.

Link called back to him, 'Ben! Wake up! Teeter's caught up behind you!' Ben rubbed his forehead, then peered nervously over his shoulder. There was Teeter, grimly hanging on.

'You, silly bugger!' snapped Ben. 'Get off!' He stood up with his battle-axe in his hand, then promptly sat down again when the restraining belt stopped him. He twisted round and called Teeter a silly bugger again.

'What are we going to do!?' Link shouted to Eydith.

'I'm thinking!' she yelled back.

'Don't take too long about it!' Teeter moaned, loudly.

'What can we do, Sprag?'

'We can't land, mistress; we'll never get airborne again.'

'We could fly over the castle and drop him on the roof?' she suggested.

'Probably our best chance, mistress. And his, I expect.'

'What if I chopped 'is 'ands off, my lady?' suggested Ben.

'If we get him close enough to the roof and he doesn't let go, Ben, you can do it then.'

'I'll let go… I promise! Just hurry up. I'm losing my grip!' yelled Teeter.

Ben turned to see if he could help Teeter in any way, after all he wasn't too far away to grab his hand. Eydith cast around to see where the castle was. It was on her left and up a bit. She pushed the stick to the left and the glider banked steeply. Teeter screamed in panic as he slid alongside and below where Ben was sitting. The glider started to rise, caught in the updraught from the cliff face.

Ben reached down beside his seat and lifted out his battle-axe. 'No! Not yet!' Teeter yelled.

'I'm not gonna chop your 'ands off. Stop panicking and grab hold of the end!' shouted Ben. 'I'll try to pull you in.'

The glider struggled to gain height at first, but, as it climbed it found more uplift. A moment later, it loomed over the battlements. 'Let him go, Ben!' Eydith shouted, urgently. There was a crumpled thud as Teeter landed, tumbling dangerously on the narrow ledge behind the wall. He sat up, hardly believing he was still alive, and watched his machine fly off. The glider, now much lighter and more aerodynamic, responded well to Eydith's control stick and soared into the sky.

***

55

The next morning, the sun was up and melting the ribbons of mist drifting in off the sea as Dennis and Florence walked down to the docks. Gulls screamed and wheeled overhead exalting in the sheer joy of flight, it seemed. And, as sometimes happens, when one is looking up at the sky instead of where one is walking, that's when one treads in something.

Dennis didn't see it. Mind you, he didn't actually tread in it either. He slid forward in it, like someone making their first faltering steps when learning to ice-skate. Florence was taken by surprise, too. One of Dennis's flailing arms caught her on the shoulder as he struggled in vain to stay upright.

Luckily, two burly seamen were passing by at the time. Florence thought they looked familiar, but was put off at first by the clothes they were wearing. Seeing the wizard on the ground, they moved quickly to his aid and pulled him back to his feet.

'Thank you, my good fellows,' Dennis puffed.

'No problem, bo… er, me hearty!' boomed a vaguely familiar voice.

Dennis looked into the face of each man in turn, noting that one of them had a moustache drawn on his upper lip with what looked like boot polish, and the other one wore an eye patch with a hole in it. 'Can't let 'im walk around like this… er, miss, can we?' said eye-patch.

Florence grinned. 'No,' she said, eyeing the mucky white stain on her father's robe. 'Do you know somewhere where we can take him to get cleaned up, er… sailor?'

'No need to be formal, miss. I'm Groundsel,' said alias Psoddoph. 'Poor old chap seems to have slipped on the, um, that *stuff*,' he grinned to himself. 'Seems to have quite a bit of it on 'im, too.' He caught the distaste with which Dennis was staring at his besmirched robe. 'Tell you what – there's a shop back there where they'll sort him out.'

A few steps along the street, they found the place: Little Jack's Outfitters. Once inside, Dennis was steered to a rack of clothes that were mainly his size. It was just a matter of picking a robe he liked that looked suitably wizardly and changing into it. He also needed to get his own robe cleaned.

'Find anything you fancy, sir?' asked Jack, circling around his potential customer. Noticing he was addressing a wizard he plucked a robe off the rail and held it up. 'This one's very popular these days, sir. On account of all the pockets in it, I expect.'

Dennis looked at it slightly bemused. *You can't be serious*, he thought.

'Look at all the sequins, sir. And all these bits of gold braid. And the tassels hanging from the shoulders, and, dare I mention them again… all those pockets, sir.' Jack paused for breath, and to give the wizard a moment to think, then added, 'You know, sir, I'd bet this robe's got pockets that haven't even been discovered yet.'

Dennis was impressed. He hadn't heard so much plausible garbage in years. He strutted up and down the shop admiring himself in the mirrors that lined the walls. Mirrors that were not so much for the customers' benefit as they were for the management to see if anyone was trying to sneak out without paying.

'It seems a bit on the short side?' said Dennis, noticing the colour of his socks between his pointy-toed shoes and the hem of the robe.

'Ah… er… that's why they're so popular, sir,' Jack stammered, trying to come up with a quick explanation. 'It'll soon reach the ground when you fill the pockets.'

Dennis hadn't considered that, and bowed to Jack's superior knowledge of gentlemen's outfitting. Florence remarked how smart he looked, adding. 'And it's so much fresher than the old one.' Dennis strutted a little more, and on impulse added a second robe to his purchase. He'd remembered he didn't much like shopping for clothes, so this was an opportunity to save himself some future aggravation. Florence picked up a cloak that she liked for herself.

The wizard paid with the change he'd forgotten to give back to Florence when he bought the horse and cart. Not quite as much as Little Jack expected, but he *did* pay. And the owner was not too upset because, after all, he hadn't planned on selling Dennis more than one robe, and thought he was never going to shift that elaborate one with all the pockets.

Dennis and Florence left the shop. Out on the sunlit street, Dennis warily surveyed the pavement. 'Where to now, Father?'

'Find somewhere to get this robe cleaned,' he muttered, holding up the bag that Jack had kindly given him.

'Sounds like a job for an expert,' she said, grinning. 'Preferably one with no sense of smell.'

Back in Little Jack's shop, Jook the sailor had slipped in. He sighed with relief. 'I didn't think 'e was gonna buy that robe, you know, Jack. But *two* – plus the cloak for the girl – that's gotta be worth a bonus, I reckon.'

Sailor Psoddoph nodded in support. Jack reluctantly gave them both a small silver coin.

Outside, Jook rubbed his hands together. 'We seem to 'ave landed on our feet 'ere.'

'Yeah. And what a good thing Dennis didn't!' said Psoddoph, raising a laugh. 'What shall we spend it on?'

Jook's brain purred gently as he floated various ideas. 'What about a couple of ales down at that inn we saw… *The Swineherd's Arms*, I think it's called… and then paying another visit to those nice girls down Onion Street.'

'Excellent idea,' said Psoddoph. 'No point in wasting it.'

Jack stood in his shop doorway and watched the two phoney sailors disappear down the street. When they were out of sight he shrugged and went back inside. He went out to the back of the shop where he kept his dogs, and gave them a plate of curry. They wouldn't normally have eaten yesterday's leftovers, but he told them it was next door's cat.

Dogs can be very stupid, thought next door's cat, watching them from the wall.

* * *

56

'Did you recognise those two sailors, Father?' asked Florence, as they strolled along the street, half looking for a cleaner and not seeing one.

'Right from the beginning,' said Dennis. 'Trying to worm their way back into my affections, I expect.'

'I thought you were a bit harsh with them,' she told him.

'Harsh? Certainly not. They'll come back, you'll see,' he said, with confidence. 'I wouldn't be surprised if they're waiting by the ship.'

'Do you think they'll have loaded our stuff?' Florence wondered.

'I expect so. Well… everything except the Drum. I told the clerk at the hotel to bring it just before we sailed.'

Captain Skillet was waiting by the gangplank. When he saw Dennis and Florence he almost stood to attention. Just straightening his back was his usual concession.

'Everything ready, Captain?' asked Dennis, trying to sound professional.

'Aye, sir. Everything's loaded.' Then he bent forward and whispered in Dennis's ear, 'Except the Drum, o'course, sir. You said you'd be dealing with that yourself.'

'Good man,' said Dennis. 'You remembered. We'll sail just as soon as it arrives.'

'Aye, aye, sir!' Skillet saluted.

Dennis strode up the plank and looked around the ship. Something was wrong. He couldn't quite put his finger on it, so he surveyed the scene again. Then he spotted it, or rather he didn't. It was something very important, and made all the more conspicuous by its absence. He turned to the captain. 'Do you intend to sail this ship on your own, Captain?' he ventured.

Skillet slapped his forehead. 'I *knew* there was something I 'ad to do, sir. Just couldn't put me finger on it.'

'Well,' Dennis prompted him, 'go and put a finger on some of your men.'

'Er, they'll be down the *Swineherd's Arms*, sir. Give me a few minutes.' Captain Skillet loped off down the road back into town.

*

Inside the *Swineherd's Arms*, there were a couple of new faces. Chickweed and Groundsel, alias Jook and Psoddoph, were eagerly spending some of their well-earned bonus. Skillet pushed the door open and stood with his back to the street. He didn't speak, he didn't have to. The men that made up his crew recognised his large silhouette against the sunlight. They drained their tankards and filed out past him. He counted them. He was still two crewmen short. He went back into the bar with three burly sailors a pace behind him.

The captain raised his hand and the men stopped where they were, folded their arms across their chests and waited while their captain looked around at the faces in the bar.

When he was short on crew, he knew he could always rely on a couple of ne'er do wells turning up on cue, and there was a likely looking pair in the bar right now. He hadn't seen them before. They looked strong enough, though probably not too well equipped in the head – just the job, in fact.

He strolled almost casually through the sparse crowd towards them. Someone tapped him on the shoulder as he past. He turned and came face to face with a pretty girl. She wasn't wearing a vest, he noticed. *Oh, dear*, he thought, *it's one of those women my mother warned me about. And today of all bloody days, just when I haven't got time.*

'Hello, sailor,' she breathed in his ear. 'Want something new?'

Skillet gave it some thought, 'I haven't got time right now.'

'Damn!' she muttered, and wandered off to look for another client.

Skillet continued his slow walk across the sea of sawdust that covered the floor, homing in on his quarry. 'Looking for a job, lads?' he asked, genially.

'No,' replied Jook. 'We got a bonus this morning. We won't be needing a job till tomo…'

His sentence was cut short. And a second later, Psoddoph also slumped forward. They'd been press-ganged.

Captain Skillet was a happy man. The ship's compliment was now up to scratch and he was ready to sail. Jook and Psoddoph were half dragged, half carried, and unceremoniously dumped onto the benches that lined the hull of the ship, each bench having its own private porthole complete with a stout pole poking through it.

The two guards were hit with buckets of cold water, which brought them both back to their senses. 'We're on a bloody ship!' said Jook.

Psoddoph wiped the water from his eyes and took in his surroundings. 'I know I said we'd 'ave a couple of ales and then go oaring, but this isn't what I 'ad in mind.'

A shadow blocked his view of the sky for a moment as someone walked by carrying Dennis's drum. 'What's the drum for?' Psoddoph asked the man on the opposite bench. The Drum looked familiar, but he wasn't sure.

'That's for beating the stroke, *darling*,' he replied in a sort of fluting voice that Psoddoph was unfamiliar with. 'When he bangs it, you dip your oar in the water. And when he bangs it again, you take it out.' After a few moments of silence, he added, 'Oh yes… and when he shouts STOP! You dig your oar in the water and hold on tight.' He winked.

Psoddoph looked at Jook, 'I'm gonna keep an eye on 'im,' he muttered.

'He's all right,' grinned Jook. 'Give the man a break. I don't think it's compulsory.'

*

A couple of hours later, the *Racing Slug* was ploughing through the waves ahead of a strong breeze. The regular crew were making the most of the opportunity to row steadily to the slow thump of the Drum. They knew that if they were becalmed, they would have to earn their keep with some *hard* rowing. They'd done some of that in the past, particularly when the captain got it into his head to take up water-skiing. Trying to row a two-masted sailing ship at thirty knots was no joke. It was only when the captain realised how long it took the ship to turn and come back for him after he'd fallen off, that he gave it up.

A shout from the look-out in the crow's nest broke the monotony of the rowing. But nobody took any notice till he shouted again. By this time, he'd clambered down and reached the deck, and was running up and down pointing anxiously up ahead.

The great crested head of the *Sea Dragon* reared out of the water a hundred yards directly in the path of the *Racing Slug*.

'STOP ROWING!' yelled Captain Skillet, just as all the oars entered the water.

There was a lot of shouting and cursing, as men were knocked from their benches onto the laps of the men behind. Most were angry, but there were some who thought their luck had changed.

Some of the crew sprang to their feet and rushed to pull down the sails, as the wind was taking them straight at the *Sea Dragon*. Others leant on their oars as hard as they could, digging them into the sea in an effort to slow or stop the ship.

The drummer at the prow was thrown into the sea, and he took the Drum with him. Using the drum-hammers as paddles as best he could, he was propelling himself back to the comparative safety of the *Racing Slug*. His efforts were futile. The *Sea Dragon's* lookout had seen him thrashing about in the water, and was determined to put an end to that bloody monotonous drumming he'd heard on their approach, once and for all. The drummer paddled faster. Then he paddled faster still, until he could get no more speed out of the Drum. Then, in sheer terror at the sight of the *Sea Dragon* bearing down on him, he hopped off the Drum and ran as fast as he could across the water on an invisible downward staircase, and wishing he'd used the privy before he left home that morning.

The great head of the *Sea Dragon* bent slowly forward and picked up the Drum, tilted its head back and swallowed, then slowly turned and moved away to the distant horizon.

* * *

57

'Why did you pick up that stupid drum?' asked Captain Dognettle, watching the old instrument being lowered into the hold.

Dognettle was captain of the *Sea Dragon*. He was heading for Port Akerbyn, on assignment from King Treadwell, to intercept Dennis and recapture a drum. Though this last part of his mission seemed to have eluded him for the moment. The ship, which was fashioned in the style of a huge dragon – hence the name – was almost a submarine. The designers hadn't yet discovered a safe way to compress air, so it wasn't fully submersible. Though air was pumped from the raised dragon's head to supply the underwater body of the vessel. The head also served as a lookout post and a crane. It's chief function, however, was to be as scary as possible.

'You told me to grab anything that looked valuable, Cap'n,' said Crimpett, the lookout. 'And in my opinion, Cap'n, it was that. Yes, sir.'

The captain thought it over. It was true, he had told Crimpett to pick up anything box shaped that looked *valuable*. Not a battered old drum, especially. Though Crimpett had unwittingly picked up the very prize that Dognettle had been looking for.

'When we get back to port, you're gonna get your eyes seen to. We must have the only par-blind lookout on the entire royal fleet.'

Which was true. Though Crimpett didn't like to say that the *Sea Dragon was* the entire royal fleet. And he wasn't bothered by all the name calling and threats Dognettle used, just so long as he could work the crane. He loved operating the crane. But the lookout part of his job was losing its appeal, not to mention becoming bloody dangerous because of his failing eyesight. Dognettle liked to think of the *Sea Dragon* as the *Terror of the Seas*, and with Crimpett's poor vision the accolade was becoming ever closer to the truth.

It was all bravado, though. Dognettle didn't actually want to kill anyone, apart from Crimpett sometimes. Or sink any ships. He knew that such actions would bring heavily armed ships after him. And King Treadwell would not be happy with that – though, if it came to it, Treadwell would probably be the least of Dognettle's problems.

Crimpett loved being in the head of the *Sea Dragon*, operating the levers that opened and closed its jaws and lifted its head, like the great big crane that it was. It was the best toy a grown-up kid could possibly have. And there, at his side, was a tube with a whistle in it. This was his connection to the engine room. There were two large propellers at the stern, which drove the ship forward, each with an independent drive to enable steering. And from the sides of the ship, flippers could be extruded to act as brakes in an emergency. In the engine room was the biggest clockwork motor ever made, and it took two of Dognettle's strongest men to turn the key that wound it up.

When Crimpett had safely landed the Drum, he helped seaman Lampitt carry it down into the hold. The captain watched them, tut-tutting at the pointlessness of stowing this useless thing. He was about to step in and order them to take it back on deck and throw it overboard when he and Crimpett had a sudden shared moment of insight. *Wasn't an old drum one of the things they were supposed to be looking out for?* They paused and held eye-contact briefly, each reading the other's thought.

'Carry on,' said Dognettle, evenly.

'Aye, aye, aye, Captain,' returned Crimpett, with a knowing smirk.

'Two ayes will do, Crimpett.'

He was about to reply: yeah, but not my two, but thought better of it.

Seeing it close up, Crimpett saw the drum was very old and had been patched and repaired many times. He thought it odd that King Treadwell would bother with a load of old junk like this. Surely he could get himself a new drum if he wanted one. Unless, of course, this one was something special. Dognettle had it taken up to his cabin.

* * *

58

Havrapsor University had been quiet for a couple of days. Hell had been occupied trying to work out how to get through the floors without the wizards noticing, and that was proving difficult.

The wizards had organised themselves into working groups, and whilst they weren't actually winning, neither were Hell and his demons.

'So you think they'll be back?' asked Pelgrum.

'No doubt about it,' replied Rumpitt. 'Just as soon as they've regrouped.'

As if on cue, the last remaining window of the west wing rattled from its frame and smashed onto the floor. The assembled wizards stared at one another in turn. Rumpitt broke the silence. 'There, told you so.'

The wizard tasked with blowing the alarm whistle blew a long blast that ended in a fit of coughing. Rumpitt, in an effort to stop his ears ringing after the whistle went silent, banged the sides of his head, though gently, of course. He picked up his staff and followed the Secretary outside.

'Out here to inspect the damage?' asked Rumpitt, looking up at the remaining crenulations on the university's towers.

'Not really,' said the Secretary. 'I just didn't want to be in there if the bloody roof came down.' A few feet in front of him, the ground welled up and a small green demon poked his head out and squinted at the sun. The hole widened and another head appeared at his side.

'Aren't you going to do…'

Rumpitt raised his staff as the Secretary spoke and muttered something under his breath. Blue sparks coruscated along his staff, and when they reached its tip, exploded in a streak of white lightning. The instant before it reached the demons, it divided and struck them both simultaneously, reducing them to a boiling puddle of gunge.

'… something?' the Secretary concluded.

Rumpitt wore a satisfied smirk. He was old, but he could still produce the goods.

'I'm impressed,' the Secretary remarked. And after a thoughtful pause, he said, 'Do you realise, in all the years I've known you, I don't think I've ever seen you do that sort of magic before.'

'Saving it,' said Rumpitt, quietly. 'And I don't usually need to zap the students – much as I feel like it, sometimes.'

Another demon gingerly peered over the edge of the hole, saw the mess and called back down, 'The soddin' wizards 'ave killed 'em… your kingliness!'

This time Rumpitt raised a shaped hand at the demon. The demon saw him, but Rumpitt was quicker. The searing and perfectly aimed bolt of lightning stopped at the top of the hole as the demon ducked, then followed it down. A few moments later came the sound of two voices cursing their luck, and wizards generally.

* * *

59

'Good thing you brought some food,' said Link. 'We've been up here for days, now.' He was exaggerating because he was irritable. The cramped flight in the glider had become a bit of a chore.

'One and a bit days,' said Eydith. 'Okay, almost two,' she conceded.

It wasn't so bad for her. Her mind was occupied with flying the glider. With Sprag's help she had become moderately skilful at it. Even her landings and take-offs were improving. Though Link and Ben still hung on tightly and closed their eyes when she brought them down on the upper slope of a hill or a mountain side, which she had to, to make launching the machine possible again. She was also adept at finding high places to land that had some foliage close by for privacy. Ben had pointed out the funnels that Teeter had installed by the seats for long flights 'for elimination', as he called it. Eydith had eliminated hers by disconnecting it and throwing it out. Link followed suit. There was no way...

On some stops they found small streams running down from melting snow and ice higher up the mountain. The water was ice-cold but drinkable, and okay for basic washing. Ben played the hardened soldier and affected to disdain all this stopping and resting, but he was invariably the last and hardest to wake whenever they napped.

'Not much further,' said Eydith, who had the best view at the front. 'I can see the sea – and a town.'

'Any idea where we are, Ben?' Link called over his shoulder.

'Nope,' said Ben, scratching his helmet rather than his head. 'Never seen it from up here before.'

Sprag buzzed into Eydith's mind. 'I think you should begin the landing procedure now, mistress. I fear I may be the only one among us who will float.'

Eydith hastily scanned the terrain below and saw a likely hill for landing. She flew over the hill, banked sharply, and approached it from the other side. She swooped low, aiming for the base of the hill, and, when she was close, she pulled the stick back hard and followed the slope upwards, allowing the glider to gradually slow and drop onto the hillside. It was more of a planned stall than a landing, but it did the trick. And it meant not using the anchor, which had proved dangerous.

'There, that wasn't so bad, was it?' said Eydith, with a noticeable tremble in her voice, but a look that suggested if either of them disagreed, they would be in serious trouble. Link and Ben remained silent, at least until she changed the subject.

She stepped a little shakily out of the glider and looked around. True to her usual form, there was a small wooded area on the slope below them. This time, though, it was needed more for hiding the glider than providing cover for a comfort break. And looking over the descending treetops Eydith could see the sea. A ship of sorts was being rowed into the port.

'I've not seen the likes of that before,' said Link, shielding his eyes from the sun.

'I can't even see the sea,' moaned Ben.

Without thinking, Link bent down and put his hands under Ben's arms to lift him high enough to see over the treetops. Nothing happened. It was like trying to lift a ton of lead. Link didn't try a second time. He looked Ben up and down, or rather down and further down, and wondered just how heavy his armour was, even without the battle-axe. He also wondered how the glider ever got off the ground. 'You'll have to wait until we get closer, then,' he had to tell him.

The idea of hiding the glider in the woods was abandoned when Sprag told them they'd have to drag it up the hill again to obtain enough height to get it airborne. Eydith solved the problem with a cloaking spell. It would last for only a day or so, but Sprag and Link were impressed. Ben just thought it was what wizards did.

Eydith picked up Sprag and the three of them ambled down the hill.

* * *

60

Dennis sat at the stern of the ship with his head in his hands. Florence put what she thought was a comforting hand on his shoulder.

'Don't cry, Father,' she whispered. 'It could happen to anyone.'

'Yes, but it happened to me,' he moaned. 'It *always* happens to me.'

Florence used to wonder how someone so detached and calculating as Dennis could be so sensitive sometimes. She'd worked it out that while he had very little pity for others, he had plenty for himself. But it somehow gave her hope for him. She saw it as the seeds of something decent that might be nurtured into something more inclusive of others. Even if they still wouldn't buy a used cart from him.

'Look, when we get back to the port, we'll get some men and go and search for it,' she said, trying to console him.

'Yes, I've still got the…' he lowered his voice for the word, '… diamonds.' His mood brightened. 'Yes, that's it, we'll get Chickweed and Groundsel, or whatever they're calling themselves these days. They can find me a ship and then I'll hunt those damn pirates down.'

'You'll have to ask them first, Father,'

'*Ask them*? Don't be foolish, child. That won't do any good. I'll have to do something drastic, I expect, like offering them *money*,' snapped Dennis, rallying perfectly. 'Though I could threaten to tell their Sergeant, when we get back, that they defected to the navy while they were with me, and any back-pay they're due should be docked accordingly.'

'Father!' she bridled. 'I hope you're not serious! And what's so wrong with giving them money?'

'I don't have any.'

Florence considered that. 'How did you pay Captain Skillet, then?' she wondered.

'Ah, I didn't. I hypnotised him into thinking I had, and he quite happily put an empty box in his safe.'

Florence frowned. 'What did you think was going to happen when he finds out?'

'I didn't think we'd be around by then.'

'Where's his safe?'

'At his lodgings.'

'That's all right then.' She was momentarily relieved. 'He won't find out until he gets home.'

Dennis smirked, annoyingly. 'Shouldn't think so.'

*

Without a drummer on the *Racing Slug* to beat the rhythm, the rowing was a bit erratic. The oars occasionally clattered into each other. And because the starboard rowers were getting fewer strokes in than the port rowers, the ship had almost completed a wide circle. Apart from shouting himself hoarse, there was little the captain could do about it.

As the vessel was about to embark on its second circuit of the same stretch of water, he had an idea. *After all*, he thought, *I'm the captain. Someone else can shout themselves hoarse.* 'That man there!'

The oarsmen looked at one another, perplexed, who could the captain mean? He seemed to be looking directly at Psoddoph, who took no notice. *Can't mean me*, he thought, *I'm not doing anything wrong. I dip the end in, pull on it and take it out again.*

'You there!' Captain Skillet called again, this time pointing unmistakably at Psoddoph. He finally twigged it was him, and stood up.

'Yes, sir?' Psoddoph replied, standing to attention, but still holding onto the oar.

'Come up here!'

Psoddoph released the oar and stepped forward. The oar slipped through the port-hole and plopped into the sea. Psoddoph looked down, and all he could say was, 'Oh.'

'Never mind that!' the captain yelled. 'Get up here!'

Psoddoph sheepishly reported to Skillet and saluted, more out of habit than respect. 'Sorry, sir. It was an accident.'

Captain Skillet shrugged it off. 'Well now,' he said, looking down his nose at him. 'Being as how you've got nothing else to do, now,' he cast his eyes at the oar drifting away on the swell, 'I have a job for you.'

'Yes, sir?' said Psoddoph, dutifully yet somehow non-committedly.

When Skillet told him what he wanted, Psoddoph's eyes sparkled at the thought of all that power. Jook saw him light up from his seat among the rowers, and rolled his own eyes.

He stood and faced the crew, cupped his hands around his mouth and bellowed at the top of his voice, 'STOP ROWING MEN!'

The crew stopped their hopelessly unsynchronised efforts and leaned on their oars.

As a soldier, Psoddoph had developed a feel for keeping time from all his parade-ground marching. 'Now,' he started, as he walked down the centre board of the ship with his hands clasped behind his back. 'When I say IN – you will plunge your oars in and pull. And when I say OUT – you will lift them up and into position for the next IN. Understand?' Nobody said no; but then, nobody said yes either. Though there were plenty of resentful looks from sailors who thought he was talking to them as if they were bloody idiots. 'Ready?' he asked in a quieter tone. 'Good. After three.' He counted slowly, then gave the order. The ship began to move smoothly again, and the helmsman steered it back to port at a slow march.

* * *

61

'Back again so soon, sir?' The clerk smiled disingenuously as Dennis walked back into the hotel lobby.

'Shuddup!' snapped Dennis.

'Father!' said Florence. 'It's not his fault.'

'Well...' Dennis whined. To him it was everyone's fault.

Florence smiled sweetly at the clerk. 'Do you still have three rooms?'

The clerk looked past them at the two guards. He examined his rows of keys, then checked his register. 'For how long?' he asked, without looking up.

She looked at Dennis. He shrugged.

'Two nights?' she asked.

The clerk ran his finger down the register again and whistled tunelessly through his teeth. 'All I can offer is one night,' he said at last.

'We'll take it,' snapped Dennis. The clerk gave him the keys and told him where to go. Jook and Psoddoph picked up the carpet, and Dennis and Florence picked up the box and the bag of clothes he'd bought in Little Jack's. They all traipsed upstairs.

Dennis laid down heavily on the bed and sighed. 'We need that Drum.'

'We'll get it back, Father,' Florence reassured him.

'How? Eh... tell me how.'

'I've still got my staff,' she pointed out.

Dennis swung his legs over the side of the bed and sat up. With everything else going on he'd forgotten about that. 'Of course!' he punched his palm with excitement. 'The *demons*.' Then he calmed down and thought about it more rationally. 'I wonder what he'll want this time.'

'Who?'

'Hell, of course.'

'Well, whatever he wants, we'll only offer him half.' Florence grinned mischievously, and anyone who knew them would have picked up a family likeness at that moment.

'We'll leave first thing in the morning and look for somewhere else to stay,' said Dennis, 'I don't want Hell wrecking this place.'

'That's a good point,' agreed Florence, recalling the demolition that usually accompanied a visit. 'And I expect Captain Skillet knows we're here by now as well.'

'I'd forgotten about him,' murmured Dennis. 'I wonder how long that hypnosis will last.'

'About as long as it takes him to try and pay his crew with non-existent money, I should think.' Florence shook her head at him. 'Shall I tell the guards what's happening, Father?'

'No,' said Dennis, absently. 'Let's surprise them with it in the morning.'

* * *

'Nice town,' remarked Link, as they walked through what must have been the main street. As the pedantic receptionist at one of the local hotels would have pointed out, this was not a town, it was a port. It was Port Akerbyn. Eydith was enthusiastic, too. But Ben remained silent as he stared open-mouthed at the multitude of coloured shop-fronts and stalls that lined the roadsides. He was also taking in the aromas of the food stalls and the noise of all the stallholders doing their best to outshout their neighbours in an effort to sell their wares. It could be said fairly of Ben that he didn't get out much.

Ben gawped at a mountain troll, as it lumbered by. It was big by most people's reckoning, but for someone Ben's size, it was enormous. He gave it a wide berth, as he did the groups of teenage barbarian dwarfs who were larking around in the milling crowds. He could have dispatched them easily with his battle axe, but their parents would have had something to say about that.

As the trio walked by a tavern, Ben paused to welcome the familiar aromas of fermentation into his nostrils. 'Fancy a drink, my lady?' he asked, craning his neck to look up at Eydith.

'What a good idea,' said Link, before she could think otherwise.

Inside the tavern, the bar was brightly lit with oil lamps and candles. The walls and ceilings had gone a very expensive shade of banana yellow from the tons of tobacco and other herbs that had been smoked in there over the years. Even now, yellow-grey smoke curled around the room.

Ben marched purposefully up to the bar, but even standing on the foot rail he was unable to attract the barman's attention. Link slapped a coin down on the counter and waited. But not for long. At the sound of money, the barman was there. 'Two ales, and a lemonade,' said Link, cheerfully. There was a tugging on Link's robe at about knee height. He looked down to see Ben looking up at him with a very serious expression on his face.

'Make that, three ales,' he whispered.

'The lemonade's for Eydith,' Link whispered, back.

'Oh,' said Ben.

Link picked up his change, studied it for a moment, shrugged and shoved it in his pocket. *No sense starting an argument on my first day in town*, he thought. He passed a tankard down to Ben, picked up the other two drinks and followed Eydith to a table.

At the next table was a man with a bushy red-beard. He stared at them for a little longer than is polite when they sat down, and then stared into the bottom of his tankard.

'Well,' said Ben, having slaked his thirst with a long gulp of ale, 'where shall we start the search?'

'Here is probably as good a place as any,' said Eydith, not wasting any time. She scanned the bar and could feel Sprag using her eyes. When the red-bearded man at the next table came into view, he noticeably shifted on his seat as if he felt her gaze.

'That man knows something mistress. I sense it.' The words went directly into her mind, but before Eydith could respond mentally, the man began trying to attract Link's attention.

'Psst…' he hissed.

Link ignored him, as you do when some oddball in a bar tries to talk to you. And, as usual, it didn't work.

Red-beard leaned towards him and whispered out of the corner of his mouth. 'I'm looking for someone… a girl with a wizard.'

Link frowned, and before he could stop himself, said, 'A girl with a wizard what?'

'Just a wizard,' conveyed red-beard, still in hushed tones, and looking about him furtively. 'You two almost fit the description.'

'Could that be because I'm *obviously* a wizard?' suggested Link. 'And she, is *definitely* a girl.'

'Well, I've got a message. Do you know…' he moved even closer to Link and whispered, 'Loosley Speekin?'

Eydith and Ben also leaned in to catch the conversation.

'I might,' Link replied, guardedly.

'I work for him,' whispered red-beard.

'Yes, all right. We know him.'

'Good. That means you're Link.' He brightened visibly, and then contained himself, feeling the need for discretion. 'I'm Greasy…

Greasy Spot.' He held out a hand. Link looked at it. It was empty, but it looked as if the man had spent the morning cleaning axles. 'Oh,' said Greasy, mildly embarrassed, 'Sorry about that. I've been cleaning axles.'

'What's the message?' asked Eydith, leaning in.

Greasy put his hands to his forehead and thought. 'Ah, that was it?' he said, lowering his hands and leaving two oily smudges on his brow. Then he said, quietly and meaningfully, though conveying very little meaning, 'The poor man fills the beggar's bowl.'

'What?' Link frowned.

'The *poor man fills the beggar's bowl*!' Greasy repeated, glancing around in case someone overheard.

Link looked at Eydith and shrugged. 'Don't mean a thing to me.'

'What about, *the flapping butterfly causes hurricanes*?'

'Nope.'

Ben chimed in, 'What about if I chopped a bit of 'im off, my lady?' he volunteered, lowering his hand to his battle-axe.

'I don't think that'll help,' said Eydith, chiding him.

'Ah,' said Greasy, at last, 'Yours must be, *Dennis is in port*.'

'Now *that*, I understand,' said Link. 'Whereabouts?'

'Hotel on Lamping Street. You can't miss it, it's the only one there.'

Link noticed that Greasy's tankard was empty. 'Can I get you another drink?'

Greasy held up a grimy hand. 'No thanks, I'm on duty now.'

'You're with the Watch, then?' asked Eydith.

'No, I'm a spy,' Greasy whispered, getting up from the table. At his full height, Greasy Spot was only marginally taller than when he was sitting down. He reached up and took his helmet off the chair next to him, and rammed it on his head just in time to protect it when it came into contact with the edge of the table. There was a sound like a small gong being struck and he reeled slightly from the impact. He shook his head, adjusted his battle-axe, and marched stiffly to the door. 'I'll be in touch,' he mouthed over his shoulder, as he went out onto the street.

* * *

Next day, Dennis woke early, before the others. He dressed quickly and snuck down the back stairs into the alley behind the hotel. Getting his bearings, he chose the direction that would lead out of the town.

He walked a little beyond the streets and buildings of the port, and followed a track across fields that still sparkled with the early morning dew. After about a mile and a half, he found himself skirting a wood to his left. Nestling on the edge of the wood was a small cottage covered in so much ivy he almost missed it. He looked around to make sure he was alone, and went to take a closer look.

The cottage was derelict, but not in such disrepair that he couldn't use it. It still had a door, and most of its windows, and a roof that was in a fairly good condition. He gently tested the door. It swung back slowly, then the top hinge snapped. The door opened only a few more inches before it twisted and fell to the floor, raising a cloud of dust.

This'll do, he thought, *for a few days anyway. Get the door fixed, sweep up a bit… Florence can do that.* He heaved the door upright and wedged it firmly against the frame. He'd considered using a restoration spell to put it back as it was, but realised it would then fall off in exactly the same way the next time he opened it. A few moments later, as he went to leave, he said, 'Bugger,' and climbed out through a window.

He didn't hurry back. It was close to mid-morning when he reached the hotel. The clerk was busy shuffling papers and the wizard slid past unnoticed. He went first to Florence's room.

He found her looking out of the window overlooking the street. She turned when she heard the door. 'Father, where have you been?'

'I've found a place about half an hour's walk from here. Get the stuff ready. I'll get the other two.' He crept along the hallway to the next room and listened at the door. There were sounds coming from inside, but one was definitely *not* a man's voice. It quickly dawned on him what was going on. Red-faced, he crept to the door of the room on the *other* side of his. That was more promising. He could hear the snoring of the two guards. The key was in the lock on the outside. Huffing at their inattention to security, he pushed the door open and stepped inside. Then slammed it shut as hard as he could.

Both men awoke at the same time, reaching for their swords as they scrambled into life. 'Oh, it's you, boss.' Psoddoph yawned, and returned his sword to its scabbard. Jook just sat there on autopilot.

'Come on,' hissed Dennis. 'We're leaving.'

The two guards stretched and forced their legs to move. 'Back door, boss?' said Psoddoph.

'Er… yes,' said Dennis. 'But first pick up the stuff in my room.'

They followed him back to his room and collected the box of troll's teeth and the carpet, then crept behind him along the hallway to the back stairs.

'Where we goin', boss?' asked Jook.

'I've found a nice little place just outside of town,' said Dennis, giving him half the truth.

*

Half an hour later – 'Is that *it*?' Jook moaned, as he surveyed the rundown, ivy-covered ruin.

'Yes,' said Dennis. 'I knew you'd like it.'

'But, boss, it's a dump,' Jook complained.

'I think it'll do, Father,' said Florence, quietly. 'I don't think there's much more that can happen to it.'

Psoddoph pushed the door. It didn't move so he shoved it harder.

'Careful!' warned Dennis, 'It's not…'

The door crashed to the ground.

'… very secure.'

'It's alright, boss, I'm not hurt,' said Psoddoph, failing to elicit any concern. 'We'll just wait out here then, shall we?'

Dennis stepped over the door, muttering an antique tidying-up spell as he went in, magically transporting the dust and grime of years to another dimension. Dennis really knew how to hone his spells when he put his mind to it.

'Now you can come in,' he said, lacing it with inevitable sarcasm.

'You did a good job there, boss,' Psoddoph complimented him. Then he thought, *I would have put money on him getting Florence to do that.*

'Put the box over there by the fireplace,' said Dennis. 'And the carpet... lay it on the floor. And stay out of the way. Both of you.' The two guards sauntered to a neutral corner and sat down.

'Are you ready?' said Dennis.

'Yes, Father.'

'Right, let's do it.'

* * *

64

'Right, you lot!' snapped Hell, as he paced along the line of five demons who were standing almost to attention in front of him. 'This time we're goin' to 'it 'em where it really 'urts.'

'What… in the soft bits, your embarrassments?' enthused a smirking, rather non-descript brown demon.

'The word is your *eminence*, you uncouth twit,' snapped Hell. 'And no, I didn't mean their soft bits. I meant that library of theirs.'

'What's the point of that, your eminence? We ain't got time to read nuffin'.'

'Or the brains, either,' he snarled, close-up in the face of the offender. 'All their magic's got from them books,' said Hell. 'If we destroy their books, they won't 'ave any magic.'

'Ah… Gottit,' said the brown demon, tapping the side of his nose. 'Then we won't get our 'eads blown off, kinda fing.'

Hell remained silent, waiting for the usual, 'your kinkiness,' or something, but it didn't come. 'Yes, go on,' he prompted.

'What?' said the demon.

'What? What do you mean, what? What about, 'your royalness?' that's what!'

'Ah… yes, sorry, *your royalness*, your royalness.'

Hell was beginning to glaze over. 'Right… now…'

Just as Hell was about to give them his next set of instructions, he got the call he'd been dreading. In fact, he was hoping that Dennis had forgotten all about him. 'Damn,' he muttered. 'That bugger's rubbed the staff.' He thrust a clawed hand to his head, then banged his ear. He didn't know why he bothered; the summoning siren wasn't going to stop until he found out what Dennis wanted. 'You!' he shouted at the brown demon, 'Come with me. You four stay 'ere till I send for you, understand?'

'Yes, your royalness,' they chorused, slowly and out of sync.

'Where are we going, your highly thingy?' the brown demon asked, as he moved to his master's side.

'To answer a call,' snapped Hell. 'Now, give me your hand.'

The demon held out his clawed hand and Hell grasped it firmly. The king then recited the spell that would take him to the staff. As usual, he forgot a part of it, and they arrived in a tunnel two hundred yards from where he wanted to be. Hell cursed the staff and crouched down while he waited for his head to stop spinning from his collision with the tunnel wall.

'Is this it? Your highly embarrassedment?' the brown demon whispered.

'Does it look like it?' moaned Hell.

'How'd I know? I've never been where we're going,' the demon replied. 'Come to think of it, you've never invited me out before, your bigheartedness.'

Hell sprang to his feet before the smaller demon could read anything more into the circumstances. Then he realised something. 'You can let go of my hand now,' he said, shaking himself free.

'Sorry, you're not-so-friendly-as-I-thought-ness,' said the demon, sullenly. 'But when you grabbed my 'and like that… and we ran away together… I just thought…'

'Well, don't *think*, alright!' said Hell, nervously. 'That shouldn't be too much of a problem for you.'

'You mean it's over between us already?' The demon sniffed.

'Shut up and come with me, you idiot.'

'Now where?' He grudgingly offered his hand again in readiness.

'Up,' said Hell, pointing up the tunnel, and, as he did so, catching a whiff of something unpleasant from his claw. 'Where 'ave you 'ad your 'and?' he demanded, realising it was the hand that had held Brown's.

'Er… places,' the demon said, evasively, as he put his hand to his nose and sniffed. 'Yuk!' He frowned and screwed up his nose. He wiped the hand somewhere behind him, and trudged up the narrow tunnel behind his kingship.

* * *

65

'You'd think he'd be here by now, wouldn't you?' Dennis griped, impatiently.

'I expect he'll be here as soon as he can, Father,' said Florence. 'He's king now, remember.'

'I'm sure he'll remind me. This really won't do.' A few moments later, a rumbling started and Dennis stood up quickly. 'He's coming!'

Florence joined him in the middle of the room. 'You two!' he shouted to the guards. 'Pick up the stuff and get outside. Quickly!'

The guards scrambled to their feet, grabbed the box and hurried to the door.

Florence glanced nervously at each wall in turn, trying to guess which one Hell would demolish when he eventually arrived. The rumbling grew louder by the second. Suddenly, part of the ceiling caved in and two very surprised demons fell to the floor, choking and cursing, in great billows of ancient dust.

As the dust settled, Hell staggered to his knees, coughing as hard as he could to clear his throat.

'Where have you been?' snapped Dennis, standing over him.

'We got lost, all right? I don't make a habit of falling through ceilings you know,' Hell growled, defiantly.

'Don't start *already*, you two,' pleaded Florence, trying to calm the situation.

'Well…' Dennis moaned. 'There's just no urgency with him, is there?'

'We got 'ere as fast as we could,' said Hell, defensively. 'It's a long way from Kra-Pton.'

'Hold it right there,' said Dennis. 'Did you just say *we*? I only summoned you, you know.'

'I've only got young Brown wiv me. 'E's me messenger,' Hell told him. He pulled the smaller demon out of the dust. It coughed as it came into the fresh air again, then politely extended a clawed hand to Dennis.

'Allo, your wizardlyness,' he said, brightly.

Dennis looked at the clawed hand and, thinking he caught a whiff of something, ignored it.

'Suit yourself,' said Brown, slightly miffed, and wiped something only he could see down the scales on his right leg.

'Well?' said Hell, standing with his hands on his hips, glaring up at Dennis.

'Well what?' said Dennis.

'What 'ave you summoned me for this time? Only we are busy you know.'

'The Drum's been stolen from me. By pirates,' said Dennis. 'I need some assistance getting it back.'

'Not again!' said Hell, despairing of the wizard's incompetence. 'Can't you look after anything?'

'We didn't see them coming,' said Dennis, ignoring Hell's attitude for the moment. They attacked us in a bloody great ship that looked like a dragon. They just plucked the Drum out of the water.'

'You were *sinking*?'

'No. The captain put the brakes on, or whatever it is that captains do, and the Drum went overboard.'

'Awful,' interrupted the brown demon.

'Nobody's talking to you,' said Hell.

'Sorry, I'm sure, your incontinence.'

Hell wasn't sure what that meant, but he took it as a compliment. 'Anyway,' he said, turning back to Dennis. 'When do you want me to start? Only we're busy right now.'

'Actually, right now would be a good time,' said Dennis.

The King of the Parallel Dimension whistled through his teeth. 'Bit short notice, ennit. As I said, we're real busy.'

'What else can you possibly have to do that's more important?' Dennis sneered.

'Well, at the moment we're trying to knock down the wizards' big buildin' at Kra-Pton.'

'What? Havrapsor?'

The brown demon looked a bit embarrassed. The pie he'd eaten earlier had just got vocal.

Dennis looked at him with a pained expression.

Then something clicked in Hell's tiny mind. 'Yeah, that's it… the university.'

Dennis sighed. 'Why are you knocking it down?'

'I 'ad this dream, see…' He looked oddly wistful for a moment. 'At the end of this dream – I decided it would be nice to rule the surface world as well. But those bloody wizards keep 'itting my demons wiv fireballs. So, I reckoned that if we took the magic away from them, then… *hey presto!…* if you'll pardon the expression… no more wizards.'

'This dream…' said Dennis.

'Yeah?'

'Did you actually see yourself leading your demons through the cities of the surface world?' Dennis looked and sounded deadly serious when he put this to the king, signalling that the demon needed to be very careful about what he said next.

Hell did think before answering, though neither long nor deeply. 'No, not really. I was leading them out of the chippies on Stove Pipe corner.'

'I see,' Dennis murmured, thinking: *I'm a master wizard; the surface world is to be mine.* But he held back. For now, he wanted the king's help, so the role of false friend was more useful to him. And for the moment, the wizards at Havrapsor would have to fend for themselves – *and rue the day they lost his leadership*, he told himself. 'Well perhaps we can help each other,' he suggested.

'Ah, a deal,' said Hell.

'Yes,' said Dennis, 'if you like.'

'I'll think about it,' said Hell.

'First,' said Dennis. 'You will find these pirates and get my Drum back.'

Hell snarled. 'You'd fink that now I'm king I'd be free of this bloody job!' He angrily slammed a wall and put his fist through it. 'I'm gonna find a way to give this job of Demon of the Staff to someone else. Someone like Brown, here.' He glared at the thing and it flinched. 'Let him get the siren summonses. There has to be a way.'

'It probably means making a deal, a trade, with the staff's owner, or current possessor. Florence or myself,' said Dennis, smoothly, seeing himself firmly in control.

Hell looked deflated. 'Yeah, maybe we can make a deal.'

'Perhaps.' Dennis nodded, though with absolutely no intention of letting the king off the hook that easily. It was hard to tell which of the two was more demonic at times.

* * *

66

The Drum lay on its side in a corner of Dognettle's cabin. He sat staring at it mystified, thinking: *Why does Treadwell want it? It looks like it's been mended more times than a poor man's socks. Perhaps it is worth something, but it's not my idea of treasure. But word will soon reach him that I've got it, and if I don't deliver it to him before long, he'll be sending someone to look for it.*

He considered his situation. He was, at the moment, captain of a very fast and fierce-looking vessel. He had a fairly reliable crew. The wages were regular and he only answered to the king. Against all that, he was trying to weigh the unknown. *Is it worth scarpering with this old Drum? How much is the thing worth? Was this an opportunity not to be missed? I'm getting a regular wage, yeah,* he thought, *but poor. Very poor. That bloody chief spy gets more than I do. That's not fair.*

There was a knock on his cabin door. He swung his feet off the desk and picked up his quill. 'Come in!' he called, pretending to be distracted from something important. Lampitt entered the cabin. 'Yes? What is it?' asked Dognettle.

Lampitt looked around the cabin and saw nothing out of the ordinary. 'Well… it must be me, Cap'n.' He was at a loss.

'Okay, let's try that again,' said Dognettle. 'What is it what you want?'

'I came to tell you, Cap'n, that we'll be docking in Port Akerbyn in five minutes.'

Dognettle swung his chair round. 'That ship we took the Drum from…'

'Yes, Cap'n?'

'Has it arrived yet?'

'Yes, Cap'n.'

'Hmm,' breathed Dognettle. 'In that case, sail up the coast another mile and we'll go ashore there.'

'B… B… But there's no dock up there, Cap'n,' Lampitt argued.

'Can you swim, Lampitt? Or do you think you can find the rowing boat?' said Dognettle, with menace in his voice. 'We don't need to *dock*, stupid. We drop anchor and row ashore. Are you new at this, or something?'

'I know exactly where the rowing boat is, Captain,' said Lampitt, levelly.

'I knew I could rely on you, Lampitt. Now tell those engineers to give the key another couple of turns. And let me know when we get there.'

'Aye, aye, sir.' Lampitt sighed almost audibly. He casually saluted and stepped outside, then angrily slammed the door behind him, ignoring whatever was shouted after him.

*

It was almost dark when Lampitt rowed the small boat across to the beach. Dognettle jumped ashore from the prow, leaving Lampitt to step into the water and drag the boat onto the sand. He muttered something under his breath as the other two crew members stepped off. 'Yer know,' he growled, 'it would be nice if I wasn't the only one round 'ere with something to do.'

'Shut up and get on with it,' rasped a young sailor with a patch over his left eye. He was unoriginally known to the rest of the crew as One-Eye. Nobody knew his real name as he never shared it. If anyone asked, he'd punch them in the face and tell them to mind their own business. At least, that's the polite way of putting it. He was just bad tempered. Very bad tempered. And as if to prove the point, he whacked Lampitt on his ear as he walked by.

The fourth member of the group had a wooden leg and a nasty habit of resting the foot end on other people's toes. He couldn't fathom why they complained so, because he never felt a thing.

Lampitt rubbed his stinging ear, and carefully helped the one-legged man out of the boat. Knowing what to expect, he stepped back a little way as the man dug his peg leg into the wet sand. He followed him up the beach to where Dognettle and One-Eye were waiting.

'Right, Cap'n,' said Lampitt. 'What now?'

'We climb up the cliff and walk to Port Akerbyn,' replied Dognettle.

'But Captain, it's almost dark,' Lampitt complained.

'You ain't afraid of the dark, are you?'

'No, Captain, sir,' said Lampitt, trying to sound brave. 'It's climbing these 'ere hundred-foot cliffs *in the dark*, is what I'm afraid of.' He stuck a thumb towards the other two. 'And these two wouldn't manage it too well in daylight, let alone…' he tapered off, not wanting to put too fine a point on it.

Dognettle looked up at the wall of granite. 'Are you *sure* that's a hundred feet? Really?'

'Give or take an inch or two, yes, Cap'n,' Lampitt nodded.

'Well… bugger that then. We'll wait till it gets light.'

*

Next morning, after spending a chilly night on the beach, and wondering why on Crett they hadn't stayed the night on the *Sea Dragon*, the four men walked along the bottom of the cliff looking for the best place to climb up. Dognettle and Lampitt clambered easily over the fallen rocks strewn around the base of the cliff, but One-Eye and Peg-Leg had to take things more slowly.

'That route up doesn't look too difficult, Cap'n,' said Lampitt, pointing at a collapsed section where a long, low slope of scree had been created. Dognettle agreed and he and Lampitt led the climb. When they were barely a couple of feet from the top, two faces peered over the edge and looked down at them. Dognettle almost teetered backwards in surprise.

'How did you get up 'ere before us!' he stormed.

'Steps, Cap'n,' said One-Eye. 'You missed 'em.' He was neither concerned nor amused as he looked down at them, just impatient. 'There's steps in the rocks just past where you started climbing, Cap'n,' Kneeling down, he hauled his captain up by his wrist.

Dognettle dusted himself down, then calmed down, and muttered his appreciation. The three started to walk off together.

'Oi! What about me, you bastards!' Lampitt yelled after them when he saw he was being left behind.

One-Eye turned back and, in a moment, hauled Lampitt onto the grassy slope of the cliff-top. Then he hit him on the ear. 'In spite of what you may have heard, my parents were married. I *know.* I was *there.*'

'Thank you,' said Lampitt, rubbing an ear that was still sore from its previous encounter with One-Eye's fist.

'Where we goin' now?' asked Lampitt, catching up.

Dognettle looked over his shoulder. 'How many times have I got to tell you?' he scowled.

'Yeah, I know. We're going to Port Akerbyn, but where in Port Akerbyn?'

'I'll tell you when we get there,' snapped Dognettle.

'You won't 'ave to tell me then, Captain. I'll know.'

'Shall I whack 'im again, Captain?' asked One-Eye.

'Do you think it'll do any good?' sighed Dognettle.

'No, sir. But I'll feel better.'

Dognettle thought about it… 'Oh, all right, then.'

Lampitt ducked the oncoming fist, only to yelp when Peg-Leg stepped on his foot. One-Eye still caught him with his second swing, though.

Lampitt silently vowed that one day he would get even. According to all the old sea stories the ruffians and bullies always met a bad end. He'd have to see what he could do to help these two get themselves immortalised in song.

* * *

67

Link walked down one side of the street peering in shop windows, while Eydith and Ben walked on the other side investigating the taverns, looking for signs of Dennis, or any disruption he may have caused. When they reached the end of the street empty handed, as it were, Ben suggested they wait in the tavern where they first met Greasy Spot, on the assumption that he would go there again and they might be able to enlist his help.

*

A pigeon settled on Teeter Gravy's hat. It was one of the drawbacks of having a workshop open to the sky. Another was rain. But he preferred to create with his mind open to the universe, as he liked to put it. Or, as King Treadwell liked to put it: there's nowhere else to put you.

Teeter stood rigidly still for a moment while he decided what it was. He'd heard the flapping of wings and felt the gentle claws scratch his head through his well-worn, floppy, pointy hat. He could still feel his heart beating so he was fairly certain he hadn't been touched by the hand of Death. He moved carefully towards the sunlight, and out of the corner of his eye he noticed his shadow on the wall. He sighed audibly when he saw the shadow of the bird. But now he had a new problem. Whilst his predicament wasn't terminal anymore, any sudden movement on his part might necessitate a trip to the cleaners. He slowly raised his hands and lifted the bird off his head. As he did so, he saw the tiny tube attached to the bird's leg. He turned it over and saw the king's seal stamped on its side.

*

Thadax pulled back the little hatch. 'Who is it?' he demanded.

'It's me. Teeter.'

'What do you want?'

Teeter sighed. 'What does anyone want when they knock on this door?'

'Well... mostly they want to see the king. But then... there's those who just want an argument,' said Thadax.

Teeter stood on tiptoe in an effort to get his eyes level with the hatch. 'Nobody *wants* an argument, it's just unavoidable with you.'

'No, it isn't,' Thadax argued.

'Look, just let me in, will you? I've got a message for the king.'

'Can't you just tell me and I'll tell him?'

'Nope,' said Teeter, 'it's sealed. Anyway, what's the big deal about opening this door? Have you got a *woman* in there?'

'No. I've got all these bloody bolts, that's what. You people just don't realise... when I've undone 'em all, I've got to do 'em all up again... then, you leave and I've got to undo 'em all again, again...'

'You're the doorman. It's your job,' Teeter pointed out. Then, he gave in. 'Here take it,' he snapped, and held the message, which was still attached to the pigeon, through the hatch.

Thadax jumped back. 'Eek! Take it away. You know I can't stand birds.'

'Oh, yeah. Well, open this soddin' door then!' yelled Teeter.

Thadax slid all the bolts back hurriedly and noisily. 'Have you got hold of it?' he asked, nervously.

'Yes,' snapped Teeter. 'Now stand aside.'

Thadax opened the door wide and stood well back. As soon as Teeter was inside, he slammed it shut and slid a couple of the bolts back into place, then ran past the wizard so he could announce him.

'Come in,' said the king, in a tone that implied sleep might not be too far away. Teeter stepped forward, still clutching the pigeon.

'I have a message for you, sire.'

'Oh, good... well? What is it?' asked Treadwell, leaning forward slightly.

'Er... I don't know, sire. The pigeon's got it.'

King Treadwell frowned at the pigeon. It ignored him. It was perfectly happy where it was. Its wings ached, it was tired, and it was being carried – what more could it want?

'Well?' said the king, almost nose to beak with the bird. 'What's the message?'

'Coo,' said the pigeon.

Treadwell looked up at Teeter. 'I don't suppose you speak pigeon, do you?'

'No, sire. The message is in the tube… attached to its leg.'

The king looked down at the pigeon again. 'Ha, I didn't think it was as smart as that… mind you… that tube's a good idea.' He gently scratched the bird's head. 'Has it come far?'

'I don't honestly know, sire. I didn't think to ask,' Teeter replied, without thinking what he was saying.

'Don't be silly, man,' Treadwell admonished him. 'Give it to me.'

Teeter held out the bird. Treadwell took it carefully and turned it around. 'Ah, here it is,' he whispered, and started to undo the tiny tube. He looked up at Teeter and grinned. 'Bit like changing a baby's nappy.'

'Wouldn't know about that, sire,' said Teeter, uneasily.

'Of course not. I forgot. You're a wizard, aren't you?'

Teeter didn't answer.

After a few irritated tugs and sighs, the king finally managed to release the tube without damaging the bird. He pulled the cap off the tube and slipped the scrap of paper into his lap, retrieving it a fraction of a second before the pigeon snatched it for lunch.

'Oh, no you don't,' snapped Treadwell. 'It's mine.'

Teeter came forward, took the pigeon and set it on the floor. It strutted about for a while, nodding its head and agreeing with everything in sight. When it found nothing to eat, it flew up into the rafters. The king read the note.

'Good news, sire?' Teeter prompted.

'Yes, they've found that wizard chappie, Dennis, at Port Akerbyn. He's chartered a ship to the Boring Islands.' Slowly he read on to himself, then turned it over. 'No! He didn't go. Someone else has stolen the Drum!'

'That's a bugger, sire.'

'Yes, but at least Dennis hasn't got it anymore.' The king read it again. 'Thadax!' he suddenly yelled. The door keeper almost collapsed from shock. He was standing right by the king's shoulder. 'Get me a pencil and paper. I want to know who's got the Drum… Teeter, call that pigeon down here. I've got a job for it.'

Teeter looked up at the pigeon, with not a clue how to get it down. 'Cooee!' he called. The pigeon might have been deaf or it didn't understand. Either way, it ignored him.

Thadax came back. 'What are you doing?'

'Trying to get that pigeon down,' said Teeter. 'The king has a message for it to take back.'

'It won't do that,' said Thadax.

'It will if the king says so.'

'No,' said Thadax. 'It doesn't work like that. They only go one way. You'll need one that's going back.'

'Perhaps it can take this one back with it,' said the king.

'No, sire,' Thadax explained. 'The idea is, that you take them away from their home, and they fly back. Then you take them away from home again, and use them to fly back again.'

Treadwell stared up into the rafters. 'Well, if that one thinks this is home, it can think again. Thadax! Call the guard and have it shot. I'm not having it up there crapping on me down here.'

The pigeon seemed to sense the danger and flew out of the window. Feeling the call of nature, it headed for King Treadwell's statue in the main courtyard.

* * *

When Eydith and her party went into the tavern, they found Greasy obligingly sitting at a table in a corner. He looked up from his ale and waved. 'Mornin',' he said, cheerily. 'Come and join me. Barman! Over here.' For a spy, he was pretty poor at being inconspicuous.

Eydith and Link sat down. Ben climbed up, then sat down. The barman came and stood by the table. 'I'll have another ale,' said Greasy, 'and one for my friend, Ben. What about you Link?'

'No, it's too early for me, thanks.'

'Do you do coffee?' Eydith asked, quietly.

'*Coffee*?' the barman repeated.

'Coffee,' ordered Greasy, in a tone that wouldn't brook a negative answer.

'How many?' the barman sighed.

Eydith looked at Link and he nodded. 'Two please.'

The barman disappeared out the back somewhere. There was a distant sound of crockery being clattered about irritably, the heavy-handed crushing and grinding of beans, and a single, long-drawn-out swearword when he splashed himself with scalding water. He brought it to their table, along with a scowl and some unintelligible cursing and muttering. They got the message, subtle as it was, that making coffee was not something the barman was interested in making. They rarely are.

'Any news of Dennis?' whispered Eydith.

'Yes,' Greasy leaned closer. 'He's back in port. But he hasn't got the Drum anymore.'

'Damn,' hissed Link. 'That means he's hidden it somewhere. Or he's lost it.'

'Not necessarily either of those,' whispered Greasy.

He was about to expand on that when the tavern door was flung open and in marched Captain Dognettle and three of his crew members. Greasy looked up.

'Ah, Captain,' he called. 'What news?'

Dognettle swaggered across the room, dragged a chair from another table, turned it around and sat astride it, almost resting his chin on its back rest. 'I've got the old Drum,' he declared, triumphantly.

'That's great news!' said Link. 'When can you get it to us?'

'And who would you be, young man, to be asking for the king's Drum?'

Eydith chimed in, 'We're old friends of King Treadwell… well, I am… well, my mother was… well… she…'

Greasy stepped in. 'The king was getting the Drum back for them… well, for him… I mean for her.'

Dognettle looked bemused, but he got the picture.

'So,' said Link, excitedly, getting back to it, 'when can you get it to us?'

'As soon as you agree to my terms,' said Dognettle.

'Terms?' said Greasy. 'What terms?'

'I'm putting the Drum up for ransom,' Dognettle announced.

'What?' said Link, not believing it.

'You can't kidnap a Drum,' said Eydith.

'I don't know what the correct terminology is,' said Dognettle. 'But that's what I'm doing.'

The others fell silent, wondering what to do next. It was Greasy who spoke first. 'How much do you want?'

'That's more like it… a thousand golds,' said Dognettle.

'The king won't pay that,' said Greasy.

'It'll go over the side, then,' Dognettle threatened. 'I'm not fussy who pays, but that's the price.' He stood up. 'I'll be around the port in the morning. I'm easy to find. In the meantime, I'm going to find that wizard who was careless enough to lose it in the first place.'

Ben stood up on the rungs of his chair. 'Shall I cut 'is legs off, my lady?' he whispered, slowly pulling his battle-axe from his belt.

Eydith rested a hand on his shoulder. 'No, Ben, not yet.'

Dognettle swept out and onto the street, his three henchmen swaggering in line behind him.

'One-Eye… will you come up here. I feel a bit of a twit walking in single file like a group of schoolkids on an outing.' One-Eye quickened his pace.

When he was level with him, Dognettle said, 'That's the first step. Now we find that wizard and see how seriously he wants his precious Drum back.'

One-Eye grinned his appreciation of his captain's scheming. 'Any idea where 'e might be, sir?'

'Nah, but the Captain of the *Racing Slug* will know.'

* * *

69

'I would suggest you try the taverns first,' said Dennis.

'Don't you fink people will notice?' said Hell.

'What?' said Dennis.

'Well, me and young Brown 'ere, bein' that much prettier than your average human, we do tend to stand out a bit, if you get my drift.' The Lord of the Parallel Dimension patted a tuft of what passed for hair on the back of his head.

Dennis squinted at them. 'I see what you mean. I'll get my guards to search the taverns first, then when they've found these sailors – these *pirates!* – you can rush in and deal with them. How about that?'

'Sounds fair enough,' said Hell. 'How many do you think there are… of these pirate people, then.'

'Oh, I don't know, twenty… thirty maybe.'

'In that case, I'll be off, then,' said Hell.

'Off?' said Dennis. 'What do you mean, off?'

'Get some more demons,' said Hell. 'We can't take on thirty bloody sailors on our own, can we?'

'All right,' sighed Dennis. 'But don't take all day about it. Or I'll be summoning you again.'

Florence dutifully waved the staff at them.

Jook and Psoddoph were watching through the window. When the demons had gone, Jook turned to Psoddoph and whispered, 'Did you see that?'

'Course I did,' replied Psoddoph. 'I've been stood 'ere next to you.'

'What do you think the boss is up to now?'

'Those looked like the demons that attacked the university.'

'Are there different sorts then?' whispered Jook.

'What?'

'Can you tell 'em apart?'

'No. What I mean is, I reckon 'e's gonna use 'em again to attack the university.'

'What, after what 'appened to 'im last time?' said Psoddoph. 'Only a fool would… Oh, 'ello, boss.'

Dennis had found them. 'Come inside, I have a job for you.'

They stepped carefully around the rubble, and looked enquiringly up at the hole in the ceiling.

'Don't worry about that,' said Dennis. 'I'll sort it out later.'

'Right, boss,' said Psoddoph. 'Not as if you found the place in good order, anyway.'

'Precisely. Now, I want you to go into town and find out where those pirates are, and where they've taken my Drum.'

'Right, boss,' said Jook.

'Then what?' said Psoddoph.

'Come back and tell me, of course.'

'Of course,' said Jook quickly, thankful they didn't have to retrieve it.

'Well, what are you waiting for?'

'Well, it might mean that we 'ave to go into taverns and places like that, boss,' said Psoddoph.

'Yes, it probably will,' agreed Dennis.

'We ain't got no money, boss,' Jook informed him.

Dennis groaned and shoved his hands into his multi-pocketed new robe. Nothing. Then he started patting it. Still nothing. He picked up a handful of cloth and shook it. Something jingled. He felt it again, lower this time. There was something coin-shaped, he could feel it through the cloth. He just couldn't find the top of the pocket that it might be in.

Seeing his embarrassment, Florence opened her purse. 'Here, take this.' She offered Psoddoph a full silver.

'You can't give them that!' Dennis intervened, alarmed. 'You'll never see them again.'

'It's either that or a gold, Father.'

'Look,' said Psoddoph. 'We won't need all of it. We'll bring you some change. Honest.'

'*Some* change? You'll bring *all* the change.'

'Don't worry, boss,' Jook assured him, 'We'll be back before you know it. Hopefully not too drunk,' he quipped, and made for the door smartishly.

*

A couple of hours and a few taverns later, Jook and Psoddoph found themselves on barstools back in a shady bar known as the *Barbarian's Codpiece*. 'Two of your best pints, please, landlord,' said Jook. Psoddoph rested his elbows on the bar and lowered his aching forehead into his hands.

'Know what?' he mumbled, looking up.

'What?' said Jook.

'I don't think I can hold much more.' Then he hiccupped, moaned, and carefully lowered his head back into his hands.

'We've gotta f… f… f… find 'em,' Jook stuttered. 'Or life's gonna be a bitch.'

Psoddoph looked at his reflection in a puddle on the bar. 'Life *is* a bitch,' he groaned.

The landlord banged two tankards down in front of them. Psoddoph jerked himself upright. 'Oh, yes, how much?'

'To you,' said the landlord. 'Thirty-eight pence.'

Psoddoph sobered up slightly, at the thought of having to count out the coins, and carefully heaped them in front of him. 'That should cover it.' The landlord scooped them up and deposited them in his till.

'Ever heard of the *Sea Dragon*?' Psoddoph asked, in a voice loud enough for everyone in the room to hear.

'Why?' asked the landlord, 'who wants to know?'

'Well… I do,' said Psoddoph.

'Any particular reason?'

'Yeah,' said Jook, 'the buggers on it have stolen something we want – a Drum.'

'It'll cost yuh,' said the landlord.

'What will?'

'Information,' he whispered.

'How much?' asked Psoddoph, leaning closer and almost disappearing between the stool and the bar.

'What's it worth?'

'What price would you put on this place?' asked Jook, looking around the room.

'What?' he said, uncomprehending at first. 'This place? Bout ten golds,' the landlord whispered. 'Why?'

'Tell us where the Drum is and consider yourself paid,' said Jook.

'How do you make that out?'

Jook took a box of yellow headed matches out of his pocket and struck one. It spluttered into flame, then he dropped it, still burning, onto the sawdust covered floor. After a moment or two, he trod on it, then leaned closer to the landlord and whispered, 'I've just saved you ten golds. You might not be so lucky next time.'

'You wouldn't dare,' hissed the landlord, nose to nose with Jook. 'I'd have the Watch round 'ere in five minutes.'

'What, to warm their 'ands?' Jook stared back and without taking his eyes off the man, took another match out of the box and struck it.

The sulphur fumes burned the inside of the landlord's nose. 'All right. All right. I'll tell you,' he said, hurriedly. Jook blew out the match and dropped it in the puddle on the counter.

'Well?' said Psoddoph, impatiently.

The landlord beckoned them to the other end of the counter.

'Look, I don't want no trouble…' the landlord whispered. 'The *Sea Dragon* – I don't know exactly where it is – but see those four men in the corner over there… no don't look now… well one of 'em's Captain Dognettle. 'E's in command of it.'

'Thank you,' said Psoddoph and rested his tankard on the counter. 'There's our man, Jook,' he said, nudging Jook in the back. Jook turned around.

'Which one?'

'The one with the feathers in his hat.'

'I'm glad I didn't become a sailor,' Jook grinned. 'That's *so* last year,'

'Yeah. Well, come on, let's get it sorted out.'

The pair crossed to Dognettle's table. Jook pulled up a chair and sat down, uninvited. One-Eye's hand moved slowly to his dagger belt.

'I wouldn't do that,' advised a voice by his ear. One-Eye felt the point of Psoddoph's knife prick his neck.

'Now, all of you. Put your hands on the table where I can see them,' barked Psoddoph. One-Eye looked pleadingly at his companions. After all, it was his neck that would be punctured first. Dognettle and his men did as they were ordered.

'There,' said Jook, 'that's much more friendly. Now, which one of you is Captain Dognettle?' The man with the feathers in his hat raised a hand. 'You were right,' Jook grinned at Psoddoph.

'And you are?' asked Dognettle.

'Jook an' Psoddoph,' Jook answered, flatly. Lampitt began to get up.

'Sit down!' snapped Psoddoph.

'But 'e just said…'

'That's who we are,' said Jook. 'Guards… for a wizard. And at this moment in time, 'e's not an 'appy wizard.'

'Who is this wizard?' asked Dognettle.

'Dennis, and 'e knows you've got 'is Drum.'

'Good,' said Dognettle. 'You've saved me the trouble of looking for *you*.'

'Well, we found you first,' said Jook. 'So listen. My boss, Dennis, wants 'is Drum back.'

'That's what I want to talk to 'im about,' said Dognettle. 'I've got an offer for 'im.'

'What sort of an offer?' asked Psoddoph.

'I want to know how much he's prepared to pay to get it back?' Dognettle smirked.

'*Pay?*' said Psoddoph, trying not to laugh. 'He won't pay anything.'

'Well, I'll just have to offer it to the girl then, won't I?'

'You're not in a position to be making deals,' said Psoddoph, his brightly-polished sword attracting their attention.

'An' if you harm any of us, you'll never see the Drum, *ever*, I promise you that.'

The stalemate lasted less than a minute.

'I'll talk to 'im,' said Psoddoph.

'Good. I'll meet you back here tomorrow, then,' said Dognettle, with a thin smile that Psoddoph longed to erase.

* * *

70

'He said, *what*?' Dennis fumed.

'How much are you prepared to pay, boss?' Psoddoph repeated. 'I told 'im you wouldn't. Then 'e said e'd offer it to that girl from the university.'

'Eydith?' said Dennis.

'Er, I do believe that's her name, yes,' said Psoddoph.

'How much does he want?' said Dennis, somewhat deflated.

'He didn't say, boss. But I think it's some sort of auction, by the sound of it.'

'Hmm...' Dennis breathed. It was a sort of covering noise while he thought about the situation. 'Right... you'll find this Dognettle character again, keep an eye on him and follow him. Chances are, he'll lead you to where the Drum is being kept. Then, we'll either take it by force, or steal it back, again. Depending on what we're up against. Got that?'

'Yes, boss,' sighed Psoddoph, thinking, *'ere we go again.*

'And if there's anything else worth taking,' Dennis added, 'we'll have that as well.'

'Don't get too ambitious, boss. Remember me and Jook 'ave got to carry it,' Psoddoph pointed out. Dennis just grunted.

The guards went back towards the waterfront and waited in an alley across the street from the *Barbarian's Codpiece*. Luckily, Dognettle was still inside drinking with his crew. They settled in for a long wait, but it wasn't long before the party emerged.

The guards flattened themselves against the wall. The captain of the *Sea Dragon* stood on the pavement outside the tavern, stuck his thumbs in his belt and took a deep breath. He swayed for a moment and leant back against the wall, then shook his head. His men staggered out behind him and formed themselves into a crooked line. They swayed down the street.

'Come on,' said Psoddoph, gently nudging Jook on the arm, 'let's go.' They followed at a discreet distance, staying close to the shopfronts and pretending to look in windows whenever one of the sailors looked as though he might turn around. After lurching and staggering for a few hundred yards, the seamen began to sober up a little. They were seasoned drinkers, after all. Then they came to another tavern and went inside. It looked like a random choice, but Dognettle knew exactly where they were going.

Eydith, Link and Ben were already sitting at a table, waiting. Greasy was watching from a couple of tables away, his axe resting across his knees.

Dognettle pulled up a chair and sat astride it. 'Come to a decision, yet?' he said, staring straight into Eydith's eyes.

'Yes,' she replied, meeting his stare. 'Sell the Drum to the wizard.'

'What?' snapped Dognettle, angrily. Realising that if Eydith wasn't prepared to bid for it, the Drum's value would drop enormously. Probably more.

'Let Dennis have it,' she said, levelly.

'Okay,' said Dognettle. 'If that's the way you want it.' He got up, slammed the chair against the table, and stomped back onto the street.

Jook and Psoddoph had been watching through the window. When they saw the captain and his men start to leave, they ducked into a shop doorway. They followed them again. But they hadn't gone far when One-Eye stumbled around and saw them. Well, Jook anyway. But by moving his head slightly, he managed to get both guards into his field of vision.

'Uh, oh,' whispered Jook. 'They've seen us.'

'No point hiding now, is there?' said Psoddoph. 'We'll just have to brazen it out.'

One-Eye grabbed Dognettle's arm and turned him around. The captain's face, at first surprised and angry, broke into a broad grin. 'Ah… it's er… Bugger off, and his pal,' he said, jovially.

'Psoddoph,' said Psoddoph, tetchily.

'Whatever,' smiled Dognettle. 'I was just coming to look for you,' he lied.

'Well, you've found us,' Jook sneered.

'About that Drum…'

'Yeah?' said Psoddoph.

'Well, the girl offered me fifty golds,' Dognettle said, over-casually and avoiding eye-contact. 'Tell your master to better her offer, and he can have it.'

'We'll do that,' Jook snarled.

'Good.' Dognettle grinned. 'I'll expect to hear from you, then.' He turned and walked away, his three crewmen reeling along close behind.

'Well,' said Jook, 'what do you think? Shall we follow them?'

'Not much point really,' said Psoddoph.

*

'Fifty golds?' laughed Dennis. 'Is that all?'

'It doesn't sound very much, Father,' said Florence.

'Not if you say it quickly, it doesn't,' said Dennis.

'What do you want us to do, boss?' asked Psoddoph.

'You can find Dognettle in the morning and tell him to bring the Drum here…' But then he had seconds thoughts. 'No. Hold on. This place is far too wooded. I don't trust this Dognettle character. We'll meet somewhere more open, where I can see who's with him.'

The guards didn't know anywhere. They shrugged. They had only limited local knowledge.

Dennis, however – ever the man with his ear to the ground – had gleaned a little folklore. 'There's an old, derelict fisherman's cottage not far along the coast. The local idiots say it's haunted…' He rolled his eyes.

Florence couldn't help butting in. 'You know as well as I do, they exist, Father. Eydith's father is a ghost.'

He held up a hand. 'Alright. But these things get out of hand. Real ghosts have better things to do than moan and rattle chains in old cottages.'

She let it go.

'Anyway – getting back to it – it must be easy to find. So, tell Dognettle we'll meet him there in the morning. And tell him I'll better the offer by five golds.'

*

'Why ever did you tell him you didn't want it, my lady?' asked Ben, curiously.

'I think it might be easier to let Dennis have it, at least for now. He knows it's no use without Sprag. When he's got the Drum, he'll come looking for me.' She thought for a moment. 'Or with Sprag's help we'll find the Drum, *and* Dennis, first. I don't relish another confrontation, but it may be the only way to settle this.'

A darkly-clad man a few tables away suddenly stood up and strode out onto the street.

Greasy slid off his chair and emerged from beneath the table to follow.

*

'Are you sure?' said Dognettle.

'Aye, Cap'n. Apparently the Drum is useless without someone called Sprag.'

'Do you think the wizard has this Sprag person?' Dognettle probed.

'The girl seems to think not, Cap'n.'

'I think he has, Cap'n,' said One-Eye. 'That's why he's keen to get the Drum back.'

'Perhaps 'e's the one who beats it,' Lampitt suggested.

One-Eye cuffed him across the ear.

'It was just a thought,' Lampitt moaned.

'Well, shut up!' snapped Dognettle. 'We'll go and meet this wizard in the morning and see what he's prepared to offer.'

'Whatever it is Captain, it'll be the best offer you're gonna get,' reckoned One-Eye.

'We'll see.' Dognettle winked conspiratorially. 'Right, gentlemen, are we staying here all day?'

'I vote we go back to the ship, Cap'n. I could do with a change of air,' said One-Eye.

Peg-Leg agreed. 'Me too, sir. I suddenly feel the urge to get the sea back under my foot again.'

Twenty yards away, Greasy fished a well-smoked cigarette butt from behind his ear and lit it. He'd forgotten he had it. He took a long draw on it. He hadn't had a smoke for a few days and leant against a convenient wall momentarily while his mind resurfaced from its unexpected swim in a sea of nicotine spiked gee-gaw. He'd almost forgotten that sensation.

Drunkenly, he stood up straight and smoothed down his chain mail jerkin, then stepped out onto the road. The four sailors turned a corner and disappeared from sight. Greasy broke into a trot. He had to be at that corner before they turned again. He arrived panting and cussed, the street didn't have any more corners. It only led into town, or from where he stood, out of town. Now it was mostly a matter of not being seen, and being only about four feet tall, it wasn't that difficult.

A mile later, Greasy was lying on his belly in the long grass on the cliff-top. Dognettle and his men went down the steps to the beach, climbed into their boat and rowed out to the *Sea Dragon*. *So, that's where you are*, Greasy thought to himself. He waited a few more minutes to watch them get on board, and when they were out of sight, he ran as fast as he could back to town to tell Eydith. He would have been quicker had he been able to run in a straight line.

*

'That's right, miss. About a mile up the coast,' Greasy told her, between deep breaths. A fresh ale in front of him was helping to revive him. Though the others doubted that.

'We should wait till morning,' said Link. 'He's got to go and see Dennis.'

'Yes,' said Ben, who seemed eager for a fight. 'Then, we'll go and get it back.'

'We'll see,' said Eydith. 'Is there anywhere on that clifftop we can watch without being seen?'

'Not on top, miss,' said Greasy. 'I could stay out of sight up there, but not you. But there are plenty of hefty rocks to get behind on the beach.'

'They'll do,' said Ben, sliding off his chair.

'Just a minute,' said Greasy. 'I haven't finished me ale, yet.'

* * *

71

That night, Eydith and her friends picked their way slowly and quietly down the cliff steps to wait among the rocks. Somewhere on the deck of the *Sea Dragon,* a match flared in the darkness and glowed intermittently for a few seconds as a sailor lit his pipe.

'There's somebody on deck, my lady,' whispered Ben.

'It's only a watchman,' Greasy reassured him. 'They won't move until dawn, I shouldn't think.'

'Well, there's no point in all of us staying awake,' said Link. 'Wake me in a couple of hours.' He pulled his hat over his eyes and leant back against the rock. Eydith sat down beside him and rested her head on his shoulder. Link smiled secretly in his private darkness. She tried to get closer. 'Cold?' he whispered.

'Hmm? Yes, just a bit,' she lied. Link put his arm around her shoulders, but sleep was proving elusive for both of them. Eventually, he felt the need to speak.

'Have you got something on your mind?' he whispered.

'Sorry?' she queried, raising her head. 'I'd rather hoped you'd be the one making a move.' She tilted he head to one side, mocking him a little coquettishly. But she kissed him lightly on his cheek, anyway.

He reddened slightly. 'I didn't mean that. I meant in the morning – about getting the Drum back.'

'Let's just see what happens,' she said. 'I think we're a match for a few sailors, don't you?'

Link flexed his fingers. 'I would hope so.'

'Let's forget about it till morning, then, shall we?' she whispered. Link opened his mouth to speak, but she put her finger to his lips, then kissed him.

Ben and Greasy moved away.

* * *

72

'What do you think about that?' hissed Ben.

'Filthy habit,' replied Greasy, looking across the water at the lone sailor on the deck of the *Sea Dragon*. 'Never could smoke a pipe meself. All that slurping, and that 'orrible brown stuff dribbling out the end.'

'Not *that*,' whispered Ben. '*That*.' He pointed at Eydith and Link.

Greasy swivelled around to see. 'The filthy, lucky swine,' he whispered.

'He's only kissing 'er,' said Ben.

'Yeah, but I can guess what he's thinking.'

'How?'

'Cos, I know what I'd be thinking,' said Greasy, smiling.

Both dwarfs sighed softly and turned their attention back to the *Sea Dragon*. After a long silence, there was another long silence that Greasy thought might go on all night if he didn't say something soon. 'You know what, Ben?'

'What?' said Ben without taking his eyes of the ship.

'It's probably the beards.'

'We've *got* beards,' Ben pointed out.

'Not us… the women.'

Ben took a long, hard look at Eydith, 'She ain't got a beard,' he said.

'Not the *tall* women… *our women*,' said Greasy.

'Well… yeah, I 'adn't really thought about it,' said Ben. So, for a moment, he did think about it. 'Mind you, they are soft, pretty beards,' he said, at last.

'Yeah.'

* * *

73

A pigeon flapped its way from Port Akerbyn.

A watery sun climbed lazily back into the sky, probably woken by screaming gulls like everyone else who lives near the sea.

Greasy and Ben were on the beach behind the rock where they'd spent the night. Fortunately, the tide didn't come that high this time of year. Greasy was dozing, while Ben was keeping a sleepy eye on the *Sea Dragon.* In the pale light of early morning, Ben saw a hatch open and a figure climb out onto the deck. The figure looked around, stretched, yawned and took some deep breaths. Then he coughed a bit. When he was satisfied he was alone, he went to the side of the ship and, after checking which way the wind was blowing, relieved himself.

Ben nudged Greasy with his foot. 'You awake?' he whispered.

Greasy stirred and turned over. 'No, not yet,' he mumbled.

'There's a crabby looking thing crawling by your ear.'

Greasy changed his mind. Not only was he awake, but he was up. 'What? Where?'

'Nowhere,' said Ben. 'I lied. But now you're up, you can come and 'ave a look at this.'

'What's goin' on, then?'

'They're stirrin'. There's someone on deck raising the sea level at the moment.'

Greasy peered over the rock as two more sailors emerged from the hatch, then a third. 'They're lowering a boat,' murmured Greasy.

Ben crawled to an adjacent rock and nudged Link. He felt that was the safer option. He couldn't be sure where the safest place to nudge Eydith was, and certainly not when she was in Link's arms.

'Hmm... what's the matter?' Link groaned, as he swam back through layers of sleep.

'Looks like they're coming ashore,' Ben whispered.

Eydith woke up.

'Already?' moaned Link. 'I haven't had breakfast yet.'

'Well, there ain't time now,' Ben told him.

Eydith yawned. 'Are you complaining again?'

'Me?' said Link, hurt. 'When do I ever complain?'

Looking at the couple sprawled on the sand, Greasy suggested diplomatically that they position themselves out of sight. 'We'll be safe here if they head straight up the beach to the steps.' He checked and saw the boat was in the water. 'They'll be here in a few minutes.'

* * *

74

Lampitt heaved on the oars, propelling the small boat towards the beach. *We'd get there a bit quicker if you lazy swabs lent a hand*, he thought. But he kept it to himself. He wasn't in the mood for a punch in the head from One-Eye this morning. The sea was calm and he made good progress. It wasn't long before he beached the boat and was helping Peg-Leg ashore.

'Have they got the Drum?' whispered Eydith.

'Can't see it, my lady,' said Ben.

'I'm glad there's not too many of them down there,' said Link.

'Yeah,' said Ben. 'I'd sooner tackle four, than all of 'em at once.'

'Don't worry,' Eydith assured them. 'We'll be all right.'

She wasn't *too* sure about that, but she didn't want to infect the others with her worries when they seemed to have enough of their own. And, in the main, she felt they could probably handle whatever might come. Sprag caught her thoughts and glowed sympathetically.

The four sailors trudged up the sandy slope to the steps and disappeared from view.

'Give them a few minutes,' Eydith whispered.

'Then what?' asked Link. 'Follow them?'

She shook her head. 'Can you row a boat?'

Link shrugged. 'I don't know, I've never tried. But it doesn't look that difficult.'

'Okay, come on then. You can find out now.' She picked up Sprag and walked down to the boat. He joined her, occasionally checking the clifftop behind them as he went, to make sure they weren't being watched from above.

Ben and Greasy followed on. Greasy had his eyes fixed on the head of the *Sea Dragon* looming up ahead of them. 'Can't be a watchman up there,' he said, raising a concern that none of them had thought of till then, 'Or there'd be alarm bells clangin' by now.'

*

A length of bow-rope was thoughtfully wound around a weighty rock to stop the tide taking the boat. Link dealt with that while Eydith stepped in and sat at the back. He held the boat steady for Greasy and Ben. Then, hitching up his robe, he leaned on the boat and pushed it back into the water.

'My feet are all wet now,' he complained. Eydith raised her hand in a magical gesture.

'No, no. It's all right. I'll see to it,' he said, and muttered a spell of his own at his soggy shoes. There was a small hiss of steam as the magic did its work, and he sat down in the middle of the boat to sort out how the oars worked. 'I suppose you just rest 'em in these U-shaped metal things,' he said.

'Rowlocks,' obliged Greasy.

'Well, I can't see anywhere else to put 'em,' said Link, indignantly.

'No. That's what they're called,' said Greasy.

Link grinned. 'Ah.'

Eydith looked out to sea. The sight of the *Sea Dragon* wallowing out there was certainly intimidating. She'd never seen anything like it.

Link soon got the hang of the oars. After splashing his passengers a few times (and quite enjoying that part of it) he got into a rhythm and rowed steadily towards the ship. His only problem was the occasional directive from Ben, who would say, 'left a bit' or 'right a bit,' without taking into account that Link was facing him, and his left was Link's right. Eventually, and by ignoring him, Link guided the boat alongside the *Sea Dragon*, and secured it to a mooring ring bolted onto the ship's side. 'Well,' he said, when nobody moved. 'Who's going first?'

Eydith stood up and passed Sprag to him. 'Me,' she said. They were bobbing on the swell a little. She'd had very little experience on water, and none at all on the sea. *This could be embarrassing,* she thought, as the boat and the ship moved contrarily. She waited her moment, and reached out hopefully for one of the iron rungs that formed a ladder up to the *Sea Dragon's* deck. Thankfully she caught hold of it. When she was safely aboard, Link followed and passed Sprag up to her as soon as he was within reach. Then he climbed up beside her.

She leant back over the side. Seeing Ben already on the ladder, she called out, 'You stay there and keep watch, Greasy. We won't be long. Yell, or something, if anyone comes back.'

They scanned the deck to get their bearings.

'There's a hatch in the middle,' said Ben, having seen the men emerge from it earlier.

Link looked both ways along the deck. 'We are in the middle.' Then he saw Ben looking at his feet and looked down. 'Oh.' And he stepped to the side.

Ben knelt down and tugged at the handle. It wouldn't budge. He looked at it again, then drew his battle-axe, which he wedged under the handle and heaved on it. The handle squeaked grudgingly as it turned, and the hatch lifted enough for him to get his fingers under it. He looked up at Link, searching his face. 'Bet you thought I was gonna knock, didn't you?'

Link actually thought for an awful moment that he was going to smash his way through, but he didn't let on. Ben lifted the hatch and laid it on the deck. It was decision time again. 'Who's going first?' he asked.

Eydith looked down the hole. It was dark. Sprag was in her mind. 'We'll go first, mistress.' He started to glow. Eydith stepped forward, in answer to Ben's question.

The dwarf stepped aside, and back a couple of paces. Until he was behind Link, in fact.

Sprag shone brighter, lighting the way to the lower decks. Nervously, Eydith descended the narrow steps. She glanced up and beckoned Link to follow. Ben waited on deck. At the bottom of the steps, the pair stopped to take in their surroundings. There were doors and more steps and ladders, leading confusingly in all directions, it seemed.

'Which way?' Eydith whispered.

Link shrugged. 'You'd think they'd put up better directions than 'mind your head', wouldn't you?'

Sprag turned in Eydith's hand. 'That way, mistress.'

Link saw the staff's gesture and flexed his fingers nervously. 'I'll go first.'

A few yards further on they faced a door. There were also ladders, one leading up, the other down. 'Which way now?'

Sprag was still pointing forward. 'Try the door,' urged Eydith.

Link pressed his ear against it and listened. Silence. He turned the handle and pushed. Nothing happened. He tried again and found to his annoyance that it opened outwards. He looked inside and peered around the cabin. There was daylight from a window. Seeing the place was unoccupied, he stepped inside. It was more of an office than a cabin. 'Come on,' he beckoned.

Eydith joined him. On the far side was Dognettle's desk, and beside it was the Drum.

The Drum!

Link was so pleased he stepped forward promptly to pick it up. But he hesitated when it glowed brightly.

'Not yet,' said Eydith, quietly, tugging on his sleeve.

The cabin brightened even more as Sprag began to glow in sync with the Drum.

Link closed his eyes tightly and turned away. He'd seen this before when the staff and Drum had merged their magic through the medium of Eydith. And it would go on for a few more moments yet. Sparks cascaded around the room as the whiteness phased down through the spectrum to the deepest indigo. A halo of golden light enveloped Eydith, and magical forces whirled in her mind. But Link didn't see any of this, he was resolutely looking away, eyes clamped. He didn't mind being present at this further transference of magic – magic that she hadn't quite learnt to control yet – but it still made his neck-hair stand on end. Suddenly the lightshow ended and Eydith fell to her knees. Her head slumped forward; her chin rested on her chest. She knelt motionless for a moment, then gradually looked up.

Link was standing over her, hesitating whether or not to put a reassuring hand on her shoulder. He knew what to expect and steeled himself for the moment when she opened her eyes again.

They shone like two golden moons. He swallowed nervously as she stared up at him. Then, just as before, the golden glow faded to a deep and disconcerting black, and finally her eyes returned to their normal blue. Link could just about cope with all that; it was what happened next that he recalled finding hard to deal with. 'Are you alright?' he whispered.

'YES,' was all she said. But it was as though she spoke with the leaden tones of the Grim Reaper himself. 'IT'LL PASS IN A MO… ment,' she added, in a voice that started huge and hollow, but shrank back to normal as she finished. She leant on Sprag and stood up. Link held her arm to steady her, but it wasn't necessary. She let out a short puff of air and sagged slightly, showing she was glad the ordeal was over.

The Drum, too, had returned to normal. Link picked it up warily, half expecting it to be hot, while Eydith opened the cabin door and looked out.

'Come on,' she whispered, 'it's all clear.' And she stepped out into the narrow passageway. Link backed out, so he could look over his shoulder to see where he was going, then turned to follow. Outside the room, Sprag lit the way again.

They came to the ladder. Now things became difficult. Both of them could climb it, but neither could climb and carry the Drum at the same time. And it was too high for one of them to pass it up to the other. And just to add to their problems, someone was coming.

Link put the Drum down. 'Now what?' he breathed, urgently. Her eyes glowed like golden moons again. 'I wish you wouldn't do that,' he said, nervously, as Crimpett walked casually down the passageway towards them.

He stopped whistling when he saw Link, but only to say, 'Good morning, I didn't expect to find anyone down here this early.'

Link acknowledged his greeting cagily, then Crimpett's short-sighted eyes saw Eydith. 'Goodness, two of you up all ready.'

Eydith fixed the little sailor with a hypnotic stare, but Crimpett didn't notice, he could only just about register the fact that anyone was there.

'Er… excuse me,' said Link, before Crimpett could get too far, 'is there another way out of here?'

'Oh, yes. Lots,' said Crimpett, brightly, as he carried on walking down the passage.

'STOP!' said Eydith, in a voice deeper than a mineshaft. Crimpett froze, then slowly turned, as if afraid of what he might see.

'Yes?' he answered, his voice trembling.

Link took over the conversation again. 'Would you mind showing us one of these *other* ways out?' Link picked up the Drum in readiness.

'Oh, has the captain sent you for the Drum, then?' asked Crimpett.

'Er, yes. That's right,' Link caught on. 'We've got to get it to him as quickly as possible.'

'We want to get out the way we came in,' said Eydith, almost in her normal voice. 'By the hatch up on deck near where the rowing boat is tied up.'

'Do you have any rope?' asked Link.

Crimpett straightened up as if he'd been insulted. 'Rope? This is a ship. Of course we've got rope. Bloody miles of it, I expect.' He pulled sharply on a cupboard door, almost tearing it off its hinges. 'Here,' he snapped, offering a coil to Link. 'That do?'

It would indeed. Link unwound what looked like enough, and Crimpett obliged with a knife. The wizard tied one end to the Drum and looped the other around his wrist, and smiled. It would be easy now. He shinned up the ladder and hauled the Drum up, with Eydith guiding and steadying it as she followed.

Crimpett stood at the bottom, not sure whether he was happy to be of assistance or not.

*

Eydith climbed down into the rowing boat, assisted by Greasy on the last step. Link lowered the Drum, and while still perched on the bottom rung of the ladder, he untied the boat. He also accepted Greasy's helping hand as he stepped down.

He was thankful for a favourable tide on the row back.

They were soon on the beach and wearily climbing the steps to the clifftop. Here they rested for a while. The walk into town didn't appeal right then, especially for Link who was carrying the Drum. But the thought of Dognettle and his crew returning got them moving. It also made them take a longer route back to the glider, avoiding the regular road.

* * *

75

Dognettle was waiting at his usual table in the *Barbarian's Codpiece* when Jook and Psoddoph turned up. One-Eye and Peg-Leg were leaning with their backs against the bar. Then Lampitt entered through the door marked 'Privy'. The two guards sat down at the captain's table.

Psoddoph opened with, 'Our boss says he'll up the offer by five golds.'

'Brought the money?' asked Dognettle without preamble.

'Um, no, actually,' said Psoddoph. 'The boss said 'e wants you to bring the Drum and meet him about half a mile out of town. By that derelict old fishermen's cottage.'

'Oh, 'e does, does 'e?' said Dognettle, sharply. 'Well you tell 'im, no money up front, no Drum.'

Jook grinned. 'Ah, 'e thought you might say that.'

'Yeah,' said Psoddoph. 'And then 'e said, tell 'im to sell it to the girl, then.' The guards made as if to leave.

Dognettle's face flushed, angrily. 'All right, all right,' he snapped. 'This afternoon. The fishermen's cottage. Three o'clock. And don't be late!'

*

Dognettle and his crew downed their drinks abruptly and stomped out of the tavern. Jook and Psoddoph followed at a safe distance. The captain was so wrapped up in his anger at the turn of events, he didn't notice he was being followed all the way back. The guards hung back to watch the sailors descend the cliff steps. And when they were out of sight, Jook and Psoddoph went to the cliff edge and saw the *Sea Dragon* anchored a short distance from the beach.

* * *

76

'They're anchored about a mile from 'ere, boss,' said Psoddoph. 'Said they'd meet us at three o'clock with the Drum.'

'Where I said?' asked Dennis.

'Yes, boss, that derelict cottage on the coast road.'

'Good. Take the box and wait for me there, we'll be along at three o'clock.' He looked sideways at Florence. 'When's that?'

'About three hours, Father.'

'Right.' Dennis was about to shoo them off when he paused. 'In case we get held up –' he said slowly, to be sure they caught every word – 'if things don't go quite to plan, that is – don't hang around on the roadside for hours with that precious box of teeth. If we don't show up in a couple of hours, get yourselves out of sight for the night and go back to the meeting place at three o'clock tomorrow. Got that?'

The guards nodded mutely.

'Good thinking,' said Florence.

'Well, run along you two. Hopefully, we'll see you later.' Dennis rubbed his hands together. 'Right, now they've gone, let's see where our demons have got to. They should be here by now.'

Florence rubbed the staff, and somewhere in the Parallel Dimension an angry voice uttered a curse. 'Doesn't 'e fink we're getting there as fast as we can?' snapped Hell.

'I must admit, your speediness, 'e is not the most patient of wizards,' the brown demon sympathised.

Dennis glanced in every direction for signs of the demon's approach. 'Can you hear anything?' said Dennis.

'Not yet, Father. But he won't be far away,' Florence tried to reassure him.

Some tell-tale dust drifted down from the ceiling.

*

Dognettle sat at his desk with his head in his hands. Lampitt thumped his fist against the door. 'Come in,' Dognettle snarled. Lampitt stepped inside. 'Got it?'

'Er, no, Cap'n,' Lampitt admitted.

'Have you checked the hold?'

'We've searched *everywhere*, Cap'n. It's gone.'

'Well, do it again,' ordered Dognettle. Lampitt started to leave. 'And send Crimpett down here.'

'Aye, aye, Cap'n,' said Lampitt, as he wandered despondently back along the passage on another futile search for the Drum.

* * *

77

Plaster dust was drifting down more heavily now, as the rumbling of Hell and his demons intensified. 'I think it might be safer to wait outside, Father,' Florence suggested, with more than a hint of urgency. Dennis didn't need to answer: he was already on his feet and heading for the door.

The walls began to rock. Florence snatched up the staff and ran. The roof of the cottage seemed to swell for a moment, then shrank and collapsed within the walls. The place appeared to settle for a moment, then one by one, the walls crashed inwards. Dennis and Florence sat on the grass a dozen yards away staring at the heap of rubble and listening to the rumbles that were still going on within. A dust cloud hung in the air like a large mushroom cloud. Then, all at once, there was silence.

After a few moments, Florence said, 'Do you think he's all right, Father?'

'Probably,' said Dennis. Then after a thoughtful pause, he added, 'He'd better be.'

A stone dislodged from the top of the pile and clattered to the grass. Shortly after, another followed. Then, with what seemed like a minor volcano erupting, Hell burst out of the top of the pile. He climbed painfully into the sunlight, rolled onto his back and collapsed, groaning. His next move was to roll down the heap onto the grass, cursing and swearing.

* * *

78

'Well, Cap'n,' said Crimpett. 'Two people came aboard this morning…'

'What people?' asked Dognettle, abruptly, his anger barely in check.

'A man in a dress.'

'Dress?' frowned Dognettle. 'Oh, a wizard.'

'Could be,' said Crimpett. 'But the other one was definitely a girl.'

Dognettle pulled the cork from a bottle and poured himself a drink. He hadn't even noticed he'd taken the bottle out of the drawer. He gulped the contents down and slammed the glass on the desk. Then he took a long swig from the bottle.

'Is everything all right, Cap'n?' asked Crimpett.

'No, it damn well isn't all right!' Dognettle lashed out. 'That wizard has stolen the Drum!'

'He told me you'd sent him to get it,' Crimpett protested.

'Of course he did!' A short, angry silence hung between them. 'Well, he *lied*, didn't he? And *you* believed him!'

'Oh, dear, Cap'n. What'll we do now?'

Dognettle screwed his eyes tightly in his frustration. Inexplicably, images of planks, yardarms and cats with nine tails came to mind, but he shook them away and tried to focus.

* * *

79

Hell sat up and angrily brushed the dust off his scales. 'Next time,' he growled, 'if there *is* a next time, do not call me unless you are in an open field.' He loped towards Dennis with a murderous look in his eyes. Dennis flexed his fingers and raised his hands.

'You can't hurt me,' Hell sneered, though not too sure about that. But he liked the sound of it. And the wizard's threat had the desired effect of halting him a few feet before he reached him. The fact that Florence was holding the staff like a club might also have had something to do with it.

'Finished?' said Dennis, ignoring the demon's tantrums. Hell, just grunted. 'Good,' said Dennis, looking past him at the demolition site. 'Now, how many demons have you brought? Thirty? Forty? Only I don't see anyone.'

The demon didn't answer immediately. In his mind he was counting the names and secretly closing down his claws as he mentally ticked them off.

'If you 'adn't called me when you did...' Hell began. 'I might've brought sixty or seventy,' he snapped.

'How many?' Dennis repeated.

'FIVE!' yelled Hell, angrily.

The colour drained from Dennis's cheeks. '*Five*?'

'Yes, five.'

Dennis slumped on the grass. 'You know,' he said, looking up, 'when I helped make you King of the Parallel Dimension, I thought you'd change – rise to the occasion – but you're still as useless as ever!'

'Huh!' Hell snorted. 'Look what I'm working with!'

Dennis looked around. There was only Florence. 'You leave her out of this!' he snapped, uncharacteristically springing to his daughter's defence.

'I wasn't referring to her,' the demon sneered.

'I think you've both said enough,' said Florence. 'This continual bickering is getting us nowhere.'

'I'll stop if he will,' said Dennis, a little petulantly.

'You started it,' whined Hell.

'No, I didn't.'

'Oh, for goodness' sake! Stop it! The pair of you!' said Florence, stamping her foot soundlessly on the grass.

'All right. All right,' said Dennis. 'I give in. Now where are these *five* demons?'

Hell swivelled his head to the heap of rubbish that was once a cottage. 'Under there,' he said. 'And I think they might need help.'

Dennis thought; *Useless. All of them. Utterly useless.* But he did step forward with the intention of helping to shift some of the rubble.

Hell gave him a quizzical look. 'Use the magic, man.'

Dennis just about held his temper. Rounding on him, he said, 'As I don't know where your people are, they might find themselves in the firing line. And we have few enough people without blasting those we do have to bits.'

'Fair enough,' said Hell, backing off. 'But don't call 'em *people* in front of 'em. They don't like it.'

Dennis moved contemptuously on. 'I suggest we move that one first,' he said, pointing at a large irregular block of stone on the top of the pile.

'Thank you,' said Hell. 'But if it's all the same to you, I'll start with the small ones and work up to that one.'

'I'm telling you it would best to move that big one first,' insisted Dennis.

Hell ignored him and started shifting the more shiftable stuff at the side of the pile. Soon, there was a hole big enough for him to crawl into. So, he did. 'Are you all right down there!' he yelled at the top of his voice.

In the darkness, about a foot from his ear, five voices yelled back at the tops of *their* voices, 'Yes, fank you, your findingness!'

The heap resonated for a moment, then the rubble began to shift again and finally collapsed under the weight of the big stone. 'Shit!' cursed Hell, as he started to dig his way out again.

Outside, Dennis just stood there. His predominant thought was, *I told you so*, but to say it would've been a waste of breath. With Hell burrowing irritably ahead of them, it wasn't long before the demons surfaced and Hell had them lined up on parade.

'Right, you lot, now listen up!' he shouted, as he walked along the very short line. 'This wizard 'ere 'as a job for you, and I want it done double quick. Understand?'

'Oh, yes, your forcefulness,' the demons chorused, raggedly.

How did they all know to say forcefulness*?* he thought, a little weird, but didn't really want to know. 'Good,' he said simply. He turned to Dennis. 'We're at your disposal now.'

'Right,' said Dennis, taking in the troops half-heartedly. 'Follow me.'

Hell suddenly thought of something and stopped in his tracks. 'Hold it,' he called, raising a clawed hand, 'I've just thought of something.' The demons sat down on the grass.

'What is it now?' said Dennis.

'We 'aven't discussed terms.'

'We can do that when you get the Drum back,' Dennis replied, dismissively.

'Oh, *no*… we'll do it now, or we're off.'

'All right.' Dennis sighed. 'What do you want this time?'

Hell had been giving this some serious thought, and now that the moment had arrived, he knew exactly what he wanted. 'I want the staff,' he blurted out.

Dennis's mouth dropped open. '*The staff?*'

'Yes,' said Hell. 'The staff. I want the staff.'

Dennis thought about it. 'I've got a flying carpet,' he said, at last. 'What about that?'

'The *staff*,' repeated Hell.

'You don't want that old thing…' said Dennis. 'Look, what about a couple of large diamonds?'

'Nope,' said Hell, bluntly. 'I want the staff.'

'What about the carpet *and* the…'

'I want the staff,' said Hell, unwavering. 'It's the only way to put an end to me being summoned 'ere, or anywhere else, by you – or anyone else.'

Dennis and Florence looked at one another. Dennis was considering it. But Florence was shaking her head. 'We'll think about it,' he said.

Hell sat down with the other demons. 'We'll wait.'

Dennis led Florence a few yards from the group. 'What are we going to do?' he whispered.

'We can't release him from the staff, Father, we'd lose the power we have over him for good. Besides, mother would be extremely angry.'

Dennis dismissed the thought of an irate Esme before it had time to settle, and glanced back over his shoulder at Hell. 'He seems determined to sit it out.'

'We'll let him wait a little longer,' said Florence.

'Then what?'

'I'll try talking to him this time.'

But Hell wasn't going to wait any longer. He stood up. 'Come on then, you lot, we're going.' Five pairs of clawed feet got ready to follow.

'Wait!' Florence called after them.

'Ah, decided to look at fings from my point of view, eh?' said Hell.

'What about this?' – she had his full attention – 'We give you the staff and you get the Drum back?' said Florence.

'That's the general idea, yes,' agreed Hell.

'But if you *fail*, you give the staff back to me.'

'*Fail?*' said Hell, raising his scaly eyebrows. 'I won't fail.'

'But if you do…' said Florence.

Hell stroked his chin. 'Hmm, yeah, all right. It's a deal,' he replied, reluctantly, and held out his claws for the staff. Florence passed it to him.

Hell felt the tingle of its magic run up his arm. He shuddered and smiled smugly.

Florence flexed her fingers and stared into the demon's eyes. 'If you fail… the staff is mine. And don't think I can't take it off you,' she finished, giving him a look calculated to remove any doubts he might have about that.

Dennis watched, concerned, but he could tell she was up to something, so he held back.

Hell looked her in the eye. He caught a glimpse of her wrath reflected back at him. Up until then, the surface world hadn't held any fear for him, but seeing his two tiny reflections in her eyes, and how they seemed to infer that she could possess him, was enough to unnerve even a Demon King. That he saw bits of himself falling off, didn't help. 'I agree,' he replied hurriedly, and stepped back as though released from an invisible grip.

*

'Follow me,' snapped Dennis, picking up from where he'd left off. Hell and his five demons fell into line this time, and followed.

After a whinge-filled, forty-five-minute, cross-country trek, they arrived on the clifftop overlooking the *Sea Dragon.*

'Nice ship,' said Hell, peering over the edge, admiring the dragon's head. 'Now what, wizard?'

Florence pointed. 'I can see steps down to the beach over there.'

Dennis looked at Hell. 'We go down.'

It was down on the beach that the next question came up.

'Anyone know 'ow to swim?' asked Hell.

They all shook their heads. Florence could, but decided to lie. There was no way she was going to strip down in front of this lot.

'Well,' said Hell. 'Can anyone hold their breath for a long time?'

Brown stepped forward. 'How long is a long time, your royalness?'

'Well now,' said Hell. 'That depends.'

'What on, your thoughtfulness?' asked Brown.

'How fast can you get to that ship and back?'

Brown agonised over the distance from the beach to the ship. He thought: *A minute? If I run, and about a minute and a half to get back again.* 'Yes, your royalness, I think I can do that all right. Two or three minutes.'

'Good,' said Dennis. 'Now, when you get there, you'll find a rope dangling in the water. One end will be attached to the ship and the other end will be attached to the anchor.'

'Yes,' said Brown, dreading what Dennis was going to say next.

'All I want you to do is pick up the anchor and bring it back here.'

'Ah,' said Brown, relieved. 'For a minute there, I thought you was going to ask me to bring the ship back.' With that, he braced himself, strutted seawards, and waded in.

'And leave the rope tied to it!' Dennis shouted after him.

The demon disappeared beneath the waves. Hell sat down. 'What do you intend to do with the anchor?' he wondered, as he idly ran a claw down the staff.

'You and your little friends here can pull the ship up to the beach,' said Dennis. 'And then we can board it.'

'Oh,' said Hell.

They sat in silence, watching the waves for any sign of Brown. The demon that is, not the effluence from Port Akerbyn. A long two minutes passed, but he didn't surface.

'Do you think 'e's all right?' remarked Hell.

'Give him a bit longer,' said Dennis, without taking his eyes off the ship. Not that he was too worried: he still had four more demons he hadn't used yet. Then, slowly, the great head of the *Sea Dragon* began to turn and glide slowly towards to the beach.

'Look!' said Florence. 'It's moving.'

Hell jumped to his feet. 'Damn! Do you think they've seen us?'

'Probably not,' said Dennis. 'Looking at you lot, they'd be heading the other way.'

They all took it as a compliment.

The *Sea Dragon* was close to the beach now and the small, brown demon's head appeared momentarily, gulping for air, as a wave crashed over him. He fell down, then staggered to his feet again, coughing up sea water and gasping for breath.

He was clutching the anchor to his chest and when the next wave hit him, he was carried forward and unceremoniously dumped in the shallows. He dropped the anchor and rolled onto his back, breathing hard. He lay there for a moment, then opened his eyes to see the bow of the ship towering above him. 'Bloody 'ell!' he yelled. And in a moment, he was back on his feet and running. As he charged up the beach, Hell stuck out a foot as he went by and sent him sprawling on the sand.

'Now get up and stop messin' about,' growled Hell. 'It's only a figger 'ead.'

'B…B…B…'

'Up!' ordered Hell. The small demon stood up and made himself look up at the figure head. Now he could see it was, in fact, a rather fearsome wood carving.

'Oh,' he mouthed.

They stood looking up at the great bulk of the *Sea Dragon*, lying in the shallows like a beached whale. They needed to get on board. Dennis scratched his head thoughtfully.

It was Florence again who was the most observant. 'There's a rung ladder on the side, Father.'

'Follow me, you lot. We're going aboard.' But their following stopped at the bottom of the rungs. 'Right, up you go,' he told Hell, who was nearest to him. Without thinking, the demon handed the staff to Dennis, to leave both his hands free to climb up.

'Thank you,' said Dennis, passing it to Florence and smiling wickedly. 'Didn't take long, did it?'

'A deal's a deal, Father,' she hissed back at him.

'But… oh, never mind.' He scowled, as the last demon climbed the rungs.

*

'Come in,' said Dognettle, as someone rapped on his door.

'It's only me, Cap'n,' said Lampitt, stepping inside.

'Find it?' asked Dognettle, despondently.

'No, sir.'

'Then why are you here?'

'We're beached, Cap'n. Didn't you feel it? And there's someone on deck,' said Lampitt, seriously.

'What! Get One-Eye, and meet me under the main hatch. Now!'

Lampitt saluted and ducked back into the passageway. Dognettle was right behind him.

*

Dennis tried the handle. It was locked.

'Now what?' said Hell. 'They're in there, and we're out 'ere.'

'How observant,' Dennis muttered.

'Well, 'ow are we supposed to get in?' moaned Hell.

'Perhaps you should knock?' suggested Dennis.

'There might be no-one 'ome,' said Brown, standing in a puddle of water that was still dripping off him.

* * *

'Are we all here?' whispered Dognettle, addressing his crew assembled under the hatch.

'All those that could spare the time, Captain,' said Lampitt. Peg-Leg hit him. One-Eye was nowhere to be found.

'There are others on the way, Cap'n,' said Peg-Leg.

'Right, when they're all here, we'll rush 'em,' said Dognettle.

Peg-Leg looked up at the hatch. 'That might be difficult, sir,' he said, weighing up the situation. 'How do you propose we rush 'em on a ladder? One at a time?'

'Ah,' said Dognettle, slightly embarrassed, and trying to figure it out. 'You know what I mean.'

'Captain?' said Lampitt, still rubbing his stinging ear.

'What now?' hissed Dognettle.

'That means they can only rush *us* one a time as well, don't it?'

'Shall I 'it 'im again, Cap'n, seeing as 'ow we can't find One-Eye?' said Peg-Leg, raising a fist.

'No,' said Dognettle. 'I think he's right. We should wait till they try to come down.'

Lampitt grinned like a Halloween Pumpkin. 'Yeah, then we can slaughter 'em as they rush us… one at a time.'

Hell rapped on the hatch door.

'Don't answer it,' breathed Dognettle.

Above them, Dennis nodded, indicating that the demon should try again. Hell knocked a bit harder. The crew of the *Sea Dragon* remained silent.

Hell shook his head. 'They must be out,' he said, resignedly.

'No… knock again!' Dennis ordered.

'Me 'and's stinging now,' he complained, and moved aside. 'Brown!'

The small demon straightened up. 'Yes? Your painfulness.'

'Open this 'atch.'

The demon knelt down and took a firm grip on the handle with both claws and yanked. There was a faint creaking sound at first, which was followed by a dull thud.

'Useful,' said Hell. '*Really useful.*'

'It came off in me 'and, your royalness,' said Brown, flinching away from Hell's flying claw.

'Now, how are we going to get in there?' Dennis raged. In his anger, he swung his foot to kick the crouching Brown. But the demon leapt away and grabbed Hell's ankle to stop himself as he started to slide down the deck. They hit the shallow water together.

Brown was up first and helping his king to his feet. Hell stood up, spitting water and coughing. 'What's *in this stuff?*' he protested. 'It's like liquid salt.'

Brown was annoyed. Firstly with Dennis, and secondly with himself. 'You all right, your wetness?'

Hell coughed again and spat out more salt water.

Brown released Hell's arm and angrily punched the hull of the *Sea Dragon.* There was a sharp cracking sound. 'Oh, no. What 'ave I done now?' he groaned.

'What's the matter now?' sighed Hell, about to mount the rung ladder and get out of the water.

'Look what I've gone an' done, your royalness.'

'Oh, well done,' beamed Hell. 'Wizard! Get yourself down 'ere. We've found a way in.'

'But, your royalness…' Brown went on.

'Hit it again,' said Hell. 'Harder. And hurry up before they try to stop us.'

Dennis appeared at the bottom of the ladder. 'What happened?'

'Brown punched an 'ole in it.'

The wizard smiled and dropped into the shallows. 'Oh, excellent.'

'See?' said Hell. 'I told you it would be all right. Now… 'it it again.'

Brown punched another hole in the side of the ship.

'It would be quicker,' said Dennis, 'if the rest of you helped.'

'What?' said Hell. 'You mean we all 'it it, like. Yeah… come on you lot, get stuck in!' The other demons scrambled down and joined in tearing great lumps away from Brown's hole.

It wasn't long before an alarm bell was clanging, closely followed by the footfalls of running men. When the hole was big enough,

Dennis stepped through. Florence followed, still clutching the staff. Half a dozen burly seamen stepped out of the shadows inside, all brandishing long, curved swords. They stood in a half circle barring the way. Dennis raised his hand and flexed his fingers.

'There's no need for that!' came a hasty voice from behind the seamen. They parted to give Dognettle room to squeeze through.

'Who are you?' asked Dennis.

'I am the captain of this ship, sir.'

'Ah… Dognettle,' said Dennis.

'The same. And judging by your dress, sir, you must be Dennis.'

'It's *a robe!*' snapped Dennis.

'Excuse me. *Robe*,' said Dognettle. 'Look, we don't want a bloody fight any more than you do, I'm sure. We're reasonable people. You'd better come to my cabin before your little friends do any more damage.' He looked at the ragged hole with immense displeasure.

'It wouldn't have happened if you'd opened the door,' said Dennis.

'We did. Eventually,' said Dognettle. 'But you weren't there.' He turned away. The sailors lowered their weapons and moved aside, allowing him to leave. Dennis followed and they closed ranks again.

Walking through the lower decks, Dennis said, 'I expect you know why I'm here.'

'Yes,' said Dognettle. 'But I would prefer to discuss it in my cabin.' He pulled the door open and stepped inside. 'Come in.'

Dennis entered, swept past Dognettle, and casually sat in the captain's chair. 'Well?' he said, 'where is it?'

'Ah. The Drum.' Dognettle sighed. 'I thought *you* might tell *me*. Being as how you sent your people here to steal it.'

'What? I didn't send anybody,' countered Dennis, not liking what he was hearing.

'Well, it would appear I've been burgled,' said Dognettle.

'This is just not good enough!' Dennis stormed. 'First you steal it from me, then you lose it!'

'I know 'ow it looks.' Dognettle was searching for words. 'But… you just can't always get good seamen these days.'

'Well, at least I don't have to pay you,' said Dennis, icily, grasping at something to his advantage from this fiasco.

'Well, perhaps not the ransom, no. But there is the small matter of a few days' storage.'

Momentarily lost for words, Dennis stood up, his face flushed with anger.

Dognettle took a couple of steps back. Dennis's stare made him nervous. 'Well, perhaps not, then. Look, I'll tell you what.'

'Yes?' said Dennis. 'What?'

'Would you still be amenable to paying for it if I got it back?'

'Maybe,' said Dennis, sitting down again. 'How much?'

'I was thinking, fifty golds?' said Dognettle, hopefully.

'*Fifty?* That was the original price.'

'I am waving the storage fee,' said Dognettle, swiftly.

'I'll give you forty,' said Dennis.

'Forty-five, and you've got a deal.'

'I said *forty*,' Dennis repeated, unblinking.

'All right, forty,' Dognettle gave way, fearing it might drop even further if he argued.

'Right,' said Dennis. 'Good. For the time being, it's in your hands. But if a chance comes my way to take the Drum, then I will.' A deal was done, but neither of them felt inclined to shake hands over it.

Dognettle led Dennis back to the hole. 'Look what you've done to my ship,' he sniped, running his fingers along the jagged edges of Brown's hole.

'You should have answered the door quicker,' Dennis reminded him.

'It'll be days before I can get her seaworthy again.'

'Days?' said Dennis, looking at the rising tide around them. 'You've got minutes rather than days, I should think.'

Dognettle suddenly realised with horror the dire strait he was in. He was about to lose his ship! The *king's* ship!!

Dennis calmly continued, 'And I want you to start looking for my Drum now.' He pointed his fingers at the pieces of the ship that were beginning to float away inland on the incoming tide, and muttered something under his breath. The flotsam paused and propelled itself back over the water. It began to move together. It assembled itself on the water into a shape that at first resembled the hole in the hull and then matched it perfectly.

Dognettle watched in fascination as Dennis performed his favourite 'party piece' restoration spell. 'We'd better get aboard,' he said, as the 'plug' began to lift itself into the hole.

'I need a drink,' said Dognettle, heading directly for his office. 'Care to join me, wizard?'

Florence cut in with, 'We'll miss that three o'clock meet-up, if we're not careful. At the fisherman's cottage,' she nudged him.

'Oh, yes,' said Dennis, faltering. Then, 'Oh, sod that,' and followed the captain.

Five minutes later, the sea had lapped above the patch and refloated the ship.

* * *

A man with a patch over one eye knocked on the gate-house door of King Treadwell's castle. That was just the beginning of his problems. From the response he got, it might as well have been a bank holiday. He tried again. Still no answer. He shrugged despondently and started to walk back down the hill. He thought he heard a voice call out to him, so he stopped and looked around. The door was still firmly shut.

'Up 'ere!' the voice called out again.

One-Eye looked up. There was a soldier leaning over the battlements on the opposite side of the moat. *Hanging on* would describe his situation more accurately. And *for dear life* might describe it even better.

'Hold on!' One-Eye called.

'I've only got two bloody options!' the soldier called down from somewhere under his armpit, 'That and fall!' One-Eye strode back to the door and thumped it hard. 'It's no good you knocking,' the soldier told him. 'I'm the one that's supposed to open it.'

'Bugger,' muttered One-Eye. He peered up at the soldier again. 'Don't go away, I'll go round the back!' and he broke into a trot around the building.

As he ran, it occurred to him, *There is no way in at the back*. He stopped. 'A ladder!' he said to himself. Then he considered how far up the wall he'd have to climb. 'Okay, lots of ladders.' He ran down the slope back into town and started to look for someone who might own a ladder, but in a town of ground floor dwellings, even the window cleaner's ladders wouldn't be more than five rungs. He needed something much longer. But what? There wasn't anything.

'Think,' he berated himself. Time was fast running out. 'There must be another way into that castle. Yes – across the moat and in through a window.' He ran back up the hill, past the moat house, and slid down the muddy bank into the murky water. 'Gods,' he complained, 'don't they ever clean this thing out.' He swam the few yards across to the wall, keeping his head high, and edged his way along till he came to a window. It was protected by a lattice of rusty iron. One-Eye cursed his luck. And not for the first time that day, either.

He reached up and took a firm hold on the grille. With his feet firmly planted against the wall, he pulled. The bars creaked. Bits of ancient iron pinged away from their bases. He paused to adjust his grip. The grating began to bow towards him, squealing as it scraped over the ancient stones. Suddenly, it came away. Just in time, he snatched a deep breath as the old iron grating sank into the depths of the moat with him under it.

His surroundings were various shades of green, which he failed to notice on account of his eyes being shut. He didn't know how deep the moat was. His instincts told him that when he reached the bottom, it would be best not to have the heavy iron grating over him. He twisted himself around and pushed himself away. His lungs were almost at bursting point as he swam desperately for the surface. After what seemed forever, he was back breathing air again. Not *fresh* air – you don't get that over a stagnant moat – but it was the best air he'd ever inhaled, and a lot easier than trying to breathe water.

After a moment to settle his breathing, he looked around to get his bearings, and swam as fast as he could to the bar-less window. He hauled himself inside and flopped to the floor, dripping water. He got up and wanted to empty his boots, but remembering the guard hanging from the battlements, he squelched out of the room and ran up the steps.

At the top, One-Eye crashed through the door and sprinted to where he last saw the unfortunate man hanging. He looked over the ledge. The man was gone. He leaned out further over the battlements, expecting to see him sprawled on the entrance pathway, but there was no sign of him. The guard had disappeared. He checked again, but he'd gone. He guessed he must either have survived and limped off somewhere, or rolled down into the moat. Either way, he was too late. The panic over, he was acutely aware how wet he was. He sat and emptied his boots.

'Ah… 'ere 'e is,' said the guard, cheerfully. 'We thought you'd drowned yourself when you went down under that grating.'

One-Eye looked up, from wringing out his socks. 'I was coming to rescue you!' he snapped.

'Yeah… I guessed that. Anyway, Alf came up and found me. Just in time, as well.'

'I could've drowned down there,' One-Eye pointed out to the two men.

'Well, we did 'ave a quick look, mate,' said the guard, defensively.

'A quick look? Is that all?'

'We're supposed to be on guard, you know. We ain't supposed to be rescuing idiots that wanna swim in the moat.'

Alf picked up on that and added. 'In fact, we're supposed to shoot people we catch swimming in the moat.'

One-Eye hit him.

Then, in frustration, and before he could react, he hit the other one as well.

They stood back, rubbing their ears.

'Now,' snapped One-Eye, belligerently. 'Take me to the king.' And after a second's pause, he added another, 'NOW!'

They still hesitated. But, then, when One-Eye reached up and replaced the eyepatch he'd removed to dry it off a bit, Alf said, 'Ere, I fink I might know this bloke.'

'I work for the king,' One-Eye said, between gritted teeth, and close to thumping them again.

'You do know you smell, don't you?' Alf remarked.

'And so will you if you don't get a move on,' retorted One-Eye.

'But you know what his majesty's like with smells,' Alf pleaded.

'Yeah…' the other guard agreed. 'Look, why don't we take you down to the kitchen and get you cleaned up first?'

One-Eye sniffed his sleeve. Reluctantly, he had to agree, it was a bit high. His anger cooled. 'Alright, one of you go and tell Loosley I'm here, and I want to see him.'

'Oh…' said Alf, quietly.

One-eye grabbed a handful of the guard's tunic and pulled him closer, and hissed, 'Yes, I'm a spy.'

'Yeah, I remember, now,' said the guard, hoarsely.

One-Eye let him go. 'Right, now we've got that sorted out, we'll go, shall we?'

Alf pulled on the new bell rope. Somewhere, a bell tolled, and the drawbridge began to lower impressively, albeit clankingly. When it was about ten feet from the ground, Alf warned One-Eye to stand further back. The spy chose to ignore him.

'It's in your best interests that you stand *further back*, sir,' Alf stressed.

One-Eye looked up, 'Ah… yes.'

The drawbridge had stopped moving. But it wasn't going to stop for long. Taking the initiative, the two guards each grabbed an arm and bundled One-Eye out of the way – just as the drawbridge suddenly slammed to the ground where the three men had been standing.

'Thank you,' said One-Eye, brushing himself down. 'Who's on duty up there?'

'Er… not quite sure today, sir,' Alf lied. 'It's just their little way, sir. You know… no harm meant… none done.'

'Find out who it is,' One-Eye ordered. 'And have him sent to me in the king's throne room.'

*

Half an hour later, One-eye was sitting in the castle's kitchen, a towel draped across his knees for modesty. His freshly-laundered clothes were hanging on the backs of chairs in front of the fire to dry out. The cooks and maids ignored him as they bustled about preparing the king's evening meal.

Tonight's meal was to be something special. It was king Treadwell's birthday, and as far as they were concerned, One-Eye was just another unwanted nuisance, and he wondered why he even bothered with the towel. For all the attention he was getting, he might as well drop it and walk around naked. *No*, he thought, *why should they have a laugh at my expense.* He leant forward and felt his clothes. *A few more minutes*, he thought, *then, damp or not, I'm putting them on.*

Mrs. Grimly, the head cook, saw him feeling his clothes and glided silently over the flag stones, wiping her flour-dusty hands on her apron. She picked up his trousers and held them against her cheek. 'Hmm,' she breathed, then tossed them to him. 'Right, young man, you can put these on now.'

One-Eye stood up without thinking and shook his trousers out in front of him, allowing the towel to fall. Mrs. Grimly clapped her hands over her eyes, not because she was shocked –she'd already buried three husbands (at least that she'd admit to) – but to save the spy's feelings. He struggled to get one leg in while hopping around on the other, and as he was about to topple over, Mrs. Grimly stuck out a hand and grabbed his arm.

'Why don't you sit down and put them on properly. I've seen it all before, you know.'

'Mrs. Grimly!' snapped One-Eye. 'I must remind you that I am one of the king's spies.'

'Yes, young man,' Mrs. Grimly replied, and before he could open his mouth again, she added. 'And I've been his cook a lot longer than you've been his spy. *I* was changing *your* nappies, young man.'

'But... Mrs. Grimly... I'm twenty-nine, now.'

'Put your trousers on.'

One-Eye turned his back to her and heaved his trousers on as quickly as he could. She snatched his shirt from the back of a chair and passed it to him. 'Thank you,' he muttered, sullenly.

'That's better,' she beamed. 'Now you look presentable. This chain mail won't be dry for another hour yet, though,' she said, moving it closer to the fire.

He smiled back while she straightened his collar and adjusted his shoulders. 'You know the way to His Majesty's room, so off you go,' she ordered, mothering him. 'I need to get on.'

'Thank you, Mrs. Grimly.'

* * *

Eydith and Link recovered the glider from the hillside outside Port Akerbyn. It took a while to find due to Eydith's cloaking spell, but Sprag finally managed to undo it, and with his help they managed to get the glider airborne again.

Even though they were obliged to spend the hours of darkness perched on the crest of a hill, they made good time on their flight back to Treadwell's castle. As before, Eydith took the pilot's seat, while Link sat awkwardly and uncomfortably nursing the Drum. Ben sat sullenly in the back, probably missing Greasy's company. But Greasy had played his part in rescuing the Drum, and had returned to his duties in Port Akerbyn.

They were soon to discover, on their arrival at the castle, that someone else had made the journey to Corin in far better time overland. One-Eye had ridden all through the night, on the moonlit roads, as spies are wont to do. His dead-beat horse was currently in recovery in the king's stables.

* * *

83

At the roadside on a grassy slope, close to a dilapidated cottage, two guards sat minding a box. 'Do you think they'll be much longer?' Jook wondered.

'He did say *about* three o'clock,' replied Psoddoph, without shifting his gaze from the point where the road met the horizon.

'He said that yesterday,' moaned Jook. 'And he didn't come. And I'm starving. What if they don't turn up today either?'

'Shall we go back and look for him?' suggested Psoddoph. 'I know we're supposed to give it a couple of hours, but…'

They were both fed up with waiting. 'Might as well.'

Both men stood up and grabbed the handles of the box. They'd only gone a few yards when Dennis appeared on the brow of the hill behind them. Noticing his guards walking away, he quickened his pace. Florence, the demons and the would-be pirates, strung out behind him.

'Come on,' Dennis nagged at Florence. 'We've got to catch them.'

'Why don't you just call them back, Father? You'll have a heart attack or something, trying to run like that at your age.'

'What? Oh… yes, good idea.' He ignored the bit about 'your age' and cupped his hands to his mouth and hollered.

Jook and Psoddoph stopped in their tracks and looked back. They put the box on the ground and sighed with relief. The wizard, though still short of breath, rushed up as fast as he dared without bringing his speed to Florence's attention. 'Aha! Thought you'd steal the teeth, did you?' he rounded on them. 'As soon as my back was turned.'

'What? Of course not,' said Psoddoph, in all innocence.

Dennis ignored him and continued his tirade. 'You didn't honestly think you'd get away with it, did you?'

'We were coming to look for you, boss,' said Jook, honestly.

Psoddoph looked pleadingly towards Florence for support.

'Father, they're telling the truth,' she interrupted. 'Why would they lie? They know you'd find them.'

Dennis calmed a little. 'All right. But I know how many there should be, and if you've taken any…'

'We haven't, boss,' Psoddoph assured him.

'Count 'em if you like,' challenged Jook, clearly offended.

Dennis shrugged and walked away to sulk on his own.

'What's wrong with him, miss?' asked Psoddoph.

'The Drum's been stolen,' she replied, and pulling a face, then added, '*again*.'

Psoddoph's shoulders sagged. 'Do we know who took it, miss?'

'Eydith,' said Florence, quietly. 'And Link of course.'

'They don't stop chasing the magic, do they?'

'That's probably because he doesn't stop stealing it,' she said, only half seriously.

'Because it's mine, that's why,' said Dennis, overhearing them.

Psoddoph lowered his voice. 'I suppose 'e wants us to 'elp 'im?' he said, with more than a suggestion of resignation. She didn't have to answer.

'Where are you heading now, then?' asked Jook, trying to keep the look of disgust off his face as he noticed the posse of demons among the seamen that accompanied them.

'We're going to King Treadwell's castle,' Florence replied. 'You know what father's like. He won't rest until he's got it back.'

'It's all right, Floren… er, miss,' said Psoddoph, kindly, almost forgetting himself for a moment – though she smiled as if she didn't mind at all – 'we know what you mean.'

The trusty guards each grabbed a box handle again and got moving. Dennis, Florence, and his motley crew followed on behind.

After an hour of marching up and down hills Dennis complained, 'It'll take ages at this rate.'

'We can always go underground, wizard,' suggested Hell.

'Er, no. I don't think so,' said Dennis. 'But don't let me stop *you*, we can meet you there later.'

Hell drew his demons aside and passed on what Dennis had suggested. They didn't disagree, because they treated anything that Hell suggested as an order. Sometimes they questioned him but they always did it. Sometimes, to their cost.

The others stood and looked on curiously as the demons clawed their way into the ground like overgrown moles. It was somehow both horrible and fascinating to watch at the same time.

When they were gone, Dennis joined Florence and the guards as they walked. He realised his daughter was still carrying the staff and smiled to himself, thinking how easy it had been to relieve Hell of it. But his good humour vanished when he realized something else.

'Where's my carpet!' he flared at the guards again.

'Dunno, boss,' Psoddoph replied, on behalf of both of them. 'Last time I saw it, it was in the cottage.'

'Everybody stop!' yelled Dennis. 'We're going back.'

'What?' said Dognettle. 'You must be joking.'

'No,' said Dennis. 'I've left something very important behind.'

'Well, we're not goin' back,' said Dognettle.

'In that case,' said Dennis. 'No gold.'

'Hold on a minute, wizard,' said Dognettle, raising a calming hand. 'I never said I wasn't going to 'elp, did I? I just said, we're not going back.'

Dennis paused and considered.

'Look,' Dognettle continued, 'we've got all we need. You go back and get whatever it is you've forgotten, and I'll take the *Sea Dragon* up the river to the city.'

Dennis didn't really trust the sailors, 'All right,' he finally agreed.

'Good,' said Dognettle. 'We'll wait for you just outside the city. And if you can't find *us*, you can't miss the ship.'

Without any undue pleasantries, the two parties went their separate ways. Jook and Psoddoph picked up the box yet again and followed the wizard back in the direction of the rubbish heap that was once a cottage.

Dennis was happier now there were fewer of them. He wasn't a great one for company. The less people around him, the less there were to distrust. He found renewed energy and was striding out. And for once he felt like they were making good time. Though, in truth, they were wasting time having to go back for the carpet.

*

When they arrived at the ruins. The guards sat down on the box and waited for Dennis to decide what he wanted them to do. They'd barely got the chill off the lid, when he started issuing his orders. There was a small shed about the size of a sentry box a short distance away. It could only be one of two things. A privy, or a tool shed. Jook opened the door and peered inside. It was, in fact, both a privy *and* a tool shed. But among the tools there was only one shovel.

'You'll just have to take turns,' said Dennis.

Jook volunteered to go first and started to dig into the heap. After a short while he saw a corner of the carpet sticking out from the rubble. 'I've found it, boss,' he called. Psoddoph came forward and started to move some of the rubble away with his hands.

'Stop wasting time,' said Dennis. 'Which way up is it?'

Jook squatted down for a better look. 'Pile side up by the look of it, boss.'

'Good. Stand back.' Dennis flexed his fingers and concentrated. Stones began to move, slipping away from the heap. 'Carpet… up,' he whispered. Nothing happened.

'Say *please*, boss,' Psoddoph reminded him.

'*Please*.' Dennis sighed. The carpet began to rise, slowly at first, still partially trapped under the weight of all the rubble, but as some of it fell off, it gained height more quickly. It was almost twenty feet in the air before the wizard remembered to ask it to stop. He brought it down again, away from the ruins. Jook and Psoddoph brushed the remaining stones and plaster off and gave it a gentle shake. Barely two minutes later, when the seating arrangements had been worked out (and Florence had nudged Jook aside to sit herself next to Psoddoph), they were back in the air, heading for Treadwell's castle.

* * *

84

One-Eye knocked on the king's door and waited. He could hear footsteps approaching from the other side. Then, the hatch slid back.

'Yep?' said the top of a head.

'I'm here to see the king,' announced One-Eye.

'Why?' asked the voice.

One-Eye didn't answer for several seconds, and when he did, he ignored the question. '*Thadax*? Is that you?' he said, leaning forward, trying to look inside the hatch.

Thadax stood on tiptoe. 'Jubnak?'

'Yes,' sighed One-Eye. He hated it when people used his real name. Spies were supposed to be nameless, faceless, elusive, beings. But, on recognition, the bolts slid back more hurriedly than usual, as Thadax threw himself into the task of opening the door. Jubnak was the only spy that the doorkeeper had any respect for. Well, not so much respect, as fear. He knew from past experience that since Jubnak had lost his eye, he'd become very short tempered, and any obstructive behaviour could result in a red ear, or a black eye. Or both.

The door swung back and Jubnak stepped inside. 'This way,' said Thadax, needlessly, pushing the door shut and ducking away as a precautionary measure. But Jubnak had raised his hands simply to shoo the doorkeeper ahead of him, as he followed him into Treadwell's throne room.

The king looked up. 'Ah… er, Jubnak. I've been waiting for you.'

The spy knelt at the foot of the dais. 'Get up, man,' said Treadwell. 'I haven't got time for all that rubbish, now.' Though Jubnak knew he'd be quick to be offended if he omitted it.

Jubnak stood up, 'I bring news, your majesty.'

'I should hope so. What's going on?'

'Well, your majesty…'

'Yes, yes, get on with it.'

'Eydith has the Drum,' Jubnak reported.

'That *is* good news,' said Treadwell, brightly. 'What happened to Dognettle? Is he in chains?'

'No, sire. But he is on his way here...' Jubnak started to explain.

'In custody, with an armed guard, I trust.'

'Sort of, sire. He has an armed guard with him, but not one you would trust. They're his crewmen. He plans to attack the castle, and steal the Drum again.'

'What?' Treadwell stood up and paced the floor. 'When does he intend to do this?'

'As soon as the wizard catches up with him, sire.'

'The wizard, Dennis?'

'Yes, sire. He's paying Dognettle to help him steal it.'

Treadwell sat down again. 'This is terrible news. What are we going to do?'

Jubnak remained silent. It seemed prudent.

The king nervily drummed his fingers on the increasingly worn-looking arms of his throne again. 'Is this wizard very powerful, do you know?' he wondered.

'He scares the sh... er, wits out of me, sire.'

'What about Teeter?' asked the king. 'Is he a match for this Dennis?'

'I doubt it, sire. My sources tell me Dennis is a master wizard, and an ex-Archchancellor of Havrapsor.'

The king sagged visibly on hearing that. 'There must be somebody,' he said, looking at the wall-hangings, as if for inspiration. 'Thadax!'

'Sire?' said the doorkeeper, snapping to attention.

'Go and get Teeter up here. Let's see what he has to say.'

Thadax bowed from the waist and left.

*

The door-keeper quick-marched himself through the castle, and was soon peering gingerly around the door into Teeter's workshop. He checked to see where the wizard was, and if he was working on or carrying anything that might go bang if he was suddenly startled. He couldn't see him at any of the benches, so went inside. He spotted him standing at the side of the slipway chute waving two table tennis bats.

Wondering if he'd finally flipped, Thadax took a step forward and slammed the door behind him, to let him know that he was in the room. But Teeter was too engrossed in watching the sky, waving the bats. Thadax crossed crablike to the other side of the room and stood at Teeter's side. 'Ahem,' he coughed, politely.

'Don't bother me now, man,' Teeter snapped, without turning his head. 'Can't you see there's a flying machine coming in?'

Thadax looked out at the sky. There was indeed a large, white cross up there, and it was approaching quickly. Thadax wasn't sure what to make of it. His lips moved silently, then his jaw dropped completely.

'Get down man!' yelled Teeter.

But Thadax was transfixed. Teeter had to rugby-tackle him to the floor. There was a loud whistling and scraping sound as the glider skated across the workshop floor and, thanks to Sprag, ground to a halt just in front of a high rack filled with bottles of assorted chemical solutions. Then there was silence, until the tip of one of the glider's wings gently tapped the stone floor.

Teeter looked up and saw Eydith standing over him. He smiled broadly and scrambled to his feet. 'You managed to get it back into the air?' he started, excitedly.

'It's a long story. But the right spell does the trick every time.' She grinned.

'Well… yes,' he said, disappointedly, hoping the reason had been more mechanical than magical.

Link stepped out and stretched, then hopped quickly as Ben's battle-axe clattered onto the floor beside him.

Ben climbed out and staggered forward, rubbing his back. 'If I never see one of them things again, it'll be too soon,' he muttered, irritably.

Thadax tugged on Teeter's sleeve. 'Come on,' he said, urgently. 'The king wants to see you.'

'Course 'e does,' said Teeter. 'He always wants to see me. Come on,' he said, turning to Eydith. 'I expect he'll want to see you as well.'

'What already?' said Link, still rolling his shoulders and stretching to get some circulation going.

Eydith wasn't too pleased to be summoned, either. She hardly felt presentable after the flight, or ready for such a meeting, but there was little choice. Link heaved the Drum out of the glider and followed.

When they entered Treadwell's throne room, the first thing to grab their attention was Jubnak, or One-Eye, standing at the king's right hand. Eydith reacted instinctively. She raised her hand and generated a fireball, but before it left her fingers, Teeter stepped in front of her with his own hand raised, though not to deliver a fireball of his own, but signalling her to stop.

'No!' he yelled, perhaps a bit louder than he intended. 'It's all right, it's all right – he's one of the king's men.'

'I saw him with Dognettle, trying to steal the Drum!' said Eydith, her eyes narrowing.

Jubnak shifted uneasily onto his other foot. 'Er… I was on the *Sea Dragon under cover* to keep an eye on him, miss.'

'Yes,' the king interrupted. 'I've had my doubts about Dognettle's loyalty for some time now.'

'That's why I'm here now, miss,' said Jubnak. 'Dognettle and Dennis are on their way here.'

'He never gives up, does he?' said Link.

'It's worse than that,' said Jubnak. 'He's bringing demons as well.'

'Ah, yes. That reminds me,' said Treadwell, anxiously. 'Are you any match for this wizard, Teeter? Could you stand up against him, do you think?'

Teeter stroked his beard, thoughtfully, uncertainly. 'I don't know your majesty,' he said. 'He was once a high-ranking wizard. Greatly feared in the wizarding fraternity.'

'Does that mean he's any good, or not?' asked Treadwell.

Eydith stepped forward. 'It means, if I might say so, your highness, that he's *very* good with magic.'

Treadwell tapped on the arms of his throne again. 'Are any of the wizards I keep here capable of taking care of this man?'

Teeter shrugged. 'I'm not even sure all of us together could do that.'

The king was crestfallen. 'So…?' He searched all their faces. 'What's to be done?'

Eydith stepped forward. 'I've beaten him before, sire.'

Treadwell gawped at her, but it was Teeter who voiced what the king was thinking. 'What? You're a *girl!*'

Link swiftly joined in, 'You're clearly not aware of what's been happening at Havrapsor these last few months.'

Eydith slipped her hand into his. 'Well, I did have help,' she said.

'Wait a moment... yes,' said Teeter. 'I heard rumours. Bits of news.' He looked closely at them, searching their faces, as if that would somehow help him piece it together. 'Oh, by all that's magical, yes. You must be two of those who …'

'Ousted the former, awful, Archchancellor,' she finished for him.

'Namely, Dennis,' added Link, completing the picture.

The king sat back and looked at the pair of them, seeing them afresh. He stopped drumming and brightened considerably. 'Then you *are* good enough,' he stated flatly. Nobody dared to argue. Well, you don't with kings, do you? And why would they? 'I take it you are willing to deal with him?'

'He has demons,' said Eydith. 'It will take more than just us.'

'My entire army is at your disposal.'

'Still not enough,' said Link.

'What?' the king was taken aback.

'We need wizards more than men,' Eydith explained.

'Then how many of those do you need?' asked the king, glancing at Teeter, not sure how many he had.

'What we really need are *all* the wizards from the university, sire. That should be enough.'

'*That* many, eh?' King Treadwell drummed the arms of his throne again.

'Yes, sire,' said Link.

'May I suggest something, sire?' asked Teeter.

'Suggest away,' said the king.

'I suggest that Mistress Eydith and, er… Link, should go back to Havrapsor as soon as possible to enlist as many wizards to their cause as they can. And they can take the Drum back to the university before Dennis gets here and tries to take it back.'

'Good idea,' agreed Jubnak. 'Then he'll have no reason to attack the castle.'

'And just how will this Dennis know we haven't got the Drum anymore?' asked Treadwell.

Heads were hung low, deep in thought for a moment.

'I know, sire,' said Teeter, brightly. 'We'll pin a note on the gate-house door.'

Treadwell considered this. After all, it was highly likely that Dennis, an ex-Archchancellor, could read. 'Hmm. That might work,' he said, at last. 'But supposing it rains and the note gets messed up, or washed away? Someone will have to keep an eye on it.'

Teeter had that covered. 'We'll also tell the guards on watch to tell Dennis when he comes that we haven't got the Drum anymore.

'Hmm... Yes, good idea. I like it,' said the king.

'I'll tell the guards now then, shall I?' asked Thadax.

The king ignored him while he spoke to Eydith. 'How soon do you think this Dennis will be here?'

She thought about it. 'A day, sire. Maybe two. He has a flying carpet.'

'Not much time at all, then,' Treadwell murmured, stroking his beard.

Jubnak gave a loud, 'Ahem.' When he had their attention, he said, 'My sources say he's travelling ahead of his demons and his seamen. They will be slower, I think. And he'll probably want to wait for them.'

'Yes, I doubt they can all get on a carpet,' said the king, sardonically.

Eydith also thought he probably wouldn't attack until all the others arrived.

'Shall I tell the guards *now*, sire?' asked Thadax, urgently.

'Oh, very well,' said Treadwell. 'And get that note organised as well.'

Thadax scurried away.

Treadwell turned his attention back to Eydith. 'How are you going to get back to your university, young lady?'

'We'll manage, sire. Just as long as Dennis doesn't overtake us.'

'You can use the flying thingy again, if you like,' Teeter offered.

Link shook his head.

'It'll be quicker,' said Eydith. 'Come on. *Please.*'

That was most unfair! One look into those big pleading eyes and he knew there was no point arguing. 'All right,' he surrendered, and picked up the Drum.

*

When Eydith and Link had left, Treadwell sat silently wondering how he could help. The best he could come up with was, *Stay out of the way and let the silly buggers get on with it. There's no point sending soldiers. Even an army. They need wizards to defeat wizards. Oh, and to defeat demons, of course.*

'You look worried, sire,' said Jubnak, quietly.

'Yes,' the king replied. 'I'm concerned there may not be enough wizards at that university.'

'What about sending Teeter and the others, sire?' suggested Jubnak.

'That's what I was thinking. But not until Dennis and his demons have been here. We don't want to be completely defenceless against his magic.'

'Ah, then let our wizards follow them back to Kra-Pton and attack them from the rear.' Jubnak grinned enthusiastically.

'That's a good idea. I hadn't considered that. Yes, why not?' agreed Treadwell. 'I'll leave it to you, then. But do remember how powerful this Dennis is! Do nothing foolish.' And he waved Jubnak out of the room. The spy bowed and took his leave.

*

In that part of the castle that was given over to the spies, Loosley was pacing the floor while Jubnak leant against his desk, watching.

'Have you heard from my replacement on the *Sea Dragon*, sir?'

'I haven't had any messages for days,' replied Loosley.

'Perhaps he's run out of pigeons,' murmured Jubnak.

'Possibly, but there's usually someone coming this way who can bring news.'

'Maybe we should send somebody back to look for him, sir.'

'Are you volunteering?'

'No, sir. Just a thought, that's all.'

'It's a good thought, too. But if not you, who else have we got left to send that's any good?' said Loosley, having racked his brains for two long minutes.

Jubnak looked up at the ceiling. There was another long, silent pause.

'No – exactly,' said Loosley.

There was a tap on the door. It was followed by two more. A short pause and another three taps in quick succession. Someone who knew the code.

'Can you see who that is,' said Loosley.

'No, not from here, sir.'

'Just answer the door!'

Jubnak slid the hatch back and peered through. A figure dressed in black stood waiting.

'Yes?' said Jubnak, warily. 'Who is it?'

The figure pushed back the hood that was flopped over his face. 'It's me, Pitiron.'

Jubnak soundlessly slid back the heavy bolts. The bolts to the spy's quarters were the only oiled and quiet ones in the entire castle. 'Come in, quickly. We were just talking about you.' He opened the door just wide enough for the man to squeeze through.

Pitiron sidled into the room and saluted his superior officer.

'Ah, good man,' said Loosley. 'I'm glad you're here. You've saved us the trouble of looking for you.'

'I had trouble getting away, sir, I…' Pitiron started to explain.

'Where's Dognettle?' asked Loosley, sidestepping Pitiron's explanation.

'About two days away, sir. He's sailing the *Sea Dragon* up the river where he plans to meet the wizard.'

'And then what?'

'Well, sir. I understand they intend to meet with Dennis and attack the castle.'

'Good work, Pitiron,' said Loosley. 'You've confirmed what we thought.' So saying, he turned on the other spy. 'Jubnak!'

'Sir?'

'Tell the king, and report back here.'

Jubnak saluted smartly and left.

*

'Have you done that note yet?' asked Treadwell.

'Yes, sire. Look.' Thadax held it up for the king's approval.

'I want it on the gate, man. Not in here.' The king sighed.

'Thought you should see it first, sire,' he said in his defence. 'To give it your seal of approval. And we've run out of tacks, sire. One of the lads is down in the town getting some now.'

'What about the guards? Have you told them what to say?'

'Yes, sire. And they wrote it down, so they'd remember.'

'Good. At last, we seem to be getting somewhere,' said the king, slightly more at ease.

'Oh, yes, sire. And they've lit the fires,' added Thadax.

'Fires? What fires?' Treadwell was beginning to worry again.

'Well, the captain of the guards said he'd heard, or seen, somewhere that when your being besieged it helps to pour boiling oil from the battlements, sire.' Then it occurred to Thadax that his captain might have seen it on a tapestry in the room, and he glanced quickly at the walls for corroboration. 'Look. There it is, sire, in that picture there.'

The king looked and nodded sagely, as if he'd known all along. 'How much oil do we have? Only they seem to have quite a cauldron of it in the tapestry.'

'Er... not very much at the moment, sire. It's cook, see. She says we can only 'ave a couple of pints, or she won't 'ave enough for chips in the dining hall, this evening.'

'Quite right,' snapped Treadwell, then, after giving it a quick mental rerun, he added. 'Oh, well. Send a boy down into town and get some more. Tell him to say it's for me.'

Thadax shifted uneasily onto his other foot, and moved closer to the king. 'We tried that, sire. Granny Wicksworth sent 'im back empty-'anded.' He lowered his voice and whispered, 'She says we 'aven't paid last month's bill, yet.'

'What?' Treadwell was horrified. 'Not paid?'

'No, sire.'

'Bugger,' he moaned, but in a regal sort of way. He drummed his fingers. 'Get my chief clerk up here now!' he ordered.

'I've already told 'im, sire. 'e's on 'is way to Granny's now.'

'It seems you have everything under control, Thadax. Well done,' the king praised him.

Thadax blushed. 'Thank you, sire,' he said, graciously, and bowed at least four times as he backed out of the throne room, thinking how clever he was, only to catch his heel on a slightly raised flagstone and finish up on his butt.

His next destination was to the office of the man responsible for the maintenance of the castle's floors.

Apart from the noise of the crew knocking flagstones back into place, the rest of the day passed quietly and uneventfully.

* * *

85

Around late morning, the next day, a small horned head pushed a hole in the side of the moat and blinked. Not because of the sunlight, but because the hole was below the water level and moat water was pouring in on him. Hell had the presence of mind to take a deep breath and brace himself against the sides of the hole. His five demons were pushed back a few feet before they managed to grab onto something secure. Hell cursed silently, and pulled himself into the murky water. He reached the surface gasping for air. Treading water and turning slowly, he looked for the nearest bank to pull himself out.

He reached out, grabbed some stout reeds and hung on while he got his breath back. It was then that he noticed the water level was going down. Slowly, but definitely down.

Foolishly, he let go and was dragged beneath the surface again. He could hear a rushing noise and the sounds of things like old tin cans and bottles clattering along the stones on the bottom of the moat. The occasional odd boot floated past. It was all coming towards him, and gathering speed. He had a bad feeling about this.

Suddenly, he was caught in the flow, and spinning. Round and round he went, caught in the whirlpool of moat-water escaping down the hole he and his demons had created. Thrashing wildly about, he barely managed to stop himself from going back down. The whirlpool began to ease, then it stopped because he was wedged in the hole like a plug. Something sharp began prodding him in the back. A claw? Could this be his worst nightmare – being torn to pieces by his own demons?

He felt the claw run gingerly down the scales on his back. He forced himself to move slightly, in the hope that the demon behind him would guess it was him, and go around, rather than try to go through him. Then he felt two clawed hands pushing him forward, releasing the pressure. Once free, he pushed himself aside from the flow and scrambled back to the surface. Then, with some difficulty, because of the lower water level, he pulled himself out onto the muddy bank, where he lay gasping for air.

The level of the moat continued dropping. As Hell lay still, he heard a series of dull clanks somewhere in the depths. The long-lost lid of Mrs. Grimly's copper was being carried by the flow on its way to getting wedged in the hole. A few feet away from him, the earth began to convulse, and a brown, horned head covered in pond weed, emerged into the sunlight.

'You alright, your breathlessness?' asked Brown, cheerfully.

Hell groaned and spat out some moat.

'Oh, good,' said Brown. Four more dishevelled demons crawled out of the hole and lay panting on the grass. Hell forced himself onto his elbows and sat up.

'I'm getting more and more fed up with that wizard,' he snarled.

Brown went over intending to put a comforting arm around him, but seeing the fire in his kingship's eyes, thought better of it.

*

A dark, rectangular shape sped across the late morning sky. Brown saw it first and gently touched Hell's arm. 'Look, your pissedoffness,' he whispered. 'Looks like your wizard's here.'

'He's not my bloody wizard,' hissed Hell. 'But one day…'

The carpet circled the castle until Dennis spotted Hell and his cohorts sprawled by the moat. The demons waved until Hell told them not to be such idiots.

Dennis brought the carpet down somewhat erratically a few yards away. 'You made good time,' he called, striding towards Hell.

The demon struggled to his feet to meet him. 'What kept you? We've been 'ere ages,' he lied.

'No, we 'aven't, your royalness,' whispered Brown.

'Shut up,' snapped Hell. 'We were 'ere before him, weren't we?'

'Well, yes, your earliness,' he agreed, then turned to Dennis and said, 'You're late!'

'I didn't know we'd set a precise time,' countered Dennis, in smart-mouth mode.

'We didn't,' said Hell. 'But bein' as 'ow I'm 'ere first, that makes you late.'

'I disagree,' said Dennis. 'It makes *you* early.'

Florence stepped in, which seemed to be her job whenever Denis and Hell were together – or whenever Dennis and almost anybody were together. 'Will you two give it a rest.'

'Alright then, you're second,' Hell conceded. 'Your pirates ain't 'ere yet, either. They're definitely late.'

After a sideways glance at Florence's pained expression, Dennis agreed to be second, but not late.

'Well?' said Hell, when nothing appeared to be happening. 'How long do you propose to wait for them?'

Dennis shrugged and looked up at the sun. 'What time is it?' he asked, looking at Florence.

'It's around midday,' she replied, shielding her eyes.

'Plenty of time till sunset, then,' said Dennis, staring back at the sun for a brief moment. When the purple and yellow floaters in his eyes had cleared, he turned back to the Demon King. 'Right! That's long enough. We'll attack the castle now.'

'What?' said Hell. 'All…' he stopped to count. 'All my six and your four of us?'

'Yes,' sighed Dennis. 'All *ten* of us. Off you go.'

Hell reluctantly ordered his five demons to their feet and told them to follow him to the castle gate. He didn't get very far. ''Ere, 'old on a minute,' he said, stopping in his tracks. His five followers shunted into his back, shuffling him forward. 'What about you lot?' he said, pointing a demonic finger at Dennis.

'We're right behind you,' Dennis assured him.

'Oh, that's all right, then.'

Hell and his demons reached the gate.

''Ere,' said Hell, 'they've left a note.'

'Who's it addressed to, your cleverness?' asked Brown, peering over Hell's shoulder.

'T-O, to T-H-E, the W-I-Z, wizard,' Hell read slowly. 'Oi!' he called to Dennis. 'There's a note up 'ere for you.'

Dennis strode up to the gate and snatched the envelope.

'Well?' said Hell. 'Who's it from?'

Dennis read it. At the bottom was King Treadwell's seal. Dennis's face flushed with anger.

'Well?' said Brown. 'What does it say?'

Dennis ignored him and turned his glare on Hell. 'It's gone,' he muttered. 'The Drum's gone.'

'Where?' demanded Hell, almost as angry and fed up as Dennis.

'She's taken it back to Kra-Pton,' he seethed.

'You mean we've come all the way out 'ere – *from Kra-Pton* – for nuffin?' groaned Brown.

'I don't believe it,' said Hell. 'They've got to be lying.'

'Why would they lie about it?' said Florence, trying to calm things.

'So we don't attack their precious, bloody castle, I expect. That's why,' said Hell.

'They can't do this to *me*,' Dennis flared. He kicked the gate, angrily, and the sound echoed around the walls unexpectedly loudly, as though the place were deserted. But there was at least one man.

*

High above them on the battlements, Alf's helmeted head peered over the edge. 'Who is it?!' he hollered down.

Dennis stood back and looked up.

'Oh,' said Alf, taking stock of the party below. 'We've been expecting you!'

'Well, open the gate!' Dennis yelled up at him.

'No! Go away,' came the reply. 'Didn't you read the note?'

'Yes, I've read it!'

'Well, piss off, then!' Alf shouted down.

'That's not what it says,' said Thadax, appearing at Alf's side.

'Means the same thing, don't it?'

'I expect you've upset him now.'

'If you don't open this gate!' yelled Dennis. 'I'll send some fireballs up there! Then I'll destroy the gate!'

'Oh yeah...' said Alf, belligerently, from the safety of the battlements. 'And I'll pour some boiling oil on you!'

'Steady on,' said Thadax. 'That's a bit dangerous, ennit?'

Alf considered this. 'No, shouldn't fink so, not from up 'ere.'

'I meant for them,' said Thadax. 'Anyway, you'd 'ave to be bloody lucky to 'it one of 'em from this distance. And we've only got one half-pint bottle and it's not boiling yet.'

'Well, it's quite warm. I've had in my pocket against me leg for an hour or so.' He leaned over the battlements again. 'I mean it, you know!' he called down, threateningly.

'That's it then,' said Hell. 'We're not 'anging around to get boiling oil flung all over us.'

'You can't leave me to fight them on my own,' whined Dennis.

'Look, he's threatening to pour boiling bloody oil over us,' Hell restated, in a slightly higher pitch.

'That doesn't mean he's going to,' argued Dennis.

'Then why do you think 'e's unscrewed the lid, then. Eh? Answer me that,' said Hell. 'An' 'e sounds like 'e means it, to me.' The demon king looked up and stepped back a couple of paces. 'And anyway, 'e said they ain't got the Drum no more.'

'You're suggesting I should believe that?'

'Yeah, I am.'

Florence nodded, just enough for him to notice.

'All right,' said Dennis, against his better judgement. 'We'll go to Havrapsor, then.'

'Now you're talking,' said Hell. 'That place has got to go.'

Dennis turned his attention back up to Alf. 'We're leaving. If you're lying about the Drum, I shall find out, you know. Then I'll be back!' he shouted, waving his fist.

Alf looked down from the battlements and grinned as he poured a spoonful of oil from the bottle. 'Oh, piss off,' he murmured, softly.

Dennis saw it coming and stepped to one side. 'Missed!' he yelled up at him. 'Is that it?'

'We're going now, then,' said Hell, seeing spots of oil on the path.

'Wait a minute… I haven't finished here, yet,' said Dennis. He looked up at Alf again, 'I'll have you for that, you…'

'All right, Father. That's enough,' said Florence, grabbing his arm. Dennis growled.

'As I said,' said Hell. 'We're goin'. We'll see you in Kra-Pton.'

'Where will I find you?' asked Dennis,

'It shouldn't be difficult,' said Hell. 'Just look around for a bit of chaos. Come on, you lot.'

The demons tramped off the path onto the grass and disappeared into the ground.

Jook and Psoddoph watched them as they sat on the box and waited for Dennis.

'Moat looks a bit low,' observed Psoddoph. 'An' them birds don't look too happy.'

Two irate-looking swans were pacing the muddy edge.

*

'You were most helpful,' said Dennis, sarcastically.

'That's alright, boss,' said Jook, the sarcasm wasted on him. 'We didn't do much.'

'I didn't notice *you* doing *anything*,' snapped Dennis.

'We guarded the diamonds, boss,' said Psoddoph. 'That's the thing about guarding, unless something actually 'appens, you don't 'ave to do a lot.'

'Oh, shut up,' Dennis snapped. 'Carpet, up, please. Gently.' The carpet rose and circled the castle, flying low over Alf's head. Before Florence could stop him, Dennis released a small fireball at the battlements. Alf and Thadax threw themselves to the floor as it hit the stonework and exploded in a shower of yellow sparks.

'Missed me!' Alf taunted him, as the carpet passed over them.

'Shut *up!*' said Thadax.

* * *

Captain Dognettle and his crew failed to show up at the castle in time for Dennis's confrontation with the guards because the *Sea Dragon* had been ploughing its way painfully slowly up a weed-choked river towards the lower parts of the city of Corin. To make matters worse, it ground to a halt on a mud bank and promptly listed to starboard.

In his cabin, Captain Dognettle, with the speed of a striking snake, grabbed the half bottle of rum before it slid from his desk. He rammed the cork back in and put it in the top drawer. *What's gone wrong now?* he wondered, a little wearily, as he made his way up to the great hollow figure head.

Crimpett was sitting in his chair, leaning forward as far as he could, trying to see through the mist that clung to the windows.

Dognettle pushed his way into the cramped compartment. 'What's wrong, Crimpett? Why have we stopped?'

Crimpett squinted through the window again. 'Not quite sure, Captain,' he said, looking at the wall of white in front of him. 'Could be an ice-berg. We've run out of water. Or, we're in a cloud.'

Dognettle unhooked the speaking tube and blew into it. This was a fairly recent addition to the *Sea Dragon's* explosion of technology and the crew members who weren't afraid of it, still hadn't got the hang of how to use it. Dognettle held on for a moment, then yelled, 'Is there anybody there?!'

A worried voice on the other end said, 'Hello?'

Dognettle put his end of the speaking tube to his ear. 'Who's that speaking?' he demanded.

'Hello?' said the voice on the other end.

Dognettle put his end of the tube to his mouth and listened.

'Hello?' said the voice on the other end. Still nothing.

Then, in desperation, and at exactly the same moment as the captain put the tube to his ear to speak, the voice shouted, 'Stop pissin' about!'

'Who's that?' said Dognettle, indignantly. 'Engine room?' There was silence, followed by some scuffling sounds as the tube at the other end was yanked from its socket. He rammed the whistle back into the tube and slammed it back in the bracket on the wall. Then, he stormed out. 'I'll go and look for myself,' he moaned, slamming the door behind him.

Out on the deck, he could make out, that the ship had definitely run out of water, because it was wallowing on mud. He shrugged his shoulders and went back inside. This time, down to the engine room.

'Don't get up,' he muttered, as he entered.

'Oh… 'ello, Cap'n,' a burly seamen greeted him. 'I'm glad you're 'ere.'

'Why?' asked Dognettle, instantly losing his train of thought.

'I want to report some silly bugger's messin' with the talkin' tube.'

Dognettle straightened up. 'Idiot! That was me!'

'Oh.'

'I'll send Lampitt down here again, shall I? You know, show you how it works,' said Dognettle, sarcastically. 'And fix it back on the wall.'

'Er, yeah. Okay, Cap'n. I suppose we could do with a refresher course. Anyway, sir, now you're 'ere, what can we do for you?'

'In case you hadn't noticed,' said Dognettle. 'We've run aground.'

One of the seamen stood up, and from the way he had to put his weight on one leg, he didn't disbelieve what his captain was telling him.

'What are you doing about it?'

'What – now – Captain?'

'Yes, now, of course.'

'Not very much. Nothing in fact.'

'Well perhaps between the two of you, you can *start* doing something. Right now,' said Dognettle.

'Oh, right.' Then after a pause, he added, 'What?'

'I don't know,' said Dognettle. 'You're the engineers. You should know these things.'

'Not a situation we've been in before, this not being too much of a river vessel.' This was a hugely toned-down version, free of colourful seafaring expressions, of what the engineer thought of taking the *Sea Dragon* this far up a river. 'Well, we could wind the engine up, sir.'

'That'll do for a start,' agreed Dognettle.

'And we could try putting her into reverse.'

'Good idea,' said Dognettle, sticking with the sarcasm.

The two men crossed the sloping deck to the rear of the engine room and began turning the huge key that wound the spring. Then, with the brake rammed tight against the cogs, one of them tugged on a lever to reverse the drive. 'Ready Cap'n?'

'Yes, come on. Get on with it,' said Dognettle. 'Skip the formalities.'

The other engineer released the brake.

The *Sea Dragon* shuddered for a moment, then stopped.

'Wind it some more!' the captain ordered. This time, the ship moved backwards. There was a great slurp from the bow, a grinding of metal amidships, and the ship was free, and gathering speed.

Dognettle panicked. 'Forward engines!' he screamed.

The chief engineer slammed his lever forwards, while the other man had the presence of mind to drop the anchor. The *Sea Dragon* righted itself and drifted to a halt.

'That was close,' the seaman remarked. 'Any chance of opening a window down 'ere, Cap'n? I don't think I was very well there for a minute.'

'We might also see better where we're going, Cap'n.'

'Yes, I suppose so. Go ahead.' He eyed the salt-smeared window, making a mental note to get a cleaning crew out there someday soon. 'It's only patchy river mist. Seems to be thinning.' He sniffed the air. Salty, as usual, but something else, too. 'And whichever one of you did that had better go and change. Good day, gentlemen.' Dognettle politely touched the tip of his hat as he strolled through the door. 'Oh,' he said, before he went out. 'One more thing.'

'Yes, Cap'n?'

'On deck in two hours. We're going ashore.'

* * *

Towards evening, Sprag faithfully steered the glider over Kra-Pton, using Eydith's eyes to avoid the taller buildings that gave the city its distinctive skyline. It was the tallest of the mismatched towers that they were looking for, those belonging to the University of Havrapsor. As the glider tilted and drifted silently around it, Eydith took in the damage below. So many tiles were missing from one part of the roof that the timbers were clearly visible. They heard the distant sound of a bell, and guessed someone on watch had spotted them, mistaking them for a threat.

'We're home, Link,' she called over her shoulder, not so much to tell him, but to share the moment.

'Yes,' he replied. 'What's left of it.'

'Take us down, Sprag,' said Eydith. The glider magically stopped and hovered in the air over the quadrangle, then gently floated to the ground. Sprag was getting the hang of it, too.

The Secretary was sitting at his desk, quill in hand, drafting a memo which the Archchancellor would unwittingly sign after dinner, and another new rule would be in force by morning. The shadow of the glider, momentarily blocking out his light, caused him to look up. *What was that?* he wondered, placing his quill back on its tray. He rammed the cork back in the inkwell and staggered drunkenly to the window.

He wasn't drunk. The excavations and burrowing of Hell and his demons had caused his part of the building to sink on one side, giving the floor an incline. All his furniture was propped at one end with blocks of wood or books of varying thicknesses. It was the cheapest option and saved shortening half the legs on the chairs and the desk. The hardest thing for him to get used to was pictures that didn't hang parallel with the ceiling. That was a word he was beginning to hate. Parallel. It brought to mind another word. Dimension. And just lately, he'd been silently wishing he was in a different one entirely.

He went to the window and looked down into the quadrangle. He saw the glider and then the people. The moment he recognised

Eydith and Link, he smiled and rushed down, as best he could, to meet them.

*

A bell clanged. 'Oh, no,' muttered Cho. 'Not another attack.' He peered into the hole he was guarding and waited expectantly for a demon to appear. It didn't. 'Anyfing on your side, Pelgrum?' he called across to his colleague guarding the next hole.

Pelgrum shook his head. 'Nothing happening here, Cho.'

Another bell clanged in answer to the first one. 'You fink there might actually be a fire?' said Cho, nervously.

'I think we'd better check.'

'I go,' said Cho. 'You guard holes.'

'Er, don't be too long,' Pelgrum mumbled, timidly.

Cho tried to leave, but struggled with an ill-fitting door. Finally giving up with his hands, he attacked it with the spade he'd been using to beat the demons. When there was enough room to squeeze through, he looked nervously up at the roof to check for any loose masonry that might come down. There wasn't any, so he stepped quickly out into the late sunshine.

Others were appearing in doorways and cautiously stepping out onto the quadrangle. Cho saw the glider, then he saw Eydith and Link. Then the Drum. He poked his head back inside. 'Pelgrum!' he called, 'Eydith back. She got Drum!'

'What? That's wonderful news!' The older wizard smiled and trotted out to see for himself.

Even Archchancellor Trinkel put in an appearance. He strode across the quad, his arms outstretched to greet Eydith. She'd dreaded moments like this for as long as she could remember. Those dreadful times when her mother's friends visited and said things like, 'My, hasn't she grown,' and 'It's been such a long time.' She cringed at the thought – and how she'd been through it all over again at King Treadwell's castle only recently.

The Archchancellor's robes billowed out behind him like a huge sail as he bore down on her. She steeled herself for the impact. But Trinkel stopped dead in front of her, grabbed her hand, and tried to shake her arm out of its socket. 'Have you got it?' he asked, bursting with excitement.

'Yes, Archchancellor, we've got it,' she said, smiling and trying to free her hand.

'Where? Show me.'

She pointed to the Drum still nestling in the glider. He gathered up his robe and scurried across to it. He peered inside, then lifted the Drum to one side, so he could look underneath, shook his head and put it down again. 'Where?' he asked, looking back at Eydith.

Eydith played along, reminding him he'd just picked it up.

'No… not the Drum,' he moaned.

'Sorry, Archchancellor,' she said, perplexed. 'I don't understand.'

'My *goat*,' he clarified. 'You said you were going to find it.'

Eydith exchanged quizzical looks with Link and shrugged. 'I'm sorry Archchancellor, I haven't. I went to get the Drum.' She looked pleadingly towards the Secretary.

He shrugged, too. He wasn't prepared for that, either. He took Trinkel's arm. 'Come, Archchancellor,' he said, quietly. 'Have a lie down. Perhaps we'll all have a look for it tomorrow.' The Secretary glanced back at Eydith, 'I'll see you in a moment,' he mouthed, as he helped the Archchancellor back to his rooms.

Link lifted the Drum out of the glider. 'Come on, let's put this back where it belongs,' he said, with some satisfaction. Eydith followed.

Outside her rooms, she touched Link's hand and bid him to, 'Just leave it here.' He rested the Drum on the floor at her door. 'Give me a few minutes,' she said, 'then we'll go and see the Secretary.' He was about to leave for his own rooms next door, when she gently tapped his arm. 'Just a minute.' She suddenly planted a lingering kiss on his lips.

The trouble with that, he thought, as he walked the few yards to his door, *is when you think back, it didn't really last as long as you thought it did while it was happening.* He smiled to himself, pushed the door open and, once inside, closed it quietly and fell onto his bed, clasping his hands behind his head and crossing his legs while still falling. He lay there for a minute staring at the ceiling, and heaved a sigh so loud that it almost drowned out the orchestra he could hear playing in his head. He smiled the smile of the very lucky.

*

In her rooms, Eydith held Sprag in both hands above her head and knelt in front of the Drum. *Dennis and his demons will be here soon, Sprag,* she thought.

'Yes, mistress,' the staff agreed, in his wavering though wooden tone.

'I need power, Sprag. Probably more now than ever before,' she whispered. 'My father's not here, and I expect Florence will want to help protect Dennis. I know she's only a beginner, but she *is* Dennis's daughter, and she'll learn fast. And I know I *have* the power, but I don't have the ability on my own to access it, or direct it.'

Sprag remained silent.

'Are you there, Sprag?'

'Yes, mistress. I was just wondering how much more you were going to say to try and defeat yourself.'

She smiled to herself. 'Do you think we can beat them again?'

'Yes, mistress. Probably.'

'What? What do you mean, *probably*?'

'Just my little joke, mistress. And *probably* is one up from *possibly*. Now, please be quiet and read the runes that I am going to show you.'

She began to protest that she couldn't read runes, but Sprag assured her that she could. She just didn't know she could.

She closed her eyes and whispered the words as Sprag scrolled them across the backs of her eyelids. The Drum began to glow as it, too, released power into her mind. She swayed momentarily before recovering her balance and dropping back onto her heels. From her memory of it, the process of transference – or update, as she thought of it – didn't seem to take so long this time. The Drum dimmed as she opened her eyes and stood up. She took a deep breath. *Right*, she thought, *let's go and talk to the Secretary.*

*

Link was ready and waiting outside for her. She brushed her lips against his cheek and slipped her hand into his.

'The Secretary?' he whispered.

'The Secretary.'

The man in question was crossing the quadrangle when they came out, so they followed him back to his office. He seemed tired as he staggered up the slope to his desk. He sat down warily, careful to avoid knocking his desk and chair in case they slipped off the books that kept them level.

Eydith and Link surveyed the room and decided it was probably safer to sit on the floor. The Secretary steepled his fingers and rested his nose at the apex.

'It's good to have you both back,' he said, eventually. 'It's been a difficult time.'

'It's going to get worse, I'm afraid, Secretary,' said Eydith. 'Dennis is on his way back with some demon help again.'

'The demons have wreaked havoc here already, as you can see. The wizards are doing their best to fend them off. And mercifully things have been quieter for a few days.' He forced a weak smile. 'Apparently, that's because the Demon King has been absent.'

Link felt really bad having to tell him, 'He's one of those coming back with Dennis.'

The Secretary stared mutely out of his window for some moments. 'How long before they get here?'

'Not long,' said Eydith. 'A day, maybe two.'

'Archchancellor Trinkel isn't so good anymore,' said the Secretary, picking his words carefully, and leaning back in his chair even more carefully. 'He spends all his spare time stuffing things. He nearly lost an arm last week. He didn't realise that bloody crocodile was only sunbathing.'

'We'll try to keep him away from the action,' said Link.

'That might prove difficult,' the Secretary warned them. 'Any commotion and he wanders out to see what's going on.'

'Can't you post a couple of wizards outside his door to protect him?' suggested Eydith. 'To try and convince him to stay put, or go with him if he won't?'

'I can try, but that'll mean being men short where it might matter more.'

'Well, he must be shielded from Dennis. He'll want the Archchancellor's job again,' she pointed out. 'That's for sure.'

That hadn't occurred to the Secretary. The idea clearly horrified him. The colour drained from his face.

'Perhaps we could take Trinkel… I mean, the Archchancellor… to the next town till it's all over,' suggested Link.

The Secretary rallied. 'Hmm. Yes. That would work. I could tell him it's a hunting trip, or something. He'd like that.' He began to sound and act purposefully again. 'Excellent idea… I'll send for somebody. We need to convince him to go this very night.'

They were all agreed on that. 'Well, there's nothing more we can do today,' said Eydith, making to leave.

'What sort of a state's the canteen in?' Link needed know before he left. He was pleased to hear it was still in service. He was desperate for some supper.

* * *

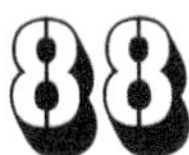

The sun crept slowly up the morning sky. A few late stars twinkled and dimmed. Somewhere, a cock crowed, and almost crowed again, but was interrupted by what sounded like the thud of a heavy leather boot. Link was awake. Well, his eyes were open. And someone was knocking on his door.

He poked his toes into his slippers and shuffled across the room.

'Come on, Link. Open this door,' said Eydith, as loud as she dare.

'It's open.' He yawned, and turned back towards his bed.

She stepped inside and quietly closed the door. *No sense upsetting the neighbours*, she thought. 'Oh, no you don't,' she said, when she realised that he was about to curl up on the bed again. 'You're staying up. Now get in there and get dressed.'

Link knew better than to argue. He got up slowly and looked at her. Suddenly, he was wide awake. She was wearing close-fitting black trousers, low on the hips and tucked into boots, with a light shirt and a short, dark sleeveless jacket. 'My word,' he said. 'You're going to get quite a few looks on campus.'

'I'm getting them now,' she said. 'This is practical. I used to dress like this all the while back home. I just remembered I'd packed the trousers.'

Link rummaged in his wardrobe for his most presentable robe. They were all about the same, so he went for the cleanest. 'You look… really great.'

That made her feel good, but all she said was, 'Get dressed.'

In the small washroom adjoining his bedroom, he looked in the mirror, 'You lucky so-and-so,' he told himself, patting his hair down. 'Hmm, could do with a trim,' he noticed, tugging at his short, straggly beard. He decided on a quick tidy-up trim.

Halfway through the trim, the building lurched, but very slowly, and he followed the little mirror as it slid along the shelf. This was not normally his best time of day, but he still had the reflexes to catch the mirror before it hit the floor. He sat down and quickly snipped away at what was left of his beard.

'It's started!' he yelled, worriedly yet excitedly, as he hurried back into the bedroom.

Eydith just sat on his bed, watching.

'Well? Aren't you going to look the other way?' he asked, trying to pull his trousers on under his robe.

'Oh, all right,' she pouted. 'But you can't hide forever.'

'I don't intend to,' he replied, and moments later he was ready. 'Come on, then.' And he raced her to the door.

Just as he was about to open it, she put her arms around his neck and planted a long, lingering kiss on his lips. 'Just in case,' she whispered, as she let him go.

He didn't like to think about the implications of what she'd said, but he was sufficiently distracted, anyway. 'Er… um…' he fumbled for words. When none came, so, he kissed her. 'You know what I mean,' he grinned.

She squeezed his hand. 'Yes… come on, let's see what's happening.'

*

Early though it was, Cho was bounding across the quadrangle waving a spade. From another doorway, the Secretary was striding out beside Rumpitt. The old wizard had a very determined look on his face, *and* he was carrying his staff.

The ground groaned under some unseen force and began to rise. Link stepped in front of Eydith, flexing his fingers and started to mutter a spell. The ancient riven flagstones became still for a moment before parting, and three demons surfaced together.

Eydith instantly sidestepped from behind Link and pointed Sprag at one of them. Her eyes flared like two angry suns, and from the fingertips of her empty hand, livid red fire spat across the air between them, completely taking the head off one and reducing the others to cinders. She was thinking that the day might get busy.

* * *

About a hundred miles away from Havrapsor, though only a mile or so from King Treadwell's castle, the *Sea Dragon* was moored at the riverside, with its dragon head playing host to a gathering of gulls who were pleased to have found a new platform from which to watch the world go by.

Captain Dognettle's crew had assembled on the deck as instructed, on the previous evening, but it had started to rain, so they'd opted to go back inside and wait until it stopped. Which, as it turned out, was this morning.

The overnight mist had cleared by the time the first sailor ventured out and it had the makings of a nice day. Dognettle climbed the steps to the lookout's station in the dragon head. 'Any sign of Dennis out there?' When Lampitt said there wasn't, Dognettle puffed. 'Well, I reckon we can do this without him. I don't want to hang around all day. He can join us whenever he gets here.'

Over in the castle, Jubnak was up and striding purposefully to the barracks. His spy in the swamp had warned him that the *Sea Dragon* had anchored upriver the previous day, and that Dognettle and his crew would most likely attack the castle today.

Jubnak stopped at the door, straightened his tunic and preened back the feathers in his hat. Then he burst through the door and slammed it shut behind him.

'All right, you lot! Wakey, wakey!' he yelled, at the top of his voice, as he walked down the aisle between the two rows of bunks. Just for good measure, he struck the flat of his sword against each one as he walked by.

His shouts were met with various groans and other military mutterings, until it became apparent that he meant business.

Hercop Vitrolly, the Sergeant, was first to erupt from his bunk.

'What the 'ell's goin' on?' he demanded to know. Then he noticed the uniform. It was one of the King's Own Spies. This didn't improve his temper in any way. *Bloody people*, he thought to himself, *give 'em a bloody blue uniform and they think they own the place.* 'Oh, it's you,' he said morosely, when Jubnak stood defiantly in front of him.

'Mornin', Sergeant,' said Jubnak, politely, and taking care to miss off the 'good' at the beginning of the greeting. *Bloody people*, he thought, *give 'em a bright red uniform, and they think they own the place. Mind you*, he added, *I'm the one with the feathers in his hat.*

'I have it on good authority, Sergeant, that the castle will be attacked today, probably in an hour or so,' said Jubnak, as plainly as he knew how.

'Oh, you do, do you?' said the Sergeant, standing up.

'Yes, Sergeant. And I want half your men to leave the castle immediately and come with me.'

'Oh, you do, do you?' said Vitrolly, pulling his chainmail vest over his head.

'Yes, Sergeant. So if you'll see to it, I'll wait here.'

'And just who's authority have you got for this venture, may I ask?' said the Sergeant, staring above Jubnak's head at the feathers, wishing he had the nerve to pluck one and stick it back where it came from.

'I have the king's authority, if you must know,' Jubnak replied, stepping back as the Sergeant stepped forward.

'Well, nobody told me.'

'Sergeant…' said Jubnak, levelly. 'If you'd been paying attention, you'll have heard me.'

The truculent Sergeant was about to argue some more when, unexpectedly, from the open doorway of the barracks, a soft, rather imperious, and eminently recognisable voice said, '*I'm* telling you, Sergeant.'

Vitrolly spun round. 'Oh… yes. Of course, sire. What a good idea, sire.'

Vitrolly glared at the spy. Jubnak wasn't certain, but what the Sergeant mouthed at him, looked very much like, *you bastard.* He grinned back and made a mental note of the score.

'Alright, you men. On your feet!' the Sergeant bellowed, 'I'm looking for volunteers to go with this… er,' he looked Jubnak up and down… 'gentleman.'

'Er, no, Sergeant. That's not what I have in mind. Not volunteers. Just half your men,' Jubnak reminded him.

'Look,' said Vitrolly, staring him in his good eye, 'you'll get half the men, but we'll do it my way, alright?'

Jubnak sighed. 'As you wish, Sergeant. Just as long as it comes out as *I* wish in the end.'

'Thank you,' said Vitrolly, smugly, though not entirely sure why.

All the soldiers were pulling on their chain mail and buckling on their swords as the Sergeant wandered down their dishevelled ranks. 'Right,' he began, as he paced. 'You'll do, and you…' he said, seemingly picking soldiers at random. In half a minute, he was standing at Jubnak's side. 'There you are, *sir*. Half the men.'

'Twenty?' said Jubnak, 'is that it?'

'I *can* count, mister,' Vitrolly replied.

'I don't doubt you, Sergeant. I just thought there'd be more.'

'Nope. Half is twenty,' Vitrolly assured him.

Jubnak put his hands behind his back and strolled down the line of 'volunteers'. The Sergeant followed closely behind. 'Are these *good* men, Sergeant?' Jubnak asked.

'You don't think I'd send *bad* ones outside, do you?'

'It had crossed my mind, Sergeant.'

'I look at it like this, Captain. If you've got men that are good at close fighting, they're the ones you send outside. If you've got men that are good at defending – e.g. *not* good at fighting up close – then you put them on the battlements. Stands to reason, does that.' Then as an afterthought, he said, 'And these fellers can run fast, too. You know… just in case.'

'Of course, Sergeant. We don't want anyone getting injured, do we?' said Jubnak.

'What? Ah… no. Right, men, get fell in.' The Sergeant marched his men to the door and out across the parade ground. Jubnak trotted after them.

'Just a moment, Sergeant. I'm supposed to be leading this mission.'

'Have you led a troop of soldiers before?' asked Vitrolly, looking over his shoulder.

'No, Sergeant.'

'Then you can lead the way... and I'll lead the men.'

He wasn't sure of the difference. 'But...'

'Just who, or what are we going to fight?' Vitrolly interrupted.

'Captain Dognettle,' replied Jubnak.

'*Halt!*' the Sergeant yelled. The soldiers stopped at so many intervals, that it sounded like a round of applause.

'One man?' said the Sergeant, pushing his helmet out of his eyes, and looking down his nose at Jubnak. 'We're up against *one* man?'

'And his crew, of course.'

'*Sailors*? A bunch of bloody *sailors*? Corporal!'

The Corporal scurried to the head of the line. 'Sarge?'

'Go back and get five more men. With crossbows. We're fighting bloody sailors.'

'Yes, Sarge.' And as the man walked away, he looked back over his shoulder, 'Sarge?'

'Yes, Corporal?'

'Can I say something?'

'What is it, Corporal?'

'*Shit*, Sarge.'

'Not sure, lad. Probably the smell of fear, I expect.' The Sergeant turned his attention back to Jubnak. 'Now, mister, let's go and sort this out. I don't suppose for half a moment that you have a plan.'

'Excuse me, Sergeant, I do have a plan,' said King Treadwell, from somewhere behind the line of soldiers.

'Oops, sorry, sire. I thought you'd gone.'

'Evidently,' said the king, as the line parted in front of him. 'It's alright, Sergeant, Jubnak will fill you in on the details.' The king turned away. 'I'll go and watch from the battlements, then. No point in me getting in the way.' *Especially of a sword or an axe*, he thought to himself.

'Yes, sire,' said Vitrolly, casually saluting as the king walked away.

'Okay, spy. What's the plan?'

'Well,' Jubnak began...

*

Across a field, sufficiently far away from the *Sea Dragon*, and sufficiently concealed by shrubbery, a small troop of soldiers lounged, while their two leaders took turns to crouch and watch for any signs of activity from the ship.

'Not much of a plan, just waiting 'ere,' the Sergeant complained.

'I assure you, Sergeant, Dognettle will be here any minute,' said Jubnak, but he didn't sound too confident.

'You said that an hour ago,' the Sergeant complained, again.

'Aha! Look! There's my man now.' Jubnak, pointed at a mud-caked figure squelching through the bushes towards them.

'Ye gods, look at the state of 'im!' Vitrolly remarked.

'I'm sure there's a good reason,' said Jubnak, hopefully.

The man stopped in front of them and saluted, splashing mud and an assortment of river weeds onto the Sergeant, who was nearest.

'Captain Jubnak, sir. Captain Dognettle and his crew are on their way,' the man reported.

'How many?' the Sergeant asked.

'I wasn't talking to you,' replied the man clad in mud.

Jubnak whacked him across the ear. 'He needs to know as well,' he snapped.

'Yes, sir. Sorry, sir. About twenty, all armed with swords.'

'Anything else?' asked Jubnak.

'Yes, sir. One of 'em's got a great big chopper.'

'That's nice,' Vitrolly remarked to himself.

'Shouldn't be a problem, Captain. We've got five men armed with crossbows.'

'Remember Sergeant,' Jubnak reminded him. 'The king doesn't want them *dead*.'

'I know,' said Vitrolly. 'But 'e didn't say anything about not making 'em bleed a little bit.'

'Captain…' hissed the muddy spy, 'they're coming.'

'Right men,' Vitrolly whispered, hoarsely. 'Stay out of sight and wait till they've gone by.'

Discretely and unknowingly followed by the king's men, Dognettle led his men stealthily up to the castle and banged on the door with the hilt of his sword. A small hatch slid back and two eyes peered through at him.

'Who is it?'

'Captain Dognettle, to see the king,' said Dognettle.

'What about?' asked the mouth below the eyes.

'None of your business,' snapped Dognettle.

'Tell 'im we've come for the Drum, Captain,' whispered Lampitt.

'Shut up,' hissed Dognettle.

'Ah… so that's it, is it? You want the Drum?' sneered the eyes. 'Well, the king said to tell you we ain't got it no more. So, piss off.'

'That's not what 'e said,' hissed another voice behind the hatch.

'I'm talkin' to 'im in *sailor*,' the voice explained. 'It means, fu…'

'I know what it means!' the other voice interrupted.

'If you don't open this door,' said Dognettle. 'I'll break it down.'

'The king won't like that,' said the eyes.

'Well, open it, then,' said Dognettle. 'He'll be okay with that, won't he?'

That caused a little confusion behind the door. 'Look, mate,' said the eyes. 'It won't do you any good. We 'aven't got the Drum anymore.'

Dognettle raised his sword and was about to thrust it through the hatch, when…

'That's enough, sailor. You're under arrest,' said Sergeant Vitrolly, firmly placing a hand on Dognettle's shoulder.

He spun round, 'What?'

'You heard, mister.'

Dognettle spun away from the Sergeant's grip, and raised his sword. 'Get 'im, men!' he yelled. Nothing happened. Without taking his eyes off the Sergeant, he repeated the order. 'I said, get 'im, men!'

'Ahem,' Lampitt coughed quietly, 'er, Captain?'

Dognettle slowly turned, and his mouth formed an O. He lowered his sword until its tip rested on the ground. The rest of his sailors had already been disarmed. They all had their hands in the air and their backs to the loaded crossbows held by the soldiers.

'That was really sneaky, Sergeant,' Dognettle complained.

'I see it this way, Captain,' said Vitrolly, amiably. 'We're all still alive.'

'For the moment, Sergeant, but Dennis will be here soon and then perhaps you'll see the error of your ways.'

'Dennis and his demons have been and gone already,' Vitrolly informed him.

Dognettle's mouth formed another O.

'Now, where were we?' said the Sergeant, scratching the back of his head. 'Ah, yes. I remember, you wanted to go inside the castle, didn't you?'

'Er, no. I don't think there's any point now, Sergeant,' said Dognettle, grinning nervously. 'So, if you and your men will just stand aside, we'll be on our way.'

'No, Captain. That's not the idea at all. Now, get inside!'

The door creaked open and the sailors shuffled into the gate house. The soldiers lowered their crossbows and shepherded them forward now that everything had become more relaxed.

But Dognettle saw his opportunity. He threw himself at the soldier in front of him and pushed him to the ground. He picked up the man's sword and ran.

Lampitt and the others saw their chance, too. A few quick knees to a few slow groins, and they were running as fast as they could back to the relative safety of the *Sea Dragon.*

It was a few moments before the soldiers recovered and fired their crossbows. The volley of bolts flew over the sailors' heads. 'Careful!' yelled the Sergeant, worried they might actually hit someone. By the time the crossbows were reloaded, the Sergeant relaxed: the sailors were too far away to bother with anymore.

He'd saved the castle and nobody had been critically injured. And that's the way he liked things. He had no ambitions for himself, or any of them, to be immortalised on a tapestry in Treadwell's throne room. He'd rather they all survived. As indeed would the King. He still wondered why, though, when he'd had the chance, he hadn't sliced the feathers off Jubnak's silly hat. *I must be getting old*, he thought.

* * *

90

'That's it!' raged Hell. 'No more Mr. Nice guy! Those towers go. Now! Brown, get all the demons up 'ere. NOW!'

'Right, your angriness,' the smaller demon replied, and scurried down the nearest tunnel.

Hell sat down on the nearest rock and rubbed his stinging forehead. The small demon was back in minutes. But when you're as impatient as Hell, the slightest delay is too long. He sprang up.

'I said, *ALL* of them, Brown!'

'Yes, your thinginess, I 'eard you. I've sent messengers to every corner of the kingdom.'

Hell surveyed the dozen or so demons standing before him, then walked back to his rock and sat down, 'Brown?'

'Royalness?'

'How many corners 'ave I got in my kingdom?'

Brown scratched his head. 'Four? Your kinkiness.'

Hell closed his mouth for a moment. He didn't think Brown would know. 'How many messengers have you sent?'

'Five, your doubtfulness. Just in case I missed one.'

* * *

91

'It's gone very quiet,' said Link.

'They'll be back,' said Rumpitt, leaning on his staff. He was the most senior wizard at Havrapsor in both years and rank, and in the absence of Trinkel, was effectively the acting Archchancellor.

'Any thoughts where they might strike next?' Eydith wondered. 'Is there any pattern to it?'

'No, they just turn up randomly,' sighed Rumpitt. 'But it's usually well away from the previous place they came up.'

Eydith stroked her chin. Which was a strange thing for a girl to do, having no beard to stroke, but she'd seen so many wizards doing it. She stopped the moment she realised. 'If you can position wizards in groups…'

'Tried it,' the Secretary interrupted. 'It worked for a while, too. Then they left us alone for a few days.'

'We could go down after them?' suggested Link, uncharacteristically. Eydith raised her eyebrows.

'What?' said Rumpitt, 'and risk upsetting the foundations even more?'

'Perhaps not, then,' Link acknowledged. 'But it might be the only way.'

'He may be right,' said Eydith. 'I think we should at least follow them back down a little way next time they surface. We might get more of an idea of how many there are, where they are, and what they're up to down there.'

'I think we know what they're up to,' said Rumpitt, grimly. 'Trying to sink the building and kill us all.'

Then, as if on cue, the ground rumbled below them. But it felt more like a dire worm passing underneath than something threatening to break into the surface world. Thankfully those big ugly worms always kept themselves to themselves. Even so, the group followed the sound with their eyes. It suddenly dawned on Rumpitt that the sound was heading towards the Library Tower.

'Come on!' he yelled, snatching up the hem of his robe and scurrying off as fast as his ageing legs would carry him.

Eydith and Link overtook him and arrived at the arched doorway about twenty yards ahead of the others. They cannoned through the doors and into the vestibule.

'Which way?' Eydith panted, urgently.

'Left and down the stairs!' replied Link, skidding on one foot as he rounded the corner.

The rumbling grew louder, and the tower rocked.

'Are you sure this is a good idea?' said Link, sounding more like his old, more cautious self.

'No, but I haven't got a better one,' replied Eydith.

Some of the stone flags at the bottom of the next landing rose up, and two demons poked their heads out. But before their eyes could adjust to the light, spears of angry red flame leapt from Eydith's fingertips, reducing one of them to something extremely messy, and singeing the horns on the other one. Screaming and holding his smoking head, the demon dropped back out of sight. Link jumped down the steps two and three at a time, and stood over the corpse of the messy demon. He nudged it with his toe, and pushed it over the edge, back to where it came from.

Eydith came to his side and peered into the pit. 'Stand back,' she said, and snapped her fingers. The flags slid back into place over the hole. She muttered something and waved Sprag in a long sweeping arc in front of her. The cracks where the flags had been joined, bubbled and disappeared as the slabs fused together creating one huge slab of granite.

'I guess we're not following them down, then,' said Link, smiling.

'I don't know how long it'll last,' she said, 'but it'll hold them off for now.'

Beneath the slab, Hell prodded it with his trident.

'Do you want us to dig around it, your thoughtfulness?' asked Brown.

'Don't be stupid,' snapped Hell. 'I don't want that bloody great thing coming down on top of us.'

'Ah, no, your royalness. I think you're right, as always,' Brown agreed.

'There are only two wizards that could do a thing like that, and one of 'em's supposed to be on our side,' said Hell, tapping the huge slab again. 'That means the girl must be back.'

'Yuk,' said Brown, remembering their last run-in with Eydith. 'I 'ope she ain't brought that 'orrible severed 'and wiv 'er, your royalness,'

Hell mouthed a yuk, too, as he thought back to their last big battle with Eydith, when her ghostly father had been with her. Wimlett's right hand was the only visible part of him back then, and when Wimlett discovered that a detached floating hand really freaked out the demons, he delighted in taunting them with it, and gesturing impolitely at them.

The demon king made no comment on that. 'I think we'll call it a day for now,' he said. 'Send someone up top to watch for Dennis, and when he arrives, we'll make a new plan.'

* * *

92

Dennis was unaware that the battle had started without him that morning. Though he hadn't missed much. He would have got to Kra-Pton sooner, but he didn't like flying at night, and, besides that, he wasn't very good with directions. Jook and Psoddoph *were*, but Dennis didn't believe them and insisted on stopping a number of times to ask the way.

Now he could see the towers of Havrapsor on the distant horizon. Was it his imagination, or was the Library Tower leaning slightly towards the Tower of Undiscovered Magic?

'Almost there now, boss,' said Jook, making unnecessary conversation. 'It'll be nice to sleep in our own beds tonight,' he added, but Dennis only half heard hm.

'What?' said the wizard, distractedly.

'I said, it will be nice to sleep in our own beds tonight, boss.'

'We might all be camped outside the city tonight,' said Dennis, gruffly. 'It depends on how today goes.'

'Yes, boss,' said Jook, glancing at Psoddoph and pulling a doleful face.

Florence pulled her robe tightly around her against the chill of the early morning.

'Are you all right, miss?' whispered Psoddoph.

She only smiled, and kept her teeth just far enough apart to stop them from chattering.

She had come to like and respect Psoddoph over the last few months, and was thinking how she might miss him when Dennis no longer required his services.

Dennis requested the carpet to land about a half mile outside the city walls, just far enough away not to be seen, and in a hollow in the ground. The air was still and no sounds were coming from the city.

'Have you noticed that tower?' asked Psoddoph.

'The one leaning?' replied Jook.

'Yeah, I wonder what's happened to it.'

'Demons,' said Dennis. 'Clumsy fools.'

'I thought you wanted the university brought down, boss,' said Psoddoph.

'Not the buildings, man! I want the leadership brought down,' barked Dennis. 'I want to be the Archchancellor again. So, I need the university to still be there. Otherwise, there's no point.'

*

The next morning, the four of them stirred and stretched in their makeshift encampment facing distant Kra-Pton.

'Are you doing breakfast, boss? Or do you want me and Psoddoph to go out and murder something?'

'No time for that. Too much to do,' said Dennis. 'Hell will be waiting for us.'

Florence handed round some fruit and other scraps she'd accumulated. The guards shared their water bottles. Dennis breakfasted impatiently, eager to get moving again. He'd have been happy skipping breakfast altogether, but Florence insisted that they should not head into a fight weak from hunger. She'd have suggested he magic something up for them all, but she knew he'd want to conserve his powers. She didn't think it would weaken him in the slightest, but she knew better than to ask.

As soon as Dennis saw the opportunity, he grunted something, then, 'Come on!' he said, abruptly. 'We're going.'

He blurted out barely polite instructions to the carpet, and it lifted gently off the ground. They set off towards the city wall, keeping low to avoid detection for as long as possible.

The demon that Brown had stationed up top was the first to notice. He was perched on a tree-stump on a mound, which gave him a fairly commanding view of the city, when the carpet flew straight at him out of the sun and almost took his head off.

'Did you see that, boss?' said Jook.

Dennis looked over his shoulder. 'What?'

'That demon. We nearly took its bloody 'ead off.'

'Carpet, stop, please,' Dennis snapped. The carpet obeyed. 'Turn, please. Stop. Forward.' The carpet did what is known elsewhere as a handbrake turn, and charged back with its passengers hanging on, grimly. When they reached the spot where Jook had seen the demon, Dennis stopped the carpet and landed. The demon had gone.

'Are you sure this is the place?'

'Yes, boss. Right there,' said Jook, pointing at the tree-stump.

'Right, Daughter,' said Dennis, turning to Florence.

'Yes, Father?'

'Call Hell.'

Florence rubbed the staff and banged it on the ground. She didn't know why, but she always felt slightly embarrassed doing this in public.

*

As it happened, Hell and his demons were already about to claw their way upwards. They'd only paused while the king dealt with a messenger who'd just scampered down with news.

'Yes, your majesty,' said the look-out demon. 'Nearly took me bloody 'ead right off.'

'Stop moaning,' said Hell. 'He's 'ere – and I've just been reminded 'e's got that bloody staff.' He began banging the side of his head as the summoning siren blasted off inside it.

He strode off, leaving them standing. 'Come on, let's get up there before I go bloody mad!'

'This must be the place the lookout meant, your wondercrisp,' said the demon, pointing up at the tunnel ceiling.

'Don't you think I know where we're going by this blasted noise in my head, idiot! Get up there and see if 'e's landed.'

'Right away, your forcefulness,' replied Brown. Minutes later, the demon's head broke the surface. Dennis turned as the movement caught his eye.

'Ah, Brown, isn't it?' said Dennis, recognising the small demon.

'Er... yes,' said Brown, grinning evilly, which was the only way he knew how, then he ducked down again.

Below ground, Brown reported, ''E's 'ere your kingliness.'

Hell smiled. Chiefly because the siren had stopped. 'Right, you lot. Up you go. It's time to kick some wizard.'

Hell and Brown were first to break into the daylight. They sprang from the hole squinting and stood facing Dennis.

'Now?' asked Brown, crouching as if to pounce on the Archwizard, and checking himself when Dennis looked disconcertingly amused by it.

'What?' said Hell.

'Kick some wizard?' said Brown.

'Not him, you fool. He's with us. Or we're with him,' he corrected himself, and wondered why he'd bothered. 'The wizards in the university.'

Hell turned his attention to Dennis. 'You're 'ere, then.'

'Obviously,' said Dennis.

'Well, what's the plan?'

'Plan?' repeated Dennis, 'you *know* the plan. How many times have I got to explain things to you? We overthrow the Archchancellor and the rest of the wizards, take the university for *me*, and leave *you* in charge of the Parallel Dimension.'

Hell gave this some thought. 'Funny sort of plan,' he said, at last. 'You're the only one that gets anything out of that.'

'What do you mean?' Dennis argued.

'Well, I'm already in charge of the Parallel Dimension,' Hell pointed out.

'Which was, in a very large part, *my* doing, I recall,' Dennis was quick to remind him.

Hell just grunted at that.

Dennis exploited his advantage. 'And if you help me now, you won't be bothered by wizards at all in future, will you?'

After the tiniest pause, he said, 'I'm only bothered by one wizard, and that's you.'

'Ah,' said Dennis, quickly, 'but *I* won't need to bother you then, will I? We'll have an alliance. Peace between our, er, kingdoms… between good and evil.'

Hell spluttered, amused by something. 'Who's the *good* in this alliance, then?'

'Well… that would have to me, wouldn't it?'

'Yeah, right,' he said, still amused. 'An' I won't be bovvered by you, either, because I'll have the staff, won't I?'

'Staff?' said Dennis. 'What staff?'

Hell nodded at Florence. Dennis turned his head slightly. 'Oh, that staff.'

Hell nodded again, 'Yeah, that's the one.'

Florence held it out to him.

'Not yet, demon. You'll get it when I'm Archchancellor, not before,' said Dennis, as he stepped between the staff and Hell's outstretched hand.

'Right,' said Hell, narrowing his eyes. 'When this is over, it's mine. Or I'll be looking for you.'

'No problem,' said Dennis, smugly. 'Oh, and before we start, there is one more thing.'

'Yes?' said Hell, warily.

'You leave the Library Tower alone, understand?'

Hell nodded, casually.

'I said, do you UNDERSTAND?'

'Yeah, all right. I understand,' said Hell, with obvious annoyance.

'Good,' snapped Dennis. 'Now it can begin.'

Hell rubbed his clawed hands together excitedly. 'Where do we start?'

'The front gates, of course,' said Dennis.

'Er… excuse me, boss,' said Psoddoph.

'Yes?' said Dennis, spinning around. 'What is it now?'

'Well, if you won't be needing me and Jook, anymore, we'll be going back to the barracks.'

'Ah, yes. I don't suppose you can fight wizards, can you?'

'No, not really, boss,' said Psoddoph. 'But when you're in charge, we'll come and visit. You know, cup of tea, pick up our bonuses, see if there's any more missions, that sort of thing. You know what I mean?'

Dennis sighed. 'No, don't bother. I'll know where you are if I need you.'

That said, he strutted off towards to the city wall. After a few steps, he stopped. 'There's one more thing.'

'Yes?' said Psoddoph, expectantly, 'What's that, boss?'

'Take charge of the box and carpet. You can bring them to me when this is over.'

'Right, boss.'

Psoddoph rolled the carpet, then he and Jook each took a handle of the box and headed off back to the barracks.

'Don't forget –' Dennis called after them – 'I know exactly how many teeth there are in that box.'

'Yeah, boss,' chorused the guards.

Jook didn't look back.

But Psoddoph did. He watched Florence leave, and smiled when she turned to him and waved. He uttered a little prayer that she would make it through the day.

* * *

93

Dennis and Florence led the way into the city, occasionally glancing behind them at an ever-increasing number of horned demons in Hell's army. *It'll be different this time*, Dennis told himself, *there's too many of us to come second.*

It was still quite early, and most of the citizens of Kra-Pton were still sleeping. But in a room overlooking the university gates, two pairs of eyes were alert.

As Dennis and his troop came up the wide road to the university, Link whispered, 'Here they come.' Eydith tugged on the rope that the wizards had rigged up to ring the great bell in the Tower of Undiscovered Magic. She gave three sharp tugs. When she tried a fourth, the rope was whipped from her hands as the heavy bell jerked off its mounting and clattered and clanged down to the sixth level.

It was certainly enough to bring the wizards to the quadrangle. Wizards were a cranky bunch at the best of times, but this time of the morning, when most were usually still sleeping off the night before, they were crankier than usual.

Eydith and Link rushed down from the room to the main gates, and slid the hatch to one side in readiness for the initial encounter. Dennis had just arrived and was standing outside, tapping a foot impatiently.

'Open up!' he yelled. 'We're coming in!'

'Is he really that stupid?' said Link.

'He must be if he thinks we're just going to swing the gates open for him,' said Eydith.

'Not a chance!' Link yelled through the hatch, and ducked down out of sight. Dennis had raised a hand. But it wasn't to deliver a fireball. He needed to halt his army of demons before they crushed him against the gates.

'That was stupid, Father,' said Florence. 'You didn't really think they'd just open up and let you in, did you?'

'It was worth a try,' he muttered, thinking there might still be a grain of respect for an old Archchancellor. 'But, if that's the way they want to play it, then that's how we'll play it.' He pointed his fingers at one of the gates. The air crackled, and a shaft of red fire discharged from his fingertips. The gate held fast and deflected the magic away.

'Here we go again,' said Link. He shot a hand hurriedly through the hatch and returned Dennis's fire. He missed, and Dennis would have deflected his rushed attempt anyway, but he struck one of the demons, knocking him to the ground. He slammed the hatch shut and stepped away with his back against the gates.

''E 'it one of my demons,' Hell complained to Dennis. 'We can't go in through there.'

'We can, and we will,' snapped Dennis. 'So, stop moaning.'

'Hang on. I've got a better idea,' said Hell. 'We'll go in underneath. There ain't no sense in getting bloody slaughtered.'

'*Slaughtered?*' Dennis sneered. 'Don't be ridiculous. It was a glancing blow, with hardly any power in it. Your demon's only *singed*.' The smoking creature was getting painfully back on his feet.

'He *could've* been slaughtered,' Hell pointed out. 'So, we're going under.'

*

The university quadrangle was filling with staff and senior students. Wizards below seventh grade were ordered to stay put. They would be a danger to everyone in a battle of magic.

'Is everybody here?' asked Link.

The Secretary looked at the sea of pointy hats in front of him. 'I can't see Cho,' he replied.

'He's looking after the Archchancellor,' said Rumpitt, and almost silently adding, 'for what good it'll do 'im.'

Eydith was concerned. 'I thought the Archchancellor was going to be taken away somewhere for his safety. That was the plan. He shouldn't even be here.'

The Secretary sighed and shook his head. 'He wouldn't budge. I tried to reason with him myself, but he kept insisting that it was his duty to be here.'

'He's kind of right,' she had to admit. 'But he's not thinking it through. He has a duty to all of us to survive this.'

'Almost my exact words to him, Eydith,' said the Secretary, despairingly.

'Well, Cho will just have to shout if he needs us.'

'Oh, he will,' said the Secretary, very sure of it. 'Right,' he said, snapping his attention back to the situation. 'What's happening out there now, Link?'

Link drew back the hatch just a slit. 'The demons are burrowing. They'll be coming up from below. Again.'

'Keep your wits about you, men!' the Secretary bellowed, relaying the news to the assembly.

The slabs in the quadrangle began to move, throwing some wizards off balance. Those closest to them dragged them out of the way, and the wizards behind them stepped forward, all pointing fingers steadfastly at the slowly tilting slabs. Rumpitt stepped forward smartly, moving like a man half his age. He held a restraining hand up at the waiting wizards.

The first demon to break into the daylight world was met with a crushing blow from Rumpitt's staff. The unfortunate creature didn't stand a chance. He slumped forward, gurgled a little, and then slowly slid back among his colleagues.

Rumpitt peered into the hole and watched the demons remove their stricken fellow. He was immediately joined by two more senior wizards. And on Rumpitt's signal, they released a trio of red-hot fireballs.

Eydith stepped forward, her eyes glowing once more like suns. She raised Sprag above her head and muttered a spell. The slabs moved grindingly back into place and fused themselves together.

'Damn!' cursed Hell. 'She's done it again.'

'Never mind, your miseryness,' said Brown, cheerfully. 'We'll just have to try somewhere else.'

Dennis leant against the wall, thinking. The gates and perimeter wall had been magically reinforced, as he expected. The buildings would gladly cooperate with that, too, because they didn't like him, for some reason. But there had to be a way...

'What shall we do, Father?' said Florence.

Dennis straightened up and snapped his fingers. A shard of fire whisked over Florence's head. 'Sorry,' he said quickly, seeing her horrified face. 'I've got it! If I can't knock the gates out of the way directly, I'm sure I can break the hinges off. Come on.'

Behind him, Hell and the demons were crawling back up onto the road. 'Ah, good. You're back,' he grinned, as Hell stood beside him.

'Got any more bright ideas?' sneered Hell.

'I recall that going underneath was *your* idea. And, yes,' said Dennis. 'Follow me. And when I say *now*... rush in and start attacking.'

The hatch slid back a fraction and Link peered through the gap. 'He's coming to the gates again!' he yelled at the Secretary. 'They're all coming!'

Dennis stepped to one side out of sight. He couldn't actually see the hinges, but the heads of the bolts protruding outside were all he needed. He intoned a spell while turning his outstretched hands at the wrists. The bolts squeaked and began to turn. One by one they twisted loose and clinked onto the ground.

'Ready?' Dennis whispered.

'Yes,' replied Hell, moving out of the way.

Dennis pushed the gates experimentally with one hand. At first they didn't move, but another push, more forceful this time, had the desired effect. One of the great gates began to fall slowly inwards, then it twisted against the bottom hinge before finally crashing into the quadrangle.

'Now!' shouted Dennis, waving the demons forward.

'Now!' echoed Hell from his position of relative safety at the rear of his army.

The horde of demons charged forward and were met with a hail of fireballs and magical spears of fire. The demons at the front fell, causing some behind to trip and add to the chaos as they ran into the thickening smoke.

On the edge of the turmoil, Dennis, Florence and Hell slipped unnoticed into the quadrangle and through the nearest unguarded door. Inside was one stairway leading down and another leading up.

'Which way?' asked Hell.

'Damn,' Dennis cursed. 'I've forgotten where we are.'

'Great Hall,' said Florence, pointing up. 'Kitchens,' pointing down.

'Up!' snapped Dennis, after a moment's hesitation, and bounded up the steps. On the next landing they passed through an arched doorway into a passage that led into the Great Hall.

'Where exactly do you want to go, Father?' Florence called after him.

'The Archchancellor's rooms,' Dennis panted.

'Oh, yeah,' beamed Hell, as realisation dawned. 'Take 'im hostage, and the others will give up, eh?'

'Something like that,' said Dennis.

'He's over on the other side of the building,' said Florence, stepping in that direction.

'Yes, I know,' said Dennis. 'I know where I am now. And we should take the scenic route. No point getting cut off before we get there, is there?' He marched off through the Great Hall.

*

More demons piled in through the gap left by the collapse of one of the main gates. Some of the wizards' magic was running low and they needed to rest and revive. They weren't used to employing their magic so intensely for such prolonged periods. But, with a combined effort they managed to raise enough firepower to repel the demons once more. The creatures stood their ground briefly, managing to hurl tridents, and even some fireballs of their own from some of the larger demons, before scurrying back outside. Those that could still walk or limp helped those worse off than themselves. Even demons had some regard for their own. But they left their dead behind.

Some wizards were wounded, but nothing serious. A few of the younger wizards and older students managed to move the fallen gate across the gap and add some campus benches to form a barricade. It was a novel experience for some of them to be vandalising benches to some purpose.

'I think they've had enough for now,' said Link, as he watched the demons retreating down the road. 'I doubt if the lull will last long, though.'

'Has anyone seen Dennis?' said Eydith, a hint of panic in her voice.

'Now you mention it,' said Link, catching her panic, 'he doesn't seem to be around.'

'I'd better go and make sure the Archchancellor's safe,' said the Secretary.

'I'll come with you,' Rumpitt volunteered. The two men headed off directly for the east wing.

'We'd better check round,' said Eydith.

'The Great Hall, first,' suggested Link, stepping in beside her as she went, not wasting a second. 'Then work our way through to Trinkel's rooms.'

The pair broke into a run, charged through the arched doorway and up the steps. As they entered the Great Hall, a door at the other end slammed shut. They glanced at each other and took off down the length of the hall. At the door, Link put an ear against it and listened. All he could hear was the sound of feet running on the stone flags on the other side, getting fainter as they receded. He twisted the brass handle and yanked the door open just in time to see Dennis and Florence, with Hell a few paces behind them, turn the corner that led to the east wing.

'There they are,' whispered Link.

'Heading for the Archchancellor's, of course,' said Eydith, angrily. 'The others may be already there. If they are, they'll need help.'

They trotted silently down the passage to the corner and peered around. Dennis was already on the steps leading up to Trinkel's rooms. They ran along the passage and up the steps. They halted when they heard footsteps coming down towards them. 'Get back,' hissed Link. Eydith didn't need telling. They turned and trotted back to the corner and waited. A moment later, Hell came into view. Not a pretty sight. Link stepped out with his hands raised and released a white-hot ball of fire. Hell dropped to the ground, letting it sail harmlessly over his head. Further back, Dennis saw it coming and stepped aside. It fizzled out noisily against a wall.

Then they both saw Eydith. And Sprag.

'We're trapped, wizard,' growled Hell.

'No, we're not,' snarled Dennis. 'You've gone through walls before. Now get us through this one.' Hell gingerly touched the wall.

Cho, roused by the commotion, appeared round the corner, saw Dennis and jumped back out of sight, releasing a bright yellow fireball as he went. It struck the wall over Hell's head and exploded in a shower of hot sparks, which burned the stones. The demon king furiously punched the wall and fell into an unoccupied room. The three rushed in, and Dennis waved his hands at the wall, causing the stones to fly back into place. He grinned, smugly. 'Now this one,' he said, pointing at the opposite side of the room.

'No need, Father. Use the door.' They went through, and quietly closed it behind them.

*

The fight had moved away from the demon army. Hell was missing and they had neither leadership nor motivation. They hung about, but there was no sign of anything happening. Or that it ever would. Dispirited, the demons formed into angry groups and set about terrorising the city.

A few of the younger wizards stayed on guard by the barricade, while the others, reluctantly led by Pelgrum, joined the search for Dennis. The seventh-level wizards were delegated to start at the top of the Library Tower and work their way down, while the others split into groups and searched the lower levels, hoping to finally meet at the bottom of the Tower of Undiscovered Magic. They were all instructed *not* to engage with Dennis, Florence or Hell if they found them. Only to get away quickly and report their whereabouts.

The trio they were looking for weren't exactly sure where they were themselves. There was no natural light in the passageway, and Dennis strained his eyes looking for a candle to light. Florence held onto the sleeve of his robe, but Hell loped forward, his eyes accustomed quite readily to the gloom.

'Bloody surface dwellers,' Hell snorted. 'No use at all, now.'

'What did you say?' asked Dennis.

'Just thinking aloud, wizard,' said Hell. 'If you can't see, you'd better follow me.' He reached out and grabbed Dennis's hand.

The wizard shrank from the touch of the claw.

'Suit yourself,' snapped Hell.

'No, it's all right. Not expecting it, that's all.'

Hell led them forward. Around the next corner they saw a light flickering at the end of the passage. Dennis quickened his pace and released Hell's hand. The light grew brighter. It was coming towards them, and they could hear voices.

'Oh, no,' muttered Dennis, realising a group of wizards was coming. Handily, there were steps leading up to a small door in the wall. The door wouldn't open, so the three flattened themselves against the wall on the steps. Fortunately, *for the young wizards*, they ambled by with their eyes fixed on the passage ahead.

'What now?' Florence whispered.

'Come on, they've gone,' hissed Dennis, and he stepped out into the passage.

Around the next corner, there were steps leading up. There was a flickering torch about half way along. Dennis removed it from its bracket and carried it.

'Where are we?' asked Hell.

'East wing,' whispered Florence. 'The Archchancellor's rooms should be on the next floor.'

'How do you know these things?' asked Dennis.

'I worked here, Father,' she reminded him.

'Hmm,' he breathed. 'So did I. But I don't remember all this.'

'Stuck in your ivory tower, probably,' she half joked.

'Absolutely. You'd better lead the way.'

At the top of the steps, Florence paused to listen at the door, then went inside. Beyond, was a short passage, brightly lit with two doors in each wall and another at the opposite end.

'Which one?' asked Dennis.

'Far end and down the steps,' she whispered.

'This place is like a bloody maze,' complained Hell.

Dennis and Florence ignored him and moved quickly across the stone flags. Moments later they were in the residential area of the east wing.

* * *

94

'What do you mean – leave?' said an indignant Trinkel.

'Archchancellor, we are being attacked by demons from the Parallel Dimension.' The Secretary was trying hard to make him see the seriousness of it.

'Where? Are they here, yet?' demanded Trinkel.

'They're everywhere, Archchancellor,' said Rumpitt. 'And Dennis is somewhere in the building, as well.'

'*Dennis*? I thought *he* was in the Parallel Dimension.'

'He was, Archchancellor, but he escaped,' said Rumpitt. 'You really need to go somewhere safer.'

Trinkel continued to pour liquid into a large bell jar balanced on a tripod, seemingly oblivious to the severity of what was going on around him. 'I didn't think anybody ever came back from there,' he said, absently, as if it were more of a curiosity than a threat. He moved a spirit-burner and placed it under the tripod.

'We all think it would be safer for you if you left the city until the danger has passed, Archchancellor,' said the Secretary, in a kindly voice.

'Where can I go at my age?' said Trinkel. 'He'll probably find me… I assume it's me he wants?'

'Not exactly, no,' said Rumpitt. 'It's your job he wants, Archchancellor.'

The contents of the bell jar began to bubble gently.

'Dennis, as Archchancellor? No, we can't have that again,' said Trinkel, turning the flame up a bit higher.

'We don't intend to, Archchancellor,' said the Secretary.

'Well,' said Trinkel, frankly, 'my leaving will amount to me relinquishing my post and handing over to him, won't it? So, no. I'm staying.'

The liquid in the bell jar turned purple and bubbled more vigorously. The Secretary and Rumpitt exchanged hopeless glances. They shrugged and made to leave.

'Oh…' said Trinkel, looking up. 'You off, then?'

'Yes, Archchancellor. We can't *make* you go. We'll leave Cho and one of the others outside your door to keep an eye on things,' said the Secretary, wearily.

'Oh, by the way,' said Trinkel, as a thought struck him. 'If you find a dead one of those demon things, let me have it, will you?'

*

The liquid in the jar began to boil, and droplets of whatever it was plopped onto his bench. Absentmindedly, he picked up a cork, rammed it into the neck of the jar, and went to get some sawdust from another room, his mind wandering to another of his many projects.

'What do you think he wants a dead demon for?' the Secretary, wondered.

'It's probably to do with his current hobby,' sighed Rumpitt.

'What's that?'

'Stuffing animals,' said Rumpitt.

'Oh, yes. But… a *demon*?' whispered the Secretary. 'No… he wouldn't. Would he?'

Rumpitt shrugged and smiled, but without amusement. The Secretary turned greenishly pale.

*

Dennis and Hell followed Florence up to the level where the senior staff accommodation was situated.

'Which one?' said Dennis, urgently. Florence nodded towards Trinkel's door.

Cho hadn't yet returned, so there was no-one on guard.

With his quarry almost in his grasp, and with the rush of adrenaline from the magic that had been coursing through him, Dennis charged at the door, shoulder first, and, to his own amazement, smashed it down and careered on through to slam into the bench.

He recoiled backwards when the fiercely bubbling bell jar on the bench exploded.

'Ooh, shit!' Dennis shrieked, as the hot liquid rained down on him. The cork was embedded in the ceiling, and the liquid was running down the walls and Dennis's face. The magical defences with which he'd been careful to protect himself before the battle, saved him from severe burns. He picked up the hem of his robe and wiped his eyes.

In a rage, he stormed back across the room, knocking a rack of phials across Trinkel's workbench, and started kicking his rickety furniture. 'Trinkel!' he yelled. 'Where are you?!' There was no reply from the other rooms.

In the passage outside, there was another minor explosion. Florence and Hell jumped into the room.

'Eydith's here!' yelled Florence.

Dennis had to think fast. He quickly intoned a refined version of his restoration spell, reassembling the door and magically strengthening it.

Hell scraped at some of the purple stuff running down the walls and tested it with his tongue. 'Yuk!' he moaned. 'Blackcurrant jam. I detest blackcurrant jam.'

The reinstated door shuddered and began to glow when Eydith hit it with a fireball.

'Come on!' Dennis yelled. 'Let's get out of here!' He raised his hands and forced livid red fire from his fingertips. A section of the wall began to smoke as the jam caught fire, then, under the sustained heat from his spell, the section of wall evaporated.

Eydith hurled a more potent fireball and Trinkel's front door shattered for the second time in as many minutes. Link flung himself inside and rolled across the floor. Dennis turned quickly and aimed a stream of white light. It went past Link's ear and hit a mirror, which deflected it up, cutting the strings of something long dead and half stuffed that was hanging from the ceiling. It fell across Link's shoulders, pinning him to the floor. Eydith saw his plight and rushed in holding Sprag in front of her, her eyes glowing white hot. Dennis allowed himself one fleeting look at her, and dived through the wall after Florence and Hell. They found themselves in a passageway on the other side of the Archchancellor's rooms. Florence instantly got her bearings, and they bounded down the steps to the quadrangle.

'Are you alright?' asked Eydith, with concern, as she helped Link get what looked like the battered remains of a half-stuffed crocodile off his back.

'Yeah, I'll live. Where did they go?'

'Down to the quad, I think.'

Link staggered to his feet and loped half-heartedly to the hole in the wall.

Eydith was right behind him. But she stalled. 'What's happened to the Archchancellor?' She checked his study, his bedroom, and his privy, but Trinkel was not at home.

'He's probably alright,' Link reassured her. 'Otherwise, Dennis wouldn't have run.'

'You think so?'

'Yeah. I reckon he'd have reinstated himself as Archchancellor then and there, and demanded Sprag from you.'

The thought stunned her for a moment.

Sprag wouldn't comment.

*

Dennis made a rush for the main gates, but his way was blocked by at least twenty wizards. And judging from their faces, they all had the same thing in mind. Stopping him. He considered his options, then turned and ran to the Library Tower. Behind him, Hell released a string of fireballs at the wizards as he ran. He just wanted to get it out his system. Most were deflected, and he scored no direct hits.

Again, more wizards. They were closing in on them from all sides. It was no use running anymore. This was it. Stand and fight, or…

Hell began to burrow into the ground.

Florence stepped forward. 'Stop right where you are!' she yelled, pointing a finger at him.

'Not bloody likely,' snapped the demon, as he continued digging.

'We need you! Here! Now!'

He ignored her.

Florence showed him her staff. 'You won't get this! I'll give it to *Eydith*,' she threatened.

Still he continued to dig.

'I'm warning you. Keep going, and I'll toss it right across the quad.' She held it tantalisingly before him.

Hell paused, eyed the staff, and suddenly lashed out and grabbed the end of it. A major tug-of-war developed.

The bigger fight went on hold as Dennis and the other wizards looked on, riveted by the push-and-pull antics going on in front of them. The demon was stronger. Florence could feel her advantage slipping away, but rather than let Hell take the staff back to the Parallel Dimension, she forced her end to the ground and stamped her foot on it, snapping it in two.

There was a thunderous explosion, and a flash of sheet-lightning lit the whole scene. The ground opened up and swallowed both Florence and the demon. The onlookers jumped back, shielding their eyes.

Dennis's jaw dropped. 'Noo…' But taking advantage of the distraction, he made a dash for the Tower of Undiscovered Magic. Eydith and Link arrived in the quadrangle in time to see Dennis disappear though the door.

The pair immediately gave chase. But they stopped short when the door to the tower was flung open and Dennis came running out towards them. He was releasing fireballs, but not at them. At something behind him. He saw them and stopped. But he was more concerned with whatever was following him. He turned and backed across the quad, directing fierce fire at the door, which disintegrated. Something or someone was coming out of the tower.

Link and Eydith sprinted away and took shelter in the nearest cloister. As they watched, Dennis continued backing away from the tower. What could have spooked Dennis so completely? He was frantic.

To their amazement, it was Archchancellor Trinkel who emerged into the sunlight, brushing aside Dennis's fireballs as though they were just minor irritants. The Archchancellor wasn't returning any of Dennis's magical fire. He was quite content just to deflect and neutralise it.

The further Dennis backed away, the more Trinkel came forward. Then, inevitably, Dennis could retreat no further and his back was against a wall. Eydith ran out from the cloisters and stood at Trinkel's side.

'Oh, hello, my dear,' he smiled, waving aside another fireball. 'Come to join in the fun? I haven't had such a good game of fireballs in years,' he confessed.

'Be careful, Archchancellor…' Eydith tried to warn him. She was worried that however good this looked it might still end badly.

In response, Trinkel gestured with his eyes for her to look at her staff. Sprag glowed strangely orange in her hands. Trinkel's eyes then signalled her to look up towards an identical glow coming from her balcony on the side of the residential building. 'Oh, my!' she mouthed, when the enormity of what was happening hit her. A feeling of awe and great relief came over her. She now knew why Trinkel was so composed and unflinching. As Archchancellor, he had used his prerogative to access the combined power of the staff and the Drum – his symbols of office – in a way far beyond what even she could accomplish.

Trinkel was effectively the most powerful man in the world at that moment as he stood beside her. And in his wise old eyes and unflappable demeanour she could see more than ever why they'd been keeping the combined Drum-and-staff power from Dennis through all his years as Archchancellor. *Only a man like Trinkel*, she thought, *could be entrusted with such power.* Inescapably, her next thought was: *A man like my father. A man like Wimlett.*

Time seemed to have slowed to a standstill since Eydith told Trinkel to be careful, and the sound of his voice set the world back in motion for her.

'No problem, my dear. Dennis's powers are running low. I'll let him have a few more pot-shots my way, then we'll show him something a little bit special.' He winked, knowingly.

Dennis could see Sprag glowing oddly, but from where he stood, he couldn't see the Drum responding, so he had no idea what was going on. Or he'd surely have given up. In his eyes, this bumbling old fool of an Archchancellor, who should *never* have been given his job, had temporarily wrong-footed him and gained the advantage, and he would shortly put an end to him. In fact, in his mind, that time had come. Angry and frustrated as he was, Dennis calmed and centred himself. He drew on every last drop of magical knowledge and power he could summon. He glared defiantly into Trinkel's serene face (*smug* face, as he saw it), raised both hands and aimed them at Trinkel's head.

'I think he's going to give me his best shot now, my dear. I think you'd better move out of the way.'

Eydith took his advice. She could see Dennis firing himself up. Almost before she'd reached the cloisters to join Link, Dennis launched the final and most lethal weapons from his arsenal. Everyone in the quadrangle had already backed away when they saw what was coming. They held their collective breath and watched in disbelief as Trinkel held up a hand and halted the formidable ball of churning, raw power. He flicked his wrist and it dropped to the ground, only to scurry away in the form of a mouse. Trinkel was enjoying himself.

The Archchancellor's next move surprised Eydith more than anyone. She looked about her wondering what was going on. *How did he…?*

Trinkel raised the still-glowing Sprag in one hand, and with his empty hand, he released the biggest, brightest ball of light Eydith had ever seen. Everyone fell back. It hovered in the air between the duelling magicians for a moment, turning slowly, swirling through all the colours of the rainbow, and beyond. Dennis watched it both hypnotised and horrified. Then it hit him like a comet. It exploded in a shower of silver sparks, in the midst of which Dennis could be seen briefly in outline as a green shimmer, then it died away.

Dennis was gone.

A deathly hush followed.

'I win,' said Trinkel.

Looking across to Eydith, he held out the staff, which had stopped glowing. 'You can have him back now.'

Nobody else spoke for a few more moments. No-one dared to even move. Dennis had gone but there was a Dennis-shaped shadow on the wall where he'd been standing, and a Dennis-shaped hole in the ground. 'That should keep him out of the way for a while,' said Trinkel, as the smoke cleared.

'Where's he gone?' said Link, arriving at his side with Rumpitt and the Secretary. 'Is he dead?'

'As to where he's gone,' said Trinkel. 'I have no idea. Is he dead? In truth, probably not.' He looked up at the balcony where the Drum still glimmered a little. 'Perhaps one day the Drum or the staff will tell us what became of him. But perhaps not. I'm certainly not going to ask.'

* * *

95

Columns of smoke hung darkly over the city. Hell's demons were busy punishing the citizens for their own failure to defeat the wizards. Leaderless gangs of horned terrors roamed the streets. All the fun had gone out of smashing windows and street lamps, now it was time to warm the place up a bit. And for that there was nothing better than torching some buildings.

The citizens had had enough. A mob was gathering at the magically repaired gates of the university, demanding that the wizards do something.

'Have you called out the City Watch?' the Secretary asked their adopted leader.

'Don't be silly, man! The Watch can't handle demons.'

'They can barely manage trolls,' the man's sidekick joined in with. 'So, no, mate. It's down to you lot in there now!'

If there was one thing that goaded wizards into *not* doing something, it was being referred to as, *you lot in there.* Rumpitt stood by the Secretary, his face flushed with anger.

'It's all right,' said Eydith, joining them and calmly laying her hand on Rumpitt's arm. 'I'll see to it.' Link arrived at that moment, too.

'A *girl*?' somebody moaned from the back of the crowd. 'You're sending *a girl*?'

Another insult, but she let it go. She was feeling frayed already from the day's events, and couldn't face an argument. She'd take it out on the demons. The mob parted to let her and Link through. The other wizards watched them go, and the fact that they were in truth 'sending a girl' struck a sensitive chord with them. They justified themselves with the thought that she was a girl whose power exceeded their own. But even so… Sheepishly, they followed after her.

'You can't all go!' the Secretary yelled, raising his hands in a vain attempt to stop them.

The ones at the back stopped pressing forward, and the ones at the front cursed their luck. Eydith turned to face them. 'We don't need all of you!' she shouted, above the noise of so much incoherent muttering. In the confusion, most of them assumed they weren't needed and turned back.

An explosion reverberated in the distance, and a few windows rattled behind them.

'That was from the *Flying Unicorn*!' yelled the citizens' mob leader. 'Go on, you lot. Get on with it!'

'Shit,' murmured Rumpitt. 'That place will be full of trolls at this time of day.' He half smiled when it occurred to him how badly demons might fare against irate trolls. But his relish was short-lived. The most likely outcome was that the half-drunk patrons of the tavern were more likely to show up venting their anger at the wizards.

Rumpitt had had enough. The last thing he needed to round off his day was a herd of trolls on the doorstep complaining. He drew himself up to his full height. 'Cho! Come with me. Pelgrum! Take some wizards and clear the north side of the city.'

'We'll take east,' said Eydith, grabbing Link's arm before somebody else decided they needed him.

'Secretary!' yelled Rumpitt. 'Sort the rest of them out! Get them moving! Make sure there are none of the little bastards left inside. Come on, Cho. We've got some demon hunting to do!'

Rumpitt strode through the gates, his eyes blazing. Shaming wizards half his age, he marched down the road and turned right into Merchant Street. Three demons were setting fire to a shop. Cho instantly reduced one of them to ashes, surprised how vengeful he felt, and Rumpitt shook his staff fiercely at the other two. They disappeared, except for some soot and smoke. The shopkeeper managed to throw a bucket of water over the flames to save his business. Rumpitt and Cho marched on, destroying every demon foolish enough to come at them.

'This is almost too easy,' said Rumpitt.

'Don't say so,' said Cho, anxiously. 'You jinx us.'

Rumpitt looked around. 'No,' he said, 'Sometimes things really are just too easy. And no comebacks.'

'I think you right,' said Cho, brightening. 'We have fun now?'

'Why not?' said Rumpitt. He'd vented most of his anger, and, although beginning to feel his age, he wasn't done yet, by any means.

'Leave this to me.' Cho grinned broadly and not in the least inscrutably. 'Ah so,' he said, pulling a white ribbon of cloth from his pocket. It had an odd-looking flower badly embroidered on it, and he tied it around his head.

'What the heck's that?' Rumpitt couldn't hide a grin.

Cho put his hands together and bowed. 'Cho-Kin Dojo. Founder member.'

'This I've got to see.'

They marched on down the street. The demons they encountered from this point on were either blasted into oblivion by a master wizard's staff or kicked and punched into the hereafter by a frenzied martial-arts maniac who didn't really know what the hell he was doing.

On the eastern side of the city, Eydith and Link weren't holding back either. As far as they were concerned, it was open season on anything from the Parallel Dimension. And there was a notable absence of prisoners. The demons either fled down hastily dug holes or they died.

Two hours later, Eydith was telling the Secretary, 'There are still a few about, but once all the wizards are back, Link and I will take one last look around.'

'Just to clear up any strays,' added Link. 'The city-folk are happy, anyway.'

The Secretary gave them the once-over. 'You two look absolutely exhausted. Why don't you grab something to eat, and take a rest before you do *anything* else. In fact, I'll join you.'

Link never needed telling twice to go and eat.

* * *

Along their route to the garrison, Jook and Psoddoph turned aside into a tavern. They sat in the gardens with their drinks and relaxed properly for the first time in weeks. They were in no hurry. They just needed to unwind. They put their feet up, sat and drank and chatted. After a couple of hours, they saw the smoke over the city and were glad to be out of whatever was going on there. It was bound to be something to do with Dennis.

Their fears were confirmed by another customer who arrived from the city and told them of the 'big ruckus at the university.' He recounted that 'some nasty piece of work' had attacked the place and that the Archchancellor himself had 'vaporised the evil bastard' in a duel.

They listened with mixed feelings. Especially Psoddoph, who wanted to know what had become of Florence. But the man couldn't help him with that.

They hadn't allowed for this. Dennis had always survived somehow. This was too unexpected. He was gone, and they sat in the tavern gardens looking at his magic carpet and his box of *extremely* valuable teeth wondering what to do next. Did these things belong to Florence now? Was she even alive? If she was, she'd be either in prison or on the run, they reasoned. They decided they should 'take charge' of the items.

Later, when they were back in their barracks still wondering what to do, Jook piped up, 'Do you think the Sergeant would let us buy ourselves out?'

'Maybe. He might be persuaded,' said Psoddoph. 'Everyone's got their price.'

Jook opened the box of teeth, to remind himself how many they had. 'Oh, look, his old robe's still rolled up in 'ere, as well.' He held it up in front of him, and jokingly mimicking their old boss, said, 'Carpet… very slowly, now… I don't want you getting any ideas. UP! Please.'

The carpet lifted gently off the floor. 'Stop! Please,' he said hurriedly. 'And sorry I shouted at you. Now… down, please.' The carpet came down again. 'It works,' They grinned wildly at each other. They almost hugged. 'We can go anywhere we like with this.' He tossed the robe on the bed.

'And with that,' said Psoddoph, indicating the box of teeth. 'Come on, let's go and find Sarge.'

*

'Come in!' yelled Sergeant Woolf, swinging his feet off the desk and dropping his whisky bottle back in the bottom drawer. The two guards marched in and saluted. 'At ease, men,' said Woolf, in a kindly voice. He'd had a couple of drams and was in a friendly mood. 'What's on your minds?'

'Well,' Psoddoph began, 'we've been thinking…' He waited a moment before delivering the big question.

'Yes?'

'What would it cost to buy ourselves out, Sarge?'

'Hmm,' the Sergeant breathed, and leant back in his chair, clasping his fingers behind his head. He eyed them curiously. 'Interesting. Don't really know. How long have you been in this army?'

'About twenty years, Sarge,' Jook lied. He recalled hearing it was cheaper to get out the longer you'd been in. The truth was nearer six. Twenty years ago he'd have been about three.

'Me too,' said Psoddoph.

Sergeant Woolf unclasped his fingers and leant forward, furrows of deep thought lining his forehead. He put his elbows on his desk, steepled his fingers and leant further forward, his nose touching the tips of his fingers. *Bloody 'ell,* he thought, *that means I've been 'ere nearly twenty-five years.* 'Thinking of retiring eh, boys?' he said, at last.

'Yes, Sarge,' the two men chorused.

'Cost? Cost? I don't know…' the Sergeant was thinking aloud. 'How much have you got?'

'We don't really know, Sarge,' Psoddoph replied, truthfully.

'That much, eh?'

'Probably quite a lot, Sarge.'

'What do you plan to do if I let you go?'

'Well, first,' said Jook, 'we thought we might see the world a bit… go travellin', you know. We'll sort out what to do next when we get back.'

The Sergeant thought quickly, *If I let them go, there'll only be me 'ere, till the rest of the regiment gets back. And it's been bleedin' deadly dull around here for the last few weeks without these two. This could be my opportunity, as well.* 'Look men…' he said, getting out of his chair and walking around the desk to stand between them. He rested a hand on each of their shoulders. 'What about… if I give you the go-ahead, and set you a very fair discharge fee… then what about you, er, cutting me in for, say, thirty percent of what you have, and I'll come with you.'

Jook and Psoddoph thought for a moment. A silent 'yes' passed between them. 'You handle it,' said Jook. 'I'm not much good at this sort of thing.'

'Fifteen,' said Psoddoph.

'Twenty-five,' countered Woolf.

'All right,' said Psoddoph. 'Twenty.'

'Deal,' snapped Woolf, spitting on his palm. 'Shake.'

Psoddoph winced and shook Woolf's hand.

'Okay, lads. Where to first?'

'We need to get a couple of things from the dorms, Sarge, and take them to a hotel to pick up later. Then we'll get out of these uniforms and into some civvies, and see you back here in a short while,' said Jook.

'Right, give me twenty minutes,' said the ex-Sergeant. 'I have some paperwork to do. Make this official, you understand. And I've a pigeon to find.'

*

'I didn't think it would be that easy,' remarked Jook, as they crossed the parade ground.

'Well, you never know until you ask,' said Psoddoph.

Twenty minutes later, Jook and Psoddoph were at the gatehouse.

''E's taking his time,' said Jook. 'The shops'll be shut in a minute.'

'When was the last time you went out?' said Psoddoph. 'Most of 'em are open all night now.'

'I suppose they've got to make up for the bad days,' said Jook.

The sound of footsteps echoed across the square. The ex-guards turned. 'Bloody 'ell!' said Jook. ''E looks like a bloody peacock!'

Psoddoph took one look and had to turn away to hide his face.

Woolf was carrying a small case in one hand and an empty milk bottle with a note sticking out of the top in the other. 'For the milkman,' he explained, as he placed it by the gate.

For what was probably the first time in a good many years, the three men walked down the street outside with a noticeable spring their step.

* * *

97

On the other side of the city, Eydith and Link watched as the last of the demons were repulsed and scrambling back into the ground. Already, city maintenance gangs on carts were touring the streets, filling holes and clearing up.

Over their meal with the Secretary, they had learned of the fate of Florence. Eydith had gasped at the news, and was still struggling with it. It was only now, as she walked back to the university hand-in-hand with Link that it all caught up with her and she sat down at the roadside and wept. Link awkwardly put an arm around her shoulder, and was so close to tears himself that he couldn't be much help. Sometimes things just needed to be cried out.

After a while she became calmer and nestled into him. He was thinking to himself that he could get used to this. How long had he known Eydith? – almost a year? They'd been through more in that time than most couples go through in a lifetime. Couples? He queried the word. Yeah, they were a couple alright. No doubt about it.

When she felt better, Eydith smiled weakly and padded her eyes dry. She looked around her, as if trying to take in the world afresh. 'What's that? she said, 'In that pile of rubbish?' She was pointing at something that had caught her eye in the rubbish piled in the entrance to an alley beside a derelict house.

Link surreptitiously wiped his eyes on a sleeve and went to investigate. There, half covered by pieces of old rag and newspapers, was an animal skin. He gently nudged it with his toe and sawdust and cotton wool spilled out. He knelt to examine it more closely. Then he smiled to himself.

'I think we've found the Archchancellor's goat.'

'That's what I thought it might be,' said Eydith, squatting down beside him. 'Come on. Let's go and surprise him.'

Link didn't fancy picking it up so they flagged down some workmen on a city cart crawling by, who kindly bagged it for them.

When they arrived back at the university, they saw that the buildings had already begun to self-repair. They were going to be madder than ever after this onslaught, thought Link. The pair made directly for the Archchancellor's rooms.

Eydith lifted the brass, cat-shaped knocker and tapped gently. As usual, it clanged loudly, echoing all through the building.

'How does it do that?' grinned Link. 'It's not even a bell.'

As they waited the minute or so it would take him to reach the door, Link had to say something: 'He's not what he appears to be, is he?'

'Hardly,' she said, and thought for a moment. 'My father once told me that the most effective, and least threatening way to wield the intimidating power of an Archchancellor was to seem weak and ineffective.'

'Well, Trinkel's certainly perfected that!' he said, laughing.

'I think the Secretary may be in on it, too,' she whispered.

Trinkel opened the door.

'Look, Archchancellor, we've found your goat.' Eydith smirked as Link held the bag at arm's length.

Trinkel reached in, pulled it out and eyed it closely. 'No, that's not mine,' he said, solemnly. 'Mine was white.' He handed it straight back to Link who took hold of the mangy pelt without thinking. 'Thank you anyway,' he said. 'Have a good night, you two.' After which he sauntered off to another room.

'Looks like we've been dismissed.' Link let the pelt slip from his grasp and wiped his hands down the back of his robe. 'I'm going to wash my hands,' he said, disgustedly. 'Are you coming?'

She did them all the favour of magically eliminating the offending item and its bag. 'Come to *my* rooms and clean up,' she suggested. 'They're a bit nearer.' This was in fact true. Link would have to walk at least half a dozen yards past her rooms to get to his own.

As soon as they arrived, he made use of the washing facilities adjoining her bedroom, and when he came out, Eydith was sitting on her bed, patting the pillows. 'I think we need a bigger bed. But this'll do for now.'

When Link looked at her uncertainly, she added, 'We've been told by the Archchancellor himself to have a good night.'

The End

CAST OF CHARACTERS

Alf	Guard in Corin Castle
Antknee	Watchman
Badger Hercop	Barbarian
Ben de Little	Dwarf and Spy for King Treadwell
Blacksmith	
Brown	A smallish Demon
Captain Dognettle	Cap'n of the Sea Dragon
Captain Skillet	Cap'n of the Racing Slug
Chickweed Scrawnier	Barbarian
Cho Kin	Student Wizard
Crimpett	Sea Dragon Crewman
Dennis	Evil wizard
Enry	Dwarf guard in Corin Castle
Eydith	Mage-ess
Farmer	A farmer
Farmer's Mother	
Florence	Dennis and Esme's daughter
Gluck	Demon at Reception
Greasy Spot	Dwarf and Spy for King Treadwell
Grandpa	A big troll
Hell	Demon king
Hercop Vitrolly	Sergeant for King Treadwell
Hotel clerk	
Jamzamin	Ex-demon king

Jubnak	(a.k.a. One Eye) Spy for Treadwell (not a dwarf)
Krumlin Droggett	Barbarian
Krystal	Troll princess
Lampitt	Sea Dragon crewman
Link	Wizard
Lionel	Watchman
Little Jack	Gents Outfitter
Loosley Speekin	Dwarf & Spy for King Treadwell
Madge	Major Domo
Paske	Librarian
Peg-Leg	Sea Dragon crewman
Pitiron	Spy
Reg	A Robber
Rumpitt	A Wizard
Secretary	To the Archchancellor
Teeter Gravy	Dwarf Inventor and Wizard
Thadax	Dwarf Herald for King Treadwell
Trevor	A Robber
Trinkel	Archchancellor
Weasel	A Robber
Wiry woman	In the cleaning dept.
Woolf	Sergeant to Jook & Psoddoph

Plus many more players who didn't get their opportunity to shine. Maybe next time?

Also available from iTunes, Amazon etc: an album of music composed and performed by Colin Attridge, inspired by characters and events from the first book in *The Chronicles of Crett* series:

Rumours of Magic

By L R Attridge